THE STAINED-GLASS WINDOW

SALLY CATTELL

LESCHENAULT PRESS
AUSTRALIA

*I dedicate this book to all migrant women
who follow their husbands wherever they go.*

~

Whither thou goest, I will go;
and where thou lodgest, I will lodge.

Ruth 1:16b (KJV)

ACKNOWLEDGEMENTS

I thank Dianne Baker for all her support to 'keep on going'; Helen Voyacek for her painstaking comments; Helen Wallis-Dunn for her encouragement; the editors at Athena Press; and Penny Plunkett for believing my novel was worth publishing. Also to all the staff at Leschenault Press for helping release this 2nd Edition.

~I~

Oh what a tangled web we weave,
When first we practise to deceive.

*Sir Walter Scott**

'**B**e watchful, stand firm in your faith, be courageous, be strong. Let all that you do be done in love.'

The words wafted past Marion Lee as she sat gazing at the cut of the stone surrounding a stained-glass window, showing a child holding a lily, below which the word 'Peace' was inscribed. Her eyes strayed downwards over the chairs with their smell of beeswax peculiar to All Saints', Laleham. Boxes, which each contained a hymn and prayer book, were attached to the backs of the shoulder rests in front of her. They infused a warm familiarity, and further down each chair was a hook upon which a dark green kneeler hung.

Marion was a smallish woman in her early fifties. She had unprepossessing brown hair, waved on a regular basis by Carol Lombard, the leading stylist at Shapers in Staines, fifteen minutes away. Her eyes were her only interesting feature, being a light grey which varied according to what she was wearing; although people who came in contact with her often felt uneasy, imagining she knew things about them which they were not about to divulge. Not being aware of this trait herself, she lived a somewhat lonely life with few friends to share her dreams and innermost thoughts. Not even her husband, Leonard, who was reading the second lesson from the Book of Corinthians in a strongly timbred voice, was privy to her deepest fears and disappointments.

---

* From *Everyman's Dictionary of Quotations and Proverbs*, London: J M Dent and Sons, 1951.

At this point in time her mind was in turmoil, her current state blocking out any comfort she could receive from the reading. Perceiving the brass eagle lectern, its form and size, with her husband standing behind it was all she would remember in the future; not the lesson, nor the Rev. Guinness's sermon. Someone in the congregation coughed; Marion's restless eyes roamed back across the aisle to the carved oak pulpit, which she and she alone adorned on all the important days in the Anglican calendar – usually with moss, ferns, and seasonal flowers from her own and neighbouring gardens. Behind and to her left stood the stone font where Anna, her daughter, had been christened. She wouldn't look now – maybe when she left the church for the last time…

The congregation mumbled, 'Thanks be to God.' The choir began an anthem. The choirboys were so small that only their white ruffs and heads could be seen above the pew. The ladies, their tricorn black hats tipping, sang lustily. Some said that their hats looked like black stars but to Marion they conjured up sinister images. Whether their cassocks were red or black would have made no difference, they seemed medieval and threatening in a way she couldn't define. Nevertheless she felt comfortable with the traditional service. The original Lord's Prayer, the sung responses, the two lessons separated, the Confession and the Gloria well known. The organ music rose to a climax. The choir resumed their seats as Marion turned her head downwards, noticing out of the corner of her eye Leonard's strong hands. She felt him shift on his seat and wondered what he was thinking, if he was worried at all.

Prayers were said, the sermon delivered and the final hymn was announced. Leafing through the hymnal to find the correct page, Marion and Leonard stood with the rest of the congregation to sing 'O Breath of God', as the green and gold collection bag was passed from row to row.

The familiar blessing was heard by all: 'May the Lord bless you and keep you, and may His face shine on you for evermore.'

As the congregation knelt to pray, the choir sang 'Amen' three times; but no prayer winged its way upwards from Marion. Her thoughts being scattered, she just went through the motions. The

choir and vicar processed out of the chancel, and by the time
Marion had returned her kneeler to its rightful home, picked up
her books and nodded to various people, the Rev. Guinness was
already shaking hands with his flock at the main door.

As she turned to follow Leonard out, her eyes strayed upwards
towards the blood-red stained-glass window high up on the
western wall. She shuddered, then looked across at a darker
painting of a man in eastern clothes being buffeted by the wind,
trying to grasp the hand of God. For some reason Marion felt
decidedly disturbed by the agony in the man's face. Noel Barker,
who owned the large farm on the corner of Ashford Road,
dressed in his neat Sunday grey suit, took her books, murmuring,
'Thank you,' and packed them into the shelves beside the large
oak door. Marion shook hands with the vicar and hoped he
wouldn't place his other hand over hers, or she would cry.

He did, looking into her eyes and saying, 'Peace be with you,
Marion, and safe journey.'

Once they were outside, various well-wishers' voices floated
on the air. The traffic hurtled round the bend of All Saints', the
garage next door completely blocked the footpath with cars, and
the 218 bus drew up opposite as the parishioners left the church.

Leonard opened the lychgate, steering Marion across the traffic towards the war memorial. He said kindly, 'I think it is safe
now.'

'You read well,' she replied and, dropping her gaze, concentrated on the roadway.

'A walk before lunch?' His brown eyes were raised towards hers.

Companionably, they quickened their pace around the war
memorial that was surrounded by a looped chain – for what
purpose no one knew, unless it was supposed to keep cars from
crashing into it. They could hear the church bells; one of the few
carillons being played on a Sunday, as they walked down towards
the river and past their house. Leonard glanced across his hedge
with relief. Soon they'd be gone thousand of miles away and he
could forget Laleham ever existed. The melodious sound could be
heard across the village and beyond.

'Josh is playing well today,' she said, and smiled. 'You trained
him well.'

He shrugged and they turned the corner from Blacksmiths' Lane on to the towpath. There were four lanes leading down to the river, all with a different ambience. Properties were hard to come by as few people ever moved away. Ferry Lane had very few large houses near the village end, whereas the lower part of the road was boarded by a field to its left and a long, high brick wall to its right, through which a narrow path joined on to Condor Road. Here again, the houses were sparse with large gardens and lime trees creating a canopy over the lane. Vicarage Lane, aptly named as it was situated across from the church, was of a different character. It had smaller houses and bungalows closely knit together, their front gardens spilling onto the lane itself. Blacksmiths' Lane had changed little over the years, apart from switching from gas lamps to neon. Marion could see from her upstairs front two bedroom windows a house at either end, joined by a high red brick wall, covered in Virginia creeper, with an orchard between. Here she had spent many an hour looking across at the church belfry listening to the tunes ringing out from the bells.

The River Thames glided by in the sunlight as Marion and Leonard shared the silence broken only by the bells, the occasional moorhen, and the crunch of their feet on the gravel pathway. She swallowed, digesting the finality of it all. They walked towards a white painted iron seat, and sat down; she savoured everything, from the quaint wooden shacks on the opposite bank, to pockets of nodding daffodils and clumps of violets rolling down to the landing stages.

Marion recalled Penton Hook Lock and its weir, which were out of sight to her right. She often went for walks there and across to the small island in her teenage years. To their left and further downstream was Chertsey Lock and its famous Bridge Restaurant. But this part of the river was their favourite, with its established houses behind them and Burway Rowing Club on the Chertsey side of the river opposite the end of Blacksmiths' Lane. In summer they watched the young men sculling in eights and fours, practising for the Laleham Regatta. Young people also took part with their dinghies. Many a balmy autumn evening they would walk their Scottie, Dougall, either towards Penton Hook

Lock or in the other direction, past Ferry Lane and up towards Laleham Park.

But that was all past now. Dougall had succumbed to old age, and the village was changing. Its male inhabitants mostly commuted to London, their wives shopping for groceries in Staines at Tesco, where they could buy all manner of items not carried in the local store. Houses had been demolished or divided into flats. The butcher's shop changed position, and the post office-cum-corner store moved further down the village, its public phone continually out of action. Only the two pubs remained the same – the Three Shoes and the Feathers – their inglenooks smelling of beer and stale smoke. There were signs erected saying 'NO PARKING', and concrete boat ramps appearing, the naturalness of the riverbank being eroded by progress, or so Marion supposed. Houseboats in the summer raced along the river far above the eight knots stipulated. Planes seemed to level out after take-off at Heathrow just above Laleham, so, on some days, depending which runway they used, the slow peacefulness of the place was shattered.

The church bells stopped, leaving gentle sounds, the lapping of the river, a dinghy bobbing in the reeds and the chugging of a barge as it came around the bend. The man at the stern raised his arm as he glided by and Leonard waved back, watching him float swiftly past. Then, reaching into his pocket, he withdrew a gold lighter and made quite a to-do lighting up a cigarette. As his fingers closed around the lighter, memories of why and from whom he'd received the gift created an unease.

The Daily Office Cleaning Company, which Leonard and his mother had worked so hard at, had grown, with ten vans and twenty employees. He'd done well and sold out a few months back. With that money and the sale of their house, 'Laleham Cottage', he was nicely cashed-up, so they could join Anna, their only daughter, now married and living in Tasmania.

Leonard was tall and sinewy, with black hair slightly receding, turning grey at the sides. This, coupled with a boyish smile, gave him an air of casualness, whereas he was anything but; not afraid of hard work, a man full of the zest for life, pragmatic and quietly spoken. As he smoked, he was sure that, as Anna had married

Nigel Crees, an Australian, and departed with him to his homeland, it was highly unlikely they would ever return to live in England.

He stole a glance at his wife. Marion was not as outgoing as himself, five foot four inches in her stocking feet, born and bred in the Thames Valley, quiet and unassuming. She was completely mystified why her daughter would first of all marry an Australian and secondly want to go and live so very far away.

He felt a twinge of apprehension about how Marion would adapt. She wasn't the sort of person who liked change or challenges. She enjoyed pottering about in their garden, arranging the flowers in the church, and looking forward to the Old Girls' Reunion, where she caught up with gossip and news. As for her friends, he wasn't too sure you could rightly call them that; more like acquaintances she met in the village or at the church.

As for himself, he was looking forward to the change of scenery in more ways than one. Grinding out his cigarette with his well-polished Clarke's shoe, he stood up and said, 'Come on, lass, time for lunch.'

Words failed her, not wanting to disappoint. The best she could achieve in a strangled voice was, 'Anna says Tadbury is on a river.' Standing beside him, she looked rather small and helpless.

Too heartily, he replied, 'I believe Tasmania has some of the oldest buildings in Australia.'

They retraced their steps, both knowing that 'old' in Australia only meant a hundred years or so, hardly worth a mention. The silence lengthened, as neither wanted to dwell on what they were leaving behind – he experiencing guilt, she feeling insecure and not understanding why.

They entered the house by the front door with its honeysuckle trailing down across the dining room bay window. Marion felt a surge of panic. She saw the packing cases in the hallway and the general chaos of a half-packed kitchen. Upstairs was no different, she knew, and willed herself to bustle about in the kitchen, preparing their last Sunday roast in the home she loved. Ignoring her empty pantry, she peeled a few potatoes, put the remains of a cauliflower in a saucepan on the stove, took the lamb from the fridge and put the remnants of a frozen packet of peas in the microwave. Finding an old battered baking tin she placed the roast in the oven and turned it to 375°.

Feeling restless, she wandered past the lounge and through the French windows out into the walled garden. It being only March, not a great deal was flowering, but she already mourned what she couldn't see. Bluebells and violets mixed with clumps of primroses were only just starting to shoot forth. Most of the daffodils had been blown over by a recent gale. Seasons and order played a large part in Marion's make-up. The quiet ebb and flow of her life created a balm that shielded her from situations out of her control.

World news was frightening. The breakdown of respect for elders and other people's property filled her with alarm. They called it 'home invasion', not theft – which it was, to Marion's way of thinking. And there was always an excuse why the perpetrator did these things. She couldn't fathom the law anymore. She couldn't fathom why Anna now lived in Tasmania. Even to go and live in Scotland or Wales would have astounded her; but to go and live in Australia – it was unthinkable.

She sat on the garden seat going over it all. The one and only time Anna had gone overseas was to Spain with a girlfriend to celebrate their graduation, before their degrees were conferred. It was there she had met Nigel, also holidaying. Later he'd come to London and luckily obtained a teaching position at Ashford Grammar, not five miles away. It was remarkable that he had been employed at Ashford Grammar, it being a few minutes' walk away from the Welsh Girls' School, now renamed St David's, where Anna was teaching. Marion closed her eyes, remembering how proud she was when Anna was approached to join the staff at her old school.

In her day it had still been the Welsh Girls' School, founded primarily for the sons and daughters of Welsh merchants in London in 1716, known then as the Most Honourable and Loyal Society of Ancient Britons. By 1852 the school had moved to Ashford in Middlesex, a country village; gradually the admission of boys was phased out, the school became 'girls only' and was renamed the Welsh Girls' School. Following the declaration of war in 1939, it was evacuated to Powis Castle and Rhiewport

Hall, Berriew, a few miles away, as the army had requisitioned the buildings.

A tear trickled down Marion's cheek as she remembered how as a day girl in the 1950s she had been so proud to enter a school full of tradition, albeit freezing in the winter, attending chapel every morning and practising the piano in the cells, suffering with chilblains. She could see herself now, learning the Welsh National Anthem from a tatty piece of paper handed to her from the girl in the row behind at singing practice. No one had any idea what the words meant, except those with surnames such as Davies, Jones, Hopkins and Pugh. The odd thing was that now, forty years later, she could remember the words and melody as clearly as the ABC. She thought of the day she enrolled Anna, walking up the massive driveway and in through the solid elm front door, and entering the beautiful hall with its curved staircase leading up to the library, where music exams took place. She could see herself standing outside the black shiny door clutching her Royal Academy exam book and waiting for the voice within to call, 'Come In.'

Not so long ago the school had been renamed St David's, the music cells giving way to laboratories. The uniforms – green pinafores and pale blue blouses for everyday, and navy skirts with white blouses for Speech Day and special occasions – were considered old-fashioned now; the students wore kilts and blouses without ties. The chapel and cloisters with their marble busts remained the same, as did the flagged floor of the corridor stretching from one end of the building to the other, sporting successful past students in black and white photographs on its walls, and the entrance hall stood majestically between the two.

Marion supposed that she would no more attend the Old Girls' reunions. How she loved those days, catching up with some of her peers, walking the grounds, remembering how happy she was there. Wiping her eyes, she tried not to feel resentful, but couldn't get out of her mind how Anna had traded all that she had achieved to go and work and live in Tasmania. She'd thought they were happy here in England. She had expected them to buy a house locally, near Laleham, and eventually she would become a grandmother. Now all her dreams had unravelled. She felt like a piece of flotsam, cast adrift, at the mercy of the tides. She had been too disappointed to ask Anna why she had decided to leave the Thames Valley, too shocked. To leave England was beyond her comprehension.

As Marion sat on the garden seat, a great heaviness enveloped her. Somehow she had been persuaded to give up everything she knew and loved – but for what reason? Just to be near Anna. She sighed aloud. 'People do this sort of thing every day,' Anna had said, obviously happy to live on the other side of the world. Who was it that suggested she and Leonard should go and join her? Oh God, I'm scared, Marion thought to herself.

Returning to the kitchen, she tried to block out the chaos around her and laid the kitchen table. Laleham Cottage looked forlorn, lonely even. She went in search of Leonard.

The house was very quiet, as though it were accusing her of leaving, silently raging at her for not standing up for herself, not caring enough. She was unhappy, and it was her own fault. She found Leonard by the bureau sorting stamp albums, and said quietly, 'It's ready.'

The accusation hung heavily in the air as she watched him carving the lamb. A slow realisation dawned, then engulfed her, that all she really wanted was to stay in her house, with Anna close by; later, perhaps, some grandchildren with whom to point out the wonders of the river and its surrounds; to tend her garden, the continuity of all she loved. Watching Leonard, a thought she had pushed to the back of her mind surfaced, no longer dormant: he couldn't *wait* to begin the new adventure! He liked the unknown, the excitement, the cut and thrust of life. A sadness swept through her, knowing he would be in his element tomorrow when the packers came.

'It will be like a second honeymoon, returning to the Swan,' he remarked. 'You remember our reception?' Sensing something was bothering her, but not wishing to hear it, he continued brightly, 'It will be good going back there for a night as oldies.' He laughed and shook his head as if he remembered their honeymoon night in detail. The phone rang and he said, 'I'll get that.'

Marion surveyed the dismantling of her home, picking at the food on her plate. Tomorrow the house would be empty. They would stay at the Swan on Staines Bridge before flying out of Heathrow, courtesy of JAL airlines, stopping at Osaka in Japan for eight hours or so. Time to have a shower, a rest, and then on to Australia… or so Anna had said.

These were the facts. She recalled a bumpy flight to Majorca, her one and only holiday overseas, vowing she wouldn't fly again.

'…thanks, John, and you will both join us for lunch at the Swan on Tuesday?' Leonard breezed on, with more mumbling, and then a click.

A sinking feeling washed over Marion, like when she wanted to work in London and her mother had bluntly said, 'No.'

'That was John,' said Leonard. 'All fixed for driving us to Heathrow.' Sensing her mood, he made his escape. 'I'll get going, sort out the garage. There will be tools John might like…' His voice trailed away as he left the kitchen and disappeared into the garage.

Feeling decidedly panicky, needing to get away from bare walls and packing cases, Marion cleared up the remains of their luncheon, slipped on her coat and quietly left the house. At the top of the lane she was perturbed to see so much traffic still hurtling past the memorial. When had it begun to be so busy, and where were all these cars going on a Sunday? Looking around, she found herself drawn towards the church again, hoping that it was not locked. Crossing the road quickly she entered the churchyard and stood for a moment in the porch, reading the notices, something she had never bothered to do before. Grasping the enormous iron handle on the oak door, she was relieved to hear the familiar clanking sound as she lifted the latch. Inside it was quite dim. She shut the door and sat down with relief at the back listening to the silence, only faintly hearing the traffic.

This was her sanctuary, so permanent, harbouring ancient stories and the past lives of the priestly and secular. Her gaze followed the flagstone nave to the lectern, the pulpit, past the choir stalls and on to the altar with its plain crucifix. Standing up, she moved towards the font, tracing her fingers around the rim. She turned and passed the solid pillars marvelling at their perfection, so creamy, fat and round – immovable, like the stone floor slabs upon which names had been carved, and next to them black intricate gratings. One would never know how many feet had trodden here over the centuries.

Crossing quickly to her usual seat, Marion removed her kneeler and, resting her elbows on the seat in front, she knelt down, steepling her fingers. She didn't pray, couldn't pray; she just stayed very still, drinking in the beauty and the familiar atmosphere. Sunshine played on the iron chandeliers, which once had held candles. Now, at Evensong, a gentle light cast shadows across the curved black beams above the chancel, contrasting against the rough white walls. She became aware of the intricate ironwork woven into the pulpit and the altar rails like a screen, and above the polished wood, where hands and elbows of many generations had leant. She wondered who the craftsman was back in the seventeenth century. What was his life like, and how much would his work cost today? She imagined men in old-fashioned clothes, churchwardens of previous centuries carrying out their tasks in the vestry. Did they see themselves as important? How much status went with the job? Snippets of past history lessons at Laleham School came to mind – around 1610, if her memory served her. She exhaled aloud. Something to do with self-government taking place within the vestry. The warders and overseers were elected annually in the church porch, receiving their commissions from the Justice of the Peace.

While in this reverie, she mused as to why now she would be thinking of these things. The churchwardens had the power to set the yearly levied rates, spending the money on road repairs, relief of sickness, and the correction of unmarried parents. Digesting this piece of information while at school, both she and Deirdre Pugh had asked Miss Wandsworth how this could be. The teacher had blushed, telling them not to be so cheeky, but as they were only nine at the time it had been a genuine question. A sheltered childhood didn't include the facts of life, didn't include 'unmarried mothers'. She recalled talking to Deirdre, saying she knew Margaret Standish didn't have a father; but their domestic arrangements apparently didn't qualify, as he hadn't returned from Normandy during World War II.

There had been a Thomas White, married to Anne something or other. It had made the class giggle. *Well-beloved* – that was it...

Anne Well-beloved. She savoured the name, turning it around in her mouth. Thomas had left £18 to the poor of the parish, quite an amount for those days. Much later, there had been records left at vestry meetings, Miss Wandsworth had shown them to the class. The second Earl of Lucan had purchased the manor and taken over the management of the workhouse. So much history, all forgotten now. Scandals were what people remembered: the present Earl of Lucan's disappearance and the murder of his housekeeper, conjecture at the time accusing him of mistaking her for his wife. The newspapers had had a field day.

Jumbled thoughts, shifting from today to people of long ago. Was there a link between those who had trodden the same spot in past times as she did now? Marion stayed very still, overwhelmed by the timelessness, aware of the flowers she had arranged close to the organ curtain. Who gathered the flowers in past decades, and were they displayed with care or just thrust into a pot? More to the point, would she arrange flowers and greenery in another church half a world away? No, she didn't think so.

Forcing herself to remember in detail everything that she could see, apprehensive of the future, thoroughly mystified that she had consented to leave all that she loved, a stumbling prayer escaped from her lips. 'Oh, God help me.'

As the tears began to slide down her cheeks, the door clanked behind her. She heard a scuffle and a giggle. Wiping her eyes, she turned to see who had entered. There, standing at the back, was a small boy of around eight years, wearing jeans, a black T-shirt and scruffy trainers.

'What do you want?' Marion's voice sounded shrill and dis-embodied.

Defensively, he shouted back, 'Just came in to look around... didn't expect to see anyone here. There's no law against that, is there?' he added arrogantly.

'I'm not deaf, you know.'

He shrugged, looking away. The silence was marred by the sound of a lorry changing gear as it negotiated the corner; a jet screamed overhead and young voices penetrated the walls from the porch.

'Your friends are calling you.'

'Yeah.'

'This isn't a playground, you know. It's a sanctuary.' Unspoken words flashed between them and then he was gone, crashing the door shut as he did so.

It was impossible now to recapture the peace. Her eyes focused on the blood-red stained-glass window above where the young lad had stood, then moved across to the painting... frightening, the hands not meeting, and the violence of the clouds, the man falling from the sky. It somehow gave the impression the distance was too great... he couldn't quite connect. She had noticed it many times before but never really understood what the picture was supposed to represent. But now, it seemed to her it was man reaching up to God, unable to grasp his hand. Depressing really, she thought, as she let herself out, closing the door, savouring the unique clanking sound for the last time.

Everything changes, she thought, especially the behaviour of the young. She spied her young intruder and his companions riding their bicycles across graves and swerving along the pathways with little thought as to where they were. Her sad eyes came to rest on the enormous yew trees flanking the porch. They'd seemed to spook her as a child, but now she was thankful for their permanence. She uttered a silent prayer, just three little words, quite unlike her usual requests, honest, from the depths of her being, something new. A fearful thought; what if she was praying to thin air? Maybe there wasn't anyone there, just wishful thinking on her behalf. Her father had once remarked that when you die there is nothing else. The worms come and eat you, and that is all there is to it. The Church preached 'faith' – in what? In some superior being, in oneself? Then she heard it very faintly in the sighing of the breeze through the pine needles of the yew tree beside her. She breathed it in gently for fear of losing something so tenuous, so personal – a thread that held everything together, even in her pathetically weak understanding. She breathed deeper allowing the message to sink in, dissolving her fears.

Turning to retrace her footsteps home, a thought occurred that maybe she had misread the meaning of the stained-glass window; but whatever it suggested eluded her. Distracted, her eyes alighted on Matthew Arnold's gravestone, leaning at an angle, its inscription worn away by the elements and time. Moreover, the gravestones in this part of the churchyard looked like a miniature henge. They were all very old, solid, and grey, whereas around the corner, being more recent, they had elaborate scrolls, and there were angels in marble perched above slabs with black inscriptions, surrounded by vases of flowers in various stages of decay. Recently, as the churchyard filled up, the deceased had to make do with small slabs, submitting just their names and dates, etched lightly. Tufts of grass had sprouted up between some and others were completely obliterated. Wryly, Marion reflected that by the time it was her turn, there wouldn't be any room. She would be squeezed under the hedge bordering the west entrance – that's if Anna would bother to bring her ashes back to Laleham and pay the exorbitant fee. At least she wouldn't be run over by boys on their bicycles. Her thoughts were meandering, troubled. Byron's lines –

> Melancholy
> She sits on me as a cloud along the sky,
> Which will not let the sunbeams through, nor yet
> Descend in rain, and end, but spreads itself
> Twixt heaven and earth…[*]

– rested heavily on her soul as she approached the lychgate. Lifting the latch and passing through, Marion glanced up and along the road. There was a lull in the traffic as she crossed over and still in a reverie, she made a detour down Vicarage Lane, savouring the ambience. Here she could touch the flowers that nodded to her as she passed by. Windows shone, curtain linings fresh and crisp with wide floral ties. Front doors looked inviting, their brass letter flaps centred in maple or oak, fitting snugly.

She turned to her right and along the riverbank towards Blacksmiths' Lane. It was all so familiar. Over on the far side stood Burway Rowing Pavilion, its boats on racks within, with oars and rowlocks being carted down to a skiff at the water's edge. Now, watching her steps, she could feel the pull of home, the primrose-coloured front door with honeysuckle not yet in bloom,

---

[*] From *Treasury of Familiar Quotations*, Avenal Books, New York.

the garden chair and the wrought iron gates, behind which there were empty packing cases needing her attention. She would have been surprised to hear that within a year, the opposite wall would be demolished, the house next door divided into two, and ugly extensions would appear above the garage of her cottage. It was called progress.

Unbeknown to Marion, Leonard's thoughts were also on the village – to be precise, on Ferry Lane, which led down to the river past fields on its left. At its top there was a short lane leading off at right angles towards Laleham Park and the Priory. Leonard was standing in the lounge by his desk sorting through past bills and notices. It was too late now to tell Marion, and probably unnecessary. The timing had never been right; maybe, just maybe, it was better to let sleeping dogs lie. After all, what she didn't know, she didn't worry about.

All the necessary documents they would need for the flight and for entering Australia he would put to one side, with $500 plus £500 in sterling to cover expenses at the Swan Hotel and other incidentals which might arise before leaving Heathrow. A second pile contained his will, various bank statements, credit card conditions, recent receipts, X-rays from his dentist, and a letter from his doctor, should he need to see a specialist. All these he put into a briefcase. A third pile contained private letters and documents referring to the sale of Laleham Cottage, a map of the village dated 1950, and some house plans relating to Number Six, Ferry Lane. These he placed in a large Manila envelope with some receipts retrieved from a small locked drawer built into the top of the desk. Going into the hallway, he placed the envelope inside a cardboard packing box, marked 'NOT NEEDED', binding it up securely with tape. Having sorted out his affairs, he picked up the money, their passports, and immediate documentation, inserting everything inside the wallet supplied by JAL. It was time to look toward the future, have some much-needed recreation. He had paid his dues; hadn't he always? Pleased with himself, he went in search of Marion.

Later that evening, as the church clock struck six, Leonard made his way to the belfry for the last time, as Marion made her way up the lane to 'Yew Corner' for a final farewell with her friend, Alice Ashby. Peering up at the newly erected sign, Marion pressed the bell, puzzled as to why her friend had changed the original house name of 'Pooh Corner' to 'Yew Corner'. In her opinion, in next to no time the fact that A A Milne had once lived in the two-storey stone house opposite the roundabout would be forgotten. Poor Christopher Robin, who lived around the corner in Staines Road, must have suffered at the hands of his fellow pupils! It was widely known that Christopher had inspired A A Milne to write; maybe he'd looked like his main character as a youngster. Marion could understand why Christopher, now in his thirties, pro-nounced his surname to rhyme with the 'o' as in go; but she couldn't fathom why Alice took an aversion to the original name of the house. It reminded her of James Barrie, who modelled the story of *Peter Pan* on children he had known and games they had played together.

'You're miles away, Marion,' said Alice, as she ushered Marion into her lounge.

The bells rang out. They heard all the variations a full carillon can play in companionable silence. Then, listening to the familiar Benedictus, they sat down, nursing glasses of sherry, each with her own thoughts as dusk descended.

At exactly 6.25, Leonard peered down from the belfry to the room below, giving a signal to the choirboy to sound the five-minute bell. Satisfied all was in order, he descended the winding stairs for the final time, mouthing, 'All right, son?' Then with a smile he walked away from what had been his saving grace for the last twenty years or so. Pulling the outside door closed, he moved silently around the back towards the entrance of the church, pausing within the wooden portal. Here he couldn't be seen by the occupants of 'Yew Corner' sipping their sherry. Marion would think he'd be sitting by the font immersed in Evensong, not walking through the village, past the butcher's.

As Leonard crossed the thoroughfare entering Ferry Lane, the five-minute bell ceased. Looking at his watch, he calculated he had just over an hour to come to some decision. Veering right and away from the exposed bend in Ferry Lane, he entered Condor Road, aware of the spreading maple trees above him, their branches creating a tunnel effect across the gravel road. His shoes crunched on its surface as he made his way down towards the river. All was quiet. It was still light enough for someone to recognise him, so he strolled along the riverbank and up through the park. The crisp spring air helped him to think more clearly about all that had gone before.

By the time he finally reached the angled arm of Ferry Lane, the street lamps had come on. He stopped, surveying the trees, the gardens, looking for stray pedestrians. It had always amazed him that the field running down to the river had never been sold for development, and only six houses built in this picturesque spot. Now, as he stood under a horse chestnut tree, its canopy of foliage spreading out to another, he fixed his attention on Number Six. Someone switched the lights on in the kitchen and lounge rooms. He lit up a cigarette and waited, undecided as to his next move. With indecision stalling his actions, lingering and deferring, he looked up and down the lane and then he heard it: the strains of Mendelssohn's Violin Concerto in E Minor coming from the back of the house. A car passed in the thickening dusk its headlights sweeping into Number Five. He ducked further behind a large elm, its leaves mingling with the horse chestnuts... It was absurd, at his age.

Standing in the shadows, he leant against the wire fence bordering the trees and the field behind, listening and watching as he ruefully fondled his lighter. The player was having some difficulty with the haunting melody, repeating the same bars of music. He saw in his mind's eye the music stand, the violin and the sixteen-year-old lad concentrating, not satisfied until the phrase sounded to his satisfaction. A shock of thick brown hair hanging over the boy's forehead, an aquiline face, and sinewy arms, youthful in their bowing, energy striving for perfection. Leonard coughed and swallowed as he heard the haunting refrain, willing his son to come through to the kitchen. He could see flickering images within the lounge room and deduced she was watching television. *'Come,'* he whispered. His conscience pricked. Was it best to leave it well alone after so long? He needed to... to what? He noticed the moon, high and full, lighting up the roadway. Anyone could walk past, so loitering was not an option.

Finally, pushing his disappointment down, he shifted his weight, deciding to make tracks down towards the river, straining to hear every last note, etching it into his memory. Wishing his life had been different would not alter salient facts. He had had enough of guilt; it had cost him dearly. His soul cried out, 'Please, son, come to the window!' and he inhaled, listening and hoping. Then he sighed as the popular song, 'Leaving on a jet plane', passed through his consciousness, the words alternating with humming the tune.

'Pull yourself together, Len!'

The echo of his mother's voice was clearly imprinted on his mind. How many times in his younger years had she voiced that remark!

'Dreams are not for the likes of us. I haven't the money for frivolities. Life is earnest, son, somehow I have to make a living… There's only you and me, and dreams are not for us!'

Memories of squalid flats came flooding back; his mother's determination to keep her head above water, there being no social security during the 1940s. Cleaning, always cleaning someone else's fancy house. Endless notes left on tatty kitchen tables to say where she was, and would he prepare the inevitable vegetables for tea? Men kept allotments, women made jam, which all helped to supplement their pathetic wages. Some houses she worked for gave them eggs as well as cast-off clothes. He glanced at the river, listening to its gentle flow, very much aware of himself and the sound of his shoes on the gravel towpath. Apart from two lamps at the end of Ferry and Vicarage Lane, it was quite dark. Curtains were now drawn, with people behind them busy preparing for an early night, watching television or laying out clean clothes for Monday morning. Children's shoes were polished, satchels packed with homework, and the occasional couple poring over glossy pamphlets depicting exotic holiday locations.

Small pinpricks of light spilled onto the water from houseboats moored on the Chertsey side of the Thames. George, the ferryman, was nowhere in sight, long gone in for his tea. Leonard would remember the sight of George, poling his punt, operating from the shingle on the Middlesex side of the river, taking customers who didn't own a dinghy back to their houseboats on the Surrey side. Or perhaps it was because they didn't like to leave a dinghy tied to the bank, where anyone could steal it, leaving them stranded. You had to call 'George!' in your loudest voice, and he would come over eventually, his red hair and florid face almost part of the landscape.

With his mind in a melancholy mood, a black and white photo of his father flashed into Leonard's thoughts. This was the father he had never known, shot down somewhere in France in April 1941, his only legacy a violin, kept mummified in its case – unused by Leonard through no fault of his own. Practicalities like rent and food on the table had taken priority.

'No time or money for music lessons, my boy,' said his mother tiredly, pushing back her fair hair from her face. The photograph showed a young man in Air Force uniform leaning against a wall, holding a violin and waving the bow with the other, smiling at something in the distance. It had stood on its own on various mantelpieces, its black frame looking much the worse for wear, never to be talked about.

'Stop dreaming, Leonard, and try to understand. Life is *work*. Find a job that makes money, puts food on the table, clothes you and gives you a roof over your head.'

And the only way to do that was to find something that everyone needs and no one else has thought about, or at the least, is offering. She had been right about that. They had begun in a small way, when he turned sixteen, cleaning public toilets, then small offices. Word got around and Johnson and Clerks, the large hardware store in Staines, engaged them on a six-monthly contract. From there they didn't look back. Businesses wanted their offices cleaned, after their staff had left for home. They were working all hours of the night. Soon a van was purchased, with 'Daily Office Cleaning' on the side in gold lettering; then two more, and in no time they were employing numerous cleaners, secretaries, and an assistant manager. Bigger premises were leased in Station Road to house the vans, and an office fitted out in Commercial Road, causing some consternation to the residents living alongside and opposite.

At about this time, his mother bought her first home in the village of Cookham Dean. Built of sandstone, with three bathrooms, a four-car garage and a lounge room stretching from the front of the house to the back, overlooking the Berkshire countryside and the river. She had been adamant about what she had wanted: a property with a circular driveway, where expensive cars would sit while their owners took afternoon tea inside, drinking from fine bone china and eating delicacies perched on doilies, arranged on a silver three-tiered cake stand. She would be acting as hostess.

That had been her dream, but it never materialised. She had no idea how to gain access to the circle of the middle or upper classes, or how to cultivate friends. It wasn't in her nature to play croquet, tennis, or attend charity functions. In the beginning, the few occasions when she did have guests were a disaster, simply because she knew nothing about travel or fashion, or what was appropriate to gossip about. Reciprocal invitations dried up. Leonard's Porsche and her Jaguar were the only flash cars ever parked in the driveway, along with the occasional delivery van. They had clawed their way up from being nobodies, but they didn't have the right accents or background to be accepted. She had changed the rules, something unheard of, and as a result was living in no-man's-land. Leonard hadn't worn an old school tie; he had gone to Matthew Arnold state school. No mentor materialised to introduce him to elitist golf clubs, nor did he meet influential acquaintances requesting his company for cocktails at six down at the marina.

Not long after the house had been purchased, two golden retrievers were added. There was a maid to answer the door, and cleaners, cooks and gardeners were hired. Leonard remembered coming home late one day to see his mother's hair dyed ash blonde, wearing jewellery fit for royalty and waving a long cigarette holder, obviously much the worse for imbibing half a bottle of gin. Now, sitting down on the riverbank close to where George plied his ferry, he felt the shattering of her dream. It had been beyond her reach; the peripheries had been attained but there was no substance: tragic, really, as she hadn't understood why. She had taken to sitting in the garden, staring blankly for hours at the view. In retrospect he should have realised what was happening. He found her there one afternoon in May, quite cold, her head dropped forward. She had slipped away, frail as a fallen rose petal drenched with rain. Few people attended the crematorium. It was just Marion, the household staff and himself. It was as if she… No, he didn't want to go down that path.

Out of all the girlfriends he brought home, his mother took to Marion. In fact she pushed them together. Marion, with her private school education, genteel manner and well-enunciated speech could do no wrong. It hadn't mattered that they had few interests in common, or that she had few opinions of her own. It was precisely that which endeared her to his mother, for Marion readily agreed with everything his mother said; there was no conflict, no jealousy. Marion didn't rock the boat, so to speak, She was the perfect wife, as far as Leonard's mother was concerned.

As time went on, he needed more; left to his own inclinations, he began going to the races alone, as Marion showed no enthusiasm, acutely aware she didn't approve of his friends, making little effort at playing hostess to those he invited back to the house. He organised office parties, picnics, joined the philatelic society, even dabbled in politics to relieve his restlessness. He became interested in bell-ringing in order to avoid attending the church services, so no one noticed whether he was there or not. In an odd sort of way, he had enjoyed playing and teaching youngsters the art of campanology.

Rousing himself, Leonard realised that time was marching on and it would seem ironic after all this time if Marion found him out. It was a futile exercise going over past mistakes. A new life awaited him in Tasmania. Ruefully, he mused that if his mother hadn't died he wouldn't have sold the house in Cookham Dean, and if he hadn't acquired so much money from the sale, he wouldn't have been tempted to buy Number Six, Ferry Lane, for illicit purposes. Rash decisions, sins not revealed, best left behind. His spirits lifted as he made for home, imagining joining a golf club in Tasmania and perhaps the Sandy Bay Yacht Club. He'd like to participate in the Sydney to Hobart Yacht Race… Now *that* would be something to write home about! He would be free for the first time in his life to do exactly what he wanted, as time and distance would erase obligations. All his life he had been beholden to women. Well, now it would stop.

He felt quite light-hearted at the prospect of the future, jangling car and house keys in his pocket as he approached Blacksmiths' Lane. In fact, was quite looking forward to seeing Anna and Nigel, even though he didn't have a close relationship with his daughter. She was assertive, knew exactly what she wanted and how to get it; for that he was proud. If Marion could accept her daughter's independence, their lives could take on a fresh turn. If she would make a life for herself… but that was hardly likely; still, he could hope. Immersed in thoughts of possibilities, he suddenly saw Marion returning from Alice's as he approached their gate from the opposite direction. With his hand on the latch, he prayed he could concoct an acceptable story to explain why he was coming up the lane instead of down it, as she would have expected at the finish of Evensong.

Alice watched Marion return home through the lounge room window with some misgivings. Apart from the fact that Marion was terrified of flying, she had hardly set a foot out of Middlesex; furthermore there was that peculiar comment she had made. 'Jesus will walk beside us; He told me so this afternoon as I stood in the churchyard. It was like a whisper through the yew tree.'

Now, although Alice attended church at Christmas and Easter, she had never experienced God, Jesus or celestial beings talking to her. Marion gave the impression she had a running dialogue with her Creator, which was news to her, as not once in their friendship had either of them mentioned religion. Alice had felt embarrassed by this revelation and wondered if Marion was heading for a nervous breakdown.

Startled by this revelation, she decided not to mention the disappointing statistics of hopeful parents following their offspring to distant lands. It would be tactless. She knew personally of one such family where the wife had hated the change and returned almost penniless, while her husband had taken up with a young woman half his age. It was too late now to recount horror stories, besides which she hadn't taken Marion seriously when she first mentioned they were thinking of moving to Tasmania. It was ridiculous at their age, in their fifties; there was always the possibility that one or the other might die within a year of leaving their homeland, thus leaving their other half bereft in a strange country.

Alice said feebly, 'I'll miss you.' The words were completely inadequate; more was needed as they stood in the porch underneath the words 'Yew Corner' embossed on a plate of oak. She needed to say something that fitted this momentous decision, less mundane, but the words were elusive, besides which Alice thought she was going to cry and couldn't bear the possibility of Marion breaking down as well on her front doorstep.

She drew the curtains with a sense of dread at what her dear friend was about to embark upon, wishing she had given Marion a small gift, like an ornament which she could stand on her new mantelpiece, wherever that may be, to remind her of their friendship. A flippant thought came to her. She would attend next Sunday morning service, and perhaps God would talk to her under the yew trees. She would kneel at the back where she couldn't be seen and pray for Marion and Leonard to have a good holiday in Tasmania, forget all their foolishness about staying permanently, and come home to Laleham where they belonged.

Retrieving their used sherry glasses, Alice rinsed them under the hot tap, remarking to herself, 'Bottoms up and all that, my friend – I wouldn't have thought you had it in you! Rather you than me.'

She sighed and sat down in front of the television, tuned into BBC1 and watched a rerun of *Fawlty Towers*.

Later that night, while lying in bed facing her bedside table stripped of its knick-knacks, Marion whispered to Leonard in a somnolent state, 'Why were you coming from the river end...?'

The lie was easy. 'Ah, I was seeing old Mrs Jessup home.' He was sitting up in bed wearing a blue silk pyjama top reading the travel section of the *Daily Telegraph*. 'She seemed a bit wobbly on her pins,' he murmured, so as not to encourage conversation.

'Oh, that was a nice thing to do. I just wondered, that's all. We listened to the Benediction, Alice and I. You'll miss playing the bells...' Her voice trailed off.

'It came a bit unstuck in the middle. Still, we managed to keep going... we just repeated the dominant and tonic.' He sighed, feigning difficulties. 'There'll be other things in Tasmania... don't you worry yourself.' Relieved, he saw she was asleep.

During the night Marion drifted into a dream where she imagined she was drowning, while Leonard sunbathed on a beach, oblivious to her cries. A bell tolled loudly as she sank to the bottom of the sea, tangled up in seaweed. She awoke late the following morning feeling far from refreshed, half an hour before the removal people arrived.

Sitting on a cardboard box in the middle of the lounge, she felt the old fear rising up to engulf her as she watched objects of love being tossed into boxes and carted out of the front door. There had hardly been a time throughout her life when she hadn't felt frightened about something or other – frightened of what, exactly, she wasn't sure. All she knew was that it was easier to please others and do what they wanted, than to voice her own opinions and desires. It didn't pay to show anger, temper, desires or wishes. Now gazing at the dismantling of her home, she tried to stay at a distance from all around her so that she wouldn't break down and annoy Leonard.

At school she had been a model student, polite, never late, did her homework, didn't run in the corridors and participated to the best of her ability. She remembered that last attribute vividly, as her mother would beam at her when reading her school report. She'd played the game to the school's satisfaction. It hardly mattered that few of her peers or teachers remembered Marion Sutcliffe; she had left without leaving her mark.

'These to go in storage, guv?'

'Storage' echoed around Marion's head as she heard Leonard's clipped reply. Visions of her kindergarten, herself shut in a dark cupboard for some misdemeanour as a child of five, passed in slow motion. Boxes of chalk, pencils, paper and textbooks piled one on top of another reached up to the ceiling. She remembered the red pencils clearly, because you weren't allowed to help yourself to them… and how she wanted to scream and bang on the door, but was too frightened to do so, for fear of worse things to come. High up in the cupboard on the far wall there was a grille, where she saw a large red face surrounded by white fluffy hair. Then she did scream.

'What are you doing in there, you naughty child?' The voice was gruff, like a man's. She learnt later the rough voice belonged to the headmistress, Miss Cooper, who supervised the kitchen staff, as luncheon was provided at the school. She didn't remember when she was let out, just the nightmare of being shut in.

Two years later she had her first piano lesson from Miss Cooper in the small library. She had sat on the piano stool next to Miss Cooper, who was large and smelled of smoke. What did adults know of childish fears? Miss Cooper had tried to impart the theory of music, but Marion was too terrified to retain much of what she said.

Now, she watched as Leonard tied a rope around some cushions… *Rope!* Fear opened up further memories. It was rope with which Miss Forbes Mitchell tied Mark Strathearn to his chair. He had been fidgeting and asked to go to the toilet, and was told 'No' – with the obvious results. He was then beaten. All this in kindergarten. She had never forgotten it.

At thirteen, she was invited to a dance at the Ashford Manor Golf Club by a class friend whose house, like hers, backed on to the golf course. She wasn't allowed a long dress. 'Too young,' her mother said. But Mark Strathearn was there, laughing and flirting with every girl. She watched him waltzing around the room and he smiled in her direction.

Everyone had to be on the floor for the progressive dances, and she came face to face with him during the barn dance. This wasn't too bad, although her shoes felt rather clumpy and she wished she had dainty pumps on her feet like the other girls. For the first time in her life she'd had her hair set at a salon in Ashford, but was mortified when she changed out of her jumper into the grown-up beaded evening top; the bouffant hairstyle was disturbed and consequently flattened. Near to tears, she remembered trying to rearrange her hair in the oak-panelled ladies' room, listening to the other girls' happy chatter. She had been too tongue-tied to find anything to talk about when partnering Mark in the veleta. He seemed so carefree that to mention their kindergarten experiences would not have been appropriate. Maybe he had forgotten the incident, but she hadn't. She didn't find out which school he went to, nor did she tell him where she had gone to school, because he had assumed she had gone to Lady Eleanor Hollis, like all the other girls. She wanted to be light-hearted, but nothing came to mind.

Mark didn't ask her to dance the last waltz, nor did anyone else. No one spoke to her when putting on their coats to leave, and everyone seemed to be laughing, making future arrangements. She slipped out of the door and ran all the way home. What was wrong with her? Why wasn't she like everyone else?

As soon as she rang the front door bell, her mother pounced. In next to no time her coat was whisked away and she herself pushed into the lounge, where her father was sitting.

'Did you have a good time?' she was asked. Bony fingers flicked imaginary specks from her shoulders.

'Oh… yes, it was wonderful,' Marion lied.

'That's good, isn't it, Ian?'

Her father had smiled, pleased his daughter wasn't a wallflower. For some unknown reason she remembered his smile now as she sat among the chaos of furniture and newspapers.

Standing there in front of her mother, who tweaked her clothes and hair as if she was on parade, Marion felt self-conscious, wearing a suspender belt for the first time. The whole experience had been a nightmare, hiding her true emotions, not being able to cry in front of her parents. Social failure would not be forgiven. And she had been a failure. No one asked her to dance – not surprising, really, when all the other girls wore pastel floaty evening dresses, whereas she wore a yellow top and purple skirt, patterned with black velvet swirls, clasped by a wide black elastic belt. Please them at all costs: pretend happiness, behave the way others expected, and then she would be accepted. She remembered it all vividly. Internally afraid, outwardly she wore a mask in case her mother flew into one of her rages at the slightest thwarting of her plans. It was safer to agree, show meekness, and don't ask or make suggestions.

'I saw Mark Strathearn there,' she had said brightly.

'Who, dear?'

'He asked me to dance.' It was only a white lie… if you consider a progressive as a personal invitation. And there had been many more embellished successes over the years.

The misery she had felt then was with her now as her eyes strayed to the staircase leading up from the lounge. A large backside was negotiating the corner, and then an iron bedstead came into view as a removal man stumbled down the last three steps. She shuddered at the prospect of damage to the paintwork, at the same moment noting the maroon velvet curtain (which was pulled across in the winter months to stop draughts) tucked into a loop to give clearer access. Leonard had said, 'Don't be silly, Marion. It won't fit anything else. We won't need the curtains in Australia. Leave it here with the house.' The same had gone for the wing-backed armchairs, the garden seat, and the front garden chair, in which she loved to sit, enjoying the smell of honeysuckle as she read a novel or did some sewing.

'It does no good hanging on to possessions, Marion. We can always buy new ones… they've had it anyway.' How *could* he?

But I want to keep them! she silently screamed. She was so ashamed she couldn't find the right words. She would comply… it was easier that way.

Shakily, she stood up and headed for the kitchen. It was un-bearable watching. Why didn't Leonard feel the same way? It came back to haunt her, this feeling of being different, being alone. The day wore on. The cleaners came. Their suitcases packed, hers with a framed picture of Laleham Cottage between two jumpers, and his hand luggage containing two small ever-lasting milk cartons, packet sugar and half a dozen Earl Grey tea bags among his overnight clothes, as instructed by Anna. It was with much grumbling on his part that these domestic items were added; however, as neither of them were partial to green tea, as offered in Japan, it seemed a wise move.

Leonard was looking forward to a pleasant evening at the Swan Hotel and the flight as he locked the front door, placing the keys in the letterbox for the new owners. Marion, on the other hand, pretended that she too was looking forward, hiding her anxieties with unusual chatter. They left Blacksmiths' Lane, she with her eyes on her lap, he with his eyes on the road.

~II~

28 April 1996 was a bright crisp Saturday morning in Hobart. Over breakfast, Anna and Nigel were scouring the Real Estate section for a property suitable to her parents' requirements. So far nothing had materialised of a standard her mother would accept, either on Mount Nelson or along the river frontage between Sandy Bay and Tadbury.

'Aha! Here's one in Tadbury, and it's on the water...' Anna replenished first her cup and then Nigel's from a steel coffee pot presented to her from the Welsh Girls' School as a wedding gift. Nigel looked away from his wife's face to where she was pointing. Her almond-coloured eyes and shoulder-length blonde hair had captivated him from the moment they met. Now, sitting opposite her at the breakfast table, he tried to concentrate on what she was saying, but all he really wanted to do was kiss her high cheekbones, rosebud mouth, take her into the bedroom and watch her hair fan out on the pillow as they made love. He had often wondered how Leonard and Marion had made such a beautiful daughter, as Anna looked nothing like her mother and was finer boned than her father.

There was a picture of a house and garden which he recognised from his early morning run. He'd watched the house – or shack, as it originally was – develop over the year into a modern structure, with enormous windows facing the river. The garden on the river side touched the pathway which the early morning joggers took, puffing along in all sorts of weather. The morning sun would light up the patio and rockery below the windows, making it impossible for strangers to see in.

On each side of the curved lawn, herbaceous flowers and shrubs grew. He could tell the photo was recent, for a flowering cherry was in bloom above the rockery and daffodils were everywhere. In the summer, he'd seen old-fashioned irises mixed in with lavender near to the path as he ran by, and a glimpse of Californian poppies, forget-me-nots and windflowers. The New Zealand flax, now pictured, had grown somewhat from the first time he had seen it, giving the garden some privacy, and recently a garden seat had been added for the weary, close to the path.

'Wish we could afford it,' Nigel said dryly. 'Probably be snapped up before they even get here. It may not be to their liking anyway.'

Anna gave him a half-smile then drank some coffee. 'Having them that close might be a drawback.'

'What? I thought you wanted them here.'

'I do… it's just that I like our life the way it is. Don't want my mum around here everyday.'

'She wouldn't do that.' He finished his coffee and said carefully, 'Well, my love, like it or not, things will change with them being here. I'd better get dressed.' Then, moving away he glanced enquiringly at her as he backed out of the room.

'Wait a minute,' she called.

'Yes, madam?' He smiled. 'I haven't forgotten. I'll clean your Laser. Anything else I need to do?' He waited.

She looked up, searching a blank spot ahead, a jumble of thoughts pressing: lavender sachets in the drawers of the small spare bedroom, enough hangers in the wardrobe, coats to remove to another area – where, she wasn't sure; fresh towels recently bought would need a rinse, and she would have to check the tea caddy for enough English Breakfast tea. Teabags wouldn't do at all for her mother, she always used tea-leaves and a teapot. Somewhere, she'd have to find an area to store their suitcases because the spare bedroom wasn't big enough to accommodate her parents, the furniture and all their luggage.

Her mind catapulted to St Mary's, where she taught English in the secondary school. Tomorrow was the school fair, and although she was horrified that it was to be held on a Sunday, there was nothing she could do about it. She was expected to organise a stall manned by students from her 'home group', and as she had been thrilled to get the position so soon after arriving in Hobart, she had little idea of the school's peculiarities. She was uneasy about participating in such an event on a Sunday, simply because it would never have happened, as far as she was aware, in an Anglican school in England. She had assumed all Christian schools were the same. At Hutchins, where Nigel taught, the only pastime that occurred on a Sunday was sport – rowing, to be precise.

'How about taking my place tomorrow?' she said coyly. Their eyes met. 'I thought not. It was worth a try.'

'I'll help you set up… after… that's if I get back in time. Could incite the girls,' he grinned.

'Charming! One sweaty, sexy male let loose with my girls. Thanks, but I won't take up your offer this time.'

He left laughing.

While Anna was looking at the picturesque house in the *Saturday Mercury* and longing to afford it herself, a young man the same age as her was seething with animosity about a piece of real estate down at Port Arthur, which he desperately wanted to buy; however, the owners, Mr and Mrs Martin, had never taken him seriously and refused his offer. He was tall, with shoulder-length blonde hair, slim with grey eyes, and could easily be mistaken for a girl from the back. He had inherited a large house in Clare Street, New Town, less than five minutes out of Hobart, plus $600,000. Money was no object; he regularly went scuba diving, owned all the latest stereo equipment, and from his demeanour appeared not to have a care in the world. But he was an awkward young man who people didn't take to. He was a loner, harbouring resentments. He wanted to be somebody of importance, somebody who stood out from the crowd; somebody people *noticed*.

Folding up the *Mercury*, Anna could hear Nigel whistling in the bedroom; how she loved Saturday mornings with lazy breakfasts. If Nigel was correct, with the imminent arrival of her parents, their weekends were about to change; and if she were honest, she wasn't too happy about that. Heading for the bathroom and a long hot shower, Anna found it inconceivable that her father had managed to persuade her mother to leave

England. She adjusted the shower taps, watching the water flow and checking the temperature before standing in the cramped cubicle. There wasn't a bath, and only a week before she had almost scalded herself. The taps were unpredictable, especially if someone ran the dishwasher at the same time. Thoughts ran through her mind… What if they stayed for months? What if her parents couldn't find a house they liked? What if her mother started on about babies!

Thoughts of activities she had to be involved with as a teacher rose like a black cloud as she dried herself and dressed. When did becoming a teacher involve all this extra activity? Wistfully, she wished for glamour and excitement, not this all-encompassing world of education. She was beginning to feel the pressure to toe the accepted line that was alien to her personality. It was suffocating.

On this sunny Sunday morning, the slender man with shoulder-length blonde hair was disturbed and angry at not being taken seriously as a teenager. He would show the Martins he wasn't to be trifled with. He would show them. He would go down to the guest house, named 'Seascape', and see how they would feel if he had the upper hand. It would be very satisfying: after all, he had sorted his father out several years ago, and a few others along the way who thwarted his desires. People had to learn they didn't mess with him and get away with it. Today the Martins would listen to him face to face: no more excuses. He left the house quietly, checked everything he required was to hand, tuned into the community radio station and drove down to Port Arthur.

Meanwhile, there was little wind over the Derwent River, its hues changing with the sun angles. The devout worshipped in the many churches across the island. Tourists revelled in the warmth of the sun, visiting vineyards in the Tamar Valley. People strolled along Richmond Village with its quaint shops, galleries and forbidding jail, now softened in time by flower beds and craftsmen bending over their respected looms and easels. Exorbitant price tags were attached to exquisite hand-woven garments which, together with unusual pottery, paintings, glassware and jewellery, lured the unwary sightseers as they listened to melodious sounds emanating from old-fashioned instruments playing gently in the background. Coffee shop proprietors enjoyed bustling trade and were happy listening to murmurs of, 'Such beautiful weather! Not what is expected at this time of the year…' interspersed with the ordering of Devonshire cream teas. Locals took friends and relations down to the Fox and Hounds at Port Arthur, its mock Tudor facade looking fresh and inviting in the sunshine, belying the area's grisly past.

Anna arrived at St Mary's College, pleased to see that her trestle table had already been assembled in the quadrangle where the fair was to take place. Four students of her 'home group' were carrying boxes laden with various oddments for their white elephant stall. The buzz of activity grew louder within a very short while, and as she looked around her, she was shocked to see one of the parents erecting a wheel of fortune. Turning away, she busied herself arranging various books, records, old board games and bric-a-brac. She called out, 'Girls, please will someone go and see if there is any more to bring from the classroom, and then go to the office to collect the petty cash?'

'Mrs Crees, can I help to price the items?'

Anne smiled, handing over a text pen and stickers. 'The list is here somewhere. Thank you.' She regarded the fifteen-year-old in front of her. Strange how some of the cheekiest students seem to flourish in extracurricular activities and be genuinely helpful, whereas you expected more cooperation from studious types.

'Where is Janice Ryan, Emily?' she asked.

'I don't know, Mrs Crees.'

'Everyone else is here. Just as well… Ah, here comes the cash box. When all is set up, girls, you can visit the other stalls. Take it in turns… no longer than fifteen minutes each.'

At around 10 a.m., an Irish folk tune came over the PA system. Students walked through the crowd of parents and friends selling toffee apples and candyfloss, their telltale marks smeared on young faces. Babies were awarded prizes for the biggest smile, and old panama hats were decorated with flowers and sold for more than they were worth in their heyday. And, as lunchtime rolled around, the sun rose higher, creating a sense of well-being. The sandstone blocks of St Mary's looked golden in the sunlight. The cathedral adjoining the school looked welcoming as visitors approached it over emerald grass, recently cut by the caretaker. Even the most pessimistic of persons couldn't help but feel happy to be alive.

And yet the unthinkable was unfolding at that very time, sixty kilometres away near to the crumbling sandstone walls of a church built in 1836. Eleven spires and a tower had been lovingly restored, so that now it looked like a piece of scenery slid into place over manicured lawns. Its peaceful slumbers were suddenly disturbed by cries and unspeakable horror. Not the whip or the lash, but an evil spirit let loose on its innocent victims, with children, adults and visitors all caught up in a carnage perpetrated by one angry young man with shoulder-length blonde hair on a sunny Sunday morning in April. He stood up after finishing a cup of coffee in the Black Arrow Café and systematically shot everyone in his path. Anyone who came into his sight was mowed down; inside the café, in the car park and on the grass. No one stopped him; no one tackled him. The church with its gleaming spires offered sanctuary to a bewildered few as the nightmare ran on for another twenty-four hours. Eventually, the killer was apprehended in the front garden of the Martins' guest house known as Seascape.

Around three o'clock the fair wound down. Stalls were dismantled and items not sold were offered at bargain prices. Anna was pleased with the amount her class had raised, but still felt uneasy about the wheel of fortune being trotted out on a Sunday. Her mind wandered to the arrival of her parents and what they would make of it all. She pictured them packing, taking their leave, and seriously began to worry having them to stay for an indefinite period of time. She and Nigel had no obligations, except to each other and their jobs. The thought of being tied down to Sunday lunch with her mother filled her with gloom. Carrying a few odds and ends already packed into boxes for the St Vincent de Paul Society she fell into conversation with Sister Anne.

'A good day had by all… and I expect you are looking forward to tomorrow?' said the nun.

Did she suspect? What would she know about families living

in a convent her entire adult life? She heard herself saying, 'Yes, Sister,' as she looked into Anne's beady eyes. She was a member of staff, wasn't she? Why did this little woman make her feel like a student? So what if she was the principal! What if she told her exactly what she thought of the fair and the wheel of fortune? She'd probably get the sack.

'You'd better hurry on home. I expect you have things to do…' Sister Anne said kindly, and with a nod she moved on.

Anna took the takings to the office and wondered idly how best to tackle Janice Ryan during roll-call as to her whereabouts, knowing full well it was compulsory to attend the school fair.

Unbeknown to Anna, around midday her recalcitrant student was lying on a plaid car rug with Gavin Armstrong, a pupil of St Virgil's. They were underneath a canopy of pine trees on a grassy knoll overlooking the penal settlement at Port Arthur. Nothing was further from Janice's mind than St Mary's. Early that morning, she had left her house in Norwood Avenue in a rush. 'I'll be off now, Mum. See you later!'

There was no reply, although Marjory Ryan thought she heard the back door slam.

Marjory turned over, luxuriating in her feather bed, thankful she had a day off from the hospital. She had just finished a week's night duty at the Royal Hobart Hospital and vaguely remembered Janice mentioning a school fair that was compulsory. It had been eight years since Paul, her husband, had drowned in a Sydney-to-Hobart yacht race; eight years of being alone and bringing up Janice. Apart from a brother who now lived somewhere in America she had no immediate relatives. She was thankful Sister Anne had accepted Janice at St Mary's, in spite of her not being a Catholic. In fact, Janice had never been christened, and she only attended the local Anglican church on Christmas Day and the occasional Easter Sunday. She would have preferred Janice to attend Fahan, which was close by, or St Michael's Collegiate, but not having the wherewithal, the next best was a Catholic school. The alternative local state school wasn't strong enough in discipline, to her mind, and she didn't like the idea that, after grade ten, Janice would have to attend one of the matriculation colleges. Neither was easy to access, living in Tadbury.

Around lunchtime, Marjory was making herself a sandwich, assuming Janice was at the school fair, completely unaware that her daughter was lying on a rug looking up at the sunshine glittering through the pine trees. Her long straight fair hair had fanned out on a rug; her clothes were askew, her jeans zipper open and her pale face flushed by the surge of warmth and excitement of the moment. Gavin rolled towards her, stroking the fingernails of her right hand with his thumb. His embarrassed brown eyes locked questioningly with two startled speedwell pools of liquid. He murmured, 'I couldn't stop!'

Janice's eyes glinted. Her throaty voice sounded foreign even to herself – 'It'll be all right.' Carried away by the euphoria of the setting and the explosion they'd both experienced, she found she could hardly speak.

'I'm sorry… I really am,' said Gavin. They were silent for a moment, each with their own thoughts; two young lovers so different in colouring – he, olive-skinned with black wavy hair; she, almost waiflike, ethereal, with eyes a dusky blue.

'It wasn't like before!' he said abruptly.

'No…' she whispered, leaning on the 'o'. A hiccup formed. She stared at his back. Janice loved everything about Gavin Armstrong. The way he walked into class, his deprecating laugh, his apparent gentleness, and most of all his inventiveness. She loved listening to him retell the dreams in a way no other boy or person had ever talked to her. By day, his physical presence carried her out of school to another realm, and her nights were filled with his hands on her body. Now, staring up at the sky through the needle-bearing branches, she was brought up short. She couldn't understand why Gavin had lost control; he never had before. He had always been so careful, withdrawing almost as soon as he entered her. Sometimes he used a condom, and that was good because the lovemaking lasted longer. Once, during the Easter holiday, when her mother was working a late shift at the Royal, they had ended up convulsed with laughter on the lounge room floor, shooing Zebedee, her Maltese terrier, away. The dog had thought they were playing a game as Gavin fumbled with a condom.

A kaleidoscope of images passed through her mind. The

lounge floor episode… the boat shed where he hauled the dinghy, away from prying eyes, romantic in a spartan kind of way; listening to the waves gently splashing on the rocks, while the tiller or the floorboards dug into their hips. The many close encounters they had shared, in parks and on riverside benches, other people's houses… and Gavin, her knight, always in control, stopping at the crucial point. But today – today was different. She should have been at the school fair helping Mrs Crees, and Gavin was supposed to be fishing with his mates.

Having lessons with the St Virgil boys was great. None of the parents had any idea they met outside class. Intuitively, Janice had sensed today would be different. Gavin had been so serious as they sailed along the coast towards Port Arthur.

She could see it in his eyes – a faraway look, keeping his distance and making sure their hands did not brush while changing positions as he tacked along the coast. It wasn't something you would notice, rather something you felt.

On landing, he'd busied himself tying up the boat and carting the blanket for them to sit upon. Then all of a sudden, it was as though he remembered she was there, and he held out his hand for her to grasp, pulling her gently up the slope. She was confused, not sure of his changing moods. They had lain out on the rug and sat in the dappled sunshine talking, not really having a conversation, more like two instruments in an orchestra tuning up. She was trying to conceal her desire by glancing at a few puffy clouds, the trees and the boats in the bay. He feigned interest in the golden ruins of past detentions. He pointed out the row of lime trees planted long ago along the large expanse of grass towards the sandstone church. To Janice, its spires looked medieval, and he was conqueror of it all with his princess beside him. Was it only a minute ago she had been carried to a height unknown, and now felt nothing?

Gavin shuddered several times. 'I didn't mean this to—'

She cut him off, putting her fingers to his lips. 'Shh, it's all right, I'm sure it will be all right.'

There was a split second of stillness before he did something with a handkerchief and she fumbled in her shoulder bag for a tissue, feeling slightly ridiculous; wishing they were near the public conveniences so she could clean off the stickiness, which was trickling down her inner thigh.

Don't turn around yet, please… The silent message wafted on the air like a caption in a cartoon for the climax had evaded her. The magic had disappeared, leaving in its wake the raw realities. She felt alone, awkward. One minute she had been flying, synchronising; the next she'd plummeted back to earth too fast. Nothing special had happened. Readjusting her clothes, she needed to fill in the silence. The gap between them grew larger as she brushed her hair, looking nowhere in particular. Then a loud crack filled the lunchtime air, followed by several more. She jumped.

'What was that?'

Relieved by the interruption, he took her hairbrush, smoothing his own hair with a wry grin. 'Ah, something to excite the tourists. Probably a re-enactment, like the ghost tours they do at night.'

'I'm hungry!'

He pulled out his wallet from the back pocket of his jeans. 'I've got…'

He was drowned out by another enormous bang, followed by several shots ricocheting across the settlement.

'Really getting into it,' he remarked. Then they heard screams and what sounded like a man yelling.

Janice shuddered, sinking down again and clasping her knees. 'Sounds ghastly.' She looked across at Gavin. More screams wounded the air.

'Doesn't sound right… I'll take a look.'

What he saw were people staggering. They were tourists, not actors. One man fell down. In the distance, two little girls were running towards the lime trees, their cotton dresses of red and yellow acting as a moving target for someone chasing them with a rifle. He saw one of the girls fall, and then was distracted by the cries from the café. Then, silence. His eyes roamed to the car park, where someone was yelling. The buses stood like statues. A car was moving off and stopped. He turned back to Janice, not sure about what he was seeing. It was too realistic.

'Come on, we're going!' His voice sounded disembodied.

'What?' She sensed he was prevaricating.

'It's not a re-enactment!' he said, and pulled her roughly back down towards the dinghy.

'Ah… pull the other one!' She was convinced his odd behaviour was because of a lack of money. She was thirsty and hungry and hadn't expected to be hustled back into the boat so soon. Instead of a nice leisurely sail back to Bellerive, Gavin had started the motor and was forcing Janice's head down in the boat. Frustrated, her fears rose to the surface that Gavin would drop her in favour of Kate Bird, the Head Prefect at St Mary's. Kate, who had a bigger bust than she, and long, light, wavy ginger hair that bounced and swayed over her delicate shoulders. She had seen a look pass between them during an English Literature lesson, where in pairs they were required to present their thoughts on the Brontë sisters and the Victorian era.

'What's got into you?' she shouted above the engine.

He pushed her head down further, hissing, 'Shhh…'

'What do you mean, *shh*?' Janice started to cry, struggling out from under his hand. His face, close to hers, looked ashen. They were going flat out skimming past trees, boulders and the bank. Nervously, Gavin's eyes scoured the other boats moored and the land around before he headed out into Storm Bay. Leaning forward, he motioned with his arm for her to do the same.

Slowly it dawned on Janice that something was terribly wrong. Fear emanated from Gavin, engulfing the boat. It was at least ten minutes before he turned the boat around towards Lauderdale and attempted to sound in control. 'Some nutter…' he began.

Mystified, Janice couldn't make head or tail of what he was talking about. They reached Bellerive much later than she had anticipated, partly because of a headwind and partly because they had run out of fuel. It was six o'clock before they hauled the dinghy up into the boat shed. He kissed her goodnight, unable to comment further on what he thought he had seen. She became indignant when he repeated again and again, 'No matter who asks you where you were today… you were *not* with me at Port Arthur!'

'OK, OK,' she replied, as his hands pressed into her shoulders. 'Right, I've got the message. Of course I'm not going to tell Mum that I was with you – she thinks I was at the school fair.'

'I'm sorry about earlier,' he mumbled.

'Will I see you tomorrow?' Janice asked.

'S'pose so… in English. I think we'd better cool it for a while.'

With that he sauntered away, leaving her to make her way to Macquarie Street and her bus stop. A sinking feeling caused tears as she waited for her bus, desperately trying to think what she had done to cause Gavin to drop her. He'd been odd all day. It was turning dark by the time her bus arrived and she wondered what excuse she could make for getting home so late. The day had turned out all wrong. She'd say she went home to Leanne's after the fair. She'd word her up tomorrow just in case…

Marjory Ryan was on the telephone to St Mary's at five o'clock. She listened to a recorded voice telling her the office would be open at eight o'clock the following morning, and didn't know who else to phone. The earliest anyone heard any news as to what was happening down at the Peninsula was around six o'clock. The news on car radios caught people off-guard. It was unbelievable – someone had run amok at Port Arthur, killing several people.

Susan Middleton, the drama teacher at St Mary's, was at home with the flu marking essays on 'The Triumph of Realism' – Ibsen being their chosen playwright. The phone rang just as she was thinking the standard was not at all bad; in fact she was quite pleasantly surprised.

'Hello, Shushan here,' she managed.

'My God, you sound awful!' said a familiar voice.

'Thanks. I've got the flu. To what do I owe this honour?'

'Just wondering if you had been down to Port Arthur today.'

'Now why would I be going down there? What with this cold, essays to mark and the school fair. Unlike you, my dear brother, I take my job home with me.'

'*Ouch!* Point taken. I was returning from a week on the Sunshine Coast – Noosa, to be precise – when I heard on the car radio that twelve people had been shot down at Port Arthur.'

'Don't be ridiculous! It's all right for some, swanning about. You're not serious?'

'No, really. Tune into your local radio station.'

But there was nothing mentioned. Telephones rang hot and furious as news trickled in from interstate; vague, unbelievable information.

Anna and Nigel, like most people in Tasmania, had no idea what had happened down at the Peninsula until the seven o'clock ABC News. Most people thought, as the death toll rose, that it was so bizarre it couldn't be true. Many people couldn't sleep that night, unable to comprehend why the gunman hadn't been caught. Information was sketchy about the sex of the perpetrator or perpetrators. Even the number was unclear. Rumours were rife, owing to the difficulties of accessibility to the Peninsula. The SAS had been called in; there had been a siege; more people were dead; it was a girl with long blonde hair; she'd hijacked a car...

Gavin went to bed as soon as he arrived home, complaining of a headache. Meanwhile, Janice sat in front of the television in shocked silence, calling to mind something Gavin had muttered when they climbed back into the dinghy: 'Worse than *Deliverance*!' It was a film he had seen several months before.

Anna Crees prayed for her parents' safe arrival, while Nigel looked grave, pouring himself a Scotch and exclaiming 'Christ!' as he watched the news.

Meanwhile, Marion and Leonard Lee, unaware of the tragedy unfolding in Tasmania, were dozing in recliner seats surrounded by dark starry skies and dimmed aircraft lights, imagining their arrival at Hobart Airport and hoping their daughter would be there to meet them. Marion was surprised at the smoothness of the flight, and pictured in her mind's eye visiting the various places Anna had mentioned in her letters. She was partial to a delicate flavoured cream cheese and was looking forward to tasting King Island Brie. Strange to think that King Island was discovered by a Captain Reid in 1798 – just a dot on the map, and now it was famous for fresh food.

One thing that concerned her was having access to unadulterated food. You could never be too careful, and for this reason she had grown vegetables herself and some fruit; the rest she hoped were chemical-free, bought at Staines Market. Now closing her eyes and, forcing herself to look forward rather than to all she had left behind, she imagined touring with Leonard the famous

Tamar Valley boutique wineries, and seeing aged craftsmen working with rainforest timbers in various hamlets across the state. All in all, she had a romantic view of Tasmania, because packed in one of their tea chests was a gnarled, richly coloured fruit bowl Anna had sent the previous year for Christmas. A small wooden bowl of various shades ranging from cream to brown was another gift, and one she had been proud to display, filled with nuts, when visitors came around, explaining to her goggle-eyed guests that it was made of sassafras wood. Glass-blowers and their delicate designs, coupled with handmade furniture, and spinning and weaving enthusiasts with their fleecy lined boots and coats, swam before her eyes. The footwear were oddly named – 'Ugg boots'. She had no idea where the word came from, but liked the sound of it.

Tasmania was frozen in time; not such a bad thing, according to the locals, but to Marion it conjured up scenes from Hardy's 'Wessex' novels, featuring enormous properties owned by the gentry. The lack of progress in some quarters, which was detriment to the whole, was the reality she would have to discover for herself. Marion didn't want to be reminded of places like Richmond Jail, Maria Island or any of the brutal penal settlements; even contemplating them made her shudder. As a child, a well-meaning aunt had taken her to the Tower of London, and for days after she had dreams of being shut in a small stone room, surrounded by unearthly screams and near-darkness, freezing to death. For that reason she disliked history, which dealt with macabre stories of past kings and queens of England. She preferred to brush over the beginnings of Tasmania and its Dickensian brutality. Hers was a wounded spirit, looking for a soft landing, unaware of the drama taking place at Port Arthur. And like those souls who regularly tuned into the seven o'clock news, she would be badly shaken for many months by the unbelievable horror now unfolding in Tasmania.

They flew into Tullarmarine Airport refreshed from their stopover in Osaka, but nevertheless irritated by the lengthy questions at passport control. Retrieving their bags and suitcases, they made their way across to the Domestic Terminal.

With their luggage checked in at the Ansett desk, they received their seating and boarding pass, then made their way towards their respective gate lounge. Leonard noticed reporters and cameramen creating quite a commotion near another counter. Something was going on. He said gently, 'You go on, love, I'll get a newspaper. *Home and Garden*?'

She nodded and had that peculiar feeling walking down the concourse of not really being there, light-headed, watching chatting hostesses with their trolleys, and groups of landing passengers rushing past in the opposite direction. Her feet felt stiff but not as swollen as the previous night, her clothes heavy. She ducked into a convenience with a picture of a lady on the door and peered into a mirror, touching its edges then her face. She was really here, in Australia, brushing her hair in the ladies, not as a tourist but as a resident. The turmoil inside of her was not apparent to those washing their hands nearby; however, on hearing a North Country accent, which she couldn't quite place, she nonetheless found it comforting.

Further down the concourse she caught snippets of conversation but found it hard to make out above the general noise at the gate lounge. Watching, she had to admit that she had never experienced complete strangers talking to each other, and thought, *How odd*, when she heard a man with an enormous camera flung across his shoulder asking anyone if they would give up their seat and catch a later plane. How extraordinary, there was a woman similarly attired doing the same. To her mind there were too many people trying to catch the same plane. Relieved, she saw Leonard approaching. He explained, 'It's very crowded back there. I couldn't get a local paper so I bought an *Express*.'

'It's very crowded here too. See that cameraman, he's trying to get that woman to give up her seat!'

Leonard ushered Marion into a corner where two seats were vacant and sat down heavily, eyeing the crowd and choosing his words carefully. He frowned. 'There seems to have been some...' – he paused; words like maniac, madman and nutcase went through his mind, but he decided on *contretemps* – '...down at Port Arthur.'

'Oh, so they are reporters,' was all Marion said, and began flicking through a magazine that was left on the chair by the previous occupants, wishing any turmoil away by staring at the glossy pictures.

The plane swooped down across the water, losing height every few minutes. Marion couldn't bear to look out of the window until they came to a halt at Hobart Airport. The glare from the pure air and the easy proximity of welcoming parties brought a tear to her eye. She could see Anna as soon as she reached the terminal, and following greetings, she was amused to be standing in a shed attached to the arrivals area, where their luggage arrived stacked on top of each other on several open-air trailers linked together. Leonard raised his eyebrows, and Marion whispered, 'How bizarre!'

It struck her immediately they were on the road, how few cars there were. She reminded herself that Tasmania was a small island with a small population, while Anna kept up a running commentary, pointing out places of interest. She'd deliberately taken a scenic route, cutting across Battery Point to Sandy Bay Yacht Club, then along Sandy Bay Road to Tadbury; however, Marion was too overwhelmed to take in much of what she said, whereas Leonard wanted to sign up at the Yacht Club there and then.

Meanwhile the senior History mistress, Pauline Attwood, was ushering in Anna's home group with her own for prayers. Janice Ryan was absent, and those in the know were aware that Mrs Crees had been given the day off to pick up her parents at the airport. Gossiping girls thought she might be pregnant and wouldn't be back for a week. No one knew why Janice Ryan hadn't been at the fair the day before, or why she was absent this Monday morning. Up on the hill at the Barrack Street Campus, Gavin Armstrong was also notable by his absence, not wanting to face anyone after yesterday's ordeal, especially Janice Ryan; and St Mary's staff did their best to quell any rumours about what was happening down at the Peninsula.

Nigel Crees found himself embroiled with other members of staff during recess at Hutchins School, working out whether or not they should call the whole school to assembly, as little work was being accomplished. The boys were intrigued by such a grotesque event, while the adults were reminded of the Hoddle

Street murders in Melbourne a few years earlier, and the more recent horror of a school in Dunblane, Scotland, where a man ran amok killing staff and children. People everywhere in the workforce and on the streets were agog with speculation, as there was only one road leading down to Port Arthur and that had been closed to all traffic except police cars and ambulances. Those living in the area were terrified, and those trying to get home were thwarted by officialdom. Many people hadn't been able to sleep the previous night, unable to comprehend why the gunman hadn't been caught. Rumours spread. The SAS had been called in to take over; there were two gunmen; there had been a siege; twenty-plus people had been shot… Information was so sketchy that even the sex of the perpetrators was uncertain.

Right across Australia, people were appalled that such a thing could happen in broad daylight in peaceful Tasmania. The irony of a massacre taking place on the very soil of a penal settlement, now a tourist destination, numbed sensible conversation, leaving many questions unanswered. Who would do such a thing, and why?

That evening, after a prawn and cheese mornay accompanied by a green salad, Anna brewed Colombian coffee as Leonard and Nigel tuned into the ABC newsflash. Marion gazed at the screen, only registering that the body count had risen. Hardly had she arrived full of optimism than this ghastly occurrence had taken place, putting a blight on the place she had elected to call home. She couldn't sit still, and began clearing the table of dishes.

'Mum, leave that, I'll do it,' said Anna, and Marion sank down on the sofa, fixing her eyes on a vase of jonquils. Suddenly she said in a strangled voice, 'So that's why everyone was talking to complete strangers!' Her voice rose. 'Complete strangers at an airport!'

She lapsed back into silence, gazing at the flowers, knowing that in any minute she was going to sneeze, as jonquils always did that to her within a closed space. For some uncanny reason her mind recalled the days her father used to travel up to London. He caught the 7.40 a.m. train to Waterloo carrying the *Daily Mirror* under his arm and a black umbrella. It was always the same train, the same time, the same carriage with the same people, and not once did anyone say more than 'Good morning' to each other throughout his commuting years to the city.

After coffee and some desultory conversation, Leonard suggested they turn in for the night, adding, 'It's been a long day.'

'Of course, Dad. Give us a call if you need anything.'

Anna and Nigel sat quietly listening to the strange noises in their house, each with their own thoughts.

Marion looked with dismay at the size of their bedroom.

'You all right, love?'

She made an effort at lightness. 'More or less. The bed's a bit hard.'

'I meant, you know…?'

'Oh, of course, it could happen anywhere.' She didn't sound convincing.

'Things will look better in the morning. Sleep tight.'

'There's a lavender bag under my pillow.'

'That's nice.' Leonard thanked God for small mercies. He was asleep in five minutes, dreaming of a house where you could hear the waves crashing on the shore from his bedroom. Marion lay awake, mulling over the day's events and finally dreaming she was back by the River Thames, walking along the riverbank and watching the water silently glide by.

The days passed, and it would be almost three months before they could agree on a house, mainly because Marion was looking for something resembling her house in Laleham, and had trouble coming to terms with the fact that most houses they saw were nothing like what she expected.

Relieved, Anna smiled for the first time in days. The population in Tasmania came to terms with the enormity of the tragedy that had played itself out on the weekend of 28 April 1996. Marion was coming to accept that her feet were on Tasmanian soil, not in England's green and pleasant land – or to be precise, the gentle Thames Valley. Leonard hoped that the horrific stories which unfolded in the newspapers describing the carnage at the Broad Arrow Café and surrounding area wouldn't colour Marion's perception of Tasmania. As it happened, he needn't have worried on that score, as she was far more preoccupied with the brightness of the light, the deceptive glare which made her squint, forcing her to wear sunglasses outside, whatever the weather, and the crisp, vicious wind which took her breath away, especially when crossing Davey or Macquarie Streets in the city. What she did enjoy was the abundance of fresh fish to choose from down at the docks, the friendliness of the people, and that houses had laundries.

Leonard, on the other hand, wasted no time joining Sandy Bay Yacht Club, the Kingston Golf Club and paying his yearly subscription to the ABC Concert Series. He made friends easily, chatting with all and sundry, no more so than at the local post office which doubled as a paper shop. This he visited daily, combining an early morning walk along the river, then up through Tadbury Crescent and back down Nubeena Crescent before returning for breakfast. An amazing feeling of freedom energised him to do anything he wanted, money being no object, as the exchange rate was in his favour.

It hadn't taken long for Leonard to feel cramped, living in the same house as Anna and Nigel, even though they were out at work all day. In exasperation, having tripped over his own belongings for the umpteenth time in their bedroom, he re-marked, 'You're far too fussy, Marion! I can't go on much longer like this!'

But as far as she was concerned, the houses they looked at in Sandy Bay didn't appeal to her: Mount Nelson and its bends, although picturesque, was frightening to negotiate in bad weather; and Battery Point, although of historic interest, seemed rather noisy.

Tadbury on the other hand was only fifteen minutes from Hobart, five minutes to the local shops, close to the beach and to her daughter, Anna. There they found a house in Devon Walk, nestled into Tadbury Beach. Even now, having settled in, Marion wasn't too sure they had made the right decision, as the house was weatherboard with a steep gradient leading to the lane behind; but she liked the ambiance. She could see from her lounge and dining windows flowering native bushes dotted along the foreshore, with tall pine trees growing along the bank. To her left a few small dinghies lay face down on the grassy verge, and in front of her house, across the lane, steps led down to the beach, sporting a newly installed handrail for safety.

Marion took to walking alone along Tadbury beach in the early afternoons while Leonard was off at one club or another. She herself wasn't interested in golf, and was terrified of sailing. There was a particularly large black flat boulder amid some smaller ones she liked to sit upon, watching the little waves eddy around her, the foam rushing into nooks and crannies as if looking for a hiding place. On this particular day in June, her gaze reached up to the enormous Allen Cliffs sheltering the bay, rising quite steeply not far from her home. She wondered who dared walk up or down, as she herself was sure she'd slip or be blown off by the relentless wind the locals called 'the sea breeze'. She stepped over the rocks to an iron-slatted seat she had seen tucked away out of the wind, from where a 180° panorama unfolded and the white lighthouse in Storm Bay was clear against the azure sky. Past experiences rose up eclipsing the beauty of the scene, and Marion was lost to its magnificence, wondering how she had ended up here, away from everything she knew.

Meeting Leonard was the most exciting thing that had happened in her life. She was behind the counter in Boots, the chemist, and he was waiting for a prescription to be filled. They had exchanged pleasantries, and she noted the scripts were similar for his mother as they were for hers. They exchanged details and began a tentative relationship... built on what? Compassion for each other's circumstances? Maybe.

Marion gazed across the river, remembering a particular visit from her Aunt Jane, who was nothing like her mother, asking her what she'd like to do when she left school. She didn't like to say and pretended she didn't know, so Doreen replied for her, with what she knew was a winning smile. 'Oh, Marion wants to get married and have babies, don't you, dear?'

'Is that all?' asked Aunt Jane sceptically.

Blushing and diffidently, Marion replied, 'Well, first I'd like to work in a kindergarten or be a nanny to a rich family in London.'

'Don't be silly, Marion! You, coping in London?' Doreen had laughed, showing irregular teeth. 'Fanciful ideas! What would I do without you nearby?' The clasp and smile had crushed all resistance from then on.

She had gone to work in Boots in Staines High Street, not three miles from their semi-detached house in Ashford. Doreen didn't see any reason for her daughter to move into a flat on her own, so she'd stayed at home, listening to her mother's complaints, attending functions her mother had a fancy for, even playing Bingo once a week at the Links Hotel, not ten minutes away. It was easier to acquiesce than to argue. Doreen was prone to violent tempers. The years wore on, and the invitations to dances petered out. Doreen developed Alzheimer's disease, and Marion found herself as chief nurse, housekeeper and general dogsbody. Two years after her mother's death, her father followed, struck down by a car in Staines High Street while crossing the road to the tobacconist.

Now here she was sitting on an iron bench, far away from her beloved Laleham and the river, watching waves crashing onto the rocks, feeling alienated, not appreciating the wild beauty, seeing little of Leonard, and less of Anna. How did you get to know people? You could hardly walk up to a complete stranger on the beach and begin a conversation. They'd think you were odd, and who could say that that person would be likeable? She thought wistfully about school reunions, decorating the church at Laleham and the people she used to know.

Sometimes in the night when the waves roared she felt quite frightened, burying herself under the covers. Stupid, really, as Leonard was there beside her. This will not do, she told herself. She'd drop over to Anna's shortly, as she should soon be home from St Mary's. Pulling her coat around her against the wind, she walked through the playground on Tadbury Reserve and down once again on to the beach. There was hardly a soul about, only a young girl standing on the edge of the waves with her shoes in her hand, gazing out to sea. By the time Marion reached the handful of steps her hands were numb. She crossed the hundred or so yards to their small white wooden gate, fumbling with the latch. The rose bushes on her left had been pruned heavily, and she wondered what colours they would be as she turned around the corner of the house, unlocking the glass-panelled back door.

On entering the kitchen, she put the kettle on for a cup of tea, took her coat off and lit the gas fire. Then she opened the desk, carefully placed to see the view beyond. It was time to write a letter to Alice.

Leonard, surprised at how easy it was to make friends in Tasmania, had paid the necessary sporting club fees as soon as they were settled in their new home. The atmosphere had become decidedly strained at Anna's, which didn't surprise him. It had taken Marion too long to make up her mind. He thanked God she had finally agreed to the house in Devon Walk, because right in the middle of its small lawn stood a Cox's pippin tree. Blackberries grew over the back fence, and several very old apricot trees grew on the rise above the courtyard. There was no accounting for what went on in his wife's mind. On this particular morning, having earlier been on his constitutional to the local paper shop, collected the *International Express* and read the *Hobart Mercury* from cover to cover, he was musing over a glass of beer at the yacht club with a fellow countryman who had moved to Tasmania some twenty years before.

'I read the Prime Minister has mooted a gun buy-back!' Leonard remarked.

'That won't go down well, I'm telling you. Just because some lunatic runs amok, everyone is tarred by the same brush. There are guns everywhere, mostly used for hunting or by farmers to keep rodents at bay.' His companion sipped his beer noisily.

Leonard regarded the white turtleneck jumper, navy blazer with embossed brass buttons and clean white handkerchief properly folded in the breast pocket. A strong weather-beaten face with piercing blue eyes didn't fit easily with shaggy grey brows and hair the colour of steel. For someone in his late forties, Bill Nash was quite slim, lanky even, which Leonard put down to all the sailing. It was good talking about current affairs with a local. It helped him to feel that he belonged somehow. Opening a packet of cashew nuts, he said, 'I read the state is moving to seize Bryant's assets – worth up to 1.5 million.'

'The whole thing's, you know, weird. How had he inherited that house in Clare Street, North Hobart, in the first place?'

'How do you mean?'

Replying, Bill leant closer, lowering his voice. 'The owner died in a car crash… Bryant was in the car at the time.' Eyebrows raised, he tapped his nose.

'Aha!' Leonard chewed a nut. 'What I can't get my head around is that he was wealthy – took overseas trips and so on. So it wasn't money… some sort of revenge thing! What kind of person does that? I mean, it wasn't one person he killed.'

'You'll have another?' suggested Bill.

Leonard nodded assent, watching his friend's back as he ambled towards the bar, thinking how relieved he was that Marion had shown little interest in the macabre stories which had dominated the papers for days, culminating in a large funeral at the Anglican Cathedral in Macquarie Street. All she had remarked at the time was, 'That is the first time I have heard a Jewish rabbi, a Buddhist priest, a Uniting Church minister and a Muslim all take part in the same service within a Christian church, presided over by an archbishop!'

He still couldn't fathom why anyone would shoot down thirty-five people at random, including children, and injure twenty more because of a grudge.

'Thanks,' he said, accepting a fresh pint, which he placed on a beer mat with 'Tooheys' scrawled in blue across the front. He would have to get to know all the Australian beers. One thing was sure, they were always ice cold.

'It was mayhem, you know, absolute mayhem!' Bill said.

'We arrived the day after. I had hoped this place would be untouched by this sort of thing. I mean England now is…' He shrugged, shaking his head.

'Oh, it is, it is, normally. This is about as sensational as it gets. Don't worry, old chap, nothing happens here. This place is as quiet as—'

'—a grave.' Leonard lit a cigarette. A pensive silence followed.

Bill cleared his throat. 'What I mean is, he was the *exception*. Intellectually limited, or so the psychiatric report read. I doubt whether some idiot will come in here blasting us all to kingdom come. Look, mate, I must dash. Lots to do.'

'Looking forward to meeting the rest of the crew. Haven't told Marion yet, but she'll be all right with it.'

'Good. Between now and Christmas you'll get to know them all. Mostly young 'uns, but if you're game, you're most welcome. It's no picnic, I assure you. See you later.'

With that, Bill stood up, buttoned his jacket, waved farewell and nodded to the barman, acknowledging others on his way out. Leonard watched him go, wishing he'd come to Australia years before. Here, he was a new boy on the block, so to speak, and was already being offered a berth to sail in the Sydney to Hobart.

Bill was a nice guy, a really nice guy. It wouldn't have happened in England; he hadn't attended the right school, and certainly had no pedigree. Life was looking decidedly better than it had for months. No one seemed to care where you were from or how much you earned. As long as you had the necessary wherewithal for subs and the suchlike, you were accepted. Still, sailing a dinghy around was not in the same league as sailing on the open seas. This would be a superb challenge.

For several weeks now Marion had contemplated joining St Luke's Anglican Church, which she passed regularly driving along the highway or visiting the local shopping centre. Unlike All Saints' in Laleham, this was a modern white building with enormous plain glass windows behind the altar, enabling parishioners when standing, to experience the view over the River Derwent through its massive windows. Leonard had shown little interest, being preoccupied with his golf, sailing and the local tennis club. She had hoped her next-door neighbour, who she had seen leaving every Sunday morning, ostensibly to attend church, would accompany her, but realised she attended the Baptist Church an hour earlier. Deciding to enlist Anna, Marion walked up her pathway at 4.30 on a Thursday afternoon.

Anna spied her mother as she was preparing dinner for Nigel and herself. She had just unpacked the groceries and begun chopping the vegetables for a Thai curry, having had a trying day at school that culminated in a difficult staff meeting. She was relishing being alone.

'Anna, it's me.'

Sighing, Anna wiped her fingers on a tea towel, set her face into a smile and crossed the kitchen, thinking the next house they rented would have the kitchen at the back, out of the sight of callers. 'Coming, Mum!' she called, and with that she flung the door wide open, startling Marion. 'What brings you here in the middle of the week?'

Marion, sensing the false atmosphere, surveyed the chopped vegetables. 'Can I help you with that?' she said, indicating a lump of brown that looked like squashed dates. 'What is it?'

'Tamarind. You soak it in boiling water to extract the juice. Here, taste it?'

'Erm… no, thank you.'

An embarrassed silence hung on the air. Anna turned away to fill the kettle. Marion felt awkward gazing at strange vegetables. She'd never had a Thai curry and looked across at her daughter, realising she didn't know her at all. She felt like a complete stranger in her daughter's kitchen. They had nothing in common, now that Anna was a mature woman.

In her confusion she blurted out, 'I haven't come for a cuppa!'

Patiently, Anna replied, 'It's not for a cup of tea, Mum.'

'Oh.'

'It's for the tamarind to soak in, but if you like I'll make you one.'

'No, no.' She stood watching her daughter cutting up various leaves, pounding garlic and opening a tin of coconut cream. Marion's diffidence was irritating Anna by the minute.

'What can I do for you then?'

'Well, I was wondering if you would accompany me to St Luke's. You do go there?'

'Occasionally.'

'Would you come with me?'

'When?'

'This Sunday.'

'What about Dad?' A small sigh did not escape Marion's ears.

'He's not keen. Seems he has plenty to occupy himself,' Marion remarked with a nervous laugh.

'It's not that I won't come, Mum, but weekends are the only time Nigel and I can have a lie-in. Besides, what with all the marking and preparation, I just don't have the time,' Anna finished lamely.

'Oh, well, it was just an idea.'

'Why don't you go?'

'What, on my own?'

'Yes, why not? I hear they're a friendly crowd.' She looked up at Marion, wondering how she came to have such a nervous mother. 'They won't eat you, you know,' she smiled.

'Oh, I couldn't walk in there on my own. Not alone.' Marion attempted to regain some dignity by forcing a smile. 'Anyway, I mustn't keep you... I can see you're busy. I'll see myself out.' Haltingly, she whispered, 'Bye, love!'

The door closed quietly behind her. Anna stood in the middle of the kitchen, feeling guilty and enraged. Exasperated with her father for landing her in this situation, she decided to call him on his mobile on Saturday morning when she knew he would be at the golf club. Something had to be done about her mother. Words like 'hopeless' and 'dependent' came to mind. She's not my responsibility. Why is she so pathetic? Vigorously she stirred the vegetables in the wok with the chicken. What with conforming all day as a teacher, and now this – it was too much.

She and Nigel opened a bottle of Hardy's Chardonnay to have with their chicken curry. Anna had gone to some effort to set the table nicely with linen napkins, a lighted candle in the middle, warmed soft bread rolls and a tossed green salad.

Nigel mentioned in passing, 'Oh, I had a letter from Matt Inglis today.'

'Oh?'

'You remember him? Done well for himself. Headship of King's Christian College in Queensland. It's co-ed, interdenomina-tional.'

'Vaguely.'

He leant back, looking at Anna over the rim of his wine glass, realising she was in some kind of mood.

'Well...?' She stretched the word out.

'What? No, you first. I haven't heard how your day went.'

'Much the same as usual. More counselling than teaching. Janice Ryan – you know, who lives around the corner – wasn't there again today; another student from my home group was caught smoking at lunchtime, and of course it's all my fault. Several staff were away, so I lost my free period and had to take a science class, which I know next to nothing about. The relevant information, such as where they were up to and what was expected of them, wasn't supplied. I found it extremely difficult. It was a nightmare trying to stay ahead of the students and keep order.

'Then we had a fire drill, which wasted valuable time out of my year twelve English class; and to cap it all off, we were inflicted with another waffly staff meeting about encouraging self-esteem in the students!' Her voice rose in indignation. 'It's the *staff* who need help, not the students!'

'Not a good day, then?' He leant over, refilling her glass.

'To crown everything, I had hardly been home before Mother was around again, wanting me to go to St Luke's with her this Sunday!'

'Oh… and you don't want to go.'

'What do you think?' she said irritably.

'It's worse than you expected, isn't it?'

'Yes,' she said with a sigh. 'It's not fair. I didn't ask them to come here. Dad's all right, he's off doing this and that, but she has no idea how to get involved, make friends or amuse herself. That's the third time she's been around this week. I don't know what to do, she seems so lonely…' Anna's voice trailed off.

'Have you rung your dad?'

'Not yet! I don't know what to say,' she wailed.

'My poor love, you've had quite a day, what with St Mary's—'

'Which is wearing me out!' She looked miserable, pushing her food around the plate. 'Everything that goes wrong involving my home group is seen to be my fault. Why should I be responsible? I'm not their mother. And another thing, we don't get a lunch hour! Half of it disappears in assemblies, sorting out problems, or doing yard duty… chasing up students to clean the tuck shop area. Honestly. Nigel, we are not supposed to leave the school grounds… it's like being watched by big brother. Teaching English is the last thing I think about. I'm not a social worker!'

'Of course not.'

'What with the school, and now Mother, I feel hemmed in.' She picked up their plates, scraping them clean before putting them in the dishwasher. 'Think I'll take a shower. Will you make the coffee? So, what did Matt Inglis want?'

Nigel busied himself with the coffee grinder, undecided whether to impart the gist of his conversation with his old friend.

'Nigel, what did he say?'

'Who?'

'Look, do you want to tell me or don't you?' Anna banged the dishwasher door closed, turned around with her arms folded across her chest and leant against the kitchen bench, glaring at nothing in particular.

'Not a lot,' said Nigel, pulling her towards himself and ruffling her hair.

She searched his face. 'There's more, I know it. He wants to come and stay for six months… stress leave or something!'

'No,' he laughed. 'It's nothing like that!'

'I couldn't put up with anyone else in our house. Maybe there's something wrong with me. Other people I know love having their houses full of people and chaos!'

'There's nothing wrong with you that a good—'

She cut him off. '*Nigel!*'

'I was going to say a good night's sleep,' he said, and kissed the tip of her nose. Silence ensued while he boiled the water, measured the ground coffee in the glass cafetière, took the milk from the fridge, and placed two dark green cups adorned with gold trim on matching saucers on the bench before looking up. 'He offered me a job.'

'He did *what*? You must be joking!'

The kettle boiled. Methodically, Nigel filled the coffee jug and replaced the plunger on the top as both of them watched the coffee granules sink to the bottom.

'Are you saying he offered you a teaching position?'

'Yes.'

'So…' she said carefully. 'What are you going to do?'

'I rang him this afternoon explaining the position here with your mum and dad.'

'Did you mention me?'

Feeling cornered, Nigel's voice rose. 'Of course I did! I said I'd have to discuss it with you.'

Puzzled, she sighed. 'But I thought you liked it here.'

'I do. But think of it – all that sun and warmth!' Warming to his theme, he went on, 'The school's not far from the beach, and set in lovely grounds. I've checked on their website.'

'So… what's the position?' Her almond eyes looked wary.

Nigel pushed the plunger down halfway, 'Vice Principal of the High School.'

'Meaning better pay and status?'

He nodded. Anna thought back to the night when Matt came to dinner. While attending a headmasters' conference at the casino in Sandy Bay, Matt had contacted Nigel. Anna had gone to bed around 10 p.m., leaving the two of them reminiscing about their school days at Canberra Boys' Grammar and the ANU. Later, after Nigel had driven Matt back to the casino, he had tripped over the bedside rug, waking her up with a start by falling across the bed in the wee small hours of the morning.

'Are you going to accept?'

He was slow in answering.

'Well, are you?' she repeated.

'To be honest I'd like to…'

'What about your mum and dad? I thought that was why we were here in Tasmania.'

He ignored her comment. 'If I don't move on it and give him a definite answer, someone else will come out of the woodwork and get the job instead of me.'

'Don't be silly, Nigel! If Matt wants you, you'd get the job.'

Pushing the plunger down to the bottom, Nigel waited a few seconds before pouring the coffee. 'As you know, my mum and dad are somewhere in Europe or wherever having a whale of a time. It wouldn't matter to them where I lived. Let's both calm down and relax. You go and have a shower, I'm going to watch *Front up.*'

With decisiveness, he switched on the television, tuned into a commercial channel and sat down in an easy chair with his coffee. Anna carried her coffee to the bathroom. The evening's conversation had been quite a revelation. She'd always assumed Nigel had wanted to teach in Australia because his parents lived there. Tonight, for the first time she realised she was wrong; he just preferred Australia to England. Australia was his home; he didn't have a close relationship with his parents, nor did he have a longing to live near them in Tasmania. What about me? she thought. What do I want? He hadn't considered her. What about my life, and where I'd like to live? The question went round and round in her head as she stood in the shower, washing away all her pent-up emotion. What am I going to do about Mum?

Similar sentiments were being echoed thousands of miles away in Alice Ashley's lounge room as she reread Marion's letter. It was like a real estate advertisement. There was a diagram enclosed, with a photo taken from the deck overlooking the River Derwent. The kitchen and lounge room had access to the deck through French windows. Strangely, there appeared to be a bathroom downstairs and a bedroom, which the Lees preferred to the two upstairs. There was a laundry room that Marion had waxed eloquently about, where she could do her ironing, and a small courtyard outside the front door, which no one used. She had gone on describing the kitchen, which had a breakfast bar that was useless; but there was a bay window behind the sink, and apple and rose trees grew upon a bank leading steeply to the lane above. Alice saw from the diagram that Marion could see the river and the next-door neighbours coming and going, because the lane finished in a cul-de-sac. Interestingly, she hadn't mentioned Anna or Leonard or anything that she was doing, nor had she mentioned attending the local Anglican church.

Concerned, Alice peered anxiously into the envelope, thinking she had missed a page. Looking for clues as to Marion's state of mind, she could find nothing to suggest she was happy – or otherwise. Finally, she propped the photo up on the mantelpiece and put the letter away, to be replied to when she had worked out what to say.

On Saturday, Leonard answered a hysterical call on his mobile from Anna just as he was about to swing his driver on the fifteenth hole at Kingston Golf Course.

'Excuse me,' he said, gazing at the golf ball. 'I'm in the middle of a game of golf, Anna! I can't talk now. I'll call you later.' He sounded nettled. 'Yes, yes, in about an hour.' He snapped the phone closed and said, 'Sorry about that.'

'Everything all right?'

'Oh, fine. A domestic issue.'

The last thing he needed was to be reminded about Marion's lack of confidence from his daughter. Here he was, having the time of his life. His partner was waiting for him to tee off, practising his swing, attempting to look nonchalant when Leonard knew he was annoyed by the interruption. It quite spoiled his game, worrying about Marion. Later that evening, under duress, he volunteered to go with her to St Luke's the following morning, but made it quite clear he wasn't about to attend regularly.

'Sunday sailing does me more good than sitting in church!' he said, leafing through the *TV Times*.

'Do you miss ringing the bells?' Marion asked.

'Not really. You move on. You don't look back. "Move on" is my motto – and so should you,' he said firmly.

Marion digested this piece of advice, turning it around in her mind. 'Don't you miss Laleham?'

'What do you think?'

'I don't know,' she hesitated. 'You seem to relax better here.'

'Too right I do. *And*,' he emphasised, 'I'm going to enjoy all the things I never could do, for one reason or another. We're not getting any younger. To be truthful I haven't been this happy for years.'

Pondering this fact while she was washing up led Marion to recall when exactly it was they had decided to come to Tasmania, only to realise it had been taken for granted she would fall in with Leonard's idea. She had never actually agreed. In subtle ways, plans for moving had occurred. Passports had been renewed, airline brochures left on the coffee table and there were more frequent phone calls to Anna. By the time she had realised Leonard was serious, it was too late to voice her opinion. It had become a fait accompli, like most events in her life; someone else had made up her mind for her. She had been persuaded against her own inclinations, and now that she was here, even her own daughter couldn't find the time to spend with her. She had made that quite clear; and Leonard was tearing around like a schoolboy, indulging in passions she had known nothing about. She moved back into the lounge opposite her husband, who was reading a yachting magazine, and announced, 'I'd like to visit Port Arthur and Richmond sometime.'

'Whatever for? I should have thought after what had happened there that would be the last place you would want to go.'

'I suppose you're right – I just thought I haven't been to any of the places we talked about before leaving England, and I'd like to see the church there – the one which sheltered some of the people – the one we saw on the television at Port Arthur.'

She wondered for a moment if Martin Bryant killed all those people as a result of loneliness. She'd often felt alone, no more so than at the present time. Meanwhile, Leonard tried to recall if there was any instability in his wife's family that he should know about. If Marion hadn't taken so long in choosing their house, they might have visited a few places.

'You're right,' he said finally, 'we haven't been anywhere. There's a very good winery up Launceston way, perhaps in a fortnight we could cruise up there. Would you like that?' Anything to ease the situation. She did look a little downcast.

At a quarter to nine the following Sunday, Leonard reversed his pride and joy, a dark green Jaguar, into St Luke's gravel car park, remarking, 'It's running well.' Going around to Marion's side, he opened her door and they walked towards the entrance. As they crossed the square, a pleasant middle-aged man alighted from an old Hillman, making towards a small door to the left of the building in a hurry. 'Looks like the minister,' Leonard remarked, and was secretly pleased he had brought his car over from England.

Before Marion had time to reply, they were being welcomed heartily by a large woman reeking of perfume, her hair in a complicated style fixed by visible pins on top of her head, and words gushing from her bright red lipsticked mouth. Books and pamphlets were shoved into their hands, while a spotty teenager stared at them without moving a muscle. Their first impression of the interior was of light and sunshine. The pews were honey-coloured, the church was bare of ornament barring a large wooden cross hanging in front of the centre windows, through which they could see coloured rooftops in the near vicinity.

A small elderly woman was sitting at a piano on the right at the front, and as they sat down on the opposite side, a competent organist was playing just in front of them. Leonard could see his

Jaguar from where he was sitting, and noticed more cars arriving. It seemed rather higgledy-piggledy out in the car park, and he hoped his car wouldn't collect a dent. Marion knelt down to pray, but found it hard to concentrate because the people in the pew behind were talking about their week's activities. When she resumed her seat, she could see the organist shuffling music, two chairs on either side of a small table under the cross, a plain wooden lectern in the centre and the pulpit to the right of it. She closed her eyes, wishing the people behind would be quiet. Books crashed behind her and there was muffled laughter.

'I dropped it!'

'Where – what?'

'My earring!' More scuffling.

'Can you see it?'

There was a bump on the back of the pew as the organist launched into the first hymn. The congregation rose.

Marion turned to see what was happening behind her. An elderly woman, smartly dressed, was bending down, as was a silver-haired gentleman wearing a hearing aid. Two women processed up the aisle with the man they saw in the car park. The smaller of the two wore a black cassock, said the prayers and preached the sermon. The other, dressed in white, said nothing until the end of the service, when she pronounced the blessing. The man, presumably the minister, although robed, sat in a pew throughout the whole proceedings. A middle-aged man dressed in rumpled jeans, sandshoes and a scruffy jumper read the lessons. He seemed to stand on one leg throughout, had some difficulty finding the various passages, made several errors and read each passage after the other without any response in between.

Sunday lunch at her parents' house was becoming a nuisance for Anna. She'd far rather be at home with Nigel, just the two of them, and here was her mother carrying on about the service.

'...she was a small woman with her hair severely pulled back into a bun. Reminded me of Charlotte Brontë, who I'm sure did not bellow at people like this woman in black did.' She looked across at Leonard for support as he carved the roast, then handed the vegetables to Nigel. 'A child of around two was banging blocks throughout the service, and what with the noise and trying to find one's place from one book to another, I was lost.'

'More like a test to see who could keep up!' Leonard laughed.

'It couldn't have been that bad, Mum.'

'I tell you it was. Where was the mystery, the uplifting? No one could come away and feel renewed spiritually. The light was so bright I needed my sunglasses!'

'I thought churches were supposed to be gloomy places,' chuckled Nigel.

'Well, this one certainly wasn't! It was more like a circus. If that is Anglicanism in Australia, you can keep it!'

'Maybe I should have gone after all,' said Anna. 'Sounds innovative!'

Leonard frowned in his daughter's direction, while Nigel busied himself with the horseradish.

'All that noise, people chatting… absolutely no reverence. I'll have to find somewhere else.'

An uncomfortable silence ensued. Leonard cleared his throat, 'And things at Hutchins – how's it going?'

'Ah, you know – much the same, keep chugging along.' Nigel seemed preoccupied with a tiny teaspoon, fishing around the jar for horseradish.

'I expect the little blighters keep you on your toes?'

Nigel caught Anna's eye, and she in turn looked down at her plate. 'Not really, they're nice lads on the whole.'

Well, at least I tried… whatever is the matter with the two of them? thought Leonard. Another awkward silence cast a pall over the meal. Marion attempted to keep the conversation going, completely mystified at the lack of normal social etiquette. 'Oh, by the way, erm… I saw that girl you are always complaining about, Anna. With her mother.' She rushed on. 'Well, I suppose it was her mother. She looked very unhappy.' Placing her knife and fork together, she looked up at Anna before wiping her mouth with a pink napkin.

'What girl?' was the response.

'The one you pointed out to me when we were in the shopping centre just after we arrived,' she said patiently, wondering why Anna was being obtuse.

'You mean Janice Ryan,' Anna said flatly. 'So, she is up and about, then. I was told by one of the girls she had German measles.'

'Oh, I don't think so, dear. She…'

'Did you speak to her?'

'Well, no, but Len's seen her too.'

Typical, Anna thought angrily, showing her up in front of Nigel because she had better things to do than be dragged along to St Luke's morning service.

'Yup, I've seen her. Girl with long blonde hair. Saw her on Friday, actually, on my walk to get the *Mercury*. Thought it was a bit odd… she was walking in the opposite direction. Then on my way home, there she was on the beach in her school uniform with her hair blowing about. Quite a looker. Sorry, forgot to mention it!'

'Oh, *Dad*!' The discussion turned to difficult students, parents who thought their little dears were angels and had expectations for them way above their abilities. Plates were cleared and a chocolate mousse appeared.

'My favourite,' beamed Leonard, enjoying each mouthful. 'Any more?'

' 'Fraid not… I didn't think to make extras.'

Nigel looked at his watch. 'Sorry to break this up, folks, but I have some test papers to mark by the morning and some tutoring to do this afternoon.' Moving to Anna, he gallantly shifted her chair sideways from the table, enabling her to stand.

'On a Sunday?'

'Sorry, but that is how it is. Great lunch, though,' he said, and leant across to Marion, giving her a peck on the cheek.

'If you must go, I suppose you must. Come to lunch next Sunday. Do come!'

Between murmurs of, 'Great mousse, wonderful lunch, sorry we have to dash,' it emerged that they'd have to consult their diaries, and of course they'd love to come, but you know what schools expected these days. Then they said their goodbyes. With a flurry of leave-taking, they were gone, leaving Marion to stare at the mess of dishes.

'I don't believe Nigel. I'm sorry, but I don't. We have come all this way, and they can't even spend a couple of hours a week with us.' Marion blew her nose, on the verge of crying.

'Don't upset yourself, love. I suppose they are used to living their way, but I agree. There's something going on between the two of them, something not quite right. Can't put my finger on it. I thought Anna looked a little drawn.

'You don't suppose she's pregnant, do you?'

'No, not for a moment. Sorry, love, you'll have to wait till the cows come home before they decide to start a family.' He laughed, while Marion could only manage a weak smile. Ineffectually he helped with stacking the dishwasher. 'Look, the sun is shining and it's only two o'clock.'

Glancing up, Marion could see Leonard had no intention of staying home now that Anna had left. 'Mind if I nip down to the yacht club for a drink or two?'

'What, now?' she sighed. 'Oh, go on! The church service was a disaster and lunch wasn't much better.'

'I wouldn't say that. Perfect lunch, my dear.'

She began folding the tablecloth. He fidgeted. 'You'll be all right, then?'

'Yes,' she said slowly, adding, 'I've plenty to do.'

'Come along if you like,' he suggested.

A drawn-out 'No' was followed by, 'You know it's not my scene.'

He nodded, relieved, then went to fetch his coat, car keys and wallet, lingering on the back door step as he slid the glass open. 'You'll be all right, then?'

'I said so, didn't I?'

The phone rang.

'Who on earth…?' Marion said, mumbling, 'On a Sunday, too!'

'I'll get it.' A premonition roused Leonard to manoeuvre past the dining table at speed, crossing the lounge room and snatching up the receiver. The familiar sound of long-distance pips, made him automatically take up a defensive stance, his back to Marion. '62278614, Leonard speaking.'

There was a pause from the other end of the line and then a husky, 'Hello.'

After the initial shock it took him a few seconds to take control. 'How did you get this number?'

'With difficulty... from the church. I enquired. Someone supplied it. What the hell are you doing in Australia?'

Leonard turned to face the doorway as Marion mouthed, 'Who is it?' Placing the handset against his chest, and giving what he hoped was an exasperated expression, he waved her away saying, 'Market research!'

'Oh.' She moved back into the kitchen and began washing the saucepans by hand.

'Are you still there, Leonard?'

'Yes. What do you want?'

'That doesn't sound very friendly. You didn't give me a forwarding address so what was I supposed to do?'

'It's very awkward at the moment... I suppose I should have told you... but life goes on, Lucy.'

'That's as may be, but I have a problem that only you can fix. Michael has been accepted into the Royal Academy of Music, and I have been made redundant... added to which, my car is out of action and I can't afford to fix it!'

'Redundant – why?'

'I should have thought it was obvious. The new boss wanted computer-literate staff.' Her voice rose unpleasantly. 'They didn't need me...'

'Well, I don't see what I can do. I'm not paying any more, Lucy. As it is—'

Lucy cut him off. 'You haven't told her about Michael, have you?' He was silent. 'You said you would. You're a bastard, Leonard. I need—'

He hung up. Visibly shaken, he stood staring at the phone, then rang Telstra to arrange a change of number, to be effective immediately. 'You wouldn't credit it,' he remarked, making for the back door again.

'What?'

His voice shook. 'Telstra! I don't intend to put up with unsolicited calls. They will be sending out a form to change the number. Don't ask me how it works, but I know several people who have had the same nuisance calls – it's beyond a joke.'

Marion noted his agitation, concerned that he could get so worked up about such a little annoyance. She said, 'Forget it, Leonard, go and enjoy yourself – and calm down, you'll have a heart attack the way you carry on!'

His behaviour sometimes was quite inexplicable, she reflected, as she continued to finish the washing up.

~III~

The best laid schemes o' mice an' men,
Gang aft agley,
And lea'e us nought but grief and pain,
For promised joy.

Robert Burns[*]

I t was a Wednesday morning in July, and Marion was pleased with the results of the perm administered by the pert owner of Caroline Coiffure. She patted her hair, applied fresh lipstick, and watched other customers having their hair done through the mirror in front of her.

'So how d'yer find Tassie?' The pleasant face caught her eye in the mirror, unwrapping the black nylon gown fixed with Velcro at her neck.

Trying not to wince at the broad flat vowels, Marion stood up and followed the stylist to the curved grey counter by the door. 'Oh, I don't know really. I mean, it is very different to where I come from.' Concerned she might have sounded patronising, she smiled. 'But I like what you did to my hair.'

As she paid the bill and made a further appointment, she was aware how different she sounded from those around her. She sensed the ease of gossip flying backwards and forwards across the room, the laughter, and the interest shown by juniors.

She left the salon, drifting into the tiny shop next door, which loaned books for a nominal fee since the library had been closed. It was manned by volunteers, mainly retired people and house-wives who could spare the time. Not sure why she had come in,

---

[*] From *The Treasury of Familiar Quotations*, Avenal Books, New York.

she made a play at looking along the shelf headed T–U. Titles swam before her eyes, registering nothing of any significance. Feeling rather foolish, she turned towards the smartly dressed gentleman sitting rather awkwardly behind a small wooden table sorting cards. He smiled; eyes of deep sea blue bored upwards, meeting hers as he murmured, 'Can I help you?'

She dropped her gaze to his shiny black shoe and some walking sticks leaning against the table, his right leg extended straight out alongside within a well-pressed grey-cuffed trouser.

'I don't know… I don't think so.' She chose a book at random, filled in a card, and as she paid the twenty cents another woman breezed in, making it easy for her to slip out of the door. All the shopkeepers here were so friendly, so nice. There was the dark-haired woman behind the counter in the post office-cum-paper shop, always helpful; the happy-go-lucky butcher, very obliging, and the courteous pharmacist who remembered her name. Certainly everyone here was more than helpful, so why did she feel so lonely, so out of place? What was the matter with her that she felt more in tune with the Lebanese couple who ran the small supermarket, with their sad faces and pain-filled eyes, rarely smiling and only speaking when necessary? Her life was spiralling out of control. Leonard had become a stranger, and Anna… well, she couldn't work out her behaviour at all.

She crossed over to the newsagent's looking for the *International Express* for Leonard who enjoyed the crossword; she, herself, liked the gossip and articles about the royal family. Sometimes she found stories about Australia which were more informative than the national or local newspapers. Her glance rested on the magazines and she decided to treat herself to *This England*, with its glossy pictures of villages and rolling hills. Paying for her purchases, she left the shopping centre lost in thought as she made her way home. The afternoon was cool in spite of the sun which shone on gardens adorned with jonquils, daffodils and white blossoms floating gently down from the fruit trees, creating lacy patterns on the footpath. With her eyes looking downwards she missed the luscious oranges, deep reds and bright yellows of the rhododendrons and azaleas flanking fences and front porches, the prize camellias at Number Twelve, Tadbury

Crescent, and the blue wrens flitting in and out of the bushes. Approaching the high side of their property on Devon Walk, she mused about the letterbox fixed to the fence rather than a slit in the front door, which she was used to. She hoped there would be news from Laleham.

Retrieving their mail, Marion unlatched the wooden gate and stepped gingerly down the concrete steps towards the sliding glass doors of the kitchen. She surmised that the letterboxes were for the convenience of the postman rather than the recipients, to avoid snapping dogs and to remain balanced on their mopeds. She herself gingerly traversed the concrete slope. Letting herself in, she placed the mail on top of the magazine and newspaper before making a cup of tea. The room was still warm, although the sun had now gone from this side of the river. Flicking through *This England* she chided herself as illustrations of the countryside, thatched cottages and tranquil streams made her more homesick. Glancing through the mail, she noticed two were from England and the third a Salvation Army request to sponsor a child. She recognised, with some pleasure, Alice's handwriting on one of the letters and sliced it open eagerly.

A shuffle behind her startled her. 'Len – I didn't know you were home. You gave me quite a fright.'

'Didn't feel terribly well so I left the golf club early. In fact, I've got an awful headache.'

'Well, you've got a letter – should cheer you up – and I've got one from Alice.' As she handed him the letter, she saw the address of the sender on the back. 'Who lives at Ferry Lane that would be writing to you?'

'Can't be doing with that now,' he muttered, and pushed it into his jacket pocket. 'Where's the codeine?'

'That bad?'

Leonard attempted a nod. 'Think I'll go and lie down again. I like your hair,' he said weakly, and turned towards the bedroom.

It was unusual for him to shuffle. She roused herself to rummage through the bathroom cabinet, and on finding the codeine, punched out two into her palm, filled a glass of water and carried it to where Leonard was sprawled out on the bed, his jacket tossed on the bedside chair.

'Can't bend down – to undo the shoes,' he said ruefully.

'Oh, Len, it's only a headache… here, I'll do them. Take these, one now and the other later.'

'It's more than a headache, I can't see out of my right eye properly!' Marion helped him swallow the pill. 'A bit of sympathy wouldn't go amiss…'

'Len, what were you doing to get into this state? My life isn't that hot either, if you cared to notice!' She sighed, pulling off his socks and shoes. Seeing there was not much more she could do, she drew the curtains and left him to sleep. Men! The slightest pain and they go to pieces. They're like children, Marion told herself, although I have to admit he doesn't look himself.

Two hours later she had laid their lap trays for their evening meal and was dishing up macaroni cheese topped with tomato and a slice of bacon sprinkled with fresh parsley. Not sure whether to pour out Leonard's usual glass of Merlot or not, she called out to him as she carried his tray into the lounge and switched on the television. As there was no reply, she called again. 'Dinner's ready, Len!' and went into the kitchen to fetch her own tray and a glass of Chardonnay.

Beginning to feel uneasy, she made her way to the bedroom, telling herself that he'd probably taken the other tablet and knocked himself out. She passed the toilet and heard him retching. Unsure what to do next, she called softly through the door, 'You all right, Len?'

'No, I'm not. I feel awful,' came the muffled reply. There was a pause. 'I'm going back to bed. I still can't see out of my eye.'

'I c-cooked your favourite…' she stammered, with a mixture of fear and annoyance. The door opened abruptly and Leonard walked straight into her, looking suddenly old and dishevelled.

'Haven't we got anything stronger than codeine? You know, for migraines?' He peered at her with his left eye, but before she had a chance to reply the phone rang. 'If that's for me I can't take it now.' And with that he shuffled back to the bedroom.

Marion stood stock-still, then turned and found herself staring at a framed painting of All Saints' at Laleham on the hall wall. How she wished she was still there! A kaleidoscope of well-loved familiar images, remembered rooms and furnishings of their previous cottage brought a lump to her throat. She could imagine the red bricks, looking solid; the primrose yellow front door, and bay window in the dining room. She missed opening windows outwards with their sturdy catches, and she disliked the sliding ones; in fact thought their steel frames were quite ugly. Now, as she lifted the receiver, to be perfectly honest, she felt insecure in her white weatherboard house.

'Hello, 62278625.' Tentatively she read the new number from a disc in the centre of the phone.

'Mum, it's me! You took ages to answer the phone.'

'Yes, well I…'

'There's something I need to talk over with you and Dad.'

'Not now, Anna. I've just dished up our dinner, and your dad's not well.'

'What's the matter with him?'

'I'm not too sure. He came home from golf with a headache, which I think has turned into a migraine. He's been sick.'

'Sounds like too much wind and sun. Did he wear a hat?'

'I don't know. I've been at the hairdresser's.'

'Perhaps you'd better call the doctor!'

'Oh, I don't think it warrants that. He's had a few headaches on and off during last summer. He'll be right as rain in the morning.'

'I still think it would be wise, Mum. Hang on, I've got the local surgery here.'

A shuffling sound came across the line as Marion watched her dinner getting cold.

'It's a Dr Ian MacIntyre – no prizes to guess where he's from! Failing him there's Dr John Appleby. They're in partnership, so the number is the same: 62278500. Have you got that?'

'Yes, but I really don't think it will be necessary.'

'Can I come around in about an hour then?'

'Well, don't expect your father to—'

'No, of course not.'

'It's not about that girl at St Mary's, is it? Cos I haven't seen her recently.'

'No, it isn't, Mum!'

'Are you both coming, because I—'

'No it's just me. Nigel has a parent-teacher night. I'm home alone. See you soon.'

The line went dead. Slowly Marion hung up, wondering what on earth was so important that couldn't wait until later. During the next hour she had picked at her lukewarm macaroni, scraped Leonard's dinner into the waste pedal bin, took one look at his agonised face and rang the local clinic. She tuned in to the seven o'clock ABC News, vaguely taking note of riots in the Gaza Strip, and a road fatality in Victoria involving a bus full of Japanese tourists, before Anna breezed in wearing a finely woven grey skirt and jacket to match with satin cuffs.

'Like it?' Anna twirled around, justifying her purchase 'I teamed it with this lime green blouse, so I wouldn't look too schoolmarmish!'

'It's very nice,' Marion said, touching the lacy collar lightly.

Anna sat down in the armchair opposite her mother, wondering how she would broach the subject of Nigel being offered a vice principal's position in Queensland. She was only half listening to what her mother was saying.

'...so I did ring the clinic, and the receptionist was quite rude. Apparently it was way past surgery hours and she wanted to get home. I had to explain why we hadn't enrolled there, and then answer numerous questions. She wanted to know if we had private coverage!' She looked appealingly at Anna. 'I don't know about those things – your father always deals with them. And to cap it all off, she suggested I took your father into the Royal, as the doctor wouldn't be in until around nine.'

Seeing she wouldn't get her mother's attention in her present frame of mind, Anna decided to take a look at her father. 'I thought you said he had a headache. That hardly warrants a trip to hospital.' She stood up, trying to remember when her father had ever taken to his bed because of illness. Marion called out, watching Anna's retreating back, 'Don't wake him up! You know how he hates a fuss.'

Sighing, she went into the kitchen to make a cup of tea, registering the three-inch grey high heels matching Anna's outfit, tapping their way down the corridor. In her present state of mind, Marion sadly acknowledged feelings of inferiority where her daughter was concerned. She was too pliable, that was her problem. No one considered her opinions worth hearing. All this fuss and waiting for a doctor she didn't even know. She was beginning to feel her age.

The kettle boiled as Anna popped her head around the door. 'He's all right, Mum, sleeping. But it's best to make certain. His face looks a bit puffy, you know, around the eyes. Had you noticed?'

Marion filled two Wedgwood cups with tea, and placed some McVities biscuits on a matching plate, with a jug of milk and sugar bowl, on a silver tray.

Back in the lounge room, Anna asked again, 'Well, have you?'

Placing the tray on the round coffee table, Marion handed Anna a cup, pouring milk into her own and popping two sugar lumps into it before muttering, 'Probably due to too much elbow-bending!'

'What?'

'As I said' – slowly, she swallowed a mouthful of tea – 'he's never here. He's always at golf or the yacht club.'

'You mean at the clubhouse?' Anna helped herself to sugar and milk before adding, 'I can't imagine Dad spending hours drinking, Mum. You must have got it wrong.' She nibbled on a biscuit, her face a mask of her true emotions. 'More like trying to improve his handicap!'

'Well, he's hardly ever here, so I wouldn't know.'

'You need to find something you enjoy doing.'

There was an embarrassed silence and Marion looked close to tears. Eventually she asked, 'You two all right then?'

'Yes, we're fine. I'm a bit tired with all the extra-curricular activities we are supposed to attend: services in the cathedral, regular lunch duty, then there was the school fair, and now, get this – take your class on camp! Me, camping? I ask you! Well, I'm not going.'

'Not your bag?'

'No, I'm an English teacher, for goodness' sake, not a sports teacher!'

'You're not expecting…?'

'*Noooo, Mum*, nothing like that.'

'So… what did you want to talk to us about?'

'I'm not sure this is the right time, Mum… what with Dad laid up.'

'He'll be as right as rain tomorrow, you see.'

And so Anna waxed lyrical about the warmth and sunshine of Queensland, swimming in the sea, Nigel being offered a once-in-a-lifetime promotion, and she not having to find a job straight away. 'So, you see, I might pick up some coaching or do something different, the possibilities are endless,' she said with a wave of her hand, and, seeing her mother's appalled expression, she added, 'Nothing's definite, that's why I wanted to see you and Dad. See how you like it here. You and Dad are settled here, and you do like it, don't you?'

'Well, I wouldn't call it settled exactly, not from my point of view.'

'You're happy here, though?'

Happy? What did that mean? She supposed Leonard was. 'Your dad is, but I'm…' She shrugged.

Anna stared at her new shoes, not wanting to share her mother's feelings. She ploughed on. 'It's a great promotion at Nigel's age, with a lot more money… and the Gold Coast. It's a gift,' she said with a flourish. 'The school is situated south of Mudgeeraba and close to Burleigh Heads beach, not fifteen minutes to Coolangatta Airport. You could come for holidays.'

'Hang on a minute! Did I hear you correctly?'

Anna made no reply.

'You two are moving to Queensland in a place called Madger or Mud-flats or something – after dragging us all the way out here to live!' She was too shocked to say more. The silence was electric. Marion choked, '*Queensland!*' Her voice wobbled with dismay.

'Well, nothing has been definitely decided, and it wouldn't be until the New Year.' Anna fiddled with her teaspoon, eyes firmly on her lap. The silence lengthened so she bit her lip and shrugged defiantly. 'But you know how these things are. If you don't grab them when they come along…'

Marion looked at her daughter in amazement. Anger and vulnerability already simmering near the surface was now exacerbated. She stood up swiftly, knocking into the table, afraid to make any comment, unable to express her true feelings and blundered out of the room.

'I'd better check on your father,' she muttered, thinking, *This can't be happening, not to us.* She stumbled along the hallway, swallowing back her tears, stricken by this turn of events, but before she reached the bedroom the front doorbell rang. On her doorstep stood a youngish man in his forties with unruly sandy hair going grey at the tips, with soft deep blue eyes set in a pleasant tanned face.

'Dr MacIntyre – and you must be Mrs Lee,' he said with a broad Scottish accent, holding out his right hand.

Marion shook his hand weakly, the cool of it steadying her. 'You had better come in.' She attempted a smile. 'Thank you for coming.'

'I'm a neighbour of yours,' he said agreeably.

'Really?'

'Aye, just up there on the cliff.' He pointed behind him towards the small ridge dividing Tadbury Beach and a row of houses. 'Position not as perrfect as you have here, being right on the beach, but we have a grrand view.' His guttural delivery, combined with the rolling r's, struck Marion as outlandish, although she couldn't say why. 'I've always *admirred* this house.' There it was again.

'Really, why is that?' asked Marion, instantly admonishing herself for mouthing an inanity.

'Och, being in a cul-de-sac, *verry prrivate.*' He smiled, moving to the bottom stair. 'Where's the patient?'

'Oh, oh no, not upstairs. We sleep in the bedroom along at the end of the passage. The bathroom and toilet are on the same level.'

Cross with herself for revealing their private domestic arrangements, even to a doctor, she watched his retreating back, passing his black bag to his left hand and knocking gently on the door with the other, introducing himself as he entered the bedroom.

Turning back towards the lounge, her eyes travelled upwards to the watercolour opposite the front door. It was of Laleham

Cottage, and it reminded her of the beautiful maple dressing table she had been advised to sell before leaving England. And now their bedroom was of mismatched woods in cramped surroundings. It was embarrassing that a complete stranger, albeit a doctor, should see their poor standard of furniture. Emotionally upset, she saw Anna peering through the lounge room curtains. Her voice raised, provoked. 'What are you looking at?' showing her outrage from Anna's previous pronouncement.

'Ah… er, I just wondered what our Dr MacIntyre drove… nothing special,' she remarked disparagingly. Glancing at Marion's expression, she sensed her displeasure. 'Shall I wait until we hear what the doctor says?'

With a great effort to hold onto her temper, Marion went into the kitchen to make a fresh pot of tea, faintly replying, 'That would be nice.'

'Mrs Lee?' Dr MacIntyre came into the lounge and Marion sped back, kettle in hand hardly registering what he was saying. She stood in the lounge holding the kettle, as the doctor repeated that Leonard should go to hospital immediately. Marion sank down onto the sofa hearing him calling for an ambulance, to transport Leonard to St John's Hospital, wherever that was, for observation, just to be on the safe side. 'To be honest, Mrs Lee, I don't like the look of that eye… Now, *trry* not to *worrry*.' Nodding at Anna, he let himself out.

Anna took over, asking numerous questions, as though Marion herself were incapable of organising her own husband. 'Where is his case? He will need shaving gear… handkerchiefs, washbag, toiletries, pyjamas.' She babbled on, and as soon as the ambulance arrived, she directed the paramedics to the bedroom.

'Don't you worry, Mum, he'll be all right. I'll drop in to see him tomorrow on my way to work, although it's a little out of the way.' And with that she left, much to Marion's relief.

Marion wandered aimlessly around the silent house finding little things to do. Washing up the tea things, locking up and finally retrieving Alice's letter, which she hadn't had a chance to read properly, though her eyes were blurred with tears as she read about Laleham gossip. The people who had bought her house owned a BMW and it had been involved in a collision outside

Alice's house. The post office had been relocated around the corner in Shepperton Road, and a woman in Ferry Lane had apparently tried to commit suicide but had failed. Did Marion know of her? She used to work for Daily Office Cleaning.

Confused by this piece of gossip, Marion wondered why Alice would imagine she would know all past employees. Alice was missing her and hoped she was happy. Finally, she went to bed worrying about the route to St John's Hospital, as she had no idea how to get there, apart from Anna telling her it was in South Hobart. She would have to find the street directory, although she was hopeless at map reading.

Around the same time as Marion turned in for the night, Nigel was absorbed in stroking Anna's luxurious hair fanned out on the pillow. She was relating in detail the evening's events. 'It didn't go down too well, but what with Dad being rushed to hospital it was hardly the right moment, I suppose. Anyhow, I handled everything. Mother went to pieces.'

It never ceased to amaze Nigel how competent his wife was, and leaning down, kissed the top of her head, murmuring 'You poor old thing.' The night was still young, and he hoped she would be in a receptive mood.

Over in Norwood Avenue, Mrs Ryan was wondering, as she cleaned her teeth, who was to finish her daughter's education now that she was four months pregnant. It had been a simple matter of deduction, catching her daughter vomiting over the toilet bowl. Janice had refused over and over again to say who the father was, and this evening Mrs Ryan had received a phone call from the school. 'As you know, this is a delicate situation, one I do not wish the girls to gossip about, so I'm sure you understand it is in the best interests of everyone if you take Janice out of school for the remainder of her pregnancy, or at least before her pregnancy has become apparent. I'm sure you would agree with me, Mrs Ryan.'

How this disaster had come about, she had no idea and blamed the school, as the father would have to be a St Virgil's boy. To the best of her knowledge, Janice never came into contact with any boys. Rinsing her mouth, she vowed she'd get to the bottom of it, and the boy responsible would have to pay. At the same time she was concerned about Janice's morbid interest in the Port Arthur massacre. Articles from the newspapers had been cut out and stuck all over the walls of her bedroom. She had even attended a memorial service at St Mary's Cathedral, along with numerous students from various Catholic schools. Marge Ryan slipped out of the bathroom quietly and observed Janice slumped in a lounge chair watching late-night television.

'Bathroom's free,' she said above the sound. 'Don't you think you should get—'

Janice cut her off. 'Yes, Mum,' she drawled. 'Don't fuss. I'll turn in soon.' When her mother was asleep, she'd give Gavin a ring; hopefully, he'd answer the phone and not Mrs Armstrong.

Over at St John's Hospital, Leonard was dreaming. He was playing the bells at All Saints', Laleham, but something was not right. Something was worrying him, something he couldn't get straight. There was something he ought to tell Marion, but for the life of him he couldn't grasp what it was. Near him, Sister Morgan, having worked a double shift, wanted a quiet night in which to catch up with her paperwork.

It was typical, a new patient arriving in the dead of night, and she was expected to check up on him every half-hour, as if she didn't have enough to do.

Across the Tasman in Bellerive, Gavin's father, Patrick Armstrong, was sipping a nightcap of whisky and dry ginger. He was tall and slim with a high forehead, wrinkles now showing around his eyes and mouth, with receding black hair turning silver. Most people attending his dental surgery would have said he was distinguished looking, unflappable. But on this particular August night, he felt tired and dispirited. He put a pine log on the fire, discussing his day's events and reaction to the Prime Minister's bill on gun buy-back.

'All because of one maniac! It's ridiculous,' he grumbled to his wife, Mary, who was sitting in the opposite chair knitting a cream matinée jacket for their first grandchild due in a month. She was thinking about their daughter, Elaine, who not long after she had received a science degree had married a doctor, and was now living in Wembley Downs, Western Australia.

'It's getting late,' she said matter-of-factly, looking across at

Patrick, her face anxious considering his dilemma. 'Maybe you won't have to sell all of your collection.'

He didn't answer, just stared broodily into the fire. She thought how thin his fingers were as he tapped the arm of the chair with his left hand. He frowned, dark eyebrows accentuated high cheekbones. 'And that's another thing,' he said looking across at her. 'I can't be putting up with patients double-booked. There was a scene in reception today.' He paused and Mary wondered where all this was going. It was most unusual for Patrick to grumble in this way. 'Sometimes extractions take longer than you'd like. You can't rush people.'

'I know, dear.'

'They get nervous!' He drank some more. '*I* get nervous!'

'What?'

'It's not good for the practice, patients discussing their treatment. I get harried. Sometimes injections take longer than usual to work. She's forcing my schedule. I've told her before, and after today… she'll have to go. And that means training up a new nurse.'

He stood up, kicking a log on the fire. There was a long commiserative silence as they listened to the crackling of the fire, the murmur of the wind and the sound of a key in the front door.

'You'll have to advertise.'

'Mmm… What's he coming home at this hour for?'

'Ah, Pat, you were his age once.'

'I didn't come home all hours of the day and night. Where's he been anyway?'

'How should I know, love!' Mary began rolling her knitting into a tapestry bag. 'If he doesn't tell me, I don't ask.' She stood up. 'You'll see to the fire?'

He nodded. The phone rang. 'I'll get it,' she said, 'although I can't think who is calling at this hour.'

She crossed to where a small table was tucked into an alcove upon which stood a replica of an old dial phone. It was cream in colour, complete with painted gold trim, above which hung a gilt framed photograph of Elaine receiving her doctorate.

'Mary Armstrong,' she said, lifting the large handset off its cradle. 'Who's speaking?' She looked across at Patrick, placing her hand over the mouthpiece. 'They won't say.'

'Hang up, then!'

'It's probably some girl,' she whispered.

'Give it to me!' Angrily, Patrick strode across, relieving her of the phone. 'Dr Armstrong here. Who is this?'

'Mr Armstrong,' said Janice in a small voice, 'please can I talk to Gavin?'

'Have you any idea what time it is, young lady?' He heard a sob. Relenting slightly, having caught Mary's eye, he added, 'Give me your number and I'll pass it on to Gavin in the morning. We'd appreciate it if you would call at a reasonable hour.' There was a muffled sound like a sniff and then a click. 'She hung up!'

'Oh, Patrick! You were a bit rough.'

The door opened. 'Was that call for me?' Gavin stood there, looking from one parent to the other.

'Yes, and I'd appreciate it if you would pass on to your friends not to ring us at eleven o'clock at night!'

'Who was it, then?'

'She didn't say. And why are you home so late?' Patrick eyed his son, lolling against the door jamb, his insolence nearly causing him to lose his temper.

'Ah, you know, nowhere in particular. Messing about with Angus and Mark.'

'Well, in future, do a little less messing about on a week-night and some serious study. This is an important year, son.'

'I know, Dad. Don't keep on.' Cheekily, he added, 'If you bought me a mobile phone I...'

'And who would be paying the bill?' Patrick sighed, raising his eyebrows. Gavin shrugged, turning to leave and then thinking better of it, gave his mother the benefit of his smile and a peck on the cheek. 'Goodnight, Mum.' Then, closing the door, he ambled nonchalantly to his bedroom, intrigued as to which girl would ring him so late at night.

'What a generation!' Patrick finished his whisky, then placed the fireguard deftly into position before locking up for the night.

Mary knew after twenty-five years of marriage that his irritability had little to do with Gavin and all to do with handing in his gun collection. She entered the kitchen to rinse the glasses reflecting on the mayhem and grief that Martin Bryant had caused by the killing of thirty-five innocent people down at Port Arthur in April. She wondered how he was faring in Risdon Prison, and if he had any idea about the repercussions of his actions. Drying Patrick's crystal tumbler, she smiled inwardly about the phone call, pleased that Gavin was taking an interest in girls. She had begun to wonder, as there was little in his room to suggest girls were a priority.

Back in Norwood Avenue, Janice wept tears of frustration. She needed to talk with Gavin, but over the last few months he always seemed to be surrounded by friends, or he skipped the classes they both attended. What was she to do? How was she going to finish school? She didn't want a baby, and her mother hadn't been much help; she'd been more worried about what the neighbours would say than what it meant to her. Why she had told Sister Anne at St Mary's, Janice had no idea, as she was sure no one would have noticed, even at seven months gone at the time of her exams. Maybe there was still time to have a termination, but she didn't know who to see or ask. Their doctor, being a staunch Catholic, wouldn't perform the task, she was sure. It was like a secret society clamming up against her. The word 'abortion' was frowned on at school. Even participating in sexual intercourse was considered a sin by Mrs Farnsworth, the senior religion teacher. Surely Gavin would help her… Round and round in her head went thoughts of herself with a baby. She sobbed into her pillow, feeling so alone, until she fell asleep.

In the early hours of the following morning, Sister Morgan was looking forward to going home, having a hot shower and six hours of sleep if she were lucky. These thoughts flitted through her mind as Nurse Philby began babbling that she had better come and have a look at Mr Lee. Dr MacIntyre was contacted, and in his sleep-befuddled state, he replied to Sister Morgan's questions as best he could. No, he didn't know Mr Lee's history, and, yes, last night was the first time he had clapped eyes on the man. He was on his way.

Nurse Philby noted that at 4.25 a.m. Leonard Lee stopped breathing. Dr MacIntyre arrived twenty minutes later at the hospital, amid the confusion of an unexplained death. Questions were put; answers given; resuscitation equipment checked. A phone call was made to Mrs Lee at 5 a.m., but the voice at the end of the line said, 'This number has been discontinued, please check with the subscriber.' Sister Morgan's confidence in her own ability began to fray, and Nurse Philby panicked.

Due to the fact that Anna found herself running late for work, she decided to visit her father after school, seeing there was no rush to be home, as Nigel was taking his grade sevens on an ecological excursion along the East Coast. Furthermore, her mother would be visiting some time in the morning. Other patients on the ward knew this was no time to bother the nurses, as word of the death travelled fast, the tension being palpable. Dr MacIntyre offered to drop by the Lee household, as it was on his way home, but despite repeatedly knocking at the front and back, no one answered the door.

As it happened, Marion was sipping coffee next door at Joy Nesbit's, waiting for her return from dropping off her children to school before driving Marion to St John's Hospital. 'It's very kind of you...'

'Not at all. Once you know where to go, you'll find it easily!' she smiled kindly, adding, 'On the way back, we'll do some shopping if you like, take your mind off things.'

'Oh, I couldn't put you to all that trouble.'

'It really isn't a problem,' said Joy. She felt rather peculiar being watched closely by Marion's serious eyes in her own kitchen. She would tell Morris tonight about her unusual grey eyes – quite unnerving. 'If you'd rather, we could stop off at Salamanca for a coffee and browse. Much more pleasant than the city,' she said breezily, clearing the table of cornflakes, dirty dishes and toast crumbs.

On their arrival in the hospital car park, Joy declared she would read a magazine and that Marion was to take as much time as she liked. Marion approached the entrance sure she would never remember the route they had just travelled. She supposed she'd have to ask for Leonard's whereabouts at the reception desk.

'Excuse me...' She looked at the back of a woman typing frantically on a keyboard.

'Yes?' she half turned at the interruption, her face bland, eyes with a faraway look.

'I wonder if you would direct me to where my husband is? He was brought in last night. Leonard Lee. I'm Mrs Lee; he was brought in for observation.'

'Ah... I'm so sorry.' Pamela Grainger recovered her equilibrium. She was not going to be the bunny to pass on the bad news. 'Mrs Lee,' she said, displaying a pearly set of teeth. 'We have been trying to contact you since the early hours of the morning, but there seemed to be something wrong with the number your husband wrote down on the admission form.' Another knowing smile beamed forth, somehow conveying to Marion that Leonard had written down the wrong number. 'Oh, no. You see, we...'

But before she had time to explain what had gone wrong, Pamela Grainger said earnestly, 'Did Dr MacIntyre catch up with you?'

'No, why would he? He only saw Leonard last night. It was he who arranged for Leonard to be admitted – for observation. He sometimes gets these headaches.' Puzzled, Marion wondered why the receptionist hadn't directed her as requested, but was speaking on the house phone.

'If you would care to wait a moment, I'll see if Sister Morgan is still on duty.' The receptionist smiled again and waved Marion towards some comfy chairs surrounding a round table partitioned off from the main waiting area. There was a tea and coffee machine, paper cups, and cellophane-wrapped biscuits, also a bar fridge. 'Please take a seat,' she said, and not wishing to be the bearer of bad tidings, she added, 'I believe your husband was moved to another ward.'

Marion sat down, trying to interpret the abstract paintings on the wall, and wondered why Dr MacIntyre would have called at her house earlier, as it was only 8.30 a.m. While thus employed, a pantomime of sorts was being played out at the desk between the receptionist and Sister Owen, now on duty.

A buxom shadow then appeared in front of Marion. 'Mrs Lee, I'm Sister Owen. Will you come this way, please.' The voice had a soft Irish lilt.

A hand on her arm, a gentle smile and Marion found herself ushered into a small sitting room, similar in size to the previous one, only this time there was a fish tank and a tape deck. Artificial yellow flowers were arranged in a circular bowl in the centre of a glass-topped table surrounded by a grey velour lounge suite.

Similar refreshments to the previous lounge were on display, and various glossy magazines were scattered about. There had to be some mistake. This couldn't be Leonard's ward. Marion said, 'Look, I would like…'

'Listen.' Sister Owen glided towards the tape deck and within seconds there was the sound of birdsong. 'I always think at times of stress there's nothing as soothing as birdsongs.' She smiled, indicating for Marion to take her pick of lounge chairs or sofa. 'Coffee or tea? How do you like yours?' She turned, waiting for a reply.

'Oh, that's nice of you. Coffee – two sugars, I'm afraid – and a little milk. Sister – er.'

'Call me Kathleen – and you are?'

'Marion. All I'm here for is…'

But before Marion had a chance to query what she was doing in this lounge, the gentle Irish voice filled her in with the details of Leonard's death from Sister Morgan's copious notes. It wasn't the first time Sister Owen had been called in to handle sad situations, and she presumed it wouldn't be the last. Privately, she felt for this Englishwoman before her, only being in the country a few months and apparently totally unaware how dangerous an embolism could be.

Stunned by the news, all Marion registered were the sounds of birds. She went into shock.

'Can I call anyone?' A long pause. 'Would you like to see him, Mrs Lee?' Getting no reply, she tried again, 'Is there anyone you wish me to call?'

'No, no,' she said very slowly. 'I have a friend outside. I need to use the bathroom.'

'Of course.' Seeing Marion's vague expression, Sister Owen helped her up and towards the door. 'I'll show you where it is.'

While Marion was washing her hands, she had the odd sensation Leonard knew this might happen to him and had planned all along for her to be near Anna.

Struck by this revelation, choking and crying, she sobbed aloud, not caring if anyone else was in one of the cubicles. But what you didn't foresee, Leonard, was that Anna and Nigel are thinking of moving to Queensland! Queensland, yes! As far away as you could imagine, and I have no intention of following them there. Nor do I wish to stay here. I wish I'd never come. You never told me… You never confided in me. She shook uncontrollably before drying her eyes and stumbling out of the hospital towards the car park.

It was the custom at St Mary's to give staff several days off if a family crisis should arise. Generally speaking, this was much appreciated, but in Anna's case she wanted to continue teaching, as she didn't care to think about her responsibility to her mother. Surprised in the first place that Leonard had even contemplated moving to Australia, she would have to admit the present scenario hadn't even crossed her mind.

'Well, what are we going to do?' she wailed to Nigel while dressing for Leonard's funeral. She was fixing a large black straw hat with an eye-catching bow at the back, not unlike those used for an expensive gift-wrapped present.

'There's little we can do at the moment,' he replied, keeping his eyes averted, vigorously brushing the fluff off the collar and lapels of a jacket draped over the back of a kitchen chair.

Taking the brush off him, she began removing the flecks off her own suit. 'It doesn't affect you like it does me,' she continued peevishly. 'Mother showed little or no interest when I told her Mrs Barnett had offered the school Senior Choir to sing "On Eagle's Wings" during the service. The least she could have done was to ring the school and thank them.'

'She's in shock still, Anna,' Nigel replied, confused by her attitude. Turning his wife around to face him, he said gently, 'I think you should spend the next few weeks sleeping over at her house.'

'Oh, God – I never thought this would happen!' Anna slipped into a new pair of high-heeled black patent shoes and reached for the matching handbag. After a last look at themselves in the hall mirror, Nigel grabbed the house keys, opened the front door and attempted to lighten the situation by intoning mockingly, 'Part of life's rich tapestry, my love.' Then, with a wry glance at Anna's face, he banged the door shut. Striding ahead, he opened the gate with a flourish, ushering her through. They walked together towards Marion's house and the waiting funeral car. He made a mental note that his own front garden needed immediate attention, as did the gate.

A fortnight after the funeral on a windy morning, Marion was seated on an iron-slatted bench gazing at nothing in particular across the River Derwent. A weak sun was eclipsed now and again by scurrying clouds, causing the river to change colour in patches from green to black. Waves bumped into giant rocks eddying into crevices leaving spume in their wake. The beach was uninhabited by human form, its wild beauty pristine apart from swirling gulls and small crabs scuttling for cover.

She sat with her hands in the pockets of her 'all-weather coat', bunching it around her against the wind, aware only of a torn tissue in the right pocket, her eyes rebelling in the clear light as she fumbled for her sunglasses. On realising she had left them back at the house, she closed her eyes, listening to the roar of the sea. She ran her tongue over her teeth, speculating as to why she chewed her food on the left side of her mouth rather than the right. She wasn't supposed to think and feel like this, not according to novels she had read or people she had known who had lost a spouse through sudden death. They had been angry, upset, even grief-stricken in some cases, unable to cope with the simplest of tasks. She, on the other hand, felt a kind of numbness, confused about what she did feel.

After a while she opened her eyes, stood up and began walking towards the northern end of the beach past the swings, slide and boat launching ramp. Ahead and higher up on the bank lying on the ground surrounded by grasses swaying in the wind, lay a whitish oblong block of stone. She quickened her pace, intending to walk past, but as she reached the spot she changed her mind. Bending down, she read the inscription.

JAS BATCHELOR
1ST OFFA
S H VENUS
JAS. BUNKER
COMR.
T. BUNKER
OWNR.
O B JAN 28TH
1810

'A mariner from the schooner *Venus*. How ghastly to end up in such a lonely place!' she said slowly under her breath. Kneeling at the gravestone, she traced the worn letters with her finger. Mistakes must have been made over the course of time. The owner couldn't have had the same surname as the Captain! Maybe errors were made when painting over the original. 'Poor man… so far from his homeland.'

A lone dandelion nodded in the wind as if in echo to her thoughts. She was not going to leave Leonard's ashes at Cornelian Bay Cemetery, not that she knew where it was; she shuddered at the thought of herself lying in 'This Timeless Land', so remote, so far away from everything they knew. 'I can't do it to you… Oh, Len!' She began to cry.

She hurried on aimlessly, hardly noticing the Crayfish Farm buildings on her left as she continued along a narrow winding path past unfamiliar windblown trees, their jagged branches sprawling from gnarled trunks. Finally, she came out into a clearing where she noticed high up a football field surrounded by a metal fence, and from its banks she caught the whiff of a pungent smell. It reminded her of what…? Ah, fennel, she was sure of it. But what an extraordinary place for it to be growing.

The river was bouncing along not a hundred yards to her right and here was fennel growing up the banks of a football field. Jolted out of her reverie, she became aware of two very different houses; their gardens both rolled down to the water's edge. The first, a tall darkly stained timber dwelling, reminded her of a Dutch building, its roof in need of paint, as did the fence, broken in places, close to the path. Here and there blackberry bushes were poking through the holes. She peered through the fence at what looked like various levels of garden, mostly overgrown. She could see rickety wooden steps and a balcony of sorts that needed a paint and repair, wondering how anyone could let a house get into this condition in so sought-after a position.

She heard voices and realised she was wrong in surmising that one of the owners must have died, the survivor losing heart. She saw a middle-aged man and woman digging over the earth at a leisurely pace, and recognised the second house from the real estate cutting Nigel had shown them on their arrival, with its enormous windows and rockery flowing down from the slate patio, ending in a circular lawn flanked by an herbaceous border. It so reminded her of home. Pity it had been sold before they started looking.

There was a garden seat placed strategically in front of a New Zealand flax, presumably by the owners for weary walkers to sit upon as they watched the river flow by. Marion sat down rather unceremoniously, as the wooden slats were uneven, being curved higher at the front than at the back. The ends were ornately moulded in iron and painted white, and she noticed the right side was padlocked to the next door's fence. Did people steal garden seats? Even here, in this quiet spot? As she looked across the river to Lauderdale and Rokeby, the clouds turned greyish, so that the river lost its varying colours and became a steely blue.

Her mood wavered, affected by the light; she too had little affinity with her house. Maybe if she moved upstairs, where she could see the river from the little bedroom, she would feel akin to something in spite of the violent changes in her life.

But there again, the upstairs bedrooms were probably designed for children. Her thoughts strayed. Children... She wouldn't go down that path. She wouldn't think about that. It was so very long ago, but the memory swam clearly into view. No, she wouldn't remember, not today, but in spite of herself she did. A trick of the light turned the choppy steel waves into a fading grey hospital ward in the Middlesex, where the doctor had said, 'Never mind, Mrs Lee. Think how lucky you are! Already a fine daughter. It happens sometimes,' and patted her on the shoulder.

She never saw her son again. Broken-hearted, she had cried non-stop, and the Sister in her starched uniform had said with impatience, 'Wipe your eyes. Whatever would the doctor think! Count your blessings, Mrs Lee. Others are not so fortunate.' What would they know about her life? So long ago... Things would be very different now if, if only... No good blaming anyone, though.

Marion got up abruptly. No sense in dwelling on what might have been; besides, she needed to concentrate on the path, which dived down dramatically to a small cove skirted by three more houses. She crossed the gritty sand and pebbles, clambering up the far bank with the help of tufts of grass and low bushes. Never before had she ventured so far from home and was surprised to see four more houses, all very different and shielded from the river by bushes close to the water's edge, so that the path meandered through private properties. She heard faint music, and a dog barked close by. She wouldn't like to trespass.

She saw no one, so she continued on her way between high bushes until, suddenly in front of her was another bay, bigger than those before, upon which a dozen beach shacks were strung together within the curve of the sand. A bitumen road bordered by five large properties and a school stood at the far end. She crossed the beach, making for some tall pine trees, where she could watch children playing sport on an oval surrounded by various school buildings. She stood still, listening to their young voices floating on the breeze and the familiar whooshing sound of wind through the pine grove.

Looking up into the canopy, a sense of being invisible to all around overwhelmed her. Tears, fragile at first, gained momentum, mixing with the rain that was now spattering down in heavy droplets. 'Where do I belong?' she said aloud, retracing her steps, confronted by visions of Laleham churchyard with its gnarled yew trees whispering to her. She stretched out her hand to touch them but nothing was there. Stumbling along with the wind now raging, she clutched angrily at those words once swept on an English breeze – 'I'll walk beside you.'

'*Where are you? Help me!*' she called in her despair. Anyone, if they cared to notice, would have seen a middle-aged woman with bent head intent on getting home out of the wind and rain; they wouldn't have seen the anguish in her heart.

By the time she reached her own back gate Marion was soaked through, but her mind had cleared and she knew enough to believe in her inner voice, to take courage. The difficulty would be explaining it to Anna. That night she set about writing a letter to her friend, Alice Ashley, tentatively enquiring if she could presume upon her hospitality, as she was now a widow. At the end she scribbled a postscript: 'You were right.'

Exhausted, she fell asleep, unaware of the storm raging or the sea pounding on the beach below. A measure of herself as being apart from others had taken hold, a leaning into the wind carrying her small but significant step of faith towards what she intuitively knew was right for her. Her prayer was answered; she was not alone, her present grief would fade with time. Her journey was just beginning, if she would accept how things were, and realise that prayers were often answered in ways unimaginable. A chink of light shone on her request. It was straight from the heart, without conditions, and her heart began to heal as she slept deep and long.

The morning brought a change of weather. Power was restored, fallen trees and debris cleared away from those unlucky enough to be affected. The inhabitants of Tadbury had sustained little damage. Nonetheless, an unpleasant job needed doing, as Anna found to her dismay. Her mother was impossible.

'I can't do this,' said Anna and sank down onto the bed amid jackets, ties and jumpers. 'I really can't. It's too soon!' She scowled at Leonard's tallboy, its doors wide open, exposing handkerchiefs neatly folded, shirts hung symmetrically and drawers containing rows of socks.

'I… I thought you might like to see if any of his things would be suitable for Nigel. They are good quality.' Marion fingered a tweed jacket, holding it up for Anna to see. 'They're about the same size.'

An uneasy silence followed, both women caught up in their own turmoil. Plastic garbage bags strewn around the room brought the finality of death to Anna; all pretences swept away into a few rubbish bags. Nothing left, only personal memories.

'Look, dear, you've done more than enough and I do appreciate it, really I do. I'm sorry that all this has happened… It's the last thing I would want.' Her thoughts jackknifed. Why was she apologising for Len's death? 'I had no idea he was at risk. He didn't share it with me,' she concluded lamely. Looking at her daughter's crestfallen face, she tried to make amends. 'I think it is about time you went back home – to Nigel. Don't you worry about me. I'll be fine, really I will.' She began moving the clothes off the bed onto a chair.

'I'm sorry, Mum.' Anne picked up a jacket that had fallen off the bed, placing it on a hanger. 'What's this?' She held out a letter, unopened, addressed to Leonard.

'That came the day your father – you know, the day we called Dr MacIntyre.'

'Aren't you going to open it?' Anna watched as her mother placed it neatly on Leonard's bedside table beside his watch, lighter and wedding ring.

'Not now. To be truthful I don't really like to, maybe later. Come on, get your night things together. There's a casserole someone left at the front door; take it home to Nigel.'

'But Mum, what are you going to have?'

She might manage tomatoes on toast. She didn't really care, wanting to be alone. 'I'll be fine, love. Take yourself off home. Go and get your things together while I get the casserole. Just remember to bring the dish back!' she called from the kitchen, noticing the words 'Car, 9 Devon Walk' Sellotaped to the bottom.

After Anna's effusive leave-taking, Marion waved until her Laser disappeared around the corner, then went inside to make a cup of tea and take stock of her situation. She sat in the lounge wondering what her life was going to be like from now on. It took several minutes before she realised that it was up to her and her alone. She wasn't going to be bullied into moving to Queensland or staying in Tadbury. God forbid! Maybe, Len, you have done me a favour – but how I go about planning or organising anything, I have no idea.

The air felt chilly and she felt cold, so, lighting the gas fire and sitting so that she could see out of the window across the river, she watched the light fade, listening to the wind and occasional wave. A line came to her: *'I am! Yet what I am, who cares, or knows?'* How did it go? And yet? *'And yet I am, I live… though I am tossed.'* For the life of her she couldn't remember where it was from or who wrote it, but she repeated the words as she switched on all the lights throughout the house, determined not to be lonely. Then she took herself to the kitchen and set about steaming some fish.

On the same Friday morning that Marion took Leonard's clothes to the City Mission, Margery Ryan cornered her daughter in their kitchen before she left for school. The appalling consequences of Janice's behaviour had resulted in sleepless nights and tormented visions of the years ahead. Marge glanced out of the window, seeing only grey skies and rain, which depressed her further, so that she sounded unintentionally angry. 'If it isn't enough your life being ruined, mine is as well!' Her freckled skin took on a suffused pink tone, her eyes slightly bloodshot. She regarded her daughter's beautiful face, now pale with blue smudges under her eyes, and filled an electric jug before plugging it in next to the toaster.

'I don't see why it affects you, Mum!'

'You silly girl!' she shrilled. 'Of course it affects me. You can't take a baby everywhere you go. It's *me* who would be minding it while you attend this or that lecture, or go out with friends. Coming home whenever… all hours of the day and night. And who will be the bunny looking after junior? *Me.* Your life is finished, my girl, before it's already started.'

'I know!' Janice shouted, and burst into tears. 'I don't want this baby, Mum.'

'Well, it's too late now. What were you thinking of?' Margery glared at her daughter's woebegone face.

'It was an accident,' she mumbled.

'*Accident*?' Marge's voice rose. 'You mean it wasn't the first time?'

Janice bit her lip looking at a piece of fluff on the floor.

'Well, this is a fine mess you've landed us in!' She unplugged the jug, pouring the water into two white fluted mugs with the Tetley label hanging over the edge. Janice stared at the labels and thought she might be sick. 'I send you to a private school, and you get knocked up by a…' She blew her nose.

'Catholic boy,' murmured Janice under her breath.

'It's just not fair, Janice. I sent you to a good school precisely so that you wouldn't get in with the wrong crowd.' Marge placed two slices of cut white bread in the toaster, wondering if she should have bought a wholemeal loaf now that Janice was pregnant. She could do without all this worry. Janice couldn't think of anything to say, so she collected the plates, knives, butter and marmalade then laid the table and sat down.

On a more conciliatory note, Marge said, 'Serviettes, please.'

Dutifully, Janice moved back to the dresser and retrieved two blue and white napkins, folded in triangles, from the drawer.

They matched the willow pattern crockery Marge had saved so long for, displayed for all to see on the dresser.

She placed a silver toast rack on the table; it had been a wedding present fifteen years ago. She cut the toast to fit, poured a little milk and stirred a teaspoon of sugar into her tea, all the time aware of Janice nibbling on a dry piece of toast.

'What, no butter or marmalade?'

'No. It makes me sick.'

Marge's eyes roamed around the kitchen, alighting on the dresser. How proud she had been when it was delivered, and the willow pattern china looked expensive, although she knew it was not the real thing. What would her friends say when they found out about Janice? And they would, sooner or later. She felt mortified. Her eyes strayed to Janice's golden hair tied neatly back with a dark green ribbon, her face distressingly sad. So young – ridiculous in that hideous uniform. Had all her hard work come to this? Soon she would begin to show…

'Have some honey. I believe that's not so bad.'

'I'm all right, Mum.'

'You're not all right. Think of the baby. What will you have for lunch?'

'Depends on how I feel. Probably a milkshake or Diet Coke.'

'That's not enough. There's no goodness in diet drinks.' Exasperated, and trying to keep her temper, Marge concentrated on spreading first some butter then marmalade on her toast and drinking her tea noisily.

'Janice, what is his name?'

'Who?'

'You know who I mean… Who did you have sex with?'

Janice winced at her words. 'Mum, I don't want to talk about it!' She stood up stacking her plate and saucer. The knife skidded onto the floor. She bent down to retrieve it, straightening up too quickly, and swayed, nearly fainting. Alarmed, Marge jumped up. 'Sit down, for heaven's sake! Oh, Janice, I wanted you to have a life… better than mine. Go places, see the world. Not be stuck struggling to make ends meet. This is your future I'm talking about! I know what it's like, believe me, and *I*' – she stressed the last word – 'was *married*. Don't you see?'

Tears welled up in her eyes, threatening to spill over. How she wished Paul was still with her. Life could be so cruel. If only he was here to talk to. If only he hadn't loved sailing so much.

'Gavin.'

'Gavin,' Marge repeated slowly. 'Gavin what?'

Janice looked down at her lap, attempting to come to a decision. 'His father is a dentist in Macquarie Street.' She wished her mother would ask what he was like, and she could then reply he was drop-dead gorgeous.

'I'm not interested in what his father does. It's what this Gavin has done to you. Please, Janice.' She tried to hold her feelings in check.

'It wasn't like that, Mum.'

'What was it like, then?'

'We were down at Port Arthur… you know, the day Martin Bryant went berserk, killing all those people.'

'Is that why you were late coming home! And I thought you had been to the school fair. Oh, God! You could have been killed!'

'We weren't near the café.'

'Oh, Janice, I don't know what to believe. So many lies…'

'It's not lies. If you must know, it's Gavin Armstrong.' Then she burst into tears.

Marge thought she knew of Dr Armstrong. He was very popular, if her memory served her rightly. Like father, like son. She handed Janice a tissue. 'Well, what's done is done, and if you don't get a move on, you'll be late for school, and I for work.' Seeing Janice's stricken face, she added, 'Get your things and I'll give you a lift up to the bus stop.'

'You won't say anything, will you, Mum?'

'Janice, get a move on! Look, if you like, I'll pick you up from school today and we'll go looking for baby clothes. I can get a pattern and start knitting.'

'Will you, Mum?'

'We'll need a crib and nappies, little vests…'

Janice stood at the bottom of the stairs, relieved she didn't have to walk up to the bus stop. She felt so tired. 'Being Friday I'll come out the Patrick Street exit. You won't be late, will you?'

'No. Why should I be late?' Marge replied gently.

'I'm sorry, Mum.'

'So am I, Janice. So am I. But I suppose we had better think of the future.' She smiled. 'We'll work something out.'

She looked away to hide her returning tears and began to stack the dishes in the sink and clear the table. She grabbed her coat, keys and bag, calling out as she did so, 'I'll wait for you in the car. Don't forget to snib the lock.'

The shift began badly for Marge Ryan. Three nurses were off sick, administration had mixed up two admissions and her pay was incorrect, according to her calculations. To top it all off, there was a continuous banging emanating from somewhere in the building, due to renovations in the maternity wing. Wryly she hoped it would be finished by the time Janice would be admitted.

At the end of her shift, Marge was ready for a confrontation with anyone who crossed her path. She had a couple of hours to kill before picking Janice up and decided to stay in town. Over a quick lunch of minestrone soup and garlic bread in the canteen, she glanced through the telephone directory and found Dr Armstrong's home address. Would she or wouldn't she? In spite of the fact that it was bucketing down with rain, she decided to visit Mrs Armstrong. No one in their right mind would be out in this weather. She would give it a try; after all, it wasn't the sort of thing you could say over the telephone.

On her way to Bellerive, she could hardly see as the windscreen wipers needed repairing. She crossed the Tasman Bridge easily enough and found the correct street, but had great difficulty in finding the exact house, as some of the numbers were camouflaged by shrubs.

Eventually she deduced which house it was, in spite of the rain and a laurel bush. Grappling with her umbrella, Marge alighted from the car only to find that the brolly wouldn't open properly. By the time she had locked the car door her hair was saturated. She took stock of the high wrought iron gates and extensive garden divided by crazy paving which wound around to the back of the house. The gates opened easily enough, but she found the path slippery as clumps of thyme and lavender spilled over its edges. Turning the corner, she saw a Mercedes parked close to the front door, and a garage attached to the side of the house. *Filthy rich* went through her mind, not helping her humour. At least there was a porch of sorts, which was relatively dry; what looked like a banksia rose trailed over its roofline, looking as miserable as she felt, its flowers squashed in the rain.

She rang the bell, getting angrier by the minute, not only because of the Mercedes and size of the house, but because of the weather and Janice's predicament. The door opened to reveal a woman quite a bit older than herself wearing a brown tweed skirt, expensive cream mohair jumper and suede shoes. Mary Armstrong wore little make-up, tiny pearl earrings and a marcasite watch. The whole effect was of someone perfectly relaxed and happy with life. She waited for the bedraggled woman on her doorstep to speak.

'I'm Janice Ryan's mother. She attends St Mary's, and your son goes to St Virgil's. Right?'

'Yes. Should I know you?'

Marge ignored her question. 'His name is Gavin, right?'

Mary nodded, puzzled by the vehemence of the woman in front of her. 'I'm sorry, I don't think I remember us meeting before…'

'No, we haven't… but as this is rather a delicate matter, I'd rather not discuss it on your doorstep.'

Realising Mrs Ryan was determined to have her say, Mary reluctantly said, 'You'd better come in out of the rain.'

At 3.45, although stuck in a traffic jam on the Tasman Bridge, Marge was nevertheless somewhat mollified. Mary Armstrong had been shocked to hear of her son's behaviour, and was at a complete loss to know how this had come about. She had provided Marge with a large mug of tea beside a roaring log fire and promised that her son would face up to his responsibilities. In fact, the afternoon went better than Marge had anticipated.

Glancing at her watch, she was aware she would be late getting to St Mary's. As the car inched along, its windscreen wipers working frantically, she noticed the petrol gauge was low and prayed she wouldn't run out before reaching a service station. It was 4.10 by the time she reached the bottom of Harrington Street, the gauge flashing. The traffic was heavy both sides, so there was no way she could cross over to the petrol station on the other side of the road. To add to her consternation, she was unable to turn into St Mary's, as there were cars blocking the driveway.

Frantically, she peered through the side window in hope of seeing Janice, but what with the rain and parked cars, she had no alternative but to continue up the steep hill, turn left into Barrack Street, flanked by St Mary's tennis courts on her left and St Virgil's campus on her right. The thought occurred to her that Janice might have given up waiting and caught the bus home, but dismissed it quickly as highly improbable. It had better be… She rounded the block once more and was held up by school buses in Harrington Street. She prayed her petrol gauge was not faulty and there would be room this time for her to enter the school car park.

Once in the car park, she found there was very little space to manoeuvre, as an island of flowers took up most of the centre, with staff cars parked at angles alongside. Knowing she couldn't stop indefinitely as there were cars on her tail, she drove slowly around. 'This is ridiculous,' she moaned, close to tears. A van reversing from alongside of the cathedral steps left a gap, and at last she spied Janice, huddled out of the rain, all alone. Her heart lurched as she beeped the horn.

A lump developed in her throat as she flung open the car door. 'Get in, quick.'

'Where've you been, Mum?'

'Going round and round trying to get a park,' Marge replied, easing out into the traffic. 'Where in this neck of the woods is a petrol station?'

'I suppose North Hobart is the closest.'

'But that's going in the wrong direction.'

'Well, try up the top of the hill. I think there's one on the opposite corner. At least, I think it's a garage. It's a corner shop-cum-everything… Yes, I'm sure it is.'

'Well, I hope you're right, Janice. Pray we get there before the car stops. In this frightful rain, I can hardly see. I can tell you something else, the car hates these hills!'

On cue, it began to sputter as they topped the rise on the intersection of Hill Street; halfway across, it died. 'Oh, God—'

Those were Marge Ryan's last words, as Janice saw a looming shadow crunch into the driver's side of the vehicle. She heard a loud tearing noise, which forced their car off the road and into a wall. Then she mercifully blacked out, to the sound of splashing rain. Was it providence or divine intervention that prevented Janice from seeing her mother mangled by a silver grille, or heard the owners of the other car laying blame, while sheltering underneath the corner shop's awning waiting for the police and ambulance? 'What idiot would stop in the middle of an intersection, I ask you. She came out of nowhere. It wasn't my fault!'

Later that night on the news, listeners were advised to stay at home and keep off the roads unless it was absolutely necessary. Numerous accidents were alluded to, and as the rain showed no sign of relenting, there were bound to be more.

Around 6.30 p.m. Patrick Armstrong arrived home, looking forward to the weekend. He had hardly stepped in the front door before Mary divulged Margery Ryan's unpleasant news. Gavin found himself in hot water. Being grilled about his amorous affair with Janice in front of his mother was embarrassing enough, but to be blamed for Janice's condition by all the adults didn't seem fair. He was shattered to hear that she was pregnant. The horror of what he had seen down at Port Arthur now came back to him, overshadowing any sensible answers to his father's questions. Mary was in tears; Patrick was beside himself.

'You've let your mother down, me down, your school down, and more importantly yourself down!' he lectured. 'You'll have to get married. You know that, don't you?'

'But…'

'No buts about it, son. Did you ever think for a minute about the consequences? God knows what this will do to my practice.' For half an hour Patrick ranted until he ran out of steam. What with the pouring rain and the atmosphere in the Armstrong household, the evening meal was eaten mostly in silence. The television was not switched on. Gavin thought it wise not to ask for his allowance.

'I suppose there's no hope this baby is someone else's?' Patrick remarked to Mary when preparing for bed.

'I don't know. I've never met the girl.'

'I blame the school. Amalgamating the senior students only asks for trouble. I expect she threw herself at him.'

'Pat, I don't want to talk about it any more tonight. Go to sleep.' She lay beside him, wondering if the call they had received the other night had been from Janice Ryan.

You never do really know your children, she thought, as she drifted off to sleep.

<h1 style="text-align:center">~IV~</h1>

Errors like straws upon the surface flow:
He who would search for pearls must dive below.

John Dryden

The same Friday evening that changed the course of Janice Ryan's life and caused ructions in the Armstrong household found Marion replying to cards of condolence. The wind and the rain kept her indoors and did nothing for her spirits. She had tried to be optimistic about her future, but, what with handing over Leonard's clothes to the City Mission, seeing the bank manager and filling in numerous forms, she felt her life was spiralling out of control. Among the many letters addressed to Leonard was the one which Anna had found. Marion sighed, staring blankly into space, listening to the wind and rain on the roof. The postmark was Spelthorne. The address was typewritten but the envelope was pale mauve and scented. The contents consisted of only one sheet folded several times in order to fit inside. Smoothing out the paper, she wondered why people couldn't get their stationary to match properly. It read as follows, there being no letterhead.

Dear Len

Thought you would like to know Michael has got his scholarship to the RAM. Everything is OK now. How do you like Australia? – you rat!

LD.

Marion placed the letter on the coffee table, not understanding a word of it, thinking her life was getting more bizarre by the minute: *you rat*... What kind of person sent letters like this? In disgust, she read it again, feeling slightly uneasy, and screwing it up, dropped it in the wastepaper basket on the way to the kitchen to fix a nightcap. The phone rang. Who now? Picking up the receiver she said tiredly, 'Marion Lee.'

'Mrs Lee?' said a jovial voice, 'David Newman from Newman and Colliers.'

'Yes?' She sounded hesitant.

'I'm sorry to contact you at this hour but we have had difficulty with the number. We tried to contact you earlier.'

'Oh, in what context?'

'Your husband's estate. I wonder when would it be convenient to you?'

'I… well, there isn't any hurry, is there?'

'No, but—'

She cut him off. 'I know all there is to know, being the sole benefactor… unless my husband left everything to the RSPCA!' She attempted a laugh.

'No, no, there's nothing like that. But legally we need to tie up any loose ends.'

'Ah, I see. You mean bequests and suchlike. We have a daughter…'

'I gather you haven't been here long. It must have been quite a shock. Very remiss of me. You have our condolences.'

'Er…' She cleared her throat. 'Thank you.'

'Shocking weather. Perhaps when it clears up, you and your daughter…'

'Anna.'

'Anna, yes; perhaps you could give my secretary a call sometime next week… to make a time and date that suits you both.'

'Yes, I'll do that. Where are you exactly?'

'Victoria Street. Close to Centre Point and the multi-storey car park.'

'I'm sorry, I didn't catch your name.'

'David Newman.' Then, sensing he was dealing with one rather confused lady, he added, 'Our number is 6235 5144.'

'Just a moment and I'll write that down. I'll be in touch shortly,' Marion said, repeating the number.

'My daughter works – you understand?' Her voice almost faded away. 'Bye.'

She hung up, sighing, 'Something else to do,' and, lost in thought, made herself a cup of hot chocolate. She felt completely isolated from the rest of the world, watching the night closing in and rain cascading down the windows. There were people to tell and letters of thanks to be dealt with, and now the solicitor. It all seemed exhausting. Sitting, she closed her eyes. By now she had run out of energy, finding little motivation to even get out of bed in the morning. She leant over to turn on the table lamp, and began idly sifting through the cards. Her eye chanced upon a beautiful card from the principal and staff at St Mary's College, and she remembered, several days before the funeral, finding on her doorstep a basket of mixed blue flowers, interspersed with gypsophila. They were the first flowers she had ever received, or so she recalled. She mused on the kindness of people she barely knew, hearing the strains of 'On Eagle's Wings' sung by the St Mary's School Choir, and reflected on the sad funeral service within the vast cathedral, herself participating as if in a dream.

'So few people… so few…' she murmured. If it had been at All Saints', Laleham, the church would have been packed. She would have ordered the flowers and probably decorated the church. There would have been an anthem sung, and special tunes played on the bells in memory of Len. People she knew would have shook her hand and some would have expected to say their eulogies. She imagined Laleham Cottage bursting at the seams with people who came back to partake of refreshments, and best of all, Anna would have come home. Anna and Nigel would have been there. Anna would have stayed, realising that England was her home. Yes, Anna would have stayed.

Reading the card through blurred eyes, Marion noticed that Sister Anne had suggested, if she would like to visit the Presentation Prayer House down at Blackman's Bay, she would be most welcome. There were nuns there she could talk with, a chapel, various lounges and extensive gardens within which she was free to wander. Tea and coffee were also available, as was a private path leading down to the beach, which previous visitors had found very restful. Why not? There was little comfort here. At least, I haven't found it yet, thought Marion.

She left the letters on the coffee table, wandering through the house, turning on lights and touching familiar objects that she had brought from Laleham. She heard nothing over the roar of the waves and wind. There were no lights on the water, no ships to see, just blackness. She drew the lounge room curtains, checked her watch for the time in England, and decided to ring Alice before she left for work.

'Please, Alice, be there! I couldn't tell you before… but now I really need to talk with a true friend.' Dialling international, the area code and then Alice's number, she listened to the ringing tone until it rang out. She replaced the receiver gently on the cradle, slumped into a chair and slowly began to cry.

On Saturday morning, Elizabeth Macclesfield, the vice principal of St Mary's College, was ensconced in Sister Anne's study, nursing a mug of coffee by a gas fire turned up to its highest level. The rain of the night before had now turned into a heavy drizzle. Looking across at Sister Anne, Elizabeth was aware how drawn she looked, an effect not helped by a severe hairstyle and the standard beige and brown outfit she customarily wore.

Elizabeth surmised that whatever the Principal had to say would have to be of some importance to be called in on a Saturday morning, as the staff had already been summoned late on Friday afternoon for an unexpected meeting, which in her view had all been a waste of time.

'Sorry about this, Elizabeth, but I wanted to run something past you.' Sister Anne looked across at the window, apparently seeking inspiration.

Elizabeth waited expectantly with what she hoped was an encouraging nod, wishing Sister Anne would get on with it, as she had grades eleven and twelve social studies to sift through and her own domestic chores to see to, there being four children still at home. She began making a mental note of what supermarket items she needed to pick up on the way home.

Sister's voice broke into her thoughts. 'Janice Ryan has been in a car accident with her mother, who was killed at the scene,' she announced, her face lacking any emotion.

'What?'

'Friday, on her way home, presumably. Just up the hill.'

'But I thought she took the bus.' And realising her remark was quite inane, owing to the circumstances, Elizabeth took a sip of tea.

'Yes, well, not on this occasion. Her mother fetched her, probably because of the rain.'

'How dreadful… poor Janice. Where is she?'

'I'm told she is in the Royal Hobart.'

'I suppose the next of kin have been notified?'

'Well, no. That's just the point… I mean, that's why I asked you in. There doesn't appear to be anyone.'

'What – *no one*?'

'It's early days yet; maybe there is someone who will know more.'

'I can't believe it. Poor lass.'

Sister Anne nodded, swallowing a large mouthful of coffee, then looked down at the spluttering fire. 'Well, not that we know of. And that's not the end of it…'

There seemed to be a long silence before Sister Anne continued. There was no easy way of saying what she felt she must. 'Janice is only sixteen and she's four months pregnant.'

'Oh no! That explains a lot of things. Her absenteeism… work not handed in. I can't believe it. What can we do?'

'I was hoping you'd come up with something,' Sister Anne said with a winsome smile.

'Does her mother own the house?'

'I don't know her financial arrangements. In any case, a sixteen-year-old girl can't live on her own, especially now… she will have to go into foster care.'

'And who is going to take on a pregnant sixteen-year-old?'

'Quite. Look, Elizabeth, the staff don't know about the pregnancy, unless Janice herself has said anything, which I very much doubt. But they must be told she has been in an accident and is in hospital.'

'The girls will want to visit…'

'Yes, I know. It's all very difficult.'

'There are various possibilities, but it will depend on Janice herself. I'll make some inquiries over the weekend.'

'Elizabeth, I don't want her here attending classes – you know, as she…'

'Yes, I quite understand.'

'Well, that's all. I don't want to keep you...' And with that Sister Anne stood up behind her desk, preoccupied with the affairs of the school.

In spite of the drizzle Salamanca Market was well patronised. Food takeaway caravans were installed at the cobbled end, close to the wheat silos and the Ball and Chain Steakhouse, their aromas wafting past stalls selling everything from books to clothing. Further along, handmade leather belts, glass-blowing, wooden toys, old maps, jewellery, handmade soaps and handmade furniture mixed with fruit and vegetables, flowers and musicians, all catching the eye as people filed past and up beyond the sandstone Law Courts terminating at Davey Street.

Mary Armstrong was not interested in any bric-a-brac, only produce. Most weekends she did her shopping here. Everything was so fresh and organically grown – especially the fruit and vegetables grown by the Hmong people.

She liked the delicate way they displayed their goods and was quite taken by their slight stature and the way they wore their colourful clothes. Today she was preoccupied with thoughts of Gavin and the girl, Janice Ryan, whom he was supposed to have made pregnant. She picked up a bunch of carrots, pak choi and small potatoes, paying for them in an absent-minded way. Then she glanced at her watch and walked towards the square behind the market, which had recently been given a makeover. There was a fountain in its centre surrounded by a patch of circular grass and on either side of the square were gourmet food shops, an expensive gift shop and a 24-hour bakery, towards which she made her way. Next to this was the much talked about Antarctic Centre which, she would have to admit, she hadn't as yet patronised.

Mary had arranged to meet a colleague, a volunteer-to-be precise, from a group she herself had instigated – 'Single Mums' Support Service'. How was she going to explain her own predicament? Their little group rented premises in Battery Point, arranged for counselling, provided baby clothes, relevant literature, and shoulders to cry on. What would she do if Janice

Ryan turned up? Would she know she was Gavin's mother? Oh, the whole thing was too embarrassing to contemplate! Mrs Ryan must be mistaken… it had to be someone else's son. Not her Gavin. And after last night, with Patrick ranting and raving about what the future held for their son, Gavin had hardly said a word, only that he hadn't seen Janice in weeks – which was hardly the point as she was four months pregnant. Mary sat quietly waiting in a window seat, drinking a long white coffee, watching the rain fall across the grass while Saturday shoppers were buffeted through the door, bringing the cold in with them. Lost in thought about the difficulties families and the mother-to-be faced, problems mostly to do with loneliness and financial hardship, she realised tragedy was no respecter of persons. If it really was Gavin's baby, then he would have to marry the girl and that was all there was to it. Oh, the stigma! What kind of life would Gavin have? Nothing like she had imagined.

'Sorry to keep you waiting.'

A hand rested lightly on her shoulder.

'Oh, Carmel, you made me jump.' Mary smiled wanly, moving her bags of vegetables off the opposite chair. 'Do sit down. What'll you have?'

'No, no. I'll get it.' With that, Carmel joined the queue at the counter, returning with a marshmallow floating on the top of a steaming mug of hot chocolate and some fruit scones.

'Thought you and I might share these.' She gave Mary a guilty smile, moving the cream to one side of the plate. 'Now, tell me, what's the problem?'

Between mouthfuls of scone, Carmel listened to Mary without interrupting, as the warmth of the bakery permeated the café so that coats were slung over the backs of chairs, faces looked flushed and feet inside boots felt decidedly hot. Carmel removed her black anorak to reveal a crimson-coloured jumper which was new, recently purchased along with blouses, vests, jeans, shoes and jewellery as a result of an acrimonious divorce. She'd had her black hair styled in a bob and her ears pierced, displaying tiny diamond flowers reflecting the light.

Mary had known about the divorce and had secretly disapproved. Now, looking at Carmel, she noticed how confident she appeared, whereas she herself felt on the back foot, so to speak. As for Carmel, she was amazed to see Mary in such a state. Many single mums had aired their problems over numerous cups of tea to Mary, and she'd always sounded calm and helpful, in a detached way, full of good advice sprinkled with palatable Catholic dogma as to how they should cope. Finally Mary came to a halt, looking at Carmel expectantly. Her friend, realising she was supposed to offer a solution, but with no idea what to say, cleared her throat. 'I assume it is early days…? I mean' – she leant towards Mary – 'if it is early days, and she is only a couple of months gone…'

Mary looked down at the table, fiddling with her knife and scone. 'That's out of the question!' she said emphatically.

'Why?'

'Because I don't believe in it. Besides, according to her mother, Janice is at least three months gone.'

'And what about Gavin? Has anyone asked him what he believes in?'

'He'll follow the teaching of the Church, Carmel,' Mary said huffily. 'I would have thought you would know where we stand on this issue.'

Carmel looked around the café, trying to think what to say next. She tried another tactic. 'Are the Ryans Catholic?'

'I suppose so… Janice goes to St Mary's.'

'Look, you asked for my advice. I'm only going on what you tell me.'

'Yes, I know.' A subdued Mary kept her eyes averted and drank some coffee. Suddenly she said, 'Gavin says he hasn't seen her for months.'

Carmel chose her next words carefully, willing Mary to look up from her plate. 'Well, in that case, it would be very unwise to force the two of them together. It would never work. If, as you say, he didn't know about the pregnancy, and he hasn't been meeting with Janice, then what about adoption? Assuming Janice would be willing.'

'Do you think Mrs Ryan would be in favour?'

'I don't know, Mary,' Carmel said exasperatedly. 'You were the one who met her. Maybe you ought to get in touch with the

Ryans. It's silly worrying yourself over a girl you haven't met, a pregnancy which may or may not be Gavin's fault, and all this just before his exams.' She paused. 'He's expecting to go to uni, isn't he?'

'Well, yes. Patrick and I have high hopes for him. Just like his sister...'

'Well, then. A round conference with Mr and Mrs Ryan, Janice, Patrick, yourself and Gavin.'

'There isn't a Mr Ryan. He drowned in the 1991 Sydney-to-Hobart Yacht Race.'

'Oh, I see. That makes things a little more...'

'Tragic!'

'Quite. Look, talk to Gavin and see how he feels about her. I can't think of anything else that may help.' Carmel fumbled with her jacket sleeves. 'I have to fly. See how my girls are getting on... and the parking meter. See you on Wednesday at the usual time.' Mary nodded. 'Now don't you worry, there are ways around every situation.' And with a smile and a pat on Mary's shoulder, she retrieved a large black leather shoulder bag, rummaging for her car keys as she turned to leave. Extraordinary! she thought. Mary in a flap. When the world doesn't work to her rules she goes to pieces. Uncharitable, I know, but fact. All this time doling out advice to others – and not once did I hear her say, 'Poor Janice.' What about *her* feelings? What about *her* exams?

Carmel arrived at the parking lot behind Salamanca Square, relieved to be under her allotted time and that it was far nicer to park under cover than be mixed up with pedestrians round the market front. She put her old Holden into gear and made for the exit and on to Sandy Bay Road to check on her business, Carmel's Coiffure. Saturday was often very busy and recently she had taken on two apprentices who were finding the hours rather exhausting.

Mary left the bakery in somewhat lighter spirits, as the rain had stopped, and made a conscious effort not to judge Gavin's conduct. She decided to stop off at Corpus Christi Catholic Church on her way home to Bellerive, as Gavin would still be rowing for St Virgil's and Patrick had gone down to his boat shed. She would pray there for a while and ask God why this calamity had happened to her family. She resolved to have a quiet word with Gavin before Patrick came home. It was going to be embarrassing.

Before leaving the square she had spotted a box of Lindt chocolates in the shop window next door to the bakery. Purchasing a box, she opened them in the car and promptly ate one after the other on her journey home. Chocolate was her weakness especially in times of stress, although she would not admit this even to Father Stephen.

By late morning the clouds began to lift and a weak sun buoyed spirits, especially those on the River Derwent. Gavin was one of those practising with the St Virgil's fours. He liked the mindless movement of arm and oar, the feathering and speed of their boat – anything to take his mind off Janice Ryan. In like mood, his father was preparing his dinghy for a sail.

Meanwhile, in the Royal Hobart Hospital, Janice was lying in a semiconscious state, drifting in and out of reality. She had a fractured arm, a broken pelvis and multiple bruises and lacerations. She wasn't aware she was haemorrhaging, but the nurses realised and she was wheeled down to theatre. No one as yet had explained to her where her mother was or how she was. This Janice had put down to the fact that they were too busy to find out for her. Everything was going wrong for her. She had been looking forward all day to buying baby clothes. In fact, throughout maths class and social science she had been dreaming what it would be like to have a baby to look after. What would her friends say? None of them had suspected that she was pregnant, only surmised that she and Gavin Armstrong were no longer an item. Someone stuck a needle into her arm and told her to count to ten. She began dreaming of sailing away into warm waters with her dad, who then changed into Gavin, where he was busy placing a lei of frangipani flowers around her neck, while she was looking down at a smiling baby nestled inside a rush basket on a tropical beach. Gavin placed on her head a garland of red hibiscus flowers, whispering, 'My queen.'

Anna was preparing lunch for herself, Nigel and Marion, having previously vacuumed throughout the house and done the weekly wash. The weather being fickle, she had hung most things in the laundry and a favourite pale blue jumper of hers over a clothes horse. Covering the round dining table was a starched white tablecloth with lace edges, upon which was arranged a small bunch of violets picked from the end of the garden by the back fence. The table was set for three, and as Anna adjusted the cloth, she wasn't sure if it was anger, sadness, loss or a combination of all three that made her feel teary. Satisfied with her efforts, she returned to the kitchen to clean up, spying her mother talking to Nigel along the front pathway. They entered the house together, he to have a shower and change from tidying up the front garden, and she calling as she entered the kitchen.

'I thought I'd find you here, Anna,' she said, gently looking around for a drying-up cloth; finding none she willed Anna to turn around. 'Where is it?'

'Oh, in the drawer there.' Anna shifted herself, banging pots, and attempted a smile.

'Am I early, dear?'

'No. No, Mum.' Anna began running fresh water into the sink, wondering when having her mother for a regular Sunday lunch had begun. She couldn't remember how it had started, but ruefully thought it was the least she could do in the circumstances. Stealing a glance at Marion, she felt guilty at her behaviour, but somehow had difficulty shaking off the mood. For Marion's part, she knew she was a nuisance, but felt it her right to have lunch on a regular basis with her daughter. After all, she didn't ask to come to Tasmania, she was persuaded by Leonard. Both were at odds and both suffering. Over roast lamb, mint sauce, peas, carrots and roast potatoes, the conversation drifted along about the weather, the difficulties of preparing students for their final examinations, and the next door's dog, which had been barking on and off since Friday night.

Nigel was all for going over there, until he remembered an altercation he had had with the owner around the time of Leonard's death. Mr Sebbens was in his late forties, Tasmanian-born from the West Coast, and had run an interstate removals business for the last fifteen years. On that particular occasion, he had returned from Western Australia late at night and had left his lorry parked across Nigel's driveway. As a result, Nigel had arrived at Hutchins School late and been reprimanded. Heated words had been exchanged while he had dragged Mr Sebbens from a deep slumber to remove his truck. He suggested Anna go and see what could be done about the dog, declaring, 'Well, we can't go on like this, not for another night.'

'So, what do you propose?' she said waspishly. 'I have hardly seen the man and don't know if there is a Mrs Sebbens.'

Trying to smooth troubled waters, Marion remarked quietly, 'It's very awkward in these situations.' Her eyes rested on her plate of apple pie and cream. 'I know, dear. You go to the front door… it might be better coming from a woman. I remember a similar incident at home with a cat yowling. It had got locked in and wanted the outside for you know what. Your dad clambered through a window to let it out. You remember the Colcloughs? Their daughter went to art school up in London; well, they – Kit and Laura – had got caught on the M25 in a pile-up. They were expecting to be home in the afternoon and didn't return until the following day. Luckily the cat didn't run away. We fed it and kept an eye on the place.'

Nigel had never heard his mother-in-law say so much and began to wonder if it was the wine. Then, to his relief, Marion's ramblings moved Anna to say, 'All right, all right, I suppose I'd better go. I hope someone's home!'

With that, Anna left the table, grabbed her coat from the hall-stand and went into Mr Sebben's overgrown garden.

Silence fell between Marion and Nigel. As far as she could tell they had never spoken more than a few words alone and she wasn't sure how to proceed. Businesslike, he said, 'I'll clear away here, Mother; you go and sit in the lounge. Coffee or tea?'

'Oh no, dear, I can help. I'd rather be doing…' She smiled up at him, then looked down at the table as they proceeded to clear the table together. Marion neatly removed the tablecloth and shook it outside the back door, replacing it beside the vase of violets. Nigel went across to the stereo system, looking for the Three Tenors CD. He popped it into the player and settled himself into an armchair with the Sunday newspaper. Marion, aware that this might be the only time she would get to talk to

Nigel alone, fiddled about in the kitchen, putting the condiments away and finally put on the kettle. It was going to be difficult to speak above the music but nevertheless she would give it a try.

She came back into the lounge, raising her voice. 'What would you say if I went back home?'

Nigel, fearing she was thinking him rude, lowered the paper, replying heartily, 'You're welcome to stay as long as you like!'

'No, I mean to England!'

'Oh, I see.' But he didn't at all, and wished Anna was there. Pavarotti was building to a climax. Nigel adjusted the volume and with his back to Marion prevaricated… 'But you've hardly been here six months.' Then, trying to mollify her, he turned away, hiding his dismay. 'What does Anna say to that?'

'She doesn't know. I wanted your thoughts.'

Nigel sat down abruptly, fiddling with the pages of the paper. He wasn't expecting this; he wished Anna would return.

'I gather – or so Anna says – you want to move to Queensland next year.'

'Well…' Nigel crossed his left hand over to his right shoulder, scratching under his collar and leaning back into the chair. He appeared to be looking for inspiration at a spot on the ceiling as to what to say next. 'Well,' he repeated, 'I'm hoping to take Anna in the school holidays up there to see what she thinks. It's not absolutely final… nothing is set in concrete.'

'But it's a step up?'

'Oh yes. Very much so.'

Marion was mystified that Nigel would deliberately move hundreds of miles away from his parents – and for what? A bigger pay packet, kudos, position? She blurted out, 'But what about your parents? Won't they expect you to stay in Tasmania? I mean, we came here to be closer. Aren't they due back from overseas shortly?'

Nigel felt vaguely uncomfortable because of Marion's circumstances. She hadn't expected to be left a widow, but he didn't think that he should change his plans to suit Anna's mother. Rallying his thoughts, he tried to lighten the situation.

'Yes, sometime in November… They've had a great time, and are thinking of doing it again. Actually I spoke to Dad the other night, and it was mooted that if we all go to Queensland they might come as well – not to Queensland, but just over the border to Byron Bay. It would be warmer in the winter, and Mum suffers with an arthritic knee. They sent their love to you and hoped you were all right. I know it is early days yet, but we would like you to consider coming up there too… either to stay with us or own a unit of your own.' He finished lamely and, leaning forward, said, 'The kettle's boiled. I'll make some coffee.'

With that, he made a beeline for the kitchen, giving Marion time to digest all that he had said. In his mind he absolved himself for having stretched the truth. Marion herself was too shocked to reply.

Her glance fell onto the headlines of an article in *The Bulletin* magazine, which was left open on the coffee table: 'Lives changed by the Unexpected'. Underneath was a picture of Martin Bryant. She picked it up and tried to imagine what drove such a gentle-faced young man to such violent rage. She studied the photo and felt the beginning of tears welling in the back of her eyes. He was apparently sitting down on some steps in front of heavy double wooden doors which were half hidden by his white fisherman's jersey, a profusion of long tangled blonde hair giving him an air of innocence.

She read the article, feeling for the families who had been deprived of their loved ones in such a senseless way. Her eyes travelled down the page. Names, pictures of people from as far as Switzerland and Kuala Lumpur, gunned down while on holiday. She thought of her first night in Tasmania, sitting on the same couch while the ABC newsreader choked out the unbelievable story unfolding down at Port Arthur. She remembered the journalists at Tullarmarine airport wanting tickets, offering to buy them from anyone, in order to get down to Tasmania before anyone else. She remembered Leonard trying to shield her from what was going on, suggesting that they'd had a very long day and it would be a good idea to have an early night. What if I had known that in a few months this would have happened to me – losing Leonard, not so dramatic, but nevertheless completely unexpected?

Her tears spilled down her cheeks as fast as she wiped them away as Anna entered the room.

'It's all been taken care of…' She stopped. 'What is it? Oh, Mum, don't cry.'

Going over to her she put an arm around her shoulders. 'What's Nigel been saying? Nigel?'

'I've made the coffee…'

'It's not him. It's…' She indicated the magazine.

Anna stared at the headlines, folded the magazine and glared at Nigel. He in turn made much of carrying the coffee and cups into the lounge. A look of puzzlement crossed his face, because even at the funeral Marion hadn't shed a tear, and now here she was in a terrible state. Defensively, he mumbled, 'I suggested to your mother she would be welcome to come with us to Queensland – that's if she wants to.'

'That's if we even go,' remarked Anna, in an attempt at lightness. 'Really, Nigel!' She made herself busy by pouring the coffee out, helping herself to two spoonfuls of sugar. She waited until Marion had taken a good sip before she said, 'They have all sorts of things available for people to be involved in, clubs and societies for this and that, not to mention the beach…'

'Anna, they have beaches here, and I don't like them particularly; besides, I really don't think I could move to another strange place.'

'But you wouldn't feel strange! We would be there.'

It occurred to Marion that no amount of stalling was going to get her anywhere, but she wasn't going to give in. This was one decision she was going to make for herself and if contact with her daughter was to be on the same level in Queensland as it was in Tadbury, she would be just as lonely.

Anna thought it was about time to change the subject. They clearly weren't going to get Marion interested in Queensland just yet. She said, 'Mum, you mentioned earlier seeing your solicitor one day this week. What for?'

'Not sure. It's not as though we don't know what is in your father's will, but apparently he wants us there.'

'Mother, you're not short of money, are you? Because if you are, we can help out until everything is…' Nigel spoke with concern, smiling.

Embarrassed, Marion interrupted him. 'No, of course not.

Financially, Len had everything sorted as soon as we arrived... which is odd, really. It's not as if he knew something like this would happen to him. I'm sure if he had known he would have told me.'

Between making much of drinking their after-Sunday-lunch coffee and the retelling of next door's drama, arrangements were made to see David Newman of Newman and Colliers on Wednesday. Marion was to meet Anna in Hobart after school.

It was just as well that Mr Sebben's Labrador, Ruby, had sounded the alarm so persistently, alerting neighbours in the vicinity. The previous night, Mr Sebbens had fallen over after imbibing a few too many beers, knocking his head on the corner of the gas stove, resulting in concussion. Right at that moment, he was being wheeled out on a stretcher. Tactfully, Anna omitted repeating what his neighbour of ten years, Mavis Brown, had relayed to her outside on the pavement. Apparently, Mrs Sebbens had gone to visit her sister in Launceston some three months earlier and had not returned. Rumour had it that she was fed up with being alone so much; however, while there, Mrs Sebbens had become friendly with the owner of the corner shop at the end of her sister's street and subsequently decided not to return.

Mr Sebbens, devastated at this turn of events, had begun binge drinking. Anna thought it unwise to mention his prognosis for the immediate future or that of his beloved dog, Ruby, as she had been taken away by the RSPCA.

Marion finished her coffee and, not wanting to discuss the move to Queensland, decided to go home, ostensibly to light the fire and warm up the house. The weather looked very threatening as it was. So, having made her excuses, she prepared to leave, declining Nigel's offer to drive her back home. 'It's no distance at all, really!' she said. Then, tying a scarf around her head against the wind, she returned to what she later described as 'her windswept holiday home'.

Daylight faded as Marion listened to FM classical radio over the hiss of the gas fire. The music soothed her frayed nerves, as she occasionally caught the sound of the waves crashing along Tadbury Beach. The scent of pine wafted around the lounge from two candles, one on the mantelpiece, roughly speckled green and white, set in a silver holder; the other squat, encased in glass and decorated with dark green leaves, given to her as a present from the ladies in the choir. She liked watching the flickering light. It reminded her of the dimmed chandeliers, their soft illumination creating a sense of timelessness and mystery at Evensong in Laleham. How she longed to return there! It seemed none of the churches round about offered an evening service. She missed the old liturgy and the peal of bells.

Thoughts fluttered in her head about what to do with Len's ashes. They were sitting in a cardboard box wrapped in blue paper (courtesy of Millingtons Pty Ltd.) and pushed under her bed. The thought of scattering them in Tasmania at the bottom of the world filled her with dismay. Alone, she spoke to Leonard's chair as if he were there. 'I'll take you home. A proper headstone standing up in the churchyard. Would you like the bells to play, and a small ceremony? I'll be happy to do that, Len… and if that doesn't seem the right resting place for you, there is always Woking Cemetery, where your mother is… I have no idea where I shall live but I'll find somewhere close by.'

She rambled on. The more she thought about it, the more she was satisfied it was the right move. She couldn't contemplate moving to Queensland and herself being buried there and Leonard in Tasmania. It was out of the question… A pleasant thought led her to find pen and paper, and she poured her heart out to Alice, imagining her friend standing beneath the respectable sign of 'Yew Corner', eagerly awaiting her news.

~V~

One day I wrote her name upon the strand,
But came the waves and washed it away:
Again I wrote it with a second hand,
But came the tide and made my pains his prey.

Edmund Spenser[*]

By Monday morning the front had passed through. The clouds had lifted and the wind had died down. Daffodils, their necks bent towards the earth, and bluebells glistening with raindrops almost ready to burst forth, seemed to say, 'Look at me! Look at me! Not at the carpets of blossom scattered on the verges and around the boles of trees. It's my turn now.'

The drain in front of Marion's house and next door's hadn't been able to cope with the rain, and as a result, there was water the length of the gutter causing severe drainage problems. Marion put a call through to Kingborough Council before discussing the situation with her neighbour, Joy Nesbit, who in turn relayed what she had heard on the radio that morning of trees crashing down onto cars and properties. There was one thing that she was reluctant to talk about with Marion; however, she felt she should mention the banksia rose.

'It is dragging our fence over. I am worried that it might collapse completely, and Skip would get out.'

'Yes, I can see. It's gone rampant. If Leonard had been here...'

'Not to worry. I'll get Morris on to it as soon as he has a moment.' Then not wishing to upset Marion, she laughingly added,

---

[*] From *Sonnets*, selected by E M Leonard, Oxford University Press, 1914.

'That's if you don't mind him coming into your garden to prune it. A bit of exercise would do him good.'

Marion attempted a thin smile. Is this what her life was going to be like from now on? She wasn't useless yet, and resolved to have a go at pruning the rose herself.

Joy broke into her thoughts with, 'If there is anything you need or anything we can do to help, you only have to ask!'

Need. All I need is to go home. I've lost my husband, and you ask if there is anything I need! Nevertheless, she replied politely, 'That is very kind of you. Thank you.'

Around 8.15 a.m. the senior staff at St Mary's were called into Sister Anne's office and told of Janice Ryan's tragedy. They were asked to quash any rumours that might be circulating and also to deal with any hysteria. No names had been given out over the news bulletin, only that a woman in her nineties had woken up to find a tree across her front porch; a car had run out of petrol on the bridge; various roads had been cut off and there had been a bad accident in Patrick Street, where a woman in her thirties was killed. Sister Anne was hopeful none of the students would be aware of what had happened and decide to jump classes to visit Janice Ryan in hospital.

A sister of Margery Ryan's late husband – Janice's aunt – had been traced, but she lived in Western Australia and had lost contact after her brother had drowned; she also had a family of her own to look after – three children to be precise – and they were quite a handful. There was no way she would be coming to Tasmania, nor did she volunteer for Janice to live with them. She had no idea what to suggest. Sister Anne repeated the conversation she had had, imitating the voice at the end of the telephone to startled staff, who were amazed she had talents in this area.

By period four, following recess, word had spread through to the senior students of St Virgil's. Gavin was relieved in some ways that Janice was absent from his English class, only to discover that she was in hospital after a fatal car crash. What did that mean? He didn't like to show too much interest but felt uneasy. No one seemed to be aware that Janice was pregnant, and for that he was much relieved; nevertheless he was distracted throughout the entire morning and couldn't tell anyone what the lesson was about. Harbouring a guilty conscience, he decided to make his own inquiries at the Royal. Not knowing where Janice was exactly proved to be another problem, embarrassing to say the least, at the service desk. 'Janice Ryan, you said? Are you a relative?' The formidable woman looked Gavin up and down, noticing his school blazer and wondering why he wasn't in class.

She sighed, aware that students were often in town, when in her day it was unthinkable. As far as she was concerned, they should be in school, not gallivanting around all over the place. Often they left their heavy bags on the footpaths, in front of shops and by bus stops, causing inconvenience to shoppers and pedestrians alike. This boy didn't appear to have anything with him, he just looked pale and shifty; good-looking too, if she was honest. Mentally she added up one and one making five, and would not have been surprised about his relationship with the girl with the long blonde hair. 'So, you're not a relative?'

'No-o,' said Gavin diffidently, 'but I really need to see her – if that's OK?'

The earnestness of his request softened the almoner's heart. 'Well, in that case I'll ring through to see if she is having visitors.' Picking up the internal phone, she dialled the Sister in charge of general admissions. 'There's a young man here wanting to see Janice Ryan. Shall I send him up? …No, he isn't a relative.'

Gavin was mystified why she had turned her back on him and was having such a long conversation – one he was not party to. Eventually, she said, 'Take the lift to the third floor, turn left at the first corridor and you will see Sister's desk before the ward. It would be a good idea to see her first. Your girlfriend is in room seven,' she added with a smile, and with that she lifted a handset and answered an incoming call.

Gavin found the ward and nurses' station easily, manned by a pretty girl whose red curls signified a young trainee. He was prepared to give her his best smile, but she didn't look up from what she was writing and he walked quickly and quietly past her to the door with a '7' on it. The door was ajar and he could see two beds in the room. The closest to him was empty. Janice was lying in the bed next to the window, her face turned towards the light. He stood for a moment watching her from the doorway, then diffidently moved to the end of her bed. As he looked at her he tried to imagine her carrying his baby, but the picture was quite different from what he could see. Her hair looked greasy and dung-coloured, and her face was ashen, accentuating red-rimmed eyelids. Where was the luscious Janice he'd imagined? This was going to be far worse than he thought.

Janice turned her head hearing a movement, just as Gavin said, 'You look a mess!'

It took him quite some time before he realised that Janice didn't see his remark as a joke. 'I mean, what happened to you?' He forced his facial muscles into a look of concern, something he had been practising in front of a shaving mirror recently as a result of his father's comment – 'And take that insolent look off your face, my lad, it will only get you into trouble. I don't know where all this is going to lead to!' With that he had walked out of Gavin's bedroom, slamming the door. It seemed that then, as now, he couldn't get anything right.

Janice stirred herself and looked into the face of her lover. The spark wasn't there any more. Listlessly, she answered, 'I don't remember much, only the sounds of the rain and the crash.' Her eyes never left his face, as she summoned up energy similar to that of prosecuting council. 'What are you doing here anyway? I haven't seen you alone since we went to Port Arthur!'

His bravado vanished. 'I know.'

'Have you ditched me for Kate Bird?'

Stung by her perception, he lied. 'No, no, it's nothing like that.'

'What then?'

'We were getting too involved, and Port Arthur... I mean, what I saw... I haven't been able to forget.'

Janice, hurt and confused, lashed out, 'Well, I needed to tell you I was pregnant!'

'It really is mine?'

Disbelief and shock crossed her face. 'Who else's could it be? How can you stand there and say that?'

'I didn't mean it like that. I'm sorry, Janice. What else can I say?'

'You never really cared! You never called. You avoided me.' She began to cry. 'Go away... it doesn't matter any more...'

'Don't be like this! I'm sorry, I didn't know. Please, Janice... we can work something out.'

'Just go away, Gavin.' She fished under her pillow for a tissue. Heartbroken, she whimpered, 'I thought you loved me.'

'Please, Janice!'

'What's that supposed to mean?' she hissed. 'Don't trouble yourself!' She started to become hysterical. Between sobs he heard, 'There isn't going to be any baby... I lost it. Aren't you glad?'

He didn't know what to say, so he waited, willing her to stop crying. This was embarrassing. He decided to change the subject, and with genuine concern made an effort. 'How long will you be in here?'

'I don't know.' She blew her nose and muttered, 'Not long... nothing that won't mend with TLC.' Then, looking up at him in full control, she said, 'If you want to be of help, please find out where my mother is, as I can't get out of this bed and no one is telling me.'

For a moment, Gavin wondered if he had misunderstood what he had heard at school that morning, but before he had time to reply, a voice behind him said, 'And what are you doing here, young man?'

'*Me*?' He spun around, and seeing someone he guessed was the Sister in charge of the ward, gave her his most beguiling smile. 'Just visiting!' he said cheekily.

'Please say your goodbyes and let Janice get some rest,' Sister Rawlins ordered. She stepped back, but had no intention of leaving the room. There was no knowing what this young man had been saying, and she didn't want her patient upset.

'I've got to go,' Gavin said, sounding awkward and completely inadequate. He wished he had never come. There was no way he could kiss Janice with the Sister standing there. 'Do you need anything?' he asked finally. The idea popped into his head, because he'd heard somewhere that it was a safe question to ask people in hospital.

'What do you think? Of course I do – nighties, clothes, shampoo and something to read. Can you find someone to get them for me?' She looked so forlorn.

'Right.' He felt better. This was something he understood. Practical. He saw the Sister becoming impatient and moved closer to the door as a kind of excuse to put a distance between them. 'Don't worry, Janice, I'll fix it.'

The Gavin she knew smiled across the room with a wave of his arm and was gone. She fell back onto the pillow, confident he would not let her down. He, for his part, had no idea who to call to collect her toiletries and belongings, and wondered why he'd said he would.

Sister Rawlins' voice broke into his thoughts. 'Janice doesn't know about her mother yet. She's had a nasty shock, of course, what with her injuries. I'm waiting for the doctor to say she is strong enough. The poor lass… she has no other relatives that we know of… And you are?'

'Er, Gavin.' Not wanting to be questioned further, he glanced at his watch.

'Well, Gavin, how well do you know…?'

But before she could continue, she was interrupted. 'Excuse me, I have a bus to catch.' And with that Gavin hurried away, having spied Mrs Macclesfield with one of Janice's close friends walking in their direction. Ducking behind the service lifts he saw them approach Sister Rawlins, then become engaged deep in conversation before moving down the corridor to room number seven.

He doubled back past the Sisters' station, entered the lift and was down on the pavement within five minutes. Slightly dazed by the turn of events, he found himself walking down Campbell Street towards the docks and the fishing trawlers, before it occurred to him all his worries had dissipated, just because of a car accident. '*Yes, yes, yes!*' he exclaimed aloud, not caring who heard him.

Janice isn't pregnant any more, and Mrs Macclesfield will tell her about her mother, I expect, and arrange for all Janice's requirements. I won't have to be involved! Needn't even visit! No one will have to know about us, and my life is back on track.

Filled with euphoria, he helped a young mother with her

pushchair, parcels and a toddler across Davey Street as he made his way towards one of the larger fishing boats tied up opposite Muir's Restaurant. He sat down on one of the seats provided, watching the gulls, the sky and the activities around the harbour. Feeling ravenous, he made his way up the gangplank and ordered fish and chips with a Coke and returned to his seat, contemplating life and its twists and turns. He made a vow never to be that careless again, and was quite looking forward to seeing his father's face as he told him the news.

Feeling much better, he deposited the rubbish in a bin and made for home, deciding against going all the way up to Barrack Street again to collect his school bag. Too bad if his assignment for social studies would not be ready by the morning, but if he got to school early the next day, maybe he could finish it then. It wasn't until he was on the bus that he gave a second thought to Janice. He wondered what would happen to her now that both parents were dead. *I'm off the hook! I'm off the hook!* went around and around in his head. Mum wouldn't give me that disapproving look any more that said, 'How can you do this to us?' And Dad wouldn't look like thunder. I'll offer to help him paint the dinghy… for a price. What's more, I am free to date who I like again.

Walking up the street to his home, it felt like a great weight had been lifted from his shoulders. There was no need for any of his mates to know, unless his mother had blabbed to Father Stephen. He'd be made to go to confession. Silly old trout; he suspected Father Stephen was gay. Entering the house, Gavin was relieved to see his mother was out. Pleased at this turn of events, he switched on the television, gazing mindlessly at a show of puppets for the under-fives. The phone rang, and not wishing to be recognised, he lifted the handset, saying in an Italian accent, 'Mario's Pizza Parlour,' and smiled as the caller hung up.

Throughout the next few days Marion was in a kind of reverie, imagining where she might live when she returned to England. How astonished her friends would be; at least Alice would be pleased to renew their friendship. Maybe, if she worded her next letter correctly, Alice would invite her to stay while she looked for somewhere suitable to live. Wandering through the house, she glanced at furniture and precious knick-knacks, talking to herself.

She picked up Leonard's lighter, feeling its smoothness, noticing how neatly it fitted into her palm. 'I'll take you with me, seeing it's engraved with your initials, Len. Nigel doesn't want it, or your watch, although heaven knows what I should be doing with either. It would be different if we'd had a son.' Feeling the tears beginning again, Marion forced herself to think of practical concerns, like the furniture and what to do with it. 'If I got rid of all this and bought fresh furniture, wouldn't that be sensible, Len? I mean, by the time I've put it into store, paid for the shipping and the removal to wherever, who's to say I'll need all this?'

She sat down on the bed, trying hard to come to terms with her present situation. Not in her worst nightmares had she envisioned being left in Australia without Leonard to take charge, and now here was Anna, calmly supposing she would move with them to Queensland. She didn't like searing heat, and to her surprise she realised she and Anna had very little in common. Anna didn't understand how she felt and Nigel, although always pleasant, gave her the impression she was a nuisance. As for seeing any grandchildren soon… that subject seemed to be taboo.

'Oh, Len, what was the point of uprooting us to here? Anna will go wherever Nigel goes, and I don't want to! I don't feel at ease… I've lost what you'd call *empathy*. Will you mind if I go back home?'

Leaning back on the pillows, the tears oozed down her cheeks as she remembered familiar faces. Quite suddenly, a dim memory of a young man wearing a navy jacket with silver buttons, beige cavalry twill trousers and matching suede casual shoes drifted into focus. His name was Andy Higgins; she had thought with his square cut jaw, brown eyes, long dark lashes and black hair that he was Adonis personified. They must have been all of seventeen. Andy had taken her by train to a so-called dance on Eel Pie Island, where you had your wrist stamped before entering the premises. It was very dark and so full of people that she had been frightened to let go of his hand in case they became separated. The music was a mixture of rock and roll and jazz, but all the young men had to wear a jacket and tie.

On returning home from the exciting evening, her mother had made it obvious that no respectable girl would be seen entering such a den of iniquity. They had argued, although that wasn't strictly true, as her mother had dominated her hopes and desires by saying, 'Good-looking he may be, my girl, but he's got absolutely no prospects. I mean, look where he works!'

'But Mum, everyone has to start somewhere…'

It was to no avail. 'I absolutely forbid you to see Andy Higgins again. Do you understand me, Marion?'

And that had been the end of the matter, as her father never became embroiled in domestic issues unless it had to do with his tobacco or beer. Marion now wondered where Andy was, and if he had married. Guilty feelings had stayed with her when dating Leonard, an office cleaner, imagining her mother's reaction if she had known. Marion wouldn't have married Leonard, or anyone else, if her mother had been alive. She would have been horrified. Leonard used to laugh when people found out what he did for a living, and how lucrative it was, amazed that now, his firm ran eight vans, and twenty staff to do the cleaning. 'Where there's muck, there's brass,' he would chuckle, tapping his nose.

Getting up from the bed, she crossed into the bathroom to wipe her tear-streaked face. This done, she stared at her features in the mirror. Such an ordinary face, she had to admit. Ordinary hair; maybe it was time for a change, as there was no one to please but herself. The thought made her smile, at her age, as if anyone was going to notice her. 'Old habits die hard,' she said aloud. 'I'm not sure I want anybody to notice me – not yet, anyway.'

She walked into the kitchen, opening the pantry door and looking for something sweet to eat. Hanging on the back of the door was a calendar picturing the canals of England, with certain days circled. Wednesday the solicitor; Thursday down at Mary Knoll in Blackman's Bay; and Saturday the book fair up at the Anglican Church. She could do with something to read, other than letters of condolence, which reminded her of the one she had received from Noel Barker. 'Very thoughtful of him,' she murmured as she helped herself from the biscuit tin, nibbling a chocolate digestive. She pictured Noel clearly, reading the lessons, taking the collection and collecting the prayer and hymn books. No extra sheets were handed out, the service being familiar to all. No one turned up in trainers or jeans, no babies banged blocks, and the atmosphere was full of reverence. What had he said at the last service she attended? 'Don't forget us,' his weathered face crinkling into a lopsided smile. 'As if I would!' melted away from her between delicate swallows of biscuit. The fresh produce displayed in the one local shop and the corn sheaves at Harvest Festival were all supplied by Noel. His farm was on the corner of Ashford Road, and anyone approaching the village from that quarter could revel in the delights of spring as the entire area from roadway to farmhouse swayed with bluebells, above which the gentle leaves of beech trees framed the scene.

Marion collected his letter from the bureau, smoothing it out on the kitchen bench. The handwriting was bold, the contents precise and simply stated; nonetheless, the spectacle of Noel in Wellingtons and working clothes eluded her as he had only spoken to her when at church, sporting a fresh flower in the buttonhole of a tweed jacket.

No one had mentioned a Mrs Barker, or children, come to think of it, or how long he had lived at Laleham. Enclosed was a copy of the Harvest Festival Service and photographs of the decorated pulpit and screen covering the north-west wall. In pencil was written, 'Not up to your standard!'

While Marion was picturing this, the phone rang. It was Anna.

'Mum, you OK?'

'Yes, dear.'

'Just touching base and filling you in with the latest.'

'Really!'

'You remember Janice Ryan – the girl who was always on the beach… long blonde hair?'

'Oh, yes. Your dad was quite concerned. Janice is her name?'

'Yes, Janice Ryan. She lived along Norwood Avenue. Well, she's been in a nasty road smash. Friday, after school, her mother was driving… and the upshot of it all was that Janice is now in hospital and her mother was killed.'

'Oh, dear! How dreadful, poor mite!'

'As I said, she is in hospital at present, nothing that won't mend but as she has no living relative here, I was wondering if I could bring her round to you, being alone and all, just for a chat…' She trailed off.

'What for, Anna?'

'Well, she'll need to study somewhere and hopefully take her HSC in a month or so.'

'Just a minute! Where will she stay? Is someone going to be looking after her?'

'Well, I thought… maybe you would; you know, it's only for a short while. She can't live in her own house alone, and we don't know whether her mother owned the house, or if she had a mortgage or if she was renting.'

'This is a bit sudden, Anna, dear. I don't think I'm ready for such an undertaking. The poor lass is probably traumatised. And a teenager – think of the responsibility!'

'You needn't decide now. I just thought I'd run it past you, see what you think.'

There was a pause during which Marion collected her wits. 'If you really want my opinion, I think you should stay well out of it.'

'Easy for you to say,' Anna rushed on. 'She's in my home group!'

The conversation continued, with Anna becoming more persistent and Marion aghast at her daughter's presumption. She wasn't looking forward to visiting the solicitor with her on Wednesday, but supposed they both had to be there. Reluctantly, she agreed to meet in the Centre Point coffee shop at 4 p.m. Still reeling from the loss of Leonard, she felt she didn't figure as a person, certainly not a mother; more like a machine without any sensitivities. In a moment of rare insight it became clear that her life seemed meaningless. Was there something about her that failed to assert her right to be loved, like a label attached to her forehead, saying, 'Walk all over me, I'm insignificant'?

She stood stock-still, recalling how it had always been thus – choosing a career, a lover, playing nursemaid to a bossy mother, and an alcoholic father. And later, having lost a son… everyone involved said she ought not to make a fuss. 'After all, you have Anna… plenty of people lose babies. It is nothing to get worked up about. Go home and get on with life.'

Now, hearing Anna's words go round inside her head, she remembered a satire she saw at Windsor Theatre entitled, *Whose Life is it Anyway?* She repeated the words aloud, savouring each one as realisation sank in to the core of her being. Tears flowed at her inadequacy in coping with recent circumstances. How come Anna had made her feel guilty, over a young girl she didn't know? Never mind about her own bereavement!

Upset and lonely, feeling like a piece of flotsam tossed this way and that, Marion was reminded of Leonard's enthusiasm to up stakes and move to Australia, and how she was unable to express any opposition as she had watched his face light up to adventure and a lifestyle change. Worn down, she had acquiesced. Besides, wasn't she his wife? How could she have stayed behind? It wasn't possible. I'm fifty plus and I'm still being manipulated – this is ridiculous! But where do I get the strength from to live my own life?

She poured a glass of sherry, turned up the radio, closed the curtains and sat down in the lounge, blotting out the roar of the waves splashing around the boulders and the shoreline on the incoming tide.

~VI~

But stronger still, in earth and air,
And in the sea, the man of prayer,
And far beneath the tide:
And in the seat to faith assign'd,
Where ask is have, where seek is find,
Where knock is open wide.

'*Song to David*', *Christopher Smart*[*]

'**W**ell I never… Dad was a dark horse!'

Marion asked Anna what she meant, as they turned into Sandy Bay Road on their way home from Newman and Colliers, the solicitors. The morning had been quite eventful for Marion. She had woken up later than usual, due partly to the roaring of the waves throughout the night, dying down just before dawn. Rushing her breakfast, she hurried up to the local shopping centre, ostensibly to catch the ten o'clock post. The first was a letter addressed to Alice sounding her out as to whether she would be welcome to stay until she found a place of her own. The second letter was to Noel Barker, thanking him for his condolences. While outside the post office she was taken by surprise when complete strangers came up to her asking after her welfare and asking, 'Is there anything we can do?'

The local Anglican vicar greeted her, wearing a silver cross in his shirt collar – that at least was recognisable. However, much flustered by these ministrations, she tripped over a dog lead as she made a hasty retreat. The dog itself was dreaming about the

---

[*] *Other Men's Flowers*, Jonathan Cape, 1944.

warmth of a hearth as opposed to the cold concrete it was lying upon, its lead attached to a hook in the wall above. The jerk of its lead surprised the dog, which began to bark loudly with fright. Helped up by a passer-by, and embarrassed by the fuss she had caused, Marion quite forgot to pick up some dry cleaning. The proprietor, who also owned the paper shop and post office, came running out after her, waving a skirt pinned to a hanger encased in a transparent plastic bag. It seemed to Marion that half the population of Tadbury was staring at her. She was mortified.

There was still more to come for this very private, grieving soul even in the sanctuary of her own home.

Hardly had she reached the house before there was a knock at the back door. It appeared one of the council workers, who was fixing the drain in Niree Parade outside her property, wished to use her toilet facilities. Not long after this intrusion, next door's whippet dog finally clambered through the broken down fence between herself and the Nesbits, and rushed out into the road, whereupon it bit one of the workmen as he was bending down to inspect the drain. This time she was rummaging through her first aid box.

These images were for some reason still uppermost in Marion's mind, so that she only very slowly realised what Anna was referring to, namely Number Six, Ferry Lane, leading to Laleham Park and the old Priory. It had been news to her also that Leonard had bought another property in Laleham, but she had no intention of revealing her ignorance to Anna. Airily, she prevaricated, 'Oh, your father owned quite a few properties – mostly shops – in Staines.'

'Good Lord! He kept it all to himself, didn't he, Mum?'

'Not at all, Anna. Don't be silly! Why should he discuss his affairs with you?' Before Anna had time to reply, she went on, 'I was amazed at the state of David Newman's office, papers everywhere, there was hardly room to sit down!'

There was a 'Hmm' of assent from Anna, as Marion lapsed into vague recollections of the events within the solicitor's office as she stared out of the car window. Anna, much surprised at this turn of events, suggested Marion stay for tea, in the hope she could wangle some of her father's estate before her mother's demise. It would be much to her and Nigel's advantage if they could make use of some of her father's investments now, or in Queensland. She could see herself living quite grandly in a house of their own, close to the Gold Coast or even at Surfers' Paradise itself. Anna kept up idle chatter all the way home, stopping off at the butcher's to buy three substantial eye fillets, plump tomatoes, button mushrooms and fresh garlic from the vegetable shop nearby, before she continued on towards The Beach House Hotel in Lower Sandy Bay.

As the sun was setting, Marion negotiated the car around to the back of the hotel, its lights reflecting across the River Derwent. In addition lights began to twinkle along Sandy Bay Road and from houses on the bends of Mount Nelson. Anna chivvied her mother to go inside the bottle shop and choose a wine to her liking. Ten minutes later, armed with two bottles of Penfold's claret, they made their way across the road to a speciality coffee and cheese shop. Anna suggested treating themselves to a coffee, as the warmth and aroma of fresh coffee beans was very enticing, before making a purchase of King Island Double Brie cheese.

Nigel arrived home from Hutchins School to find his wife in good spirits for the first time in weeks. His mother-in-law, fortified by several glasses of claret, related the traumas of her morning, which in hindsight struck her as humorous. Anna and Nigel, much amused by the extraordinary behaviour of Joy Nesbit's whippet, retold the story with many embellishments the following day in their respective staff rooms.

At ten o'clock, Marion returned home accompanied by both Nigel and Anna, declaring they needed the fresh air and the exercise. Marion had the best night's sleep she had experienced since arriving in Tasmania, and the deepest since Leonard had died.

Anna and Nigel retraced their steps, deviating along the foreshore, caught up in the moon's glittering path which danced across the River Derwent like a magical pathway. That night they made love, buoyed by fantasies of wealth and happiness.

Marion, on the other hand, dreamt of moving into Number Six, Ferry Lane, completely unaware of the relationship between the tenants and her late husband. Morris Nesbit was in his wife's bad books because he had failed to fix the fence between themselves and Marion. He, on the other hand, was more worried about the fact that the council workman might sue them for negligence.

Marion found the drive to Mary Knoll along the Channel Highway enjoyable, much to her surprise, it being the first time she had driven to Blackman's Bay alone. Previously, Leonard had driven, and then only to Coles supermarket in Kingston. She had to admit it was a very pleasant drive from Tadbury. Convolvulus grew up the bank to her right, above which she caught glimpses of houses through her windscreen. Along the winding road to her left were hawthorn bushes and lush green fields leading down to the water's edge; from here she could see right across Storm Bay, the lighthouse no longer in use but shining white in its pristine beauty. Now, sitting within the gardens of Mary Knoll, she appreciated the various blues and greens that shimmered across the water, as there were few clouds to bar the sun. A gentle smell of thyme and boronia emanated from a bush nearby. Leonard's sudden and untimely death took on a less threatening aspect as she sat watching the early bees, the odd blue butterfly and a gardener at work in the distance. Confidence began to grow within her as she recalled recent encounters with Anna; how she had presented her own wishes against strong opposition.

'Truly beautiful,' she whispered. 'If Leonard was still here, maybe I could settle, but without his presence it is all too remote. Too wild, and unpredictable.' She glanced across at the gardener tending the remnants of daffodils and jonquils, his collie dog sitting obediently by his side, and wondered if he felt lonely with only his dog and the occasional seagull for company, swooping towards the beach below.

There was a narrow pathway to her left, presumably winding around to the back of the Prayer House. This she meandered along, astonished to see further units clustered together, and the shadow of someone moving behind a tulle curtain. Normally she would have averted her eyes, but on this occasion she began to feel the first stirrings of self-worth. 'It's all right to be here and it's all right to be me,' she murmured to herself. There was no need to explain herself to anyone – least of all to Anna. She, Marion, needn't be on the defensive all the time.

It was very quiet sitting in the chapel at Mary Knoll. The peace and tranquillity washed over Marion like a comforter. Looking around, she put it down to its location, rather than its substance, as the chairs were mostly the type you see in schools. The windows were plain; there was an unprepossessing lectern in some kind of golden wood, and only one statue of the Virgin Mary. The only other pieces of furniture in the room were a small organ at the back, and next to the doorway a small cardboard table with bundles of pamphlets upon it. She expected it to be more ornate, being a Catholic chapel, with numerous icons, and was relieved to find that this was not so.

'Take your time… wander wherever you like through the gardens. I shall be here if you want me.' The unassuming, gentle-voiced woman had said, when she arrived. The smooth unlined face combined with the darkest eyes, like berries, so dark brown that they were hard to read. The awkward moment evaporated as she watched her hostess silently glide away through the garden towards a red-bricked single-storey house.

Marion moved closer to the left window, praying hard for a few moments – or was it longer? – but at last she admitted to herself that nothing was connecting, and it was a futile exercise. Glancing up, she could see a garden seat through the shrubbery, tucked away out of the wind and decided to leave the chapel and, finding a doorway to the verandah running around the Prayer House, she lifted the latch, leaving the snib up so that she could re-enter the chapel easily again. Now, pushing through the bushes, she sat down once again inside what felt like a secret garden. From this vantage point she could see the gardens laid out before her, her car parked close to the nun's brick home, the sea, and Opossum Bay far into the distance.

Her thoughts returned to Anna. If only this guilt feeling would go away. Why shouldn't she live wherever she liked? After all, it was Anna who had left home and come to Australia, not the other way around.

If Len was here, I wonder what he would make of all this? He wouldn't be too happy, either, with Anna and Nigel up and going to Queensland. It really is quite inconsiderate of them to expect me to tag along. If the truth be known, I wish to return to Laleham, and to take Len's ashes with me. I could always visit Anna in the future… That's if they ever get around to having a family. That way I can call the tune…

Lost in her reverie, Marion was surprised to hear an Irish voice behind her saying, 'If you'd like a tea or coffee, there is a kitchen just to your left.' Looking up, she saw an elderly, pleasantly round-faced woman with wispy grey hair tied back into a bun. She was carrying some bluebells and what looked like wild chervil with its profusion of fern-like leaves and lace-like flower heads. 'Help yourself to biscuits if you like,' she said with a smile and disappeared along the path in the direction from which Marion had come.

Half an hour later, replenished and feeling the need to talk with someone, Marion found herself sitting opposite Sister Ruth in her small sparse bedroom, one of five within the red brick house she saw on her arrival. Never in all her life had anyone given her their complete and undivided attention as Sister Ruth did at this present moment. Marion became emboldened as Sister Ruth sat perfectly still, looking across at her and listening intently to her. She didn't stop to think about what to say to this kind unassuming woman, but just poured out all her anxieties.

'And then when we arrived in Tasmania – all those people were shot down by some maniac – at Port Arthur. It was on the ABC News the night we arrived!' She clasped a tissue on her lap, twisting it to shreds. 'All those people dead… little children. No rhyme or reason. Why them?' She stopped abruptly, attempting to use her torn tissue.

'Death seems to be all around me,' she went on, 'what with Leonard dying suddenly.' Her voice taking on a different tone. 'And now this girl…' she paused. 'I wish—'

'You wish?'

'I wish I had never come,' she whispered.

Abashed at what she had just voiced, and not wishing to sound rude, she tried to explain. 'I mean, I wish Leonard had told me about his health and how precarious it was. I just wished things were different.'

'How different?' Sister Ruth prompted, as she reached across to a small bedside table and, retrieving a tissue from a box that was decorated with pink flowers, handed it to Marion.

Marion blew her nose and wiped the corner of her eyes. 'Well, I was just beginning to settle in… then there were all those awful accounts on television down at Port Arthur, and Len suffering with what I thought was a migraine. We didn't have time to say goodbye. I went to visit him the following morning, at St John's, and – and I had no idea…' She trailed off.

There was a long silence without either of the two women saying anything; Sister Ruth, because she knew better, and Marion, because unburdening her soul was an entirely new experience.

'I'm taking up your valuable time.' Marion looked up into the Sister's face, seeing compassion and something else there which she couldn't put her finger on.

'No, you are not,' she replied gently. 'There are at least another fifteen minutes before we hear Mass. You mentioned a girl…?'

'Yes. I think her name is Janice. She lives near me – or should I say, she *lived* near me. She's in Anna's home group.' Her voice took on a despairing quality.

'Anna seems to think, as I have the room, that this girl can come and live with me.'

'I believe her mother was killed in a recent car accident,' remarked Sister Ruth quietly.

Marion continued, 'She was often seen on the beach at Tadbury during school hours, even though this was her last term, with important examinations coming up. Why me? I can't, I really can't!' And with that she burst into tears.

'It's all right, Marion.' Sister Ruth stretched out her arm, placing her hand gently on Marion's sleeve. 'The school will take responsibility – if no relatives can be found.'

She handed another tissue to Marion, as she cried, 'I seem to be surrounded in death!' Sister Ruth could see platitudes would not help the grieving woman opposite her, so she remained silent until Marion was composed. 'Your daughter, Anna – what does she teach?'

'Oh, mostly English. Nigel, her husband, teaches at Hutchins, but it appears he wants to take up a position in Queensland in the New Year, so they'll be moving. I don't want to follow them there… What's the point?'

'You don't want to go?'

Marion looked up at the kindly woman opposite her, and felt she was drowning in those two dark brown pools, which had widened at her last remark. 'No,' she said apologetically.

'It seems to me you have been dealt a very unsettling hand. Your life has been turned upside down. It is quite all right to feel the way you do, you know,' said the kindly nun.

'Is it?'

Sister Ruth opened a book that was on the bed and handed a small card to Marion. 'Read this when you get home. I hope it will help you. And now I must attend Mass. Would you like to join us?'

'What, me? I'm not a Catholic.' Marion stood up, not sure how to leave the room with some dignity. However, her companion spared her any awkwardness by saying, 'There will only be six of us in all, if you care to come. Two of our Sisters are away at present, and our housekeeper sometimes joins us. I know you're not a Catholic, but Father Martyn won't object, as this is on our property. Please, don't imagine we stand on ceremony here. The service is like your Eucharist, except we hand the Host to each other. We sit in a semicircle… and the service is quite simple. You will be very welcome.'

And so she was. It was a revelation to Marion, the sincerity and quiet certainty that emanated from those elderly nuns. She returned to Tadbury by lunchtime in a much calmer frame of mind. In fact she felt happy for the first time in months.

Now, as she made herself a cheese and ham sandwich, she even began to hum various hymns; she walked with a lighter step and marvelled at the encounters she had had that morning. She dug out the card Sister Ruth had given her, carrying it, the sandwich and a cup of instant coffee towards the dining table.

Between nibbling her sandwich and sipping coffee, she read the text several times.

Come to the water, you who are thirsty, though you have nothing. I bid you come! And be filled with the goodness I have to offer. Come! Listen! Live!

Marion felt the stirrings of friendship with the Sisters, something she would never have imagined. Seeing them and participating in the Eucharist service had been an uplifting experience that she couldn't define.

The uncertainty of her future no longer loomed as a nightmare but rather a challenge. The nuns had a much stronger faith than she, in spite of what looked like simplicity on the surface. She sensed they were closely in tune with the world and their own spirituality. How she wished she could obtain what it was they had! Collecting her dishes, she left them in the sink, feeling a kind of excitement as she changed her shoes, put on an anorak, tucked a scarf into her pocket (in case of violent wind) and headed down to the beach in anticipation of whatever elements came her way. She was quite looking forward to the sea breeze, and for the moment her fear was in abeyance. She would return to Mary Knoll next Friday. How come she hadn't appreciated before the wildness of the river, the ever-changing hues, the lichen-coated rocks and the freshness of the air? Laughingly, she said to herself, 'Oh, the freshness – a bit too much for my liking!' A buoyant spirit, coupled with a sense of direction, gradually changed her persona. Slowly it dawned on her that she had been a victim of emotional blackmail, first with her mother, next with her husband, and now with Anna. She needed to stand firm against what others thought she should or shouldn't do. Generally it was their own selfish desires they wanted to fulfil.

Inwardly, she had seethed with humiliation, but had never acknowledged she was an easy target for persuasion. Now, outwardly she consciously engaged in conversation, with a smile and a gentle interest in other people's affairs. This interest even surprised herself, as she began to realise that nearly everyone with whom she came into contact had tales of disappointments, woes and disasters. Several more visits to Mary Knoll helped her personally along her spiritual journey, opening up new avenues within her prayer life. Understanding dawned. Meaningless ritual, religious piety, and dogma she now recognised as stumbling blocks to her own spiritual journey, things she had never thought to question before. Armed with this new awareness, she wondered how many other people of her generation had been misled as to what 'religion' was supposed to be about. Why did most regular worshippers even bother to attend, as so many seemed unhappy? Somehow what was heard on Sunday during the hymns, the prayers and sermons made little impact on their everyday lives. There was no inner peace or joy, and in her case, no growth past her Sunday school days. Her restless spirit was thrashing around in a vacuum. The God she had revered was taken from sermons abounding in 'the wages of sin', condemnation, and remoteness. For a gentle soul, this only compounded her alienation and disgust at the human condition.

She remarked to Sister Ruth on her third visit, 'I never knew God wanted us to be happy. I thought we had to earn our way into his good books.' Devouring as much reading matter as the Prayer House offered, both religious and secular on the subject, a new world of joy was opened to Marion. Prayers telling the Almighty what should be done to rectify a situation were an insult.

'Please God, this is what I want…' or 'this is what should happen,' or 'Make so and so do this or that…' had to fall on deaf ears, for God didn't ordain personal calamities, but by giving us free will, worked with us for the best possible outcome, which might be unclear to us at the time.

The quest for mind and body harmony through trials and tribulations were the same the world over, Marion realised, whatever one's religious persuasion. It was up to man to reach out to God humbly and without reservation, denying the ego and asking for the fruits of the Spirit. God in His compassion would always answer, even though many didn't realise that this was so.

'God wants me to be happy.' She kept repeating as she opened up her damaged spirit and bruised soul while gazing across the ever-changing waters of the Derwent. The thought seeped through her whole being so that the cool breeze which caressed her face, the choppy waters and wildness of the coastal scenery no longer threatened her. Instead, her depressed spirit vanished. She slowed down, meandering along the beach, feeling an entirely new sensation growing up within her of something she couldn't name. She sat down abruptly on an enormous black rock, watching spume eddying around its base, seeing, yet not seeing and felt peace reach tentatively towards her damaged soul. This is what she had been longing for, and she had done nothing to bring it about – well nothing obvious that she could pinpoint. Was it this easy to speak with God? What if she had died before knowing this profound truth?

A vision of the painting hanging in Laleham Church of the frightening sky, and violent turmoil on the man's face while floating in the ether, still seemed to evade her understanding. She longed to discuss with the vicar its true meaning, and smiled to think that there was nothing stopping her from actually doing so. The tide was coming in, and with a laugh she spun around on the flat top of the rock and leapt across to the dry sand. 'God loves me – just the way I am,' she whispered to the wind, cherishing this entirely new feeling: that of joy. It permeated her soul, and her life took on a different hue.

~VII~

We learn new courage, stifle our old fears,
Stand with stiff backs, take part in every broil,
It may be that we love, that we are blest.
It may be, for a little space of years,
We conquer fate and half forget our tears.

Wilfrid Scawen Blunt[*]

'I couldn't concentrate properly on the questions!' Janice looked away from Marion and out across the River Derwent.

'I'm so sorry, dear, but you must remember you've had a terrible time, what with the accident. Exams are stressful enough.' Marion looked down at the sand as she made room for Janice on the boulder, wishing she could find words of comfort. Tadbury Beach was deserted apart from a stray black Labrador nosing in the creeping vegetation.

They had met abruptly while Marion was returning from a walk along the water's edge by Batchelor's grave – the lone mariner. There, right in front of her, was Janice, looking like a piece of flotsam washed up by the sea. Her blonde hair flying around in the wind, her pale face accentuating expressive blue eyes that in a few seconds spoke volumes, of loneliness and wounded emotion. An awkward moment lapsed before the pair assisted each other down on to the beach. Exchanging pleasantries as they walked along the foreshore, Marion was amazed to find she was willing to listen as Janice began to unburden herself to a complete stranger – and to her of all people. Now, as the wind

---

[*] *The Century's Poetry*, Penguin, 1938.

whipped up the waves, Janice was reminded of the previous morning, waiting to enter St Mary's Hall at 8.30 for the English Literature examination. It had been cold then too. The door had finally been opened by Mrs Macclesfield, and eighty or so students from her school and St Virgil's College streamed inside. She had hoped to find a desk against the wall, but they were all taken and so she was forced to sit near the back in one of the centre aisles.

She had just written her number and date on the paper and was checking the length of time that was allotted written up on a blackboard, centre stage, when her eye was caught by a familiar head of wavy black hair. An unbearable ache ran through her body as her eyes travelled down from his cheek, jaw, shoulders and arm resting on a desk, and then down to the floor, where one long familiar leg was stretched out towards the desk immediately in front of him. She tried to concentrate on the sequence of events from *The Thirty-Nine Steps* by John Buchan, but everything was a jumble. Any sense of the narrative eluded her, as her eyes strayed back to that form, to Gavin Armstrong, as the minutes ticked away. The rest of the questions seemed a blur; she had no idea what she had written down and was sure she had failed.

Ringing in her ears were his words, 'Do you need anything?' She could see him now, standing at the end of her bed at the hospital, promising to bring what she requested. His head was cocked to one side, his hair flopping over one eyebrow, and with a wave and a smile he had left the hospital ward. She had waited in high expectation but he never came back. It was as if their relationship had never taken place. That fatal day down at Port Arthur! She had been so frightened by his behaviour. No, she wouldn't go there... She began to shake.

Marion placed a tentative arm around the girl, feeling her sorrow, but not sure what she could do. The wind was insistent, if anything getting stronger. Tears spilled down Janice's cheeks as she remembered the day down at Port Arthur. She wiped them away with her fist, whispering, 'No, no. It wasn't just the accident and my mum being killed, it was why we were in the car in the first place. Mum was late picking me up because of the storm.' She stopped; and then relived her last conversation, seeing and hearing the driving rain. 'We were going to buy baby clothes.'

'Baby clothes?'

Janice looked down at the sand tracing a pattern with her shoe. 'Yes, baby clothes.' She seemed to jerk the words out with a hiss between sobs.

'Look, Janice… it is Janice, isn't it?' The girl nodded. 'Come with me up to my house and I'll make us a cup of tea.'

'You live close by?'

'Yes, up there.' Marion indicated with her head and then added, 'I'm Mrs Crees' mother.'

Janice jumped off the rock, backing a step. 'Oh no. I couldn't! What would she think? I mean, I was absent a lot… she wouldn't like it.'

'If you are worried on that score, don't be. She wanted you to stay with me after the accident.'

'Did she?'

Nodding, Marion clasped Janice's hand in hers, saying as she did so, 'I'm sorry, at that time I wasn't up to having anyone to stay – as I had just lost my husband.'

'Oh.' Janice looked at Marion in a new light. 'I'm getting cold.'

Marion held out her hand, attempting to smile.

They climbed the dozen steps, holding onto the handrail, to Niree Parade. Janice was surprised and pleased that the gate Marion opened led to a house she had often fantasised about – who the owners were, and what kind of lives they led. She never dreamed she would get an invitation one day to go inside. Half an hour later, sitting by a roaring gas fire and nursing a cup of tea, she confessed, 'I've always wanted to see inside this house.'

'Well, you'll have to come more often.' There was a pause while they both felt the intimacy of the moment, listening to the hiss of the fire. 'Actually, Janice, I'm not going to be here that much longer. I'm thinking of returning to England.'

Janice stared at her host, trying to work out why. 'Don't you like it here?'

'That's a hard one to answer.' Marion smiled. 'But what about you? Have you made any plans?'

'Not really. It depends on my results. You see, I wasn't… I mean…'

Gently Marion asked, 'Are you staying at the Convent?'

'No. With a family, thank goodness – the Pascoes. Angela is in our home group. She's in grade eleven. It's all right,' she said dully.

'Oh, I see.'

'I'll probably go out on my own next year, share a flat, you know. I've got enough stuff to furnish one.' Janice replied with a dry laugh. 'I've got all Mum's china… it's willow pattern. Cost her a small fortune!'

They sat in companionable silence for a few minutes, Marion imagining the china set and Janice picturing everything as it was in her home. 'I won't need a thing,' she said brightly. 'I suppose I'll get a job.'

Meeting her mood, Marion said, 'You'll probably be eligible for an allowance.'

Janice didn't respond; instead she looked moodily at the fire.

'Tell you what,' said Marion, 'would you like to stay and have supper with me? It won't be very exciting, I'm afraid! Poached eggs on toast, with some ham off the bone. Afterwards I can run you back to… where?'

'South Hobart. Thanks! I better not be back too late, as I've two more exams to go…'

'Perhaps you should ring the Pascoes.' Janice looked puzzled. 'Tell them where you are, for tea…'

'Oh, I suppose so. Where is the…?'

She jumped up, nearly knocking over her cup, at the same time as Marion indicated the whereabouts of the phone. 'Through there by the bookcase on your left.'

It was as they finished supper and cleared away that Marion found some After Dinner Mints in the pantry. 'Help yourself.'

'Oh, great. I haven't had chocolate for months.'

'Tuck in.'

'It made me sick. I didn't know that being pregnant felt so awful.'

'Oh, I thought…'

'What?'

Feeling rather foolish, Marion prevaricated.

'Oh, you thought it was Mum expecting a baby!'

Marion nodded.

Janice stifled a gasp. 'No, it was me, that's why I was asked to leave,' she whispered. 'It wouldn't have worked, anyway. His family would have been shocked and blamed me that their precious son had caused an unwanted baby. My mum was already wailing about having to mind it, so maybe it was all for the best.' Her eyes filled with tears. 'He only found out I was pregnant after the accident! I can't understand it, I mean after the day at Port Arthur he never contacted me, and I could never get hold of him to tell him. Oh, Mrs Lee, I feel so miserable… He came to the hospital after the accident and I told him about the baby. And what does he do?' Her voice rose in despair. 'He goes on living his life as if nothing has happened! I thought he loved me…' She sobbed and hiccupped.

'Come.' Marion took her hand and led her over to the daybed near the fire. 'Shh,' she whispered, stroking her hair.

'I'm all alone… no mum, no dad. No one loves me!'

'Shh, shh,' Marion murmured, rocking Janice, as she listened to her sadness. After a while Janice's sobs died down and she rested her head on Marion's shoulder.

'I've got something to tell you. Something I've never told anyone before. I too lost a baby. It was a boy, and because of various complications I couldn't have any more babies. No one understood how I felt at the time. No one wanted to know; even my husband seemed to think it was something to get over easily. It took me years wishing that things had been different. I so wanted a son. But you, dear, are young and have your whole life ahead of you. One day, you'll meet someone who really cares about you and understands. I'm sure of it. You'll see.'

'I wish you'd stay here…'

Later that evening, at Janice's request, Marion drove her down Norwood Avenue to steal a glance at what had been her home for the last sixteen years, before driving her back to South Hobart and the Pascoes.

Three weeks later, Anna was soaking up the Gold Coast sun, walking along Burleigh Beach towards the Heads watching the board riders catch the elusive waves. Nigel was sitting in Matt

Inglis's sumptuous office learning about his duties as Vice Principal of King's Christian College. Much impressed by the college grounds and the design of the school buildings, he could see that the job would more than satisfy his yearning for advancement, and that the surrounding area would be an ideal place in which to settle down. Looking at his old friend, he remarked, 'Who would have thought that this is how my career would have turned out?'

Matt agreed with a slow smile. 'Just you and me, mate, in sunny Queensland!'

'I do appreciate this. I mean, there must have been lots of applicants.' He looked across the desk at Matt.

'Mmm.' There was a long pause while Matt scrutinised his friend. Then he smiled. 'But none quite like you, my old mate. By the way, I never thanked you for your wedding invite. I was surprised to get it… sorry I couldn't come.'

'Good Lord, that seems aeons ago!'

'Well, you know how it is, our terms and holidays don't exactly coincide with the UK.'

'You never took the plunge?'

'No,' Matt said abruptly, with a laugh. 'Too many beautiful women in the world to choose from… no time, no time, mate. Come on, and I'll show you the rest of the school.'

They discussed surfing, sailing, and horse riding, all of which Nigel was keen to become involved in, and although he was mainly interested in the high school, he appreciated the two on-campus facilities for pre-school education. The class sizes were smaller than what he had become accustomed to, and he was pleasantly surprised by the 120-seat tiered lecture theatre with its air conditioning.

During the walk around, Matt enquired after Anna, and Nigel filled him in on recent circumstances.

'Oh so you'll be bringing your mother-in-law with you?'

'No, it doesn't look like it.'

'Oh, I hadn't realised.' Matt stopped in his tracks, looking away across the fields.

'But, Anna… she'll be coming with you.'

'Of course she will. I mean, she will have to hand in her notice, just as I will on returning. Could be a bit tricky; we've left it rather late. As for Mother-in-law, she wants to return to England.'

'That will be hard on Anna.'

'More awkward, really. She'll be going back on her own. Have to buy another house. Can't think why she won't come with us.'

'Oh, I think I can understand. You didn't bring her with you this time?'

'No. It wasn't for want of asking. She doesn't want to stay. Anyway, Anna is more than happy to move here after what she spied on the beach earlier today!'

'Good.' He chuckled. 'Accommodation OK?'

'Very nice, thank you; I'll settle up tonight. Be our guest.'

'Thanks. And after I'll take you both to some nightlife on the Coast! Tell Anna to wear something glamorous.'

'Not sure if she's brought anything. I suppose that means a trip to a boutique.'

Matt chuckled. 'Look, I've an appointment. All right if I leave you here to potter about on your own?'

'No problem. See you at eight.'

Nigel watched Matt lumbering across the nicely manicured lawn, then wandered into one of the staff rooms. As no one was about, he made himself a cup of black coffee, careful to rinse the cup thoroughly before putting it back in the cupboard. That reminds me, he thought. My coffee mug at Hutchins – better not forget it. He pictured it clearly, engraved with his name and the year 1991, a trophy from The Burway Rowing Club, where he'd won the Singles Sculls on the River Thames at Laleham.

Nigel returned to Hobart and placed his resignation on the headmaster's desk the very next day. He advised Anna to do the same, as strictly speaking they should give a complete term's notice. He hoped it would suffice.

They had enjoyed their brief visit to Queensland, with its bright colours and relaxed way of living, not to mention its modern shopping centres, especially Pacific Fair, with its hanging baskets and tall shady trees. Sitting close to a pond with water lilies and ducklings skimming across its water, they marvelled that they were actually in a shopping complex. Anna had pointed out small children riding miniature cars, and a sightseeing train which took visitors around, ringing a large brass bell, warning of its approach. Numerous coffee shops, restaurants, and takeaway food outlets were scattered among the laneways, and an enormous six-auditorium cinema showing all the latest films stood at one end, close to one of the largest car parks Anna had ever seen. Matt had explained that petrol was cheaper here in Queensland than anywhere else, as was the government stamp duty on purchasing your first house. The common expression referring to the weather was, 'Beautiful one day and perfect the next'. In fact, Nigel couldn't wait to begin his new job – if only he could persuade his mother-in-law to come too.

But this was not to be. Marion was adamant. It had been a mistake coming to Australia in the first place. He had heard it all before: 'If you had only stayed in England. But no, you drag my daughter over here, and so we come… and look what happens!' To be honest, he had never given it a moment's thought. 'If I had a grandchild, that would be a different story,' she stated firmly on more than one occasion.

It was as they were leaving Midnight Mass on Christmas Eve at St David's Cathedral in Hobart, surrounded by jostling worshippers, that Marion had touched Anna's hand, whispering in her ear, 'You have a baby and I'll come and visit.'

'I don't want to have a baby yet, and I won't be blackmailed into having one!' Anna spat out between mouthfuls of toothpaste as they prepared for bed. She lay awake, making out the dim shapes in their bedroom, listening to Nigel's regular breathing and imagining the horrors of childbirth, tales of which she had been subjected to during morning recess in the staff common room. There was another fear factor, herself swelling up into a grotesque shape and never really returning to her original weight; nor had she contemplated giving birth without her mother being there. Why was she being so selfish? Why couldn't Marion understand? She fell asleep eventually, wondering how they were going to get through Christmas Day, with herself grieving for a father she so admired and a mother suddenly acquiring opinions and decisions of her own.

Mary and Patrick Armstrong, meanwhile, were spending Christmas in Perth, West Australia, with their daughter, enjoying their first grandchild and having left strict instructions for Gavin to behave himself while they were away. Both were secretly pleased to be going away on holiday, Patrick because although he had grudgingly agreed to the buy-back gun laws that Prime Minister Howard had stipulated, he had no intention of doing so. As he had fumed to Mary on several occasions, 'It's grossly unfair that collectors such as I have to comply just because some maniac goes berserk! These firearms have cost me a lot of money. If I could get my hands on the son of the bitch, I'd screw his neck!'

'Yes, dear. It is unfair, but there is nothing you can do about it. Martin Bryant was a very disturbed young man,' she would reply vaguely, her mind focussing on Gavin's sexual exploits with Janice Ryan. Visibly shaken, she had blurted out the whole sorry saga in the confessional box to Father Stephen. 'And heaven knows what else he has been up to!'

'Don't do anything foolhardy, son,' were Patrick's parting words. Secretly, he was proud that Gavin had been chosen as one of the crew on the yacht, *Mirabella*, which was to sail in the Sydney-to-Hobart classic; also, he hoped that some sense of maturity and responsibility would be knocked into his son. It meant he would be flying up to Sydney on Christmas Eve, and staying on the yacht Christmas Day in order to meet up with the rest of the crew on Boxing Day. No time for larking about, he hoped.

Janice Ryan hadn't enjoyed the end-of-term celebrations, nor did she want to stay with the Pascoes any longer. 'It was a stroke of luck, really,' she recounted to Marion on one of her many visits. 'At Mum's funeral there were quite a few nurses, and one who I'd seen on several occasions, cos she came to the house sometimes. Well, she and Mum were quite close, and she whispered to me that if I ever needed a place to stay, to call her. I'd forgotten about it. Her name is Barbara, and she has this cottage in Sandy Bay. It's divine... and there's a gorgeous cat called Precious, and I've moved into an annex at the back with my own kitchenette and bed-sitting room!'

'Good gracious me, aren't you the lucky one!'

'And that's not all. We eat our tea on our laps while watching TV, on the nights Barbara is off-duty, and I can come and go as I like! I've got a job in the children's department at Myer's for the holiday.'

'Good for you, but what about your studies, Janice?'

'I don't think I've matriculated. Barbara said she will support me to redo the subjects again... at Rosny College. She even let me choose the furniture I like for the annex, and I can put up posters and use all the crockery we had at home. Oh, Marion, you must meet her. You'd like her.'

'All these new experiences! Have you heard from...'

'Gavin? No.' She smiled, looking up at Marion's worried face. 'Don't worry. I've realised how some things are not to be.' Then quickly she changed the mood, saying how she was looking forward to Christmas, as she and Barbara were going to decorate the tree and go carol singing and, some of Barbara's friends were coming round for drinks and she had to help with all the arrangements.

'Mum used to say Barbara was quite dotty. I can still come and see you, before you go, can't I?'

'Of course you can.' The awkward moment passed as Janice prattled on.

On Christmas morning, while making preparations of bread sauce, Marion had that sinking feeling that comes when things are not what they seem, when people talk banalities and you wonder how you are going to get through the day. The three of them sat around her dining table attempting conversation. Nigel waxed eloquently about Queensland and his new position. Anna was amazed as to how quickly affairs had taken shape, and Marion wished her first Christmas in Tasmania was anything other than it was. Memories engulfed her of earlier times.

'I looked everywhere for the Nativity scene,' she babbled on, trying to reduce the tension. 'You know, the one we used to place on the hall table, with straw and yew branches which we collected, and your dad fixed the lights around. But I couldn't find it. Probably it's still in a box in the garage,' she mumbled, smiling wanly.

The day wore on. They watched the Queen's speech on television and then exchanged presents. Anna, attempting to lighten the mood, showed cards and gifts from students who weren't to know she wouldn't be teaching at St Mary's the next year. Nigel put a call through to his parents, now that they were back in Tasmania, after which he announced he intended to travel up there before going to Queensland. 'We could go tomorrow, or for the New Year, Anna,' he suggested.

'What, Boxing Day? You've got to be joking, and I don't know about the New Year.' She looked stonily across at her husband. 'What about Mum?'

'Well, I ought to go sometime before we leave.'

'You go, Anna. It's all right. He ought to see his mum and dad.'

'No, Mum, I'm not going. Nigel can go if he likes.'

There was an awkward silence. Anna was angry that Nigel could be so insensitive and that he could so casually suggest arrangements she knew nothing about in front of her mother.

Emotions charged the air, so with foresight Marion suggested a walk along the beach. Nigel said, 'You two go... I'll watch the television.' Nigel caught Anna's glare. 'Maybe some footie on...' He gave Anna his best smile.

They walked in silence along Tadbury Beach, passing a few familiar faces nodding and murmuring 'Happy Christmas' past the grave of the lone sailor, the crayfish farm, the sewerage treatment works and down through the copse until they came level with the house that had enormous windows and a picturesque cottage garden. Here they sat down, as Marion had done before, on the garden seat placed by the pathway, presumably by the owners.

'This was the house I had hoped you and Dad would buy,' remarked Anna, looking across the Derwent River to Lauderdale.

'It would have been nice. But it wasn't to be, was it?'

'Talking of houses, Mum. Will you sell yours?'

Marion sighed. 'I don't know, Anna. It's too early to say. Probably at some later date.'

'I just wondered. And... what about Dad's businesses?'

'What about them?'

'Well, I didn't know he had so many. They must be worth a bit.'

'There was no reason for you to know. Even I was surprised.'

Anna tried another tack. 'If you freed up some of Dad's assets now, it would help us buy what we would really like in Queensland.'

Marion thought for a moment before replying. 'I dare say it would.' She got up and they retraced their footsteps.

'You know,' she said, 'I don't wish to discuss money on Christmas Day.'

'Why not?' Exasperated, Anna raised her voice.

'Keep your voice down! Because I don't, right now. These considerations are for the future... when I return home to England. You are going to Queensland. That's your choice.'

'You could come with us.'

Marion gave her a withering look. 'Please, Anna, let it rest.'

They reached the lone grave and stopped for a moment before heading down to the beach. 'Did you know it was here that I first met Janice Ryan?'

Picking her way down over the roughly made steps, Anna turned and offered her hand to Marion. 'You talked to her?'

'Oh, yes, on many an occasion. Thank you, love. I wouldn't want to slip here. Quite dangerous, don't you think?'

'I suppose so. But why didn't you tell me?'

'I don't know, really. It never seemed important enough at the time to mention. She comes around quite often. Poor lass, what she has been through.'

'Do you think you'll miss Tadbury – the beach and all?'

'Probably not, as most of the time my memories have been sad.' Laughing, she added, 'And I definitely won't miss this wind!'

'I had a great time on Nobby's Beach. It was nothing like this one. Miles and miles of sand and dunes. There were cafés at one end, and shops. It wasn't as interesting as this one with its rocks and plants close by, but at least it was warm!'

'There you are, you see; you'll enjoy Queensland, love. Me, I prefer the gentle flow of the Thames. It's where I belong.' There was a slight thawing in Anna's manner as Marion added, 'I'm taking your father's ashes back to where he belongs, and don't worry, my dear, you'll get your share. Everything will be left to you.' Then, staring out to sea, she said firmly, 'But not right at this moment.'

'And the property in Ferry Lane?' asked Anna.

'That's something I'll be looking into as soon as I get back. It's very odd about owning that house. The businesses I vaguely knew about – well, one of them…'

'Oh, Mum!'

'Anna, you have to understand, your father never discussed money.'

'You'll have to deal with solicitors and agents… and the occupants.'

'Yes, I know. Don't you think I'm capable?'

'Don't be silly, Mum. Maybe Dad thought he'd told you about the house.'

'Maybe; however, I can assure you he never mentioned it.'

'I wish he was still here.'

'So do I, Anna, so do I… but wishing doesn't change anything!' Emotionally wrung out and in need of some support, Marion clasped Anna's hand as they reached the steps leading from the beach to Niree Parade. 'I want you to know,' she began, looking down at her feet. 'Your father could be very persuasive. If it had been up to me, I wouldn't have come to Tasmania in the first place. So you see, I couldn't come to Queensland. I just couldn't – not without him. I'm sorry.'

As they reached the top, there, about to open the gate, stood Janice, carrying a large box wrapped in Christmas paper. Seeing the strain on Marion's face, she stammered, 'Oh, I hope – I mean, I bought you this. Happy Christmas.'

Reflecting on all that had transpired, the awkward conversations, finding Nigel asleep in the chair on returning from their walk, and Anna's snappishness, it hadn't been too bad a day. So now alone, as Nigel and Anna had taken Janice back to Sandy Bay, Marion recounted the good moments to Leonard's empty chair. 'I was glad Janice came, she had so much to say and seemed so positive about her life. We all had a glass of sherry to celebrate her Christmas bonus, and she made us laugh about the goings-on at the department store. I missed you, Len… but all in all, you would have been proud of me, as I have managed to get through the day without crying. By the way, what do you want me to do with the house in Ferry Lane? Maybe you kept it for an occasion such as this, with me going home again… You always look after me.'

With that, she nibbled the last mince pie, cleaned up the debris and carried the sherry glasses into the kitchen. On impulse she decided to ring her old friend, Alice Ashby, in Laleham to wish her a Happy Christmas before turning in for the night, but she forgot the change in time zones. Alice, as was her custom at Christmas and Easter, was sitting at the back of All Saints' Church, fumbling for the hymn, 'Christians, Awake, Salute the Happy Morn' in an *Ancient and Modern* hymn book.

~VIII~

Samuel Daniel

'**M**a'am, it is dinner time. Please, will you put your table down?'

Marion opened her eyes to see a stewardess wearing a bright red scarf pinned to her jacket shoulder leaning towards her with a tray of food. This was the second leg of her flight to England with JAL. She had been dozing, reflecting on her last two months in Tasmania.

Anna had been persuaded by Nigel to visit his parents in Devonport before they caught the ferry to the mainland, driving on through Victoria, New South Wales, and on up the coastal road to the Gold Coast. She held misgivings about their old Laser Ghia being up to it, however, Nigel assured her all would be well. Hopefully, they would arrive with enough time to spare – to find a house or flat to rent before Nigel had to attend staff meetings at King's College and the 1997 school year began.

It was January, so it would be quite hot driving through Australia; whereas Marion would be going back to quite the opposite with possibly fog. In retrospect, their parting had been easy. The usual pleasantries were said, while loading the Laser.

'You will be OK, Mum?'

'Drive carefully you two, there are so many idiots on the roads, especially at this time of year.' Maps were checked and kisses exchanged through the car window, and then they were gone.

As far as Marion knew, all her furniture and effects were in a storage shed in Blackman's Bay, or so the nice removal man had said. She had his card somewhere in her purse, that she remembered.

The Jaguar had been sold to a dealer, and Marion's clothes were few. They filled two suitcases which she had with her, plus Leonard's documents, his watch, his ashes and the painting of Laleham Cottage.

'Oh, I'm so sorry.' She smiled at the hostess, at the same time pushing the armrest button, releasing the folding table. 'Thank you.' She took the tray and began opening the little plastic sachets holding cutlery and lifting the lid off the plate containing something called Chicken Cacciatore. She peered at the other objects on the tray, a serviette and two small ramekins, one with a steamed pudding topped by a doubtful sauce, the other containing a salad – at least what she deemed passed as a salad.

While tackling this meagre fare, she thought of Janice. A face-to-face farewell was out of the question, as she was afraid she would break down, having grown fond of this plucky teenager. She had telephoned Janice the night before she left, hinting that if she ever wanted a holiday in England, she only had to ask and Marion would buy the ticket.

The passenger on her right was stabbing at her food, which caused the sauce surrounding her meat to splash in Marion's direction. At the same time, the man immediately in front of her decided to push his chair into the reclining position, causing a thump to her tray.

'Just as well I haven't ordered any liquid refreshment,' she remarked wryly to the woman on her left, whose large frame encroached into Marion's seating, while a child in the row behind kicked her seat. This was going to be a trying flight, so Marion ate her meal quickly and tossed up whether to accept tea or coffee or neither from the hostess. The flight was full. She could hear from somewhere near the back a child wailing, and a teenage sports team were becoming noisy just ahead of her. Marion closed her eyes as she heard a woman hiss, 'Don't do that, Andrew.'

'Why not?'

'Because I say so.'

'There's not enough room!' This was followed by more of the same.

The hours dragged on as Marion reminisced over her arrival in Tasmania, the horrors of the Port Arthur massacre, and Leonard's sudden death. It came to her that she hadn't visited any of the areas she thought she would see. There never seemed enough time or opportunity to visit the Tamar district and its wineries. Then there was the quaint village of Richmond and its gaol, now turned into craft shops, and even the summit of Mount Wellington. Leonard was too busy, either sailing or playing golf, and Anna seemed so involved at St Mary's she didn't like to ask her after Leonard had died. Nothing had turned out the way she had imagined. How strange she felt, sitting here without Len next to her; but at the same time she was a little excited, looking forward to her future now that she was going home. The vision of the lone sailor's grave swam before her; the poor soul, buried on a riverbank in unconsecrated ground, far from home, all those years ago.

'Excuse me?'

'Oh, I'm sorry, I was talking to myself,' she replied to the fat lady next to her. She was pleased she had placed a Peace rose, picked from her garden in the early morning, on the gravestone before she left Tadbury for good. She had said a prayer for the sailor, secure in the knowledge that she was taking Len's ashes home with her to Laleham where he belonged. No way would she have his ashes buried at Cornelian Bay Cemetery, so far from his homeland. At All Saints', Laleham, she would arrange a Memorial Service. Her mind drifted – seeing the interior, the enormous stained-glass window, the smaller ones, the stalwart pillars and the blackened oak door. She could feel the heavy iron latch in her hand, sense the flagstones through her feet and smell the pervasive mixture of polish and old woodwork – something unique to the church – something she loved and had so sorely missed.

She could see the lychgate, hear the whisper of the yew tree that everything would be all right, and reluctantly accepted that in the scheme of things her life was as unimportant as a grain of sand. But it was her life, and she wondered why it had been turned upside down.

The journey was over. Throngs of people spewed out of the metal doors at customs, Heathrow, pushing their trolleys laden with luggage. However, she thankfully spied Alice and tried to stay dignified. Her tears spilled over and she was oblivious to all around her except that she was finally home. Emotionally exhausted, by nine in the evening Marion had retired to Alice's spare bedroom. Conversation had been strained, due to the fact that Marion had talked incessantly about the journey, her companions and very little else. 'And as it's Sunday tomorrow, I suppose you'll be going to church?' Alice said diffidently.

'Oh, yes. After experiencing what constitutes for a service in Tasmania, I will. But Alice, could I persuade you to come with me?'

'You know me. Easter Sunday… Christmas Day.'

'Please, Alice, just this once? It would mean a lot to me.'

'I could make an exception, just this once,' her host said with a smile, feeling cornered.

Following a simple meal of poached eggs on toast, fresh per-colated coffee and liqueur chocolates, Alice had ushered a protesting Marion up to bed.

'Let me…'

'No, no, it's not necessary. There's hardly anything to wash. Really, Marion. You get a good night's sleep.'

Alice turned the kitchen sink taps on, and squeezed some Fairy Liquid into a blue plastic bowl inside the sink. 'Pink towels are on the heated towel rack in the bathroom for you,' she called, swishing the soap suds around, relieved to hear Marion climbing the stairs.

It had been one of those difficult days, she mused, as she washed up the dishes. Finding a car park at Heathrow close to the terminal from which she guessed Marion would emerge was tricky and she'd not been quite sure what to talk about. Luckily, the day had been crisp and fine. The fog hadn't as yet fallen. As it was, she needn't have worried. Marion avoided any discussion about Leonard or Anna. Thank heavens she only had Sunday to get through, as on Monday she would leave the house at 8 a.m., and be at her receptionist's desk until 5.30. Then there were only the evenings for conversation. She couldn't quite remember how long she had been at the Thames Street Surgery in Staines, but remembered she'd started there shortly after her mother had died.

Alice liked the work. It made her feel part of the bustling world. At one time she almost handed in her notice in order to marry Guy Forbes, a struggling farmer she had met on a holiday up in the Yorkshire Dales. But she had dithered so long that he upped and married someone else. Since that time, there was the occasional date but no one special. To be quite honest, Alice liked living alone. Maybe she was like her father. He had walked out one day, carrying all his possessions and clothes in a battered suitcase when she was quite small, leaving her mother and herself to make the best of it.

She was quite content living in the village close to the River Thames and working in Staines. She liked the quiet life, free of emotional entanglements. Look where it had landed Marion! She wouldn't like to be in her shoes. Now, with Marion in the house, she wondered how long she would be staying. Poor Marion would get quite a shock to see what the new owners had done to Laleham Cottage. First they demolished the front hedge, replacing it with a black iron paling fence, so now you could see into the kitchen and dining-room windows. They had torn down the honeysuckle from the front door and painted it white. But that wasn't the end of it. Someone had added a glass-walled room above the garage, which didn't seem at all in keeping with the brick and tile house.

Tipping the suds out of the blue bowl down the drain, Alice set about drying the dishes and putting everything carefully away. She felt quite strange hearing someone else in the house.

Normally in the winter months on Sundays she would take in a film with a friend and then go on to the Swan Hotel for dinner or drinks at the bar. She liked going there because it was one of the oldest buildings on the river that hadn't been turned into a modern monstrosity.

Hopefully, tomorrow would not be too much of a strain. She could hardly ask Marion what her plans were, so soon after arriving. Alice went around the house, checking on the locks of the front and back doors. Happy everything was in order, she switched off the downstairs lights and made her way up to bed.

With hindsight, she wished she had asked Marion, while she was still in Tasmania, how long she expected to stay.

Marion was standing in Alice's spare bedroom wrapped in a terry towelling white robe she had found on the back of the bedroom door, feeling rather odd. She thought about her house just down the lane with strangers sleeping in her bedroom. Telling herself to thank God that she was safe and sound rather than dwell on the past, hearing traffic as she walked towards the window. Opening the casement, she breathed in the familiar Thames Valley air, now tinged with fog and fumes from cars still careering around the bend in the road avoiding the War Memorial. Lights from the traffic threw up ghostly images of the church and trees, creating a surreal effect. Was she really back in Laleham, staying in a strange bedroom? It was quite noisy, whereas in her old bedroom you couldn't hear anything. What a difference a few hundred yards made! She would make sure her next house was in a quiet area. Closing the window, she climbed into bed and then turned off the bedside light while listening to the traffic. She drifted off to sleep, seeing herself walking along the towpath beside her much-loved River Thames.

Sunday morning dawned grey and misty. The inhabitants of Laleham village peeped around their curtained windows and resolved to stay in bed, barring one returned native who was oblivious of the dull cold day. Alice hated the cold; as a result she had installed central heating. In all Christian charity she felt it her duty to accompany Marion just this once to the draughty church. She glanced at her friend over the breakfast table and was surprised to see a different side to her. There was a determined resilience in her face, and her gaze was less apprehensive, if anything, optimistic and more alive, so that she, Alice, felt she need no longer fear that Marion was going to collapse on her doorstep, so to speak. Relieved, she remarked, 'You'll have to tell me all about Tasmania.'

'I can tell you one thing now. It's cold!'

'Cold?'

'Mm,' said Marion chewing a piece of toast. 'Windy… well, it was in Tadbury, being on the coast.'

'Oh, I didn't expect it to be cold.'

Marion could see Alice was genuinely interested, and although she didn't want to remember much about the last nine months, felt she ought to make an effort.

'Well, it's a different kind of cold to here. The air is clearer, somehow, which makes the wind seem fresher, coming from the Antarctic.' Marion looked across at Alice over the lip of her coffee cup. 'It's difficult to explain, but I used to take long walks along the beach at Tadbury. I felt so lonely... I felt as though I was living on the edge of the world, miles away from anyone. I tried very hard to settle there, but what with one thing and another, it was too big a decision – too lonely – so I came home, where I belong.'

She was silent for a while, sipping her coffee slowly, both women aware of the water bubbling in the pipes, the ticking of a grandfather clock close by and the noise of an occasional truck changing gear as it negotiated the curve in the road around the church.

Marion broke the silence. 'I've brought Len's ashes home. I'd like to have a Memorial Service for him, with bells. So that's the first thing to arrange.' Although composed, her eyes glistened and her voice was just a whisper. 'Next, I must find somewhere to live – hopefully here in Laleham.'

Alice found herself wanting to ask what Anna felt about her mother returning to England, but one look at Marion's face suggested this was not a good time to bring Anna into the conversation. Instead, she said breezily, 'Stay as long as you like. There's no rush.' Then she wished fervently she had kept her mouth shut.

Marion leant across the table patting Alice's hand. 'I do appreciate your kindness.' The idea came to her unexpectedly, 'Perhaps you'll help me find a house, nothing too big... something with loads of character.'

The church clock struck ten as they began clearing the table, with Alice murmuring compliance to Marion's suggestions. In fact she was quite looking forward to the next few weeks.

In the space of twenty minutes, visits to the bathroom were made, make-up applied, coats and gloves retrieved from the hallstand, and the front door key located in Alice's handbag. Then they crossed the road as the church bell tolled, reminding parishioners they had five minutes before the service started. They entered by the gate below the bell tower round the western end towards the porch, with Marion leading the way.

As they approached, they saw that the great solid oak door was open. A sidesman thrust the blue hymnal and red prayer book into Marion's hand. She moved along the aisle and sat down in the same row and close to her old seat with Alice on her left. She fixed her gaze on the window she remembered to her right, showing a child holding lilies with the word 'Peace' written underneath.

The organ was playing quietly, the congregation whispering, as word was spreading, 'Mrs Lee has come back, poor soul, without her husband.' Alice felt like a kind of bollard protecting Marion from surreptitious glances.

The watcher felt only deep emotion, wondering if the light was playing tricks on him. Noel Barker had to sit down just as the choir processed in, singing 'Dear Lord and Father of Mankind', causing Graham Watts, his off-sider, to ask if he was feeling ill. Marion was blissfully unaware of his discomfort or that anything was amiss. In her heart she thanked God everything was just the same. Nothing had changed.

Noel Barker thanked God too for bringing Marion back to Laleham. He couldn't believe that this was so. He kept looking in her direction, just to make sure she was really there, and beaming at Graham as he sang, '…and let our ordered lives confess the beauty of thy peace.'

Graham thought Noel's behaviour was bizarre and wondered if he was having a breakdown, seeing him look white as a sheet one minute and singing lustily the next. He hoped that Noel was up to reading the lessons, otherwise he would have to step in.

The sung responses soothed Marion's soul. It had seemed an age since she had heard them, and the cultured voice of the Reverend Peter Guinness gave off an air of dependability and permanence.

Between the lessons read by Noel were the appointed collects, just as it always was. Marion wanted to say 'thank you' for not placing the lessons and psalm together without a break, as she had experienced in progressive churches in Tasmania. She had never seen the point of it. Looking across at the lectern, she thought Noel Barker looked quite handsome. She liked his tweed jacket, which she was sure she hadn't seen before. The deep timbre of his voice rang out clearly and everyone was quietly listening. There was no noise; no children grizzling or making noises with toys. Of course, they wouldn't be here disturbing the adults. They would be in the Village Hall. There would not be a children's talk while adults looked on in a benign way. *Silence*. Here there was a strong sense of hallowed ground where all who entered came to worship, not to gossip. She was glad the Reverend Guinness had not singled her out with false bonhomie at her return, as she had seen happen in Tadbury. She could once again concentrate on her relationship with God, and feed her tired batteries, rather as she had experienced with Sister Ruth at Mary Knoll. She would write to her thanking her for guidance… Wistfully, she imagined Sister Ruth sitting next to her. She would understand. It occurred to her that most people would be shocked she had visited a nun while away and found comfort from a Roman Catholic.

The service was over all too soon for Marion, but not soon enough for Alice. She was frozen. She couldn't see for the life of her what Marion saw in all these 'thees' and 'thous', not to mention listening to a man wearing a dress droning on about a prophet who lived hundreds of years ago. Where was the relevance? Still, if it gave Marion solace, who was she to criticise?

'Would you mind if we waited till everyone has left? There is something I want to do,' Marion whispered into her ear.

Inwardly, Alice groaned. 'Not at all,' she replied. Thrusting her hands into her gloves and then into her pockets, she watched as Marion replaced her kneeler, collected their books together and turned to see the last person leave the church. Footsteps on the flagstoned floor faded. The organist had stopped playing, and the only sounds now were of someone stacking books onto the shelves at the back of the church.

Alice stood up to leave. If she didn't move soon she would be glued to the seat. Marion followed, but stopped in front of the stained-glass window high in the western wall. She moved closer and was shocked to realise she had confused the enormous painting behind the font with that of the window. It was nothing like what she remembered. Yes, the painting was just as disturbing… but why had she imagined it as the window? How could she have mixed them up? Thoroughly perplexed, she turned quickly and almost collided with Noel Barker.

'Marion, what a lovely surprise! When did you arrive?'

Jolted by Noel's close proximity, she attempted to move backwards, but almost lost her balance as her legs came into contact with a row of chairs.

'Here, let me take those.' Noel turned to stack the books on the shelves. She found herself smiling at his broad shoulders. 'Yesterday,' she replied, and sank into one of the chairs, from where she could see Alice talking to the vicar in the porch. She closed her eyes, attempting to block out improper imaginings of those strong arms around her. 'You have no idea how good it is to be back here.'

'Oh, I think I do…'

'It's the air – the light – sounds silly, but…' Opening her eyes she met two kindly blue ones. They held each other's gaze. Noel leant on the back of the chair in front of Marion shifting his gaze up to the stained-glass window and back again.

'Somehow or other I had mixed up the painting with the stained-glass window.' She frowned. 'I still can't understand why I did.'

Noel smiled back at her, his thoughts on a different subject. 'An easy enough mistake. You worry too much. It's not important.'

She stood up turning to look once more at the window.

Another voice behind her said, 'St Christopher, St Cecilia and St Eustace look a little dull in this light.'

'I remembered it as blood red…' she said, turning to the vicar.

'It is when the sun is setting, but on a dull day like today not easily imagined.'

Marion looked at the kindly ageing face of Peter Guinness, noticing the lines around his eyes and mouth, but was relieved to see that his enigmatic smile was still the same. Holding out his hand, he said, 'Welcome home, Marion. If there is anything I can do you know where to find me.' His hand was cold and smooth as she took it in hers.

'Well, yes there is. I've brought Leonard's ashes home and...'

'No problem. You'd like a Memorial Service?'

She nodded.

'Contact Lisa at the office. She'll make the arrangements. She has my diary. I see you are staying with Alice Ashby.' He nodded in Alice's direction. 'Good for you.' He paused and smiled brightly. 'Well, I must away, see what the Sunday school has been up to!'

She watched him walk swiftly up the aisle towards the sacristy, his white surplice billowing out around him.

'Are you coming, Marion, it's freezing!' called Alice, stomping her feet on the porch mat.

An electric current from Noel seemed to bore right into Marion. She felt herself blushing, and looked at the flagstone floor. 'Sorry! Come over here. See that painting? It has haunted me all the time I was away.'

All three stared at the large dark oil. Finally, Alice said, 'I can't see what's so threatening. A man with a flowing beard, leaning down to another who appears to be on a wave. Can't say I've noticed it before.'

'It's of God leaning down to save Saint Peter from drowning, and I guess it represents...' Noel paused, 'hope. Look, if you two are ready,' he coughed, 'I'd like to lock up now.'

They moved out into the porch, where traffic could be heard hurtling around the corner. Marion wasn't entirely convinced she was wrong about the painting. To her, it was of man drowning, unable to reach the hand of God. 'Oh, I didn't know you locked the church?' she said to Noel.

'Unfortunately, yes. Not long after you left, the CMS money box was stolen.' She watched as he slid the enormous key into the lock, heard the click, and felt both angry and sad, for now she wouldn't be able to walk in to pray when she felt like it.

'Sign of the times!' he said, dangling the key from his fingers. 'Marion, if you need anything, anything at all, I'm only a phone call away. I mean it.'

'Thank you, Noel.' She tried to sound businesslike. 'Regards to Mrs Barker...'

Her words were drowned out by the traffic, as he abruptly

turned on his heel, bounding up the three steps to the left leading to the graveyard. It began to drizzle as the two friends hurried in the opposite direction before crossing the road and entering Yew Cottage.

'Not your usual church goer, was he?' said Alice, as she put the kettle on.

Marion was consumed with curiosity as to what Noel Barker's wife was like. She murmured, 'Do you think so?'

'I can't say I have ever spoken to him before. Where does he live?'

'The farm on Ashford Road. He's been a churchwarden for as long as I can remember.' Still in her coat and gloves, Marion sat down abruptly. 'Alice, I know it sounds silly, but I feel terribly tired. You won't mind if I go back to bed? I think I was a bit premature going to church this morning.'

Alice glanced at Marion's white pinched face and hoped she wasn't going to pass out. 'Of course not. You take yourself off upstairs and I'll bring you up a cuppa. I'm not at all surprised; anyway, the weather is inclement. There is plenty of time for you to take a walk down the lane. If it doesn't fine up today, you've got all of tomorrow.'

She bustled about, taking Marion's coat and ushering her up to bed. 'You sleep for as long as you like,' Alice called up the stairs, hoping she didn't have an invalid on her hands, and that it was only jet lag affecting Marion. Alice set to making the tea, found a couple of digestive biscuits, and placed the items on a small tray. She opened a new packet of paper serviettes, folding one that displayed forget-me-nots next to the biscuits and carried the tray up the stairs, knocking gently on the bedroom door.

There was no sound from within, so she opened the door and, finding Marion asleep tucked up in bed, put the tray down on top of the bedside table. She crossed the room to close the curtains and decided to put on the bedside light so that when Marion awoke she wouldn't be disorientated. Looking around, she adjusted the eiderdown, then went downstairs to sip her tea and read the Sunday papers.

~IX~

For Marion, returning to Laleham was serendipitous. Her nights brought dreams of fulfilment, her day's frantic activity. She tried to justify her feelings of loss for Leonard, but had to admit it wasn't the essence of him she missed, it was simply not having someone else to rely upon. She probed further. Did she love him? Had she ever really loved him? The questions rose up through her consciousness. There was time to think now and, as much as she pushed these thoughts away, they kept arising of their own free will like the head on a glass of beer. Every time she travelled on the 218 bus to Staines, these painful thoughts reared their ugly heads, with visions of Leonard pursuing his own interests and herself tagging along. Dining with friends – his friends – she had felt like a handbag, an appendage for Leonard, something he dragged around. She had known his guests thought her dull, with their talk of the latest gossip, of films she had no wish to see, and shenanigans which she could only smile and nod at, knowing full well she had nothing to contribute.

And then Anna had married an Australian and gone away. She couldn't remember when she felt aware that she was superfluous to Anna's life. It wasn't what she had imagined would happen when she married Leonard. Come to think of it, she was amazed

---

* From *The Treasury of Familiar Quotations*, Avenal Books, New York.

Leonard had wanted to move to Australia. She thought he was perfectly satisfied with the way his life was turning out. A few days later, while returning on the 218 bus from her solicitors, Muckeridge and Associates, she was pleased with the way she had conducted herself, and having brought herself up to date with what was going on financially in the various businesses, she would visit each and decide which one to sell. 'Yes,' she whispered, looking out of the bus window, 'I will decide.'

Pondering about property and cottages in general, she began to see in her mind's eye the type of house she would like. Emotionally it would not be sensible to live back in Blacksmiths' Lane, even if a house there came on the market, she mused to herself. What the new owners have done to my house, I'd rather not think about – and those bungalows! Three of them squeezed into a cul-de-sac opposite where I used to look at an orchard bounded by a wall covered with flaming Virginia creeper in the autumn! There were other changes too: there was a sign forbidding cars to park at the river end of Blacksmiths' Lane, and the post office and shop had moved from one side to the other on the through road to Shepperton.

Something seemed to remind her of the house she had left in Tadbury. Peering out of the grimy bus window as it stopped to pick up passengers, she looked into a garden, but the bus moved off before she could identify whatever it was. She smiled, recalling her visit to Brown and Banks Real Estate offices in Sandy Bay. They would look after the house in Tadbury and collect a good rent. She wasn't too sure how long she would keep it; however, she had been advised to hold on at least until she wouldn't get stung for capital gains tax. The bus was nearing Laleham when two young girls in school uniform got on, their skirts up to their thighs, giggling as they made for the back seat.

She thought of Anna, casting her mind back to when it was she had had her first niggling feeling that they had little in common. But now… Someone rang the bell. She gathered up her bags and followed the line to the front of the bus. Returning home to England, she had at least gained some dignity. The bus came to a stop outside the church, and she thought of Anna soaking up the sun in Queensland. Struggling with her shopping, she alighted down the two stairs and glancing up saw a young man waiting his turn to jump on. He was the spitting image of Leonard as a young man. The shock made her lose her footing. The bags fell on the pavement and she went down too.

'Are you all right?' A vaguely familiar voice reached her ears. A strong arm helped her up. She had gone quite white. People in the bus were looking out the nearside window, tut-tutting about the safety of public transport.

Leaning on the arm for support, she pulled herself up. He handed the shopping bags to her. She dusted herself down. 'I... er... live across the way,' Marion said, indicating Yew Cottage, her eyes riveted on the young man's face.

'Well, that's good then,' he said with a smile.

'Are you coming or not?' a terse voice from the inside of the bus called.

With relief, the young man noticed the colour coming back into her face, and swung himself up onto the bus. 'We don't have all day, son!'

Marion watched as the driver took his fare. The bus set off and the young man peered between the two teenage girls looking out of the back window. He noticed she was standing exactly where he had left her, staring after the bus as it retreated around the bend towards Shepperton.

Marion collected her thoughts and told herself she must be imagining things. She dodged the traffic, crossing the road to Alice's house, and resolved this was one incident she had no intention of sharing with her friend. 'What would she think?' she muttered as she put the key into the lock.

However, it was while they were having supper on the Saturday night and Marion was immersed in the Property section of the weekend paper that Alice stabbed at an article on the social page. 'Good heavens! We have a *Talent not to be missed* living in Laleham, according to the paper!'

'Really?'

She continued to read aloud. ' "Michael Driver, only seventeen, has been offered a year's study in Vienna." Here' – she waved the paper at Marion – 'there's a picture. He's playing with the Philharmonic Orchestra in the Albert Hall!'

Marion recognised the young man instantly as Alice chatted on. 'Fancy that! He lives in Laleham-on-Thames. Let's go up to London to hear him, Marion. He's only playing for one night – Wednesday.' Alice leant towards her friend expectantly.

'Oh, I don't think so. I mean, I've the Memorial Service on Monday, then later in the week two houses to see…' She looked up at Alice's crestfallen face. 'You go, and then you can tell me all about it.'

'I don't want to go alone.'

'Please go; I have overstayed my welcome, I know. Don't pretend! Yes, I have. It is taking me longer than I thought to find a property. I thought I'd find one easily, but so far nothing has come up. Maybe this week.'

She prattled on, hoping to distract Alice from her shaking hands. With an abrupt movement she handed the paper back to Alice and began clearing their dishes away. Her mind was in a spin, as she now had a name to fit the young man at the bus stop, and wondered if Alice would see a likeness to Len.

She needn't have worried. Alice was thinking of who she could ask to come with her. Having Marion to stay was good in some ways, someone to talk with at the end of the day, but she liked to go out at least once a week, and since Marion had arrived, she hadn't even popped into the local.

'Well, I'll think about it,' said Alice, and with that she tuned in to BBC2.

On the Sunday after Evensong, Marion was deep in conversation with Noel Barker in the vestry. Handing her a pile of pamphlets, he said with a smile, 'These are your Order of Service sheets for Leonard's Memorial Service, at eleven o'clock tomorrow. They're done in just the way you asked for, I hope.'

Her eye examined the topmost one. 'Thank you, Noel. They are just what I wanted.' Looking at him anxiously, she added, 'I expect you wonder why I'm not doing the Eulogy?'

'Not at all. It's quite common these days for friends to do them. Less traumatic for the loved ones.'

She looked up at him and noticed his concern. 'You've been so kind,' she said softly.

'Rubbish, anyone would do the same.' Turning away to hide the effect her close proximity had on him, his voice was barely audible, 'I've taken the liberty to tee up a bell-ringer for ten minutes before and after the service. Would you like that?'

Her eyes filled with tears. 'You've thought of everything.' Her voice shook as she looked down at the sheet in her hand.

'The wake?'

'Mmm, I thought in the Village Hall. I couldn't expect Alice to... There could be lots of people from Leonard's old firm, and some friends of his I barely know.'

'May I make a suggestion?'

She laughed, breaking the tension. 'The Three Shoes?'

'Not quite...' He leant against the wall, eyeing her seriously. 'You are welcome to have it at the farmhouse.'

She spun round to face him. 'Oh, I couldn't do that. Your family don't even know me.'

'What family?'

'Your wife. I spoke to her on the phone the other day!'

'That wasn't my wife. It was Mrs Davies, my housekeeper.'

'Oh, I didn't know. How silly of me.'

'Marion, I thought you knew...'

She shook her head. 'No, I didn't.'

He shifted his position and moved closer. 'My wife ran off with an old flame many years ago.' He cleared his throat, 'This being a village, I thought everyone knew... Gerald, my son, would have been about five at the time. He now works at Heathrow. He's a loader and works with computers.'

She looked blank.

'Checking plane loading. He lives at Colnbrook. I see him now and again.' He paused and gently said, 'I'd like you to have it at my farmhouse. Plenty of parking... and Mrs Davies wouldn't mind. In fact she'd quite enjoy having a lot of people to cater for.'

'Well, I'd thought of getting up early and making sandwiches and savouries.'

'You'll have enough to do decorating the church without worrying about the catering,' Noel pointed out.

'Yes, but there may be quite a number...'

'Exactly. I'll call Mrs Davies tonight, and she will knock up hors d'oeuvres and other finger food. I'll provide the liquid refreshment, so you don't have to worry about a thing.' There was a pause, and as Marion was sorting out her jumbled thoughts, he said, 'If it makes you feel any better, I'll get Mrs Davies to call you early tomorrow morning.'

'Could it be before nine, please.'

'I think that could be arranged.' He smiled down at her.

'I don't know what to say.'

'If you are happy with that arrangement?'

'Yes. Thank you,' she whispered.

Noel moved closer and for a moment looked as though he would touch her, but changed his mind and turned towards the door. 'Well, that's settled, then; better make a move and catch Mrs Davies before she goes to bed.' He laughed, ushering her through the door, turned off the light and locked up.

Outside it was quite dark. Marion was grateful he had a torch to light the path. 'Oh, by the way, you'd better have this.' He handed her a smallish key. 'It opens the bell tower door. You can give it back to me tomorrow at the farmhouse. I'll be there to welcome any people who arrive before you do.'

'Aren't you coming to the service?'

'I'm afraid not, the farm calls.'

'Can I get into the church from there?'

'Yes, you just need to unbolt the inside door.'

'You think of everything!' She looked up at this amazing man and he smiled. They had reached his car parked on the pavement close to the 218 bus stop. Marion felt that she should say something. 'I'm sorry I didn't know about your situation.' She stood awkwardly on the footpath, waiting for him to unlock the car door. 'What would Mrs Davies think of me? I feel quite embarrassed.'

'Don't be – an easy enough mistake. She'll call you in the morning.' He hesitated. 'You'll be all right then? Don't worry. Goodnight.' And with that, he opened the car door.

'Night,' she replied and walked up to the corner before crossing the road. She was aware he had started the engine and put on the headlights, watching her arrive safely at Alice's pathway before driving off home.

Thoughtfully, she let herself into the house. Alice was sitting by the fire watching the television, sipping a glass of sherry. Marion didn't feel like having the same, so she divested herself of her coat in the hall and made for the kitchen cupboard where the Milo was kept. While waiting for the milk to warm she mulled over the recent conversation she had had with Noel. She liked the way he spoke, the timbre in his voice and the habit he had of running his hands through his hair. Highly sensitive herself, she marvelled that he should bother with her. Surely he couldn't feel anything towards her. She knew she was rather ordinary, and no spring chicken. And yet the way he looked at her sometimes made her heart flutter, something she couldn't remember experiencing very often in her life.

The milk was ready, and as she poured it into a mug with spoonfuls of Milo she remembered what she had heard whispered in the yew trees before she had left for Australia. '*I am with you. Do not fear.*'

With a spring in her step, she joined Alice by the fire. Seeing her sparkling eyes, her friend knew a change had taken place, something deep and personal.

'Evensong all right then?'

'Oh, yes,' Marion replied. 'The best yet.'

'Going to tell me about it?' Her eyes were raised in Marion's direction.

'Not tonight. Soon, perhaps,' she teased, before taking a mouthful of Milo, savouring the sweet taste as it slithered down her throat.

A weak May sun was shining through the stained-glass window on the north aisle depicting St Nicholas, the patron saint of children. Specks of dust bounced about within the beam of light as Marion knelt on a dust sheet surrounded by flowers and foliage. Most of the inhabitants of Laleham were having their breakfast, whereas she was completely absorbed in decorating the church for Leonard's Memorial Service.

Gently sorting the apple blossom from the mass surrounding her, she sent up an arrow prayer to God, thanking him for sending Noel Barker her way. She had discovered armfuls of bluebells and lily of the valley resting in the kitchen sink to the right of her, as she entered the bell tower. She had filled up various jam jars with water and carefully placed them behind the rood screen and the pulpit, wondering how Noel could know that she would use only blue and white flowers. Picking up the apple blossom with some ferns and ceanothus, she delicately placed them to cover the lower part of the rood screen. Then, she entwined some yew branches around the pulpit before placing the lilies in the centre. Next, she made up small posies of grape hyacinths with small irises, which she placed around the inside of the font. Finally, on either side of the altar rails, she arranged the flowers that Noel had provided with some maidenhair fern. Standing back, she was pleased with the result. The bluebells, lily of the valley and ferns gave the impression that they were growing together out in the wild.

Reluctant to leave this haven, she gathered up the remnants within the dust sheet, went outside and shook it under a yew tree, then folded it neatly away in the cupboard under the sink.

Satisfied all was as she'd like it, she left the church, carefully locking the door before returning to Alice's house to dress for the service. She tried to keep at bay her imaginings of what Noel's reception room was like, hoping above all else she could hold her own among the expected gathering.

Marion surveyed herself in front of a long mirror on the landing and was pleased with what she saw. She had pinned a cameo brooch onto her lapel, one which Leonard had given her before they were married. As she did up the buttons on her jacket she hoped Leonard's friends had seen the notice in the paper. She tucked a lace handkerchief in the jacket pocket, smoothed down the knee-length skirt, recalling her foray into Staines to carry out some 'retail therapy'. She was thankful that the gentle heather hues of her outfit had caught her eye, and was now pleasantly surprised at its snug fit. The shoes and handbag were of a darker hue, the former a soft leather with a dainty 'Louis' heel. A mulberry rinse brightened her hair, which was now down to her collar and kicked out at the ends, giving the impression she was ten years younger than her fifty-six years. She supposed she was one of the lucky ones to be the same size ten now as she had always been. Weight was not her problem; nervousness was, though, and that she was dealing with as best she knew how.

Adjusting a patterned silk scarf of various purple shades, she descended the stairs, took a last glance in the hall mirror, touched up her lipstick and let herself out of Alice's front door.

Someone was playing 'The Lord's My Shepherd' on the bells to the tune 'Crimmond'. Marion stood still, amazed how the sound drowned out the traffic hurtling around the corner. Glancing up at the tower, she could see by the clock there would be at least another five minutes of playing, and wished Leonard could hear it. Her heart lurched at his memory. 'This is for you, Len,' she murmured. 'I've brought you home.'

Waiting for the road to clear, she crossed over into the churchyard and stood for a few moments listening to the bells before entering the porch. The door was wide open and she was relieved to see a crowded church. Suddenly she was being ushered towards the front rows, left empty for family, something she hadn't anticipated. She demurred and, spying a seat vacant on the right aisle three rows back, sat down. No way could she sit in front of everyone all on her own.

Marion composed herself and said words of greeting to the gentleman on her right. The bells stopped. The organist played Pachelbel's Canon in D Major softly as the Reverend Peter Guinness took his place on the chancel step.

'We welcome you all to the celebration of the life of Leonard Charles Lee.' Nodding in Marion's direction, his eyebrows raised in understanding, a fleeting smile giving her encouragement. 'Shall we pray. Dear Lord…'

The service washed over Marion like a balm. The congregation joined the choir singing 'Amazing Grace', chosen especially, as she was sure very few of those present attended church on a regular basis.

'Leonard has been sorely missed since he moved to Tasmania, but we are pleased to see Marion back again with us, even though it is under such circumstances.'

The eulogies were shared between Desmond White, now Manager of The Daily Office Cleaning, and an acting church server, Matthew Carghill, the former speech invoking several smiles. And then, to Marion's surprise, a young chorister was introduced.

'And now my friends, there is a young man here, Mark Bartlett, who rather looked up to Leonard as his mentor. Not only does he sing, but I gather is a budding campanologist! He would like to show his appreciation for all the time Leonard gave him and his friends. No doubt those of you who live in the village have heard their practice every Wednesday evening!'

Marion could just see the youngster standing near the organist. Her spirits soared as she listened to the Benediction, 'God be in my head'. Mark's voice rang out as only a young boy's can, touching the souls of all present. People murmured, 'How beautiful,' as they gazed at the flowers or closed their eyes.

At the end there were a few coughs, and the rustle of the service sheet being handled as the vicar returned to the chancel steps. 'My friends, we have with us another humble musician, who would rather stay anonymous; nevertheless, he would like to play the first song he learnt on the violin – encouraged again by Leonard.'

From behind the rood screen came the strains of 'The Londonderry Air'. It was too much for some, tears flowed and handkerchiefs were in evidence. Moved by the haunting melody, Marion stared at the lilies around the pulpit for fear of breaking down. Transported back in time, she could hear Leonard's voice singing at the firm's Christmas functions. Beautifully played, the emotive melody gave rise again to voices singing quietly those well-remembered words to 'Danny Boy'. A hush fell. It was as though no one dared to breathe in case the spell was broken.

Quietly, the Reverend Peter Guinness stood up from his seat in the choir stalls and moved towards the chancel steps. When he spoke, his voice was a little shaky. 'We will now sing our final hymn, which you will find on the back of the Service Sheet. But before we do,' he smiled, 'I would like to invite anyone who wishes to join Marion and myself along to the short burial of ashes ceremony, which will take place over in the Rose Garden.' He paused. 'For those of you wishing to go straight to Home Farm, Noel Barker informs me you will be most welcome. Please ask for directions if you are unsure as to the location. I am informed by Noel that everyone is most welcome.' Raising his right arm, he then intoned, 'And may the Peace of God be with us all, now and forever more.'

'Amen,' resounded.

'Let us now raise our voices with that well-known hymn, "Abide with Me".'

It was during the singing of the line, 'Shine through the gloom and point me to the skies', that a fair-haired woman dressed in a dark suit silently moved from her place beneath the stained-glass window and left the church. No one seemed to notice except the Reverend Guinness, as he was facing in her direction; several days later he remembered how pale and forlorn she looked in contrast with Marion. There was no accounting for grief; some hid it well, while others just went to pieces. Leading Marion outside towards the Rose Garden, he was amazed at her fortitude. She was holding up well, better than he expected.

Bells wounded the air, ringing out with 'Rock of Ages' as Marion scattered Leonard's ashes. Shortly after, she and the Reverend Guinness entered Noel Barker's farmhouse. She stood for a moment in the hallway, not sure of which way to go. A voice called out from a room on her left, 'There's a loo upstairs, first right...'

Suddenly, a young woman burst out of the room, almost colliding with the vicar. 'Excuse me!' she exclaimed, and pushing past ran up the stairs.

Peter Guinness cleared his throat while watching her disappear, then balanced his coat on top of others already covering the hallstand. Two more people entered the front door, divesting themselves of their coats, looking for a suitable hook. As none could be seen, they added theirs to the stand that was already precariously overladen.

'Shall we?' Peter Guinness pushed open the same door from which the young woman had appeared, gesturing for Marion to pass through first.

'Beautiful service, Mrs Lee, knew your husband – business wise,' murmured a portly man, now revealing a shiny suit that had seen better days.

They stood in an awkward gaggle within the doorway until

Mrs Davies looked across from where she was collecting glasses. 'Mrs Lee, do come in, and Reverend too.' She bustled across the enormous reception room. 'Come closer to the fire. Now, what can I get you, Mrs Lee?' she whispered.

'Marion, please!' She estimated there were about forty people engaged in various conversations around the room as she perched on the arm of a green leather chair, its double similarly placed opposite an enormous log fire. Various people were warming their toes, sitting on a couch of matching leather between the two. A large, jolly-faced man thrust a glass of sweet sherry into her hand, waving a plate of savouries past her. 'Get this down you, Marion!'

She helped herself to a stuffed egg with what looked like red caviar on top of salad cream. Abashed, she couldn't recall the man's name, so she nodded a thank you.

'Ah, I see you are taken care of… Good.' Mrs Davies smiled. 'Be back in a jiffy.'

She disappeared through the throng of people. Feeling hungry, Marion helped herself to various finger food on offer, amazed at the variety Mrs Davies had rustled up in so short a time. Worried by her own lack of social repartee, Marion steered quickly away from the more loquacious, and in doing so she noticed a large bay window seat covered in green velvet, several small antique-looking tables scattered about and various platters of food arranged along a sideboard. Wall bracket lights lit up numerous paintings and the parquetry floor was of a honey colour. As the guests shifted around she was aware of priceless artefacts, knick-knacks and delicate china. Beginning to feel she had stepped into an Aladdin's cave, and wondering if Noel's offer was such a good idea, her glance happened on the far end of the room, where several men had congregated. As they moved apart she saw a gas fire with a mantelpiece and an exquisite mirror above. There was a chaise longue and two high-backed armchairs covered in a floral print, in front of which was a large Indian rug. At the same moment as she looked towards the mirror, one of the men also looked up. It was Noel, who, on seeing Marion, excused himself. She felt as though her heart missed a beat, and that he knew exactly what she was thinking.

'I'm so sorry, I didn't see you arrive,' he told her.

'There's quite a crush. I didn't expect that. So many… but I'm glad they came.' She attempted a smile. 'For Len's sake, I mean.'

'Marion, darling!' a woman gushed. A heavily made-up face loomed into view. 'How ghastly for you! Never mind, now you are home again with friends.' She patted Marion's shoulder absently and moved on, her presence insinuating herself between the table of food and the Reverend Guinness.

'Who was that?' asked Noel.

'Rita Mollock. One of Len's many acquaintances.' Marion stopped abruptly. 'Chris Mollock owns a chain of lingerie stores. We used to meet as a foursome. I hated it, but it was all good for the business. He's over there.' She nodded towards a tall, white-haired gentleman dressed in an expensive dark grey suit, holding forth between two youngish women in the bay window. 'I think I'm going to cry.'

Noel steered her towards a quiet corner. 'Wait here and I'll get you a plate of food. Top-up?'

She nodded and sat down, fumbling for a handkerchief. The Reverend Guinness extricated himself from Rita Mollock and sat down next to her.

'I'm sorry you were cornered by Rita Mollock,' she said, her eyes swimming in tears, looking down at the twisted handkerchief on her lap.

'Think nothing of it, Marion.' Leaning forward with his elbows on his knees he surveyed the motley group of people, then studied his shoes. To an onlooker they could have been planning a conspiracy. 'I'm used to her ilk.'

'You're smiling.'

'I'm just surprised Leonard was…'

'Oh, I see. Well, we weren't exactly friends. It's just that Chris was Len's first client, and somehow we ended up having dinner once a month on a regular basis.' She knew it sounded pathetic, but to be fair to Leonard, she had never voiced her dislike of Rita, and so pretended she enjoyed those evenings, when in fact she secretly felt completely out of her depth.

Someone murmured, 'Beautiful service, Marion.' Condolences passed.

'If you need anything, do ring.'

'Look after yourself.'

'Love the house.'

'It isn't mine. It's Noel's.'

'Oh, I'm so sorry. Silly of me, of course it isn't yours.' Mildly embarrassed, a youngish man, obviously having had too much sherry, muttered something about, 'I forgot your move to the Antipodes,' and hurried away, nearly colliding with Noel, who was carrying a tray of canapés, sandwiches and coffees.

'You'll join us, Reverend?' Handing him a glass tumbler, encased in filigree silver, Noel said, 'Sugar? Milk?'

'No, thank you. Just how I like it.'

Noel handed Marion a sherry and poured milk into his own coffee, then indicated for her to help herself from the tray, offering the milk and sugar.

'I can't remember when I've felt so hungry,' she said, attempting a smile and trying to look at the plate of sandwiches rather than at Noel's kindly face.

Seeing that people were taking their leave and Marion was in good hands, Noel stood up. 'I'd best see off those already departing. Be back shortly.'

For a while Marion and Peter Guinness ate and drank in silence, watching as the room divested of its assembly, like a classroom suddenly denuded of its pupils.

'Well, I must be going too.' Peter wiped his mouth with a serviette. 'I hope all went to your satisfaction, Marion?' He rose awkwardly, bumping into the table, rattling the china. To him, Marion looked exhausted, worried about something.

He did so hate having to deal with emotional women. Meanwhile, she was thinking, How did it come to this, sitting in Noel's sumptuous living room, when she herself had no home as yet? A house in Tasmania not sold, a daughter in Queensland, a suspicion that Leonard was not the person she'd thought him to be, and that if she hadn't come home to Laleham she would never have known.

'He couldn't have asked for anything better,' she replied in a trembling voice.

Breathing a sigh of relief, he saw Noel approaching. 'My goodness,' he exclaimed, 'is that the time!'

'Everyone seemed to think I knew who the violinist was, but I'm afraid to say I didn't.' Noel shrugged. 'Why they thought I should know, I can't imagine. I wasn't even there. Said they'd never heard it played so hauntingly. I said to ask you, Vicar.'

'Well, there you have me, Noel. Marion?'

'I—' She coughed. 'No, I didn't know, but they were right. It was beautiful.'

'My secretary said she received a phone call late yesterday afternoon. She passed the message to me this morning, saying he wouldn't give a name. I said it was highly irregular, but he was brilliant, as it turned out...' He beamed at them both. 'Now I really must be going.'

And with that he followed Noel into the hall, wondering if his coat, a fine Harris tweed, was still on the hallstand. As it was, someone had hung it over the banisters while searching for their own.

Marion crossed to the settee by the log fire, watching the flames, pondering on the morning's events. Presently Noel returned, having discarded his tie and rolled up his shirtsleeves. He didn't say anything, just stretched out his legs towards the fire, sipping a whisky. Grateful for his silence, Marion nibbled on a tasty celery boat, while listening to Mrs Davies clearing up behind them, transfixed by the sparks of the fire. Eventually she said, 'Your flowers were beautiful.'

'Think nothing of it. I grow them.'

'Len couldn't have had a better send-off.' She smiled, tears glistening her eyes.

Noel felt something was not quite right. It wasn't grief, more like an unreachable sadness. At a loss as to what to say or do, he stood up and saw the pain, some memory in which she seemed to be engulfed. Holding out his hand, he grasped hers and said gently, 'Come with me.'

They walked out of the room and down the corridor to the kitchen and through into the scullery. 'There is something I want to show you. I hope you like animals?'

'Animals? Oh, oh I see...' She knelt down to a basket on the floor where three Shetland sheepdog puppies were scrambling about, their mother lying down, looking up at the intrusion.

'Will she let me touch them?'

'Yes, but don't move quickly.'

Marion watched for a while, then reached out with her hand open towards the nearest one, who staggered across and sniffed her hand, whereupon she stroked its back with a finger, then lifted the puppy up towards her face. 'Is it a she or a he?'

'Have a look!' he said laughingly. 'I've called her "Intrepid".'

'Why?'

'Because she is the bravest; not afraid to explore. Perhaps when you are settled you'd like to have her.'

'Oh, I couldn't! I've never reared a dog, but she is rather beautiful.' She put Intrepid down with the others and immediately the puppy ran back to Marion.

'See, she knows where she wants to be,' said Noel.

There was a movement in the doorway. 'I'll be off now, Mr Barker.' A flushed Mrs Davies popped her head around the door.

'Excuse me a moment,' murmured Noel.

Left alone, Marion found herself talking to the proud mother of the puppies, and gradually all her turmoil drifted away. The bitch got up from the basket, nudging her offspring and then, shaking her coat, she wandered over to Marion who was looking out of the window across the backyard towards swathes of bluebells beyond two greenhouses. She stroked the dog's head and was rewarded with a lick, and suddenly her perceived problems and what she knew she had to face seemed only as big a she liked to make them. There was nothing unusual about unfaithful spouses.

But her Len? No, she wouldn't go there. The thought did cross her mind that if she hadn't returned to Laleham she'd never have known.

The door opened and Noel remarked, 'I see you've made a friend. Dorcas is very choosy.' At the sound of her master's voice, Dorcas went back again to her pups. Marion gazed at the scene while Noel looked in her direction, pleased to see that the distraction had apparently made her sadness disappear. 'Stay as long a you want,' he added.

'I must be going, Noel, but thank you for everything. Please thank Mrs Davies – she did a much better job than I would have done.'

'I'll run you home… I mean to Alice's.'

'If it's all the same to you, I'm quite happy to walk,' she replied, smiling.

They stood on Noel's front doorstep, emotions masked, discussing the weather, the Memorial Service, which Noel didn't attend, the guests, and if Marion needed a car. Finally, Noel watched Marion's trim figure retreating along his driveway, having secured a promise that if she needed a second opinion on rising damp, faulty foundations, and dubious plumbing on any house she was keen to purchase, she would call him. He closed the door softly, surmising now that Leonard had been laid to rest, Marion could begin to think about her future… *their* future, if he didn't rush things.

Marion listened to her new shoes tap-tapping along the pavement, hoping they wouldn't pinch on the walk back to Alice's, consoling herself that it was a good idea to wear them in. As she walked along she glanced at the cottage gardens on her left, with their spring flowers and peeping apple blossom. She passed what used to be her primary school, now turned into offices. Across the road still stood the Village Hall and the 224 bus stop, which was usually crowded early in the morning with commuters as the bus took them straight to Staines Station to catch the 8.15 to Waterloo. Memories tumbled through her mind as she grappled with her present circumstances, so she concentrated placing one foot after another, hardly registering the Rectory, with its iron gates and high brick wall, above which two enormous yew trees towered.

A car whistled past, and as she approached the corner of the Staines Road, two young men appeared, looking her up and down before entering the Feathers for their lunchtime beers. A motorbike hurtled around the corner, its rider pulling up beside Marion. Removing his helmet, he revealed greasy, shoulder-length blonde hair. He leered at her as he leant on the door, before stomping inside the pub. Disconcerted, she hurried across Staines Road. All Saints', now silent, stood on her left. It was as if everything that had taken place earlier in the morning had never happened. Traffic flowed around the Memorial, as she let herself into the house. The hallway seemed impersonal, the staircase adding to her numbness.

Chaotic thoughts enveloped her as she changed into slacks, polo-neck sweater and flat shoes, pulling them out of the wardrobe and drawers at random. 'Pooh Corner' felt stifling, and knowing Alice wouldn't be back from work for several hours, she collected her anorak from the hallstand and left the house, careful not to look up at her previous home as she passed by towards the river. One day she would be able to look at it dispassionately, but not today. I have enough to deal with… one step at a time, she reminded herself.

The air was still crisp, with just the hint of a breeze, the watery sun bouncing off the river as it rippled by. The River Thames was predictable, and that was how she liked it. She smiled to herself, remembering Leonard's words that the River Derwent in Tasmania was similar. But it was nothing like it, with its ferocious winds and small sandy beaches strewn with enormous boulders and treacherous waters. Here she felt safe, sad but safe. Gradually her mind calmed down as she listened to her shoes crunching on the familiar gravel, watching the gentle flow of the river.

Presently she found herself sitting on the seat she and Leonard had occupied on the Sunday just before they left for Tasmania. No bells rang out to wound the air. She was alone, and yet that wasn't strictly true. With a jolt she realised there were several people who cared what happened to her: Alice, Noel, various parishioners, and, if you counted words spoken at that morning's service, she was surrounded by kind, well-meaning souls. And yet there was this feeling within her, a hollow that had never been fulfilled, if she was to be completely honest. It was one that she hadn't acknowledged before, because deep down she hadn't expected anything better. What with her domineering mother ruining any self-expression, and a father showing little or no interest in her, only in his next drink, it wasn't surprising; and here she was in her fifties, still sorting herself out. She tried to get some perspective on her situation, and came to the conclusion that by trying to fit in with other people's dreams and desires, she had stifled her own.

Her thoughts turned inevitably to Leonard and the baby boy she had lost all those years ago. Ruefully, she realised that it was Leonard's deception that was gnawing at her heart. If what she suspected to be true was fact, she would have to deal with it, and the sooner the better. Until she did so, she would never be completely at peace, and would have trouble reconciling herself to an action that she presumed had taken place some eighteen years ago. Anything more was unimaginable; besides which she might need the proceeds from the sale of Number Six, Ferry Lane, her own pecuniary interests being rather in the balance at the moment. However unpleasant, she would have to visit very soon and confront the occupiers face to face. Whether she needed to sell the property or use it for investment income, gleaning a sizeable rent was neither here nor there. The present arrangements could not continue indefinitely.

Having come to a decision, she felt a load lifted from her shoulders. What she would tell Anna was the next worry, but for the moment she would shelve referring to it in her letters. Tomorrow was going to be a turning point. She was to inspect two houses at the Shepperton edge of the village. Staring out at the river, she watched two swans gliding along, their wings half raised as if in battle to where it appeared several ducks were congregating. She smiled as the swans made short shrift of the interlopers on their patch. Like me, she thought; I only hope I handle the situation with the same aplomb.

If she lived close to public transport she wouldn't need a car. If she had sold the house and car in Tadbury she wouldn't have to worry about the confrontation in Ferry Lane or about transport, although she could see the sense of not doing so immediately. She wasn't sure which business to sell in Staines, but then maybe she didn't need to sell just yet; again, it all depended on what she would do with Number Six, Ferry Lane.

Marion stood up and continued walking towards Penton Hook Lock. A family of coots were foraging in the bulrushes as she approached Beech Tree Lane.

She could see that the lane abutted on to Staines Road at its furthest end, with only a handful of low-lying houses tucked behind hedges of hawthorn. She knew the one facing her on the river frontage was owned by a spinster in her eighties, now living in a nursing home in Chertsey. Miss Amelia Jones had been a stalwart of All Saints', Laleham, and as far as she knew, a distant niece was looking after the property. But by the look of it, the house was in need of some repairs and new paintwork; the garden was much neglected and choked with bindweed. What an ideal spot! It was a disgrace to let a property get into that state. She passed two other bungalows before reaching the end. Then, looking to her left, saw a bus stop not fifty yards from the corner.

Retracing her steps, she glanced to the other side of the lane, where from the back of a house, a conservatory opened on to a stone patio, with steps leading down to a lawn, surrounded by rose beds. Along one side was a dell, and a pathway led to a thatched summer house. She studied it for a while, then walked around to the front, where a bay window looked across the river, wistfully wishing she'd be able to afford it – that's if it ever came on the market. Marion decided to mention to the estate agent the next day her interest in the run-down house; maybe it was for sale. This was where she'd like to live – close to the village but far enough away in peaceful surroundings, preferably with a river frontage.

By the time she had returned to Blacksmiths' Lane, her spirits had lifted. She would have a great deal to talk about with Alice that evening. There was a spring in her step and a confidence in her own ability to make decisions, at least for the moment. As she let herself in, she could hardly wait for Alice's return. Today had been a turning point, and at last she felt more in control of her life. The feeling of dread had finally dissipated. She felt optimistic; and then laughed at herself, for she couldn't remember when she last felt so good. And there on the doormat was a letter at last from Anna.

It was twilight a few days later, and still quite cool as Marion walked through the village towards Ferry Lane. Clouds were forming and a crisp breeze had sprung up blowing litter along the gutters. Traffic was zooming around the churchyard, presumably commuters on their way home from work heading towards Staines and beyond. She thrust her hands into her anorak pockets for warmth and, with head bent, she negotiated the edge of the pavement before crossing over Vicarage Lane, musing over the five houses shown to her by Patricia Clerk of Clerk and Gamble Estate Agents. Two houses had been on the busy Staines Road; one was semi-detached, and another, although right in the middle of the village, had a lethal staircase. They were totally unsuitable. The remaining house had a well-kept garden, large lounge, well-appointed kitchen and three bedrooms. However, it was situated opposite an army depot shielded by a row of fir trees that ran the length of the road, added to which there wasn't any public transport. She had stood in front of the house looking down the road from left to right. In the distance was the Ford Bridge, Kingston Road, and five miles to the nearest shops. In the opposite direction was Laleham.

She could see herself as a youngster riding her bicycle along the road to the Welsh Girls' School; no matter which direction she was going the wind always seemed to be against her. One dark afternoon coming home there was a storm, with lightning and thunder. She remembered being terrified, praying hard as the wind and rain lashed at her legs as she pedalled furiously. Her green velour hat was saturated, but at least it hadn't blown off, as it was secured with elastic under her chin. She had been so relieved to see Barker's Farm up front with a street light on outside that she had cried with relief. After that episode she wore a green beret, not recognised as correct uniform!

How strange that she now knew the owner of the farm, and had actually been inside all these years later! Finding a house was going to be much harder than she imagined. At this rate she would have to be more specific with the criteria.

Location wasn't enough to go by; ambience was just as important. What she wanted was a house in Beech Tree Lane. Maybe she should try another agent, or even do some door-knocking. As this thought occurred to her, she passed the Three Shoes and could hear and see the patrons through the dimly lit windows. She turned the corner as the church clock struck six. Nearing Lucy Driver's house, she forced herself to concentrate on the moment at hand. What to say when the door was opened? How did she begin? Was it wise to stick strictly to the economics and keep away from the emotions? When it all boiled down to it, she was going to sell Number Six, and the occupants would have to make other arrangements. She could feel her stomach churning at the prospect of an unpleasant situation. Then there was the near certainty of Michael Driver being Len's son. The pain of her husband's betrayal was still niggling at her. She said quietly, 'Oh God, help me handle this with compassion, I don't feel very charitable.'

As she rounded the corner, her thoughts tumbled around incoherently. She could see the half-dozen houses on her left and horse chestnut trees flanking the right side leading to Laleham Park, behind which a field led down to the river with two ponies over in the far corner. An eerie gloom descended as a tabby cat suddenly appeared, wrapping itself around her legs, nearly tripping her up. 'What the—?' she exclaimed, and watched it saunter away, jumping onto a wooden fence post close by and blinking at her.

Idly she stroked its head and thought of joining a t'ai chi or yoga class. She almost laughed to think how amazed Anna would be if she knew. She, Marion, meditating – not her thing at all! Anna had written that they had found an apartment not five minutes away from King's College in Burleigh. Nigel was ecstatic, enjoying his job, and she spent most of her days on the beach. It seemed the sun shone every day.

A street lamp came on as an old Metro drove past, pausing at the rusted gate of Number Six. A woman got out dressed in a raincoat, pulling at the gate to open it. She drove in and parked on the driveway, then returned to the gate.

She looked fortyish with blonde hair tied back at the nape of her neck, fairly tall and thin. Marion observed her from the shadows, surprised at the differences between them. It seemed the gate was too heavy for her, and she struggled to close it, scraping on the driveway, teetering on delicate high-heeled shoes. Marion gave her a minute or so before walking up the broken pathway to the front door. The doorbell didn't work and the knocker was broken. Lights came on. She could hear a kettle being filled, the chink of china. She rapped clearly on the glass pane beside the door.

The house was cold. A recently lit gas fire hardly delivered any warmth in the lounge where they stood. Lucy Driver had taken off her coat and was wearing a bright pink jumper, her breasts straining at the wool, emanating hostility. Marion refused to be intimidated, secretly disgusted by the short, tight navy skirt straining over Lucy's hips.

'…so you see,' she pressed on, 'I have no alternative but to sell this house. I'm very sorry, but there it is. This situation can't continue.'

'But where am I expected to go? I can't afford to rent in this area. This house has suited us fine.'

'You surely didn't expect this situation to go on indefinitely?'

'Len promised me I would be taken care of.' She added, as an afterthought, 'And, of course, Michael.' Red spots suffused Lucy's cheeks as her anger welled up.

Marion stood still, staring at the grubby carpet, its hues long ago faded, before replying. 'As far as I can see and hear, Michael is doing fine. I think my husband, under the circumstances, shouldered his share of the responsibility as best he knew how. However, whatever arrangements you thought you had with… Len… are terminated as of now. There was nothing in his will to the contrary.'

'No provision for Michael?'

'No. I'm sorry.' Marion's eyes rested on a formation of three ducks above the gas fire.

'He promised me we'd be together one day. He was going to get a divorce, leave you…' The air was thick with hate.

'I thought by coming to see you, rather than you being suddenly contacted by my solicitor, by mail, would make things easier. It would give you time. I need hardly tell you what a shock it was for me. I had no idea… eighteen years…'

'So, he pissed off to Australia without a word,' Lucy hissed, hands on hips, her pelvis thrust forward.

The front door banged and into the lounge walked Michael.

'Mum, what's going on? The kettle is boiling away. Oh, hello – I know you, don't I?'

Lucy pushed past him, crossing the hallway into the kitchen.

Reeling from shock, Marion hardly heard him. He seemed to

fill the room with his presence, smiling quizzically at her. 'I…
er…' She swallowed. He waited. 'I came to…' She couldn't go on.
'To thank you for playing so beautifully at my husband's
Memorial Service. It was you, wasn't it?'

'Oh, that.' He shrugged. 'You're all right since your fall?'

She smiled, looking up at the all too familiar eyes. 'I'm afraid
your mother's upset and… I seem to be the cause of it.'

'Oh?' He frowned, putting down his violin case.

Time seemed to stop still as Marion focused her eyes on the
initials 'L. L.' embossed on the side. Sorrow was reflected as she
looked up at Michael then back at the case. 'I'd better go; you
have things to talk over with your mother.'

She turned, looking back at him as he followed her to the
front door. 'Keep in touch if you like. It's what Len would have
wanted. I'm at Yew Cottage, opposite the church, until I find
somewhere.' She fumbled with the lock. The words 'I can see
myself out' were cut off as the door closed behind her.

Michael leant against the banister, staring at the closed front
door. Suddenly everything clicked into place. All his suspicions
over the years had been finally confirmed. What a fool he'd been
to believe his mother's lies! 'Dead from a car accident.' And all the
time, Uncle Len… so trusting. He'd adored him. His mentor. He
grabbed the violin case and entered the back room, slamming the
door.

~X~

Expecting Him, my door was open wide:
Then I looked round
If any lack of service might be found,
And saw Him at my side:
How entered, **by what secret stair**
I know not, knowing only He was there.

T E Brown[*]

'**I**s it what you want?'

'Oh, yes. I can't believe it. After looking so long and getting nowhere. All this…' Marion indicated to Alice the beautiful lounge where they stood, looking through a bay window at the River Thames flowing swiftly past, flanked by the grassy bank, not a stone's throw from where they were.

'Come, I'll show you round.' The furnished house was on the corner of Beech Tree Lane, situated on the opposite side from the dilapidated house belonging to Miss Jones. Two weeks had gone by since Marion had called on Lucy Driver and endured the painful conversation which had followed. Wheels had been put in motion for the sale of Number Six, Ferry Lane, and Marion was thankful she wouldn't have to deal with Lucy face to face again. The experience had shattered her confidence, giving rise to a bout of insomnia that caused Alice some concern, suggesting she visit a doctor. And, as Alice was not party to what had transpired, and had no idea that Leonard Lee was Michael Driver's father, she was secretly relieved that Marion would be moving out sooner rather

---

[*] From Rita Snowden's *While the Candle Burns*, Epworth Press, 1942.

than later. There had been only one other house Marion had considered, between Vicarage and Ferry Lane with river frontage; however, it was not to Marion's liking, and exorbitantly expensive. The style had not appealed, among other points, leaving Patricia Clerk, the agent, exasperated and convinced this particular buyer was not going to be a pushover. She could forget a quick sale.

Having nothing else to offer and not wanting to lose a buyer, Patricia Clerk rang Marion on a wild chance that she might be interested in renting a property just listed, with the faint possibility to buy at a future date. Yes, the house was in Laleham, and yes, it was rather special, with river frontage. The following day as Marion sat in Patricia's uncomfortable red sports car, its soft roof not fitting properly and letting in a draught, she had discussed the rent and filled her in with the owner's plans. Finding it hard to hear everything Patricia was saying, Marion kept her eyes on her face as the little car roared down the road, not noticing where she was going, only to be somewhat shocked when Patricia pulled into the driveway of River's End, Beech Tree Lane.

'The house,' she explained as Marion inelegantly pulled herself out of the car, 'is owned by a Mr Philip Sloane, who has taken up a position in Canada for two years.' Patricia looked across the roof of the car at Marion's shocked expression as she reached inside the back seat for her briefcase. 'Are you all right?'

She nodded. 'It's just that this is exactly the spot, the place…' Her voice trailed off as her eyes roamed from house to garden and back again, and for the first time she smiled.

Thank God, thought Patricia. The rest was easy, as Marion enthused about the attic bedrooms with their sloping ceilings. The old-fashioned kitchen had a large wooden table, now bleached almost white with years of scrubbing. There was an inglenook fireplace and a conservatory glowing in the morning sunshine. Within twenty-four hours, Patricia had to open up the house again – Marion was insistent Alice had to see River's End.

Now, as Marion showed her friend the quaint cupboard under the stairs, the cloakroom off the hall and a gazebo at the bottom of the garden, Alice remarked, 'I suppose he wants a fortune.' They were sitting on a low brick wall. Three wide steps led down to the lawn bordered by spring bulbs. Creepers of honeysuckle hung over the back fence, and strands of clematis, still in bud, climbed up the gazebo.

'Maybe,' Marion replied, smiling. She gazed at an apple tree beginning to blossom, wondering if she would be able to afford the house. 'It gives me time to organise my finances. In the meantime I can afford the rent.' Looking to her left, she squinted at a flowering cherry with its delicately curved branches covered in a mass of double white blossoms tinged with pink. 'I should have brought my sunglasses.'

'Sunglasses?'

'Yes. It was the first thing I needed in Tasmania. Looks like I ought to carry them all the time. Look at that, Alice!' She waved her hand. 'A ceanothus: it's beautiful!'

Twisted branches were overhanging the driveway above Patricia Clerk's sports car, with pale clouds of delicate blue puffs hanging along the boughs.

'Looks quite old – the trunk, I mean, all gnarled and grey.'

'Don't you like it?'

'Not much. But I can see you do.'

'Well, what do you think?'

'I think it is very you,' said Alice generously, amazed at the transformation in Marion. Now full of excitement and brimming over with life, she could hardly believe this was the same person. She stood up and turned to see Patricia Clerk coming towards them from the conservatory.

'Have you seen enough, Mrs Lee? If so, I'll lock up. Meet you at the car.'

'I love it!' She beamed at Alice. 'Can you put up with me for another fortnight?' They strolled towards the driveway, exchanging light banter. 'Because that's the earliest I can move in here.'

'Marion, as I said before, I think it is very you, but don't you think you should get it checked out first. You know – rising damp, plumbing, electrics…?'

'I didn't see any signs of rising damp.'

'There probably isn't any, but to be on the safe side. I mean, God knows what it's worth. You might get a nasty shock if there is something structurally wrong.'

'Mmm… I'm more worried that Philip Sloane might change his mind.'

Patricia was unlocking her car as they approached. Marion said, 'If you don't mind, and it's not too much of a nuisance, I'd like to show a friend of mine through River's End before signing on the dotted line. He knows about houses, and I must confess I used to leave all that sort of thing to my husband.'

Irritated by this turn of events, Patricia threw her briefcase into the car. 'You know it's a six-month rental, Mrs Lee, I hardly think…'

'Yes. But you did say there's an option to buy.'

'Mr Sloane was fairly sure that would be the case, but in the event his wife doesn't like Canada, he would return to England. Whether he would move back in or sell would be up to him; however, he will be in contact. I can always put your offer to him at a later date…'

'I suppose there is no hope he would settle earlier?'

'Not that I know of. I suppose I could make inquiries. Don't forget, it's fully furnished. How soon can this friend of yours view the property? Because I have other clients who would rent it tomorrow,' she said abruptly.

'Within two days… at the latest, the day after.'

'Call me at the office, then, and we'll go from there. I can't guarantee to hold the property for longer than this week. Look, I must dash.' And with a wave, Patricia reversed down the driveway and roared up the lane.

'Home and a glass of wine, I think,' said Alice.

'Oh, Alice, it's a bit early in the day.'

'Nonsense! I can feel it in my bones. River's End belongs to you – you have every reason to celebrate. If you don't mind my saying, I didn't care much for Miss Patricia Clerk.'

'Nor I. Do you suppose Noel will think it an awful cheek if I ask him to check the house over?'

'Course not.' They ambled back along the towpath, Marion starting to worry.

'I couldn't bear to move in, and then find I had to move out!'

While Marion made her call to Noel, Alice had her doubts about how well her call might be received. She had seen the two together on various occasions. If it wasn't clear to Marion what Noel's interest was, it certainly was to her. Still, it was none of her business, and as Marion hadn't confided in her, she wasn't about to mention her observations. Privately, she was happy that at last she would be able to return to her normal pattern of living as soon as Marion moved out.

'…and then there is my china and linen.'

Alice realised she hadn't been listening. 'Your furniture?'

'Oh, I sold most of it. Kept the paintings, though; they are in storage here. I shall have to send for all household effects. But, don't you see, with a house fully furnished it won't matter when it arrives! What does concern me is the rental part of the contract. I just want to settle down, make it my own. Those curtains would need changing, and some of the carpets aren't what I would choose. I prefer fitted ones, and then I know just what kind of furniture I would like in the conservatory.'

'Oh, I see,' Alice said lamely.

'And then there is the dog.'

'*Dog?*'

'Didn't I tell you? Noel has a sheepdog who had these gorgeous puppies, and one of them I just fell in love with.'

'Oh… Will you be allowed a dog, in a rental?'

'I don't know.'

'I didn't think you liked animals.'

'Well, I don't dislike them. I've never had a pet,' Marion said wistfully.

'Really? I thought all children had pets. I did: a rabbit, and it…'

'Died,' Marion said. 'That is why my parents wouldn't let me have a dog, a cat or even a goldfish.'

They passed Marion's previous home deep in discussion about animals before she was aware of doing so. Alice drew a sigh of relief as Marion displayed no qualms. She hadn't even bothered to look up.

'Feather your oars!' the coxswain's voice called from the stern of the skiff. Eight oarsmen acted as one, the boat gliding to a halt in front of Burway Rowing Club. Dandelions mingled with bindweed along the riverbanks; roses and forget-me-nots dotted gardens rolling down towards the River Thames. Young lovers ambled arm in arm along the towpath as the river sparkled under bright sunshine. It was one of those magic Saturday evenings in late June where everyone smiled. 'This year we have a summer. No rain at Wimbledon... can't remember when we last experienced such a phenomenon!' was remarked, as winter clothes were discarded and bare limbs soaked up the sunshine. Marion relished every day, not quite believing her luck. Each morning she would wake up savouring the ambience of River's End and the beauty of the garden. She took photographs and wrote long letters to Anna, describing each room in detail, and now that Number Six, Ferry Lane, had sold so quickly, a new confidence surrounded her.

It seemed everything she touched turned to gold. The parking lot close to Staines Bridge had become a valuable piece of real estate. Two buyers had desperately wanted it, and a third had offered a substantial amount, surpassing anything Marion had imagined. Her agent in Tasmania had suggested she sell her house on the banks of the River Derwent, contrary to his previous advice, as house prices on the riverside were soaring after many years of stagnation. 'So, all I need now is to persuade Mr Sloane to accept my offer on River's End,' she breathed softly to the collie by her side.

'Come!' Marion gently pulled on the lead as Intrepid snuffed at some exotic smell in the grassy riverbank. True to his word, Noel had given her the puppy at Easter, and it was hardly ever out of her sight. She had no idea what joy the puppy would bring, and apart from a few mishaps at the onset, Intrepid settled down to a routine: an early morning and late afternoon walk along the towpath; and a comfortable night on the end of Marion's bed. This last situation she felt no need to mention to Noel when he enquired about Intrepid's habits.

She found herself looking forward to Noel's visits. He made her feel that what she had to say was worthwhile. The way she cooked, what she wore, and the simple things of life that made up her day seemed sufficient to keep his friendship. Not once had he forced her into situations she would feel ill at ease with. Who would have imagined that she, Marion, could find contentment after all that had gone before? She murmured to God, 'Thank you. Thank you, for sending Noel my way.'

Letters arrived from Australia. Anna revealed she and Nigel had found an apartment to their liking, but she couldn't find a teaching position, so in the meantime she was doing some modelling, and had been snapped up by Myers, a large retail store located around Australia. She hoped to be noticed by international magazines… and no, they hadn't started a family yet. A letter from Janice Ryan prompted Marion to invite her to stay for a holiday during the winter in Tasmania, as this was an exceptional summer in England; and now that she had found a house (which she was sure Janice would love), she must come. An open return ticket was sent to Janice who, on receiving it, burst into tears of gratitude. All she had to do was to make the booking and Marion would meet her at Heathrow Airport.

'I think we have gone far enough today, Intrepid.' Marion turned homeward, enjoying the long summer evening, imagining Janice tucked up in the spare room, cosy evenings together and walks along the towpath with Intrepid, so different from the violence of the River Derwent. No doubt they would have a lot to talk about. How different she felt now to when Anna had asked her to take in Janice, all those months ago. Now Marion felt competent, growing in the knowledge of who she was and where she truly belonged.

There was only one small cloud on the horizon, disturbing her serenity: the church's inevitable change towards modernisation. The rood screen had been removed and in its place a children's corner, complete with electronic organ, had been established. A large screen attached to the rafters was lowered over the chancel steps, on which the words of hymns, readings and prayers were displayed. The projector was installed within the back two rows of the church underneath the magnificent stained-glass window. This meant the churchwarden had to stand up every so often to start and stop the selected tracks.

All this had taken place within a fortnight of the Reverend Guinness succumbing to a fatal heart attack. The new vicar, the Reverend Simon Smith, had not wasted his time on conventions, and the congregation was encouraged to partake of refreshment at the back of the church. Marion disliked the changes. She mourned the loss of the *Book of Common Prayer* and *Hymns Ancient and Modern*. In their place was a pamphlet containing the hymns, prayers, general business and what was being offered during the week.

'As if we didn't know,' said Marion to Noel. Later, she confided in Alice, 'It seems what I had experienced in Tasmania – barring a formidable female priest – has happened here!'

She was on her way back from Sunday morning worship. It had become a ritual to call in to Yew Corner, first to collect any mail still arriving, and then to resume their friendship over a glass of sherry. 'Some parishioners have stopped going!'

'Will you?' asked Alice.

The continuity and strength Marion had drawn from the familiar service was no longer there. The effect of recent technology alienated her thought process. Even the white surplice had flown away with the Reverend Guinness (so to speak); the Reverend Simon Smith wore everyday clothes. Somehow what he preached about was lost on Marion as she gazed irritably at his strange garb. Then there was a layperson who read the prayers from the chancel steps. Why this was so, she had no idea. The whole service felt disjointed, somehow. The final annoyance were the lessons; once they were spaced between the prayers, so you had time to digest the Old Testament reading from the New. But now all three followed one another, with the psalm squeezed in between.

'I don't suppose Jewish worship has changed in over 2,000 years. That's why it has survived,' Marion told Alice. 'In answer to your question,' she added, smiling ruefully, 'No, I'll still go. Where else is there? I expect the same has happened at St Peter's in Staines, and the Anglican church in Chertsey.' She paused. 'I'll just have to find another way to feed my spirituality. I wish you could have met Sister Ruth. I was at my wit's end before I met her. Now, *there* was a spiritual person, and she invited me to join in their Mass!'

'Really?'

'It was the most spiritual communion service I've ever experienced.'

And Alice had remarked, 'Then all was not disaster going to Tasmania.'

'Far from it,' Marion had replied. 'Sometime I'll tell you about Mary Knoll and everything that happened there, but not yet. It's hard to put into words.' With each successive Sunday saga, Alice became more intrigued.

Now, as Marion opened the gate to River's End, she wished she could invite Sister Ruth over to see how she had changed. She leant down and let Intrepid off the lead, watching her bounding around the garden before closing the gate. She would make herself grilled tomatoes on toast, after which she and Intrepid would settle down to listen to the ABC Saturday evening musical concert, while watching the sun go down through the bay window.

Tomorrow, after church and her drink with Alice, Noel was coming to Sunday lunch. She would pick Peace roses from the garden and arrange them on the dining table. Everything was back on track, or so she thought. Life was as she wanted it to be: predictable.

At about the same time as Marion was grilling her tomatoes, Alice was getting ready to meet some friends in Staines; they'd take in a movie and try out a club recently opened above the Thames Hotel. She was about to enter the shower when the doorbell rang. 'Oh, shit!' Alice exclaimed.

Putting on a dressing gown, she hurried down the stairs. On opening the door she was surprised to see a young man she recognised from his picture in the local paper, Michael Driver.

'Excuse me…' He shifted from foot to foot. 'I'm sorry to bother you, but…'

'Yes? What can I do for you?'

Faintly annoyed and embarrassed at standing on her front doorstep for all to see in her bathrobe, Alice's hands fluttered to the top of her wrap. 'I was just getting ready to go out…' Why she found herself explaining her attire to this young man, she had no idea.

'I was wondering if you could help me. I mean, Mrs Lee said I could look her up, and this is where she lives, isn't it?'

'I didn't know you knew her?'

'Oh, I don't, not really, but I would very much like to speak with her.'

'I see. You do know she lost her husband not so long ago, and I'm not sure…'

'Yes. Leonard. He taught us campanology.' He indicated the bell tower.

Caught between asking the young man in while she wrote down Marion's address, or standing on the doorstep as cars whistled around the War Memorial, Alice said, 'She has moved. I didn't think to ask her whether she wanted her address given out…' She paused. 'You're Michael Driver, aren't you?'

He nodded.

She took in his unkempt appearance and decided to give him Marion's details on the doorstep. 'She has moved to River's End, Beech Tree Lane, right on the towpath.' She waved her arm in the approximate direction.

'Oh, I didn't know.' The young man looked dispirited.

There was an awkward pause. 'Do you think she'll mind if I go and see her?'

He looked so unsure of himself that Alice realised he wasn't going to do Marion any harm. Mystified why he wanted to see Marion, she said, 'Why don't you go round there and see? Look, I've got to hurry off, I'll be late. You've got that? River's End. Go down the lane and along the towpath.'

He nodded and backed a step. 'Sorry…'

With that she closed the door. How mysterious. Marion never said a word.

She raced back up the stairs and jumped in the shower, mulling over what she had just done. She smiled, imagining Marion's face when Michael Driver turned up on her doorstep. Then, pushing the incident from her mind, she dressed and left home within the half-hour. It wasn't until she was sitting in the cinema watching a murder taking place up on the silver screen that she felt uneasy about sending a young man around whom Marion didn't know – or so she was led to believe. The whole thing was peculiar, to say the least.

Michael hesitated on the threshold for a minute before deciding he had nothing to lose; besides, he had nowhere else to go. He slunk along Blacksmiths' Lane, turned right along the towpath and thought of what he would say to Marion if he found her at home. The beautiful evening was completely lost on him as he kept his eyes down on the gravel path and his hands in his pockets.

She saw him coming up the garden path before he knocked on the door. Oh God… What do I do? An invisible force propelled her towards the door and out across the porch, her arms open wide. A diminutive figure, unsure, her face registering a gamut of emotions, her voice shaky with welcome. Intrepid ran in circles around Michael's feet. He picked the puppy up and was rewarded with a slobbery kiss. He sensed the charged emotion emanating from the small woman standing not twenty yards away.

Their eyes locked and he, feeling rather foolish, was rooted to the spot with a puppy wriggling in his arms. All he could manage was, 'Hello.' Before opening the gate he had surveyed the neat garden, roses blooming, scents on the evening air, a herbaceous border a riot of colour and texture. He wished he had at least put on a clean T-shirt. With one swift glance, Marion took in his appearance, and something touched her heart beyond any feeling she knew. He was similar in frame and manner to Leonard, but with the hopes of youth, eyes still reflecting uncertainty.

'You'd better come in. Are you hungry?' And with that he followed her into the kitchen. It seemed the most natural thing in the world to do.

~XI~

'Forgive us our trespasses, as we forgive those that trespass against us,' was all Marion felt capable of recalling from the following Sunday morning's service at All Saints'. As to what the Reverend Smith preached about, she had no idea. Michael's vulnerability of the previous evening had overridden any anger she still harboured towards Leonard. As he sat in the lounge room scoffing down scrambled eggs, juice, and numerous coffees, she had been overwhelmed by his appreciation. That he should come to her after their previous encounter touched her deep down. He needed her, this young man caught between the sins of Leonard and his mother.

To be perfectly honest, she was at fault too. She'd been only too ready to put Leonard on a pedestal, as he was the only male to have taken an interest in her and had saved her from becoming an old maid. She had allowed it to happen by transferring all decisions to him, just as she had acquiesced to her mother. Maybe if she had shown less rigidity, building impenetrable walls and remaining terrified of human behaviour, Leonard would have told

---

* From *The Century's Poetry*, Penguin, 1938.

206

her long ago about Michael. So many guilty thoughts crowded in her mind. She felt ill-equipped… and yet here was a situation calling out for a 'meshing of the spiritual and physical worlds', as Sister Ruth would have said. Here she could either make things right as best she could, or refuse to forgive Leonard's infidelity.

Before turning her bedside light off, she had stroked Intrepid's silky head. The dog's large liquid eyes fastened on her mistress, who said, 'Well, this is a turn-up for the books, isn't it? You liked Michael.' Intrepid surreptitiously snuggled up to Marion, hoping she could stay put. 'Go on with you, down the end of the bed! Whatever next?'

Marion was pleased to discover she was actually looking for-ward to whatever transpired in the coming months, for life and all its complexities had been dumped on her doorstep, so to speak. There was no need to feel afraid. She could give body and soul to it – if she chose to do so. Before switching off the bedside lamp and falling asleep, her last thought filled her with joy: I have a ready-made son – even if it is by default.

Sunday morning found Alice impatiently waiting for Marion on her doorstep, consumed by curiosity after the previous day's encounter with Michael Driver. Aware of a change in Marion's demeanour, but not sure what to make of it, she launched straight in as she poured their sherries. 'That young man, Michael Driver, called here yesterday looking for you. I gave him your address. I hope I didn't do the wrong thing… but I was in a hurry to go out.'

She thrust the glass into Marion's hand so that some of the amber liquid spilt over the edge. 'Oh, I'm sorry.' Alice mopped ineffectually at Marion's wrist. 'Did he find you?'

Marion sat down and smiled at her friend's fluster. 'No, you didn't do the wrong thing, and yes, he found me.' She sipped her sherry, trying to think what to say as she knew what the next question would be.

Sounding slightly peeved, as her visitor was so unforthcoming, Alice sat down opposite and tried to read Marion's expression. 'I didn't know you knew him,' she ventured.

'You're right. I didn't know him before last night, but—'

Alice interrupted her. 'What did he want?'

Marion looked down at her glass, twiddling the stem. 'He wanted to come and live with me.'

'But why?'

Marion coughed, fussing about with her handkerchief and pretending she didn't hear. Not being able to leave the topic, and sensing some skeleton in Marion's cupboard, Alice blurted out, 'Is he your son?'

'No. Not really…' Seeing Alice's bewilderment, she said simply, 'He's Leonard's son by Lucy Driver.'

'He's *what*?'

Marion waited a moment before adding, 'I've only recently found out myself.'

Stunned by this turn of events, Alice was speechless. Eventually she pulled herself together, murmuring, 'Oh, you poor thing.'

'You're wrong there. He's the son I've always longed for. May I have a top-up?'

And while Alice obliged, she continued diffidently, 'I trust this will go no further. I wouldn't want the whole village gossiping.' Marion parried further questions, but on the whole she was pleased how she had handled the difficult encounter. She felt sure Alice would not divulge anything within the village. What she might do was pass on juicy titbits to patients in the dentist's waiting room, but that she would have to bear.

She headed back to River's End, looking forward to preparing lunch for Noel as Alice drank the remains of the sherry, enthralled to think that because of her friendship with Marion, she had a link with an up-and-coming virtuoso.

Noel drove his much-loved Aston Martin over to Marion's for Sunday lunch. He wasn't in church that morning primarily because, like her, he didn't find the changes beneficial, nor could he take to the Reverend Smith; besides which, if he was honest with himself, the only reason he still attended was to see Marion, and now that they were meeting regularly there was little reason to do so. Soon, quite soon, he would pop the question, he mused, as the scents of honeysuckle and mown grass wafted on the air around his head. It was a glorious day. His spirits rose above the mundane, imagining Marion ensconced within his farmhouse,

Marion presiding over the antique dinner table, Marion floating around the bedroom in diaphanous apparel, Marion snuggling up to him on winter days beside a roaring fire, the dogs asleep at their feet.

The bay windows were open, letting in a gentle breeze. Bright pink hollyhocks could be seen peeping over the window ledge as Noel helped himself to home-made mint sauce, while Marion revealed who the violinist was at Leonard's Memorial Service. For a moment the Peace roses swam before his eyes. Very slowly, Noel cut through the slice of lamb, piercing it with his fork, then dipped it into the mint sauce before placing the morsel into his mouth. He was in shock.

'Run that past me again,' he said, slicing through a roast potato and carrot, giving the vegetables far more concentration than they warranted. As he stretched towards the gravy boat, he caught his host's embarrassed expression, but there was something else as well. Marion's face shone with zeal – or was it love? Carefully, he put down his knife and fork, looking straight at her across the table, as she seemed to be running all sorts of information past him.

'And you see, with his mother gone to live with her new partner down in Wiltshire, Michael has no home. I'd like to offer him one. What do you think?'

She didn't wait for his reply as he sat there amid their Sunday lunch, the roses and the sunshine. Their intimacy had been invaded by some lunatic scheme which put paid to all he had planned.

'The long and short of it is that Michael is sleeping on a friend's couch. There is nowhere to practise, and from what I can gather not enough money to rent in London.'

'His mother is *where*?'

'Oh, Noel, you haven't been listening! Because I sold their house, she has up and gone to live with a friend – according to Michael. There is no room for him.'

Noel looked puzzled. Marion seemed to be talking at a great speed, as though if she didn't, she wouldn't be able to talk at all. 'You see, Leonard bought the house for them many years ago.' She swallowed. 'I had no idea who was living in it, until I decided to sell the property.' She pushed her food around the plate with her fork, then made a great fuss of pouring iced water into her glass. Noel wiped his mouth with a yellow napkin that matched the roses in the centre of the table. Marion had run out of steam. He was expected to say something.

'So, are you telling me that Leonard kept a mistress in Laleham for the last, what, sixteen, seventeen years – and you didn't know?' It was at times like this he wished he hadn't given up smoking.

'Yes.' She was close to tears.

Noel leant back in the chair and absent-mindedly stroked Intrepid, who happened to be sitting as close to the table as she could, hoping some morsel would come her way. 'What about Anna?'

'She doesn't know… and there is no need to tell her.'

'But there is, Marion. You can't keep this a secret. She might not like the idea of a stepbrother – or whatever he is – living here with you.'

'She didn't care about me when they decided to move to Queensland!' Her voice rose angrily. Noel had never seen Marion angry or quite this upset. Suddenly, the afternoon took on a different mood. He wasn't quite sure what to say. All he knew was that Marion had some hare-brained scheme that would put paid to any plans of his.

'But are you sure about this? Do you have any idea what you are taking on?'

'Oh, don't be so stuffy, Noel. Michael won't be here all the time. Next year he's going to Vienna to study… and before you know it, he'll be gone earning his living.'

'What do you know about teenage boys?' Noel asked, clutching at straws.

'I was hoping you'd tell me,' she replied, her voice softening a little. They finished their meal almost in silence apart from hearing each other's knives and forks scraping their plates. Finally Marion got up from the table to make coffee.

Noel cleared away, then returned to the lounge, fully aware that nothing he said would change Marion's mind. He loved this woman, and somehow or other she seemed to be slipping away from his grasp. He wasn't about to share her with anyone.

Marion carried two cups, sugar and milk in on a tray, then went out into the kitchen, returning with the percolator. She began to pour. The silence was intolerable. Noel said, 'So, I suppose you won't be coming with me next Saturday to the car boot sale?'

'Of course I'm coming with you. Why wouldn't I?'

Noel muttered a few words to the effect she would probably find herself too busy. Marion fiddled with her coffee spoon, wondering how she could explain that offering Michael a home was something she knew was right, without losing Noel into the bargain. This man had stood by her from the moment she had returned from Australia; he had been there for her every step of the way, and if she was honest, made her far happier than Leonard ever had. Her days sparkled with laughter; it was as if they were meant to be a couple. Oh God, please don't let me lose him! I couldn't bear it! Was he *jealous*? She had never thought of him in that light. No, he couldn't be; it was just an unexpected situation he wasn't prepared for, and yet...

'You know that painting I confused with the stained-glass window in the church?' He looked wary. 'And you said I had misinterpreted the message. Well, I realised your understanding was correct. We don't have to reach up to clasp God's hand. He reaches down to clasp ours.'

Noel couldn't quite see what this had to do with Michael Driver moving in to upset his plans. Marion continued, while gently stirring her coffee, 'Well, in the same way, we are God's hands to others. Michael reached out to me and I realised I could help him. He wasn't to blame... he's only seventeen, for heaven's sake.'

'I was hoping we'd spend more private time together – just us,' he said, leaning forward earnestly.

'Why would this make any difference?'

Of course, it would make all the difference to what he had in mind. He decided on a different attack, forcing a laugh. 'You know, teenage boys need constant supplies of food. Their socks walk into the washing machine, and as for their rooms... they take on a distinct resemblance to a tip!'

She relaxed a little. 'He did look rather grubby, but that's not his fault. I don't mind doing his laundry. He can have the spare room.'

'Hang on, I thought Janice was to have the spare room! Wouldn't do, you know…'

'Oh, Noel, of course not.' She half-smiled, too embarrassed to meet his eye. 'Janice can have the attic room – she won't mind. Anyway, Michael may not be here when she comes. He said something about going up to the Edinburgh Festival and playing there. He seems to be booked for various concerts around the country… I'm afraid I didn't pay much attention to what or where last night.'

'You were more interested in his welfare.' He sighed, resignedly.

'Like you have been about mine.' Her eyes pleaded with him to understand. He was about to say, 'But there was more to it than that,' when she began clearing the cups and setting the dishwasher.

Noel followed her into the kitchen with some light-hearted banter about teenagers, hoping she would realise there was a lot more to looking after teenage boys than she had imagined. But he could see her mind was made up, so, no doubt, he would offer his support to this wonderful selfless woman. He wanted to take Marion into his arms, and maybe try out the spare room himself, but hesitated to declare his hand in case he frightened her off. Seeing her standing there, rinsing out the coffee pot so close to him, was sheer torture. Instead, he brushed her hair with his lips, murmuring, 'You are wonderful…'

Pleased, but slightly flustered, her hands splashed about in the sink. 'I wouldn't have considered doing this a year ago – it's really all down to you. And this house which I feel will be mine.'

She pulled out the plug, wiping her hands on a tea towel printed with recipes from orchards in the Tasmanian Huon Valley, then carefully hung it over the oven rail, avoiding his gaze.

The space between the two of them forbade any form of intimacy. Intrepid snuffled her bowl. 'Have we forgotten you?' Marion said. She bustled about, filling one bowl with leftovers, the other with fresh water.

Noel looked on. 'When does he arrive?'

'Probably Wednesday.' She turned to look at him. 'He will ring before. He said he hasn't much to bring, some small items of furniture which are in store in Staines. I've got a spare bed, so we'll see…' She smiled, looking for his approval.

Then, watching Intrepid's shiny black coat and fluffy tail sweeping the floor, Marion remarked, 'She needs a walk. I don't suppose you'll…'

Noel pulled himself together. 'Sorry, duty calls. I ought to be getting back to Dorcas. She'll be needing hers.'

'Noel, I want you to know how much I appreciate everything you have done for me. Having Michael here won't change anything.'

Won't it, he thought, ignoring her comment. 'I'll be seeing you on Saturday, then. Pick you up at eight.' And with that, he tore his eyes away from Marion's as he let himself out of the back door.

She followed, watching him as he climbed into his Aston Martin. He didn't wave as he normally did, nor she reflected, as she clipped Intrepid onto her lead, did he say, 'Call you during the week.'

By the time Noel reached the farm he had calmed down somewhat. He called Dorcas and went out to check on the flowers in the greenhouses. Here, he could think straight. The farmhouse lacked something, and to his thinking, that something was Marion. He walked up and down, going over the things they had in common, trying to work out why this turn of events had so upset him. They both disliked the new innovations within the church service, and neither of them had taken to the Reverend Smith. They both liked classical music, the same types of food, and a quiet life. They both read a lot and he liked doing the *Times* crossword. She loved gardening and so did he – quiet pastimes that didn't require other people – and yet, being human, they both needed someone else to care for, to share life with, to love… to *love*, that was the crux of the matter. She was now going to pour out her love on someone other than himself! Maybe she didn't love him, or not enough to warrant a full relationship. He loved her, and he'd known that ever since she'd come back home. He couldn't lose her now just because she had some crazy altruistic notion. He began to speculate on her relationship with Leonard, then found himself getting angry at how the man had deceived Marion for all those years.

Leonard had seemed a decent sort of chap, a bit noisy for his liking, but obviously he had fooled everyone. He would never have guessed it of him. Noel pottered about the farm for the rest of the afternoon, picking off a flower head here and inspecting a leaf there. Then he looked in at the chickens and picked six punnets of strawberries, which he would later deliver to the local grocer's with fresh leeks, lettuces, beetroot, carrots, potatoes and onions. Returning to the chicken coop, he filled half a dozen cartons with eggs for the local butcher, and keeping four out for himself, he took them inside to make an omelette.

Around seven, and feeling restless, he called Dorcas, locked up and ambled across the fields towards the Bridge Inn on the Chertsey side of the river. It being a warm Sunday evening, the place was packed. Gnats and dragonflies swarmed above the river, oarsmen were sweating it out, their coxswains calling out orders, their small bodies hunched in the sterns wearing their team colours. Along and below the riverbanks, wild irises grew, their leaves swaying from the ripples caused by the eights, and ducks foraged for food. Traffic rumbled across the bridge, mindful of cyclists, and rented houseboats slowed, their occupants looking for somewhere to moor.

Noel pushed his way towards the bar, ordering a pint, holding Dorcas on a short lead. A voice called, 'Noel, join us!' He waved them away, preferring to be outside. What would they say, if he confessed to his dilemma. 'Go on – you're joking!' Or, 'You are a dark horse – get stuck in – what are you waiting for?' And more of the same. He couldn't confide in any of this lot, and come to think of it, he would be hard-pressed to find anyone who would understand. He returned to the bar, leaving Dorcas tied to the leg of a chair, while he bought another pint. Meanwhile, Dorcas had slipped her lead and was now barking furiously at a boat moored alongside the bank, preventing its occupants from alighting. Patrons were laughing at what looked like a very corpulent captain with one leg on the bank, the other in the water, swearing at Dorcas. 'Who's the bloody owner?' he bawled.

Noel emerged from the pub, hearing shouts of outrage and seeing Dorcas snapping at the ankles of a man dressed in expensive yachting gear. 'This is all I need!' he said to those closest to him. 'I'm most awfully sorry…' Noel lunged at Dorcas, pulling her away. 'It's not like her!' As he pushed through the crowd he heard a few titters, and the odd remark about 'bloody dog owners'. Someone had purloined his beer during the ruckus.

'Come on, Dorcas, home!' She didn't like all those legs, and attempted to snap at any close by, but Noel kept her on a very short lead. Before she realised it they were back over the bridge, away from people, traffic and noise. It was quiet here in the field, apart from rooks flying high above in formation. The occasional rabbit poked its head out of its burrow, but Dorcas could sense that now was not the time to chase rabbits. 'What got into you?' Noel asked. She slunk along beside him. Didn't he know she was frightened by that huge white thing? She had tried to protect him from its roar, and coming too near. 'What a day!' he moaned to the evening air. 'I've met a woman I finally want to marry, and would you believe it, she has taken it into her head to fill her life with strays!'

Dorcas kept her nose close to the ground as her master rambled on.

'Doesn't she realise I want her to live with us? But she wants to buy River's End. I don't want any teenager dropping by, and certainly not under my roof. One was bad enough.' Dorcas sat down, refusing to budge. She had had enough. She wanted to run. Dog and master came to a halt in the middle of the field. 'Oh, all right.' He let her off and she was away, bounding and woofing at anything that moved.

That night Noel sat up late watching television. If asked what he had seen he would have been hard-pressed to recall. He drank several whiskies before retiring and dreamt about birds nesting, cuckoos commandeering other birds' nests, taloned eagles hovering, and himself fending off swooping magpies. He awoke the following morning feeling decidedly out of sorts; by contrast, Marion slept peacefully and awoke looking forward to the arrival of a new day.

Overcome with bonhomie, the glorious summer weather and

the direction her life seemed to be taking, Marion felt sure River's End would soon become hers. What she hadn't banked on was noticing traits similar to Leonard's being exhibited by Michael. The timbre of his voice, certain facial expressions, even how he sat in a chair, were all familiar, but they were things she would rather forget. She took to visiting the churchyard and talking to the plaque lying above Leonard's ashes, now settled into the lawn, telling him all about Michael and what she had done. Sunday service found her sitting in a seat on the opposite aisle from where they used to sit. She hired a Mr Symmonds to cut the lawns and do the pruning at River's End, while she herself became involved with the Laleham Heritage Centre. She enjoyed meeting strangers, handing out leaflets, explaining the memorabilia, the seventeenth-century pond, the wildlife garden, and 'Walks around Laleham'. This she did two mornings a week, giving her something else to think about… besides Leonard.

Michael had moved in a fortnight before with two large green refuse bags full of clothes, a fishing rod, a box of books, his violin, a music stand and numerous CDs, but no player. Now, as she stood in his bedroom, she noticed how neat the room was, but then he owned very few possessions. When he was home he spent most of the time practising in the conservatory, something he hoped didn't disturb her. On the contrary she would sit in the lounge with Intrepid, enjoying the music as it filtered through. Most weekdays he went up to the Royal Academy, coming home on the last train; what he did all day she couldn't imagine. All she knew was that he was lead violinist in the orchestra. She was very proud of his success. He had mentioned something about playing a solo with the rest of the orchestra accompanying him, but hadn't divulged what, where, or when. She couldn't say he was a difficult teenager, because he wasn't. It was just that they had few meaningful conversations. Generally, she would ask him if he needed dinner and what he would like; it couldn't go on indefinitely.

There was a certain awkwardness in their relationship, which made it difficult for Marion to know whether he would be affronted if she asked questions. She wanted to know all about his upbringing and couldn't understand how his mother, Lucy

Driver, could have gone away with her current lover, leaving Michael to virtually fend for himself. Wasn't she proud of her son? Did she dare ask how often Leonard used to visit them? Maybe Michael was embarrassed too – this she could understand. Maybe he wasn't sure how she would take any further revelations.

This was going to be far more complicated than she had imagined. With the advent of Michael, Marion was acutely aware of a change in Noel's behaviour towards her. Their relationship had stalled, so to speak. It was as if Noel refused to accept Michael's existence. She had hoped the two would become friends, but something in Noel's manner showed her this was not going to be the case. Could he be jealous? She so wanted them to be friends, especially since her feelings for Noel had deepened in ways she hadn't known before. Here she was in her fifties, and was experiencing a profound love, a love she just knew was right. It was like a river flowing through her, shaking, shimmering, plunging into realms unknown and lifting her above the mundane, although very much a part of ordinary living. And yet neither she nor Noel had voiced or physically shown any of these emotions. Maybe she was simply imagining he loved her. Maybe he was just lonely. Oh, she hoped this was not so. She told herself, maybe he is waiting for a sign from me. I wouldn't know where to start… it's been so long. Absurd, really, at my age! What if I kiss him and he pulls away? I'd be mortified. Does he know that when he holds my hand I can hardly think straight? If only I was younger with a beautiful body I'd feel more confident. Dear God, help me! Am I right to love this man? Thank you for sending him to me. He has filled my life with happiness, such that I have never experienced before… Thus she prayed, as she placed a freshly ironed shirt on top of Michael's new green bedspread with matching pillowslips, and wondered what else to do to bridge the gap between them. She looked across to the window and seeing Michael's books lined up across the sill, decided he could do with a bookcase. She'd get a bedside lamp to match the greens of the bedspread and a clock radio. She left the fishing rod propped up against the wall and went down to the kitchen to make elevenses for Mr Symmonds in an ambivalent mood.

~XII~

Trust in the Lord with all thine heart;
and lean not unto thine own understanding.

Proverbs 3:5

It was a Saturday morning in July when Marion and Noel were wandering up and down between the various lines of cars at a car boot sale within an enormous field on the outskirts of Walton-on-Thames. Michael had gone fishing for the day with Scott Weir, an old school friend, from Matthew Arnold Secondary Modern. Scott Weir had his own runabout, and Marion wasn't to expect him home for tea. She stopped by a rack of men's clothing, pulling a black leather jacket from its hanger. She held it out. 'Do you think this will fit Michael? Noel squinted in the sunlight and shrugged. 'Here, try it on – he has so few clothes.'

'Marion, I don't think I…' Noel grumbled, as she thrust it at him.

Wriggling his shoulders and feeling decidedly uncomfortable, he pulled the jacket on. 'It's a bit tight for me…'

'You could say that!' she laughed.

'What's so funny?'

'Take it off, then. I just thought… I could do with a bit of help here.'

'Sorry.' He smiled ruefully and added, 'I just can't get used to – you know.' He handed the jacket back to a bewildered stallholder. Attempting to recover some dignity in her eyes, he pretended to look further along the rack. 'If it's too tight for me, it probably is OK. What size is he? Does he like leather jackets?'

Marion stared at the back of his head. 'In answer to both questions, I don't know. I just thought he has so few clothes… and don't ask me when his birthday is or what shoe size he takes, because I don't know. He seems to have only one pair of trainers, and those he wears every day!'

'If I may suggest…' Noel guided Marion away, continuing gently, 'I think you should sit him down and find out these things. What does he do for money?'

Marion confessed she had little idea, only that he was on a scholarship to the Royal Academy, he had a bus and train pass, and that she believed he helped out in a bookshop in Fleet Street.

'Does he pay you board?'

'Well, no. I don't expect him to… I know this sounds odd, but I'm trying to treat him like a son.'

'But he isn't your son, is he?'

'He fills the gap of the son I lost. Also, I'm trying to forgive Leonard, and then there's Anna so far away.'

'Look, all I'm trying to say is I think you have some sorting out to do, and go slowly. Things may not turn out exactly as you had in mind.'

'I know that.' She smiled weakly, disentangling her arm from his and crossing over to another stall with vases. Noel remained separate, moving on to the next table, rummaging through some books. She purchased a small cut-glass vase, then moved back closer to him, watching. 'You were right. I had no idea how difficult this would be… but I still feel it was the right thing to do. I mean, he had nowhere else to go.'

Noel made no reply, preferring to keep his own counsel. He paid for a small brown leather-bound book and turning, offered it to Marion. 'This is for you.'

'For me? Oh… *Sonnets*.' She opened it. 'Donne, Keats, Shakespeare.'

He smiled looking down at her. 'Let's find somewhere for lunch. The Anchor do?'

'Where's that?'

'Surprise. Not far.'

They drove in companionable silence with the roof down, drawing in the scents, the light breeze and their surroundings. Marion wanted to shout, 'I love you. You understand… at least, I think we understand each other better,' but she didn't.

They skimmed through leafy lanes, their tangled canopies

letting in shafts of sunshine, and at other times past enormous banks covered with bindweed, ivy and rotted tree trunks, completely blocking the view to whatever lay on the other side. Suddenly, the lane ran out, and there in front of them was a gravelled car park. The Anchor, with its modern additions, nestled into the riverbank, and close to a very old bridge which took the through traffic across the Thames, its narrow road only accommodating vehicles in single file.

'There's nothing else here!' she exclaimed in surprise as they climbed out of the Aston Martin.

'I hope you like it,' he said, as he dipped his head through a very low doorway. Marion followed, marvelling at the large windows through which she could see a courtyard set with small tables and chairs clustered around, behind which hanging baskets were attached to the walls, trailing red and pink geraniums, sprinkled with gypsophila and blue lobelia. Completing the picture, on a small island, opposite the courtyard, cascading willows brushed the river.

'It's magic, Noel. How did you find this?'

'Ah, well... that's another story.' He ushered Marion into a chair, from where she could enjoy the view. He followed suit, leaning his arms across the table.

'There are other places beside Laleham, you know,' he chuck-led. 'Shere and Gomshall, Friday Street, Abinger Bottom...'

'What a funny name – Friday Street! You're having me on...'

'No, it exists. It's a little hard to find, but worth persevering. Didn't Len ever take you to lunch in the countryside?'

She shook her head.

'Peaselake... surely?'

At that moment a waiter arrived to take their orders, sparing Marion further admissions. 'We're not quite ready yet.' Noel flipped the menu across to Marion. 'You choose for both of us. I'll get the drinks. Chardonnay all right?'

She nodded, feeling embarrassed while the waiter stood beside their table, notebook at the ready. At the bar, Noel debated whether to buy a bottle of champagne but decided against it. He ordered two glasses of house Chardonnay, then changed his mind and asked for a bottle of Australian wine – Piper's Brook – much to the confusion of the bar attendant. 'Oh, and I would like it in a bucket of ice, please.'

He returned to find Marion leaning back in her chair, eyes closed, her face lifted towards the sun. He felt his pulse race on seeing her profile and the rich tones of her hair, now slightly windblown from the car ride. She opened her eyes. He smiled, relishing the unusual greyish blue of her eyes, reflecting the blue of her dress. It had a large stand-up collar and pockets on either side of the skirt, her waist neatly nipped in by a wide belt of the same fabric. Caught out, she looked down at her lap.

'I've ordered salmon on a bed of jasmine rice with side salad, and…'

'Marion.'

'Yes.'

Someone placed an ice bucket on a tripod next to their table. Neither of them looked at the waiter or the wine being opened. 'Sir?'

Noel indicated he should pour for Marion. Then he reached out his hand across the table, enfolding hers. Marion sipped, murmuring, 'Mmm,' then smiled across at Noel, gently biting her bottom lip with dainty white teeth. With their glasses full, their eyes only for each other, he said, 'It's Australian… I thought you'd like it.'

The food arrived. As he gazed at Marion, a memory of his courting days flashed across his mind, for the life of him he couldn't fathom why. He recalled summer evenings spent at pubs in Twickenham or Richmond, and clandestine meetings within the grounds of Hampton Court, where he was employed as a gardener, and Judy Jenkins was in the souvenir shop as a trainee. A mistake had been made under an oak tree which cannoned Judy and Noel into marriage. With the advent of Gerald looming, Noel took an instant dislike to oak trees. From the start, nothing went as he had imagined it should. Young and inexperienced, struggling to make ends meet, they constantly quarrelled; furthermore, Judy had eyes for 'Gerry' alone.

Mr and Mrs Jenkins doted on their daughter and grandson, completely ignoring Noel's existence. His mother, who avoided arguments at all costs, said, 'You'll be all right son, the farm is yours, you know… when we're gone.' His father would sit in his favourite armchair wagging his head, pronouncing in mock derision, 'Marry in haste, repent at leisure,' in such a tone that Noel wasn't sure if he was disappointed in him or thought that his troubles were funny. He remembered how they were completely mismatched. Judy neither cooked nor cleaned. She merely fussed over Gerald and read women's magazines. She'd said detergents ruined her hands, and that she hadn't married him to become a domestic. She'd wave her fingers in front of his face displaying lurid red nail varnish. Then she told him over spaghetti one evening that he was boring with his talk of soil, trees, bulbs and plants.

By the time Gerald had turned four, Judy had taken him and the contents of their joint savings account to live with her widowed mother in Barnes. The few times he had spent with his son had been difficult. Summoned to a parent-teacher night, Noel had admitted to a guidance officer at Northolt High that Gerald was moody, fractious, and uncooperative. In turn, he was told that this was an unfortunate attitude to take.

Eventually he inherited the farm. He was thirty-six and lonely. Judy had run off with a hairdresser, or so he was led to believe, and Gerald shared a flat with a mate in Colnbrook not five minutes away from Heathrow Airport, where they both worked, staring into computers all day.

Now, as he savoured a tasty piece of salmon, with devilled artichokes and goat's cheese, he studied the woman opposite him. She was still wearing her wedding ring. He noticed because she had beautiful fingers wrapped around a fork, lifting salmon into her mouth with her right hand as Americans do; her left was twiddling the wine glass.

'This is delicious,' she smiled. 'Is something wrong? You seem miles away.'

Noel hesitated, not wishing to divulge his thoughts, and attempted to change the subject. 'Tell me about Tasmania, and that girl who's coming to stay.'

'Oh, you mean Janice. It's rather complicated, in a way.'

'Maybe some other time, then…' He sounded disappointed and for want of something to do and to cover what was apparently a faux pas, he refilled Marion's glass. He decided to lighten the conversation and, looking around at all the noise and chatter said, 'I hadn't realised all the tables here are full.'

'We've been engrossed,' she said shyly, sipping her wine, also looking around. 'When we first arrived in Tadbury, Janice was seen wandering along the beach when she should have been at school. Later I learnt from Anna that she'd been in a car crash and ended up in hospital. Her mother was killed, and she didn't have a father… he was drowned in one of the Sydney-to-Hobart yacht races.'

'Sounds sad.'

'Yes, it was. I met her on one of my walks and we fell into talking – this was after Len died – Janice was in the middle of her final exams. You can imagine how those went! Well, anyway, she didn't have any guardians or any relatives who could be found in Tasmania, so the school arranged for her to stay temporarily with another family; their daughter was also attending St Mary's. Anna wanted me to take her in, but it was too soon after Len… I could barely cope.'

'Of course you couldn't! Rather tactless of Anna, if you don't mind my saying so. But now you feel you can cope, I mean.'

'Well, she's only coming for a holiday.' Marion gave a half laugh, pushing back her hair and rubbing her forehead. 'She was pregnant at the time of the crash, apparently, but luckily in a way she lost the baby, and that's about it.'

'Another waif to take under your wing! You seem to have a penchant for it!' His eyes twinkled as he reached for the menu. 'Crème brûlée, lemon tart, mixed berries and cream, profitéroles, or Cheddar cheese and biscuits. Madame, what is your desire?'

'Sorry, I…' She didn't register everything Noel said, as she was picturing the lone sailor's grave and recalling her own desolation at the time.

'I shall have the Cheddar.' He repeated the menu, and Marion said, 'Lemon tart, I think. I like that,' she added, trying to pull herself together. 'Not much point in making a whole tart for oneself, is there?'

'And coffee?'

'Yes.' Unwittingly, the memory of Janice, clasping a mug of

hot chocolate sitting opposite her in her Tadbury home, intruded, with tears streaming down her face, so alone, trying to be brave.

A voice spoke in Noel's head. 'Go gently, not now. Now is not the time.'

Later that evening, Marion opened the book of sonnets while sitting in a comfortable wing-backed chair, with Intrepid at her feet. She treasured the feel of the leather binding, stroking it back and forth with her fingers; she loved the closeness of Intrepid, and the warmth of the long summer evening. A mug decorated with nasturtiums containing Earl Grey tea was beside her on a walnut table as she listened to Michael practising in the conservatory. He had mentioned an Intermezzo she thought was by Brahms, which sparkled and echoed against the conservatory windows, or so it sounded to her. Should she tell Anna about Michael? Noel seemed to think so. Maybe he was right. She wasn't ready to do so. She'd do it soon though, but not now – soon. She noticed it was nine o'clock as her eyes fell on a Shakespearean sonnet.

'Let me not to the marriage of true minds/ Admit impediments. Love is not love/ which alters when it alteration finds/ Or bends with the remover to remove…' She read the fourteen lines aloud to Intrepid. 'Well, what do you make of that?' she said. Then she drank the rest of her tea and closed her eyes, immersed in the day's astonishing events.

On the night the weather broke in the Thames Valley, far away in Queensland, Anna and Nigel Crees were sunbathing early in the morning on Burleigh Beach, reading the *Gold Coast Bulletin*, a large weekend paper divided into sections. Nigel was perusing the Property section, where lavish houses were pictured on the side of canals, and the seafront, worth over a million dollars. Blue pools and tranquil ocean were predominant, coupled with spacious living areas of marble and stone exhibiting various open-plan kitchens, their bench tops made out of free-form granite or an imitation laminate.

'A bit out of our league, isn't it?' she said leaning over his shoulder and pointing to a five-bedroom, three-bathroom house with DVD lounge, games room, horseshoe pool and jetty. A houseboat was pictured nestling alongside. 'Mmm… maybe one day. I'd prefer somewhere in the hinterland.' Nigel lay back on the rug, arms supporting his head. Anna went on reading in companionable silence. Nigel said, 'I like the birds,' then, turning his head towards her, lowering his sunglasses provocatively and peering over the top he said, 'I mean the feathered variety.'

She gave him a gentle push, thinking how happy they were. The lifestyle, the sunshine and the easy access to shopping malls with boutiques sporting famous names suited them; not to mention the up-and-coming designers from all around the world. She had mentioned this to Nigel on several occasions. If there was one indulgence Anna succumbed to on a regular basis, it was buying clothes. She loved modelling, the feel of different fabrics, the excitement and chaos before a show. Her own wardrobe was stacked with shoes and accessories – too many, in Nigel's opinion.

He would return from a day's teaching at King's Christian School to see bags and boxes strewn across the bedroom floor, their contents neatly laid out on the bed. If asked, he would say he was happy for her; however, he had been feeling uneasy about all her gadding about, as he didn't know where she was half the time. He'd approach Matt with Anna in mind, to see if there was any chance of a vacancy at the school in the near future, in the senior English department. Clasping his knees, he rocked into a sitting position, looking at the surfers away to his right, the early body-boarders closer in and the walkers wearing an assortment of shorts and bathers revelling in the sunshine, sand and surf. Nearer to him, he saw two children under five digging in the sand, their mother sitting close by, reading a book.

'I like large houses,' said Anna, 'with lots of rooms. The only thing I miss is a garden. Don't get me wrong, I love the apartment.' She kissed his neck, tasting the salt and running her hand through his hair.

'Anna, not here!' He wriggled away. 'Large houses contain lots of bedrooms.'

'So…?' she laughed.

'Lots of bedrooms require children to fill them. There's no point, otherwise.'

Anna didn't reply, shuffling the paper, wondering what had

got Nigel on to the subject of children. He knew she wasn't keen to start a family, not yet anyway.

'Good heavens!' she said. 'There's more about Martin Bryant here… It says he's becoming a danger to himself. He's been in hospital! Poor Mum and Dad, arriving in the middle of all that – a bloody massacre. When I think of that girl – you know, Janice Ryan – being down at Port Arthur on that very day…' She shuddered.

'Yes, but she wasn't exactly involved, was she?'

'Still, the boy she was with saw things.'

'Just goes to show.'

'Show what?'

'Well, if she had been at the school fair, where she should have been, she wouldn't have got herself pregnant.'

'What do you mean, she wouldn't have got herself pregnant? It takes two, you know. Anyway she could have been somewhere else. I don't think you can generalise.'

'Bit touchy, aren't you?'

Anna chose to ignore his comment. 'She's going to stay with Mum in Laleham, or so her letter led me to believe. I'm amazed.'

'Why?'

'You don't know my mum. She would hardly speak to anyone she didn't know. She shied away from new friends. As far as I know, she never joined a club – only attended her Old Girls' reunions and decorated the church. When I suggested she take Janice in, she fair chewed my ear off. I mean, she had that house and I thought it would be nice company for her after Dad died.'

'Maybe she needed—'

Anna interrupted. 'I mean, why would Mum invite her over there? She's just a teenager. What would they have in common? I bet she's paying for the ticket – not that I mind, of course – but when I asked if we could have some of Dad's capital, she went all funny on me.'

'Oh, Anna, you didn't! You never told me. What would she think?'

'I'm sure she's sold the Tadbury house but she's not letting on.'

'It's none of our business if she has…'

'That's where you're wrong! It is *our* business. I'm their only child, and I expect to inherit what is mine – not have it frittered away on strangers. I know it was a mistake them moving here to Australia, but Dad loved it.'

'Pity he didn't live long enough to enjoy his sailing. I liked your dad; mine has never taken much interest in anything I do.'

They sat for a while, each with their own thoughts, until Anna muttered, 'She seems to have settled back in Laleham as if nothing had happened. I can't get over how busy her life is now – she's even acquired a dog! My mum with a dog – it's quite bizarre!'

'People change, you know. Maybe she's met someone else.'

'Oh, don't be ridiculous.' Anne laughed quietly, tossing back her hair, then inspected her nail varnish, pleased with the whiteness of the tips.

'She wouldn't be the first. She's not that old and she's still attractive.'

'Not my mum.' Anne began foraging around in a capacious raffia bag.

'Different from mine!' he laughed. 'Can't wait to see the world, never settling. Bit of a joke if they decided to move to England. She loves it. They'll probably look your mum up when they return from the Cotswolds, back up to London. I gave them her address.'

'That's nice! I'd love to be a fly on the wall. The jet-setters meet the stick-in-the-mud!'

'What are you looking for?'

'My camera.' Suntan lotion, a soft floppy hat, make-up bag, a packet of tissues, and purse and then a comb and hairbrush were discarded in a heap before she extracted a piece of cheesecloth decorated with blue swirls, then neatly tied it around her hips with a knot. Thrusting her hand back into the bag she retrieved her Nikon and a flask of coffee with two cups. 'All yours,' she said, handing Nigel the flask. 'I'm going to take photos to send to Mum! I should have done it ages ago.'

As she felt the warmth and firmness of the sand under her feet she pictured her father walking along Tadbury Beach each morning, and wondered if he had known how little time he had left. She felt bad about not making more of an effort to ease her parents' transition from England to Tasmania, especially where her mother was concerned. She walked along, deep in thought, seeing but not registering the little waves at her feet. She missed her father, feeling guilty she hadn't made more of an effort. It was extraordinary that she should think of him on this particular day. Feelings of irritability crept in where her mother was concerned; after all, they had offered to bring her to Queensland. She wished he had known that. He would have been shocked to know her mother had returned to England, not wanting to stay; maybe it was just as well, as she would have been banging on about grandchildren and expecting to be included in all they did. Anna turned and began taking photos of the beach, children jumping little waves and body-boarders riding the swell further out. 'Morning!' called a couple of smiling walkers, thinking she was a tourist.

Locals and tourists alike would have been astounded to know that within eight years a law was to be passed forbidding strangers to take pictures of unsuspecting children on the beach. Pornographic pictures of children would be sold over the Internet causing an outrage within the community. Panicked parents would hear of paedophiles within churches, schools and homes for the unwanted. Nigel watched his wife while sipping coffee, envisaging his garrulous mother arriving unannounced on Marion's doorstep, and wished she were a little more refined or at the very least, more restrained. Then, turning his attention towards the two children playing nearby, he imagined himself as a father, making sandcastles with his son, a smaller replica of himself, running down to the waves with a red plastic bucket, filling it with water and hauling it back to their sandcastle; his younger sister squatting on her haunches, patting the sand.

Anna returned, flushed from her task, flopping down beside him and waving her hands in the general direction of the children. The dream was dashed; happy families was not on the menu. 'Kids! Who'd have them. Look at those two, whingeing away! That poor mother... no peace at all.'

Nigel stared at his wife, appreciating her physical attributes, but not at all sure he liked the things she said. The children were quarrelling – so what? He saw children quarrelling all day. That's what children did, didn't they? Or so it seemed to him.

Anna poured herself a coffee, thinking about her next modelling assignment. It beat teaching any day, and lying down on the rug, she closed her eyes, dreaming of fame and glamour.

Nigel read the financial pages, attempting to push from his mind Anna's negative attitude towards having children. He came to the conclusion she wasn't about to make a mistake with the Pill, and felt cheated, knowing there would be scenes and tears. What her aversion was to having a baby, he had no idea, unless she had a fear of being pregnant and becoming unattractive. The sooner she returned to teaching the better, and then all this nonsense with modelling would hopefully stop.

All over the Thames Valley people commented on the break in the weather. 'Lucky this downpour didn't happen for Wimbledon,' said a tennis enthusiast to a lawn keeper as they sheltered from the rain. Total strangers on the 5.10 from Waterloo to the outer suburbs discussed the unpredictable elements, and were then moved to voice their opinion on the scandalous behaviour of the Princess of Wales. Marion, like everyone else was shocked to see a photo, splashed across the front page of the *Daily Express*, of Princess Diana holidaying on a yacht with Dodi Fayed, son of Mohamed Al Fayed, whose name was synonymous with Harrods of London. She wondered if the Queen ever read such damaging reports about the Royal House of Windsor; as she listened to the rain gushing over the gutters and splashing the windows of River's End, she reflected, the Queen would not be amused to see her estranged daughter-in-law cavorting with a Muslim.

Mr Thomas, the Laleham butcher, read how Diana was holidaying in the Bahamas with the notorious Dodi Fayed and, not wishing to be seen as an ignoramus, commented on it to Lady Smythe-Browne, over the telephone, after she had placed her weekly order. She replied that such behaviour was unprecedented, and wondered what Diana's two sons, the Princes William and Harry, would make of it all. He acknowledged he wouldn't know.

The Reverend Smith the previous Sunday had preached a sermon on adultery for the benefit of the newlyweds within his flock. He had grave misgivings about the forthcoming wedding between Sally Cox and Wayne Weller, as they had exclaimed raucously during a preparation class that those in high places disregarded all rules, and furthermore, the Church was behind the times.

Mrs Ponsonby remarked to Alice Ashby as she was pulling on her mackintosh at the reception desk, while making a dentist appointment for root canal treatment, that the antics of the Duchess of York were bad enough, and now it was the Princess of Wales. It was an utter disgrace! Her opinion wafted behind the closed door of the surgery, to the discomfort of a frightened patient.

Sheltering from the rain, senior students from Sir William Perkins' huddled together inside the bike sheds, embellishing the romance between the Princess of Wales and Dodi Fayed. 'Wish it were me holidaying with a gorgeous rich and handsome man on his yacht,' said Cathy McDowell. 'She has all the fun!'

'Can't say I blame her,' said her friends. 'Prince Charles is right boring!'

Each in their own way dreamed through their afternoon classes of sophisticated lifestyles, with sunshine, sex and scandal.

'It is appalling, the filth you read about in the papers!' shouted Mrs Davies over the vacuum cleaner as she reached around a settee. Noel regarded the rain gloomily through the lounge room window. 'What?' The heavy downpour wouldn't do his tomatoes any good, nor the fruit now lying in puddles. Thank God he had put in greenhouses; not all his crop would be ruined.

'I said...' She switched off the Hoover, regarding her employer. It was a mystery to her why Noel hadn't married that nice widow, Marion Lee. 'I think it is a disgrace taking pictures of Royals like this.' She indicated a picture of Princess Diana and Dodi Fayed sunbathing on a yacht, on the front page of the *Daily Telegraph*.

'Ex-Royal,' he said dryly, turning from the window and picking up the paper.

Feeling slightly put out, Mrs Davies shrugged. 'Whatever.' She was not content to leave it there. 'First, it was Margaret and all those shenanigans after that photographer fellow, then Anne and that horsey type, next Andrew and Fergie – totally unsuitable.' She sniffed, warming to her theme. 'And now Charles and Diana! They have it all and expect us to be sympathetic… the hoi polloi.'

She stopped in her tracks, wondering what Noel meant by 'ex'. He loafed around the farm, using peculiar words, hardly speaking. 'As I was saying. Is it worth it having a royal family, I ask you? They're all at it, barring the Queen herself, God bless her.' And with that she pushed the button on the Hoover, resumed vacuuming feeling decidedly out of sorts concerning the royal family, her employer and the rain.

Noel absently flicked through the paper, contemplating the ease with which some relinquish all sense of propriety, grabbing what they wanted, regardless of upset to others. He ruminated on the lack of excitement in his life. Apart from a mild fling while holidaying in Provence, which really was an unsatisfactory one-night stand of which he had only vague recall, nothing of any significance came to mind. He was appalled at his own lack of initiative, but then nobody had stirred him to passionate escapades. He read the article, again feeling depressed. He began to fantasise about what he would say to Marion on the telephone. It was easier that way; no embarrassing silences. 'I love you… and can't wait any longer. Will you marry me?' Then he thought to himself, This is ridiculous, a man of my age!

Mrs Davies interrupted his musings. 'I'll be going now, sir. Your meal is on the stove-top… I've taken the liberty of airing the sheets for the adjoining bedroom… cleaned the room and the en-suite. See you next week.'

Noel heard the door bang, wondering what she was twittering on about, and decided to investigate. It was a pleasant room with a sloping ceiling above the queen-size bed. Opening the door, he stood transfixed. Mrs Davies had found some pale pink lawn sheets with matching blankets and a white eiderdown. Four plumped-up pillows and small mauve cushions adorned the bedhead. A white doily sat perkily on top of a small Queen Anne table, with a bowl of pinks and gypsophila. On either side were two upright cane chairs and a three-cornered mirror of the same wood was perched on a kidney-shaped dressing table. 'What the...?' said Noel. Opening the door into the en-suite, there was more of the same: pink and white fluffy towels, Cussons soap and floral toilet paper. Sinking down into one of the chairs, he couldn't fathom where she had obtained all the linen and towels. The furniture looked vaguely familiar, but the eiderdown...! He was stunned, and chuckled at her audacity.

All around the globe, humankind read avidly about the romantic attachments of the Princess of Wales. From farm workers to secretaries, sports enthusiasts to musicians, everyone had opinions about the Royals, but none more damning than what passed as an aside between Anna and Nigel while sitting on a Queensland beach.

'I think the royal family have had their day.' To which he replied, 'Roll on the republic!'

In Laleham, Marion sighed, turning the page of the *Daily Express*, musing as she did so that hardly a day went by without some scandalous reference, relating to the royal family. She read that a horse had created mayhem on the M25. There was a picture of the horse and a pile-up of cars with a caption, 'Horse Power not appreciated'.

'How extraordinary!' she exclaimed, disturbing Intrepid, who was lying in her basket feigning sleep, not wishing for a repeat performance of the early morning, where she was unceremoniously bundled out into the rain. She shifted her position, burying her nose in the blanket and dreamt about chasing butterflies in sunny weather.

Further down page two Marion saw a photo of a Member of Parliament entering a gay bar. There was a comment about the garbage strike and pictures of refuse lying up and down a street in Putney. The caption read: 'Can you smell it?' Idly, she turned the page, distracted by the rain, mulling over whether she ought to buy a car. Waiting for the 218 bus in this kind of weather was no joke. Sometimes she had stood for twenty minutes, and there was no shelter. There was also the fact that now she was manning the Laleham Visitor Centre three mornings a week, quite often she didn't feel like the long walk home to River's End.

She read about a drought across Australia, which put her in mind of Janice, who would be arriving soon. How would she fetch her from Heathrow without a car? In her predicament about who she could ask to collect Janice, Noel's kindly face came into view. She would have been amazed to learn that he was thinking of her at that precise moment in time, as he sat on a cane-based chair in a bedroom with walls painted pale pink, flowers in a bowl and a white eiderdown, visualising Marion as the occupant; but remaining just as hesitant to make his request known as she was. Intuition nagged at the back of her mind that it was not fair to rely on Noel so much. Janice was her responsibility.

'I suppose I could ask Alice,' she said aloud. Intrepid opened one eye, then closed it quickly as her mistress stayed seated. Silence reigned, as Marion recalled how well Alice knew her way around Heathrow. It was mind-boggling, with the roads always seeming to be altered or under repair; furthermore Terminal 4 was about to be opened, to add to the chaos. Her thoughts flew to when Alice had met her. How thankful she was to see her familiar face among the crowds as she emerged from Customs!

What am I thinking of? Two years ago I wouldn't have dreamt of asking anyone in the lane if I could borrow a cup of sugar – let alone pick up a complete stranger from the airport. I need a car, and that's a fact! A vision of Leonard sitting behind the wheel and filling up at the local garage swam before her eyes. Leaving the table to make some minestrone soup, she decided to visit Robert Morell and see if he could point her in the right direction for a second-hand car. He might even have something suitable on the forecourt – something reliable, not too flashy. She imagined a dark blue car with CD player and matching upholstery.

Rummaging through the vegetable stand, she collected a carrot, onion, a cabbage and some fresh tomatoes that Noel had brought over at the weekend. She cut up the vegetables, thinking wistfully about Leonard and their relationship. It was nothing like the emotion she felt for Noel, but in a funny sort of way she missed him, usually at the oddest times. She took the saucepan over to the cold tap, considering whether to talk her problem over with Alice. After church would be a good time. At the very least, Alice could give her some pointers about which signs to look out for, so that she didn't end up in Cambridge. Then, adding some water to the vegetables, she imagined places she and Janice could visit. Windsor and its castle; the Queen's Doll's House; and St George's Chapel where kings and queens were buried. They could take a steamer up to Runnymede, and Marion could show Janice where Magna Carta was signed by King John. She pictured herself and Janice taking tea at Hampton Court and wandering around Kew Gardens. Then there was the picturesque town of Marlow, and peaceful Lechlade – so many possibilities if, and only if, she had a car.

Crumbling up a stock cube in the saucepan, Marion turned the gas on low, having noticed the rain had eased. She decided to go for a walk along the towpath. There was much to think about. Pulling on her raincoat, hood and small green boots, she bent down, whispering into Intrepid's ear, 'I know you don't want to come; shan't be long.' Then she left River's End by the front door, pocketing the keys as she did so.

Rose petals mingled with wisteria on the sodden grass, laburnum tails hung low, their branches weighed down by the rain, and forget-me-nots attempted to hold up their tiny blue heads as Marion savoured the fresh moist air. Swans and coots busied themselves in the reeds of the river, while the grass along the riverbanks glistened with silver droplets.

Imagined intimacies between Leonard and Michael's mother, Lucy, upstairs at Number Six, Ferry Lane, zoomed through her consciousness as her boots pressed into the soft squelchy gravel. With her imagination running riot, she found herself already at Penton Hook Lock. She could hear the weir, its waters thrashing in a thunderous roar, amply fitting her mood. Within minutes she was standing along the parapet looking down to the river below, a smallish insignificant woman, her face hidden by a rain hat. Her thoughts raced on, trying to recall any time she had felt suspicious of Leonard's behaviour, but none came to mind. How was it possible that two people could live together for so long and not know if the other were cheating? Either she was wrong in her assumptions or she was quite stupid. Neither equation seemed to fit the facts as she knew them. There was only one thing for it: she would have to ask Michael, something she was loath to do.

Tonight, over minestrone soup she would talk to Michael. Michael, who reminded her so often of Leonard, was caught, poor lamb, in the middle. It wasn't his fault and yet he had to carry the consequences.

'Fools rush in where angels fear to tread' went through her mind as she turned away from the weir, mulling over accepting Michael under her roof. And yet it wasn't her roof... Tomorrow she'd go into Clerk and Gamble and put pressure on Patricia to get an answer from Philip Sloane concerning her offer on the house. She couldn't wait until Christmas to know whether he was due to return or not. It didn't bear thinking about, having to move in the middle of winter... and where to? It really was impossible to contemplate. Lights came on as she passed the handful of houses set back from the lock, the sound from the weir fading as she gazed at the river rushing by in full spate. A light mist fell, creating a magical aura, this river, this place which she so loved. How she wished Sister Ruth was close by; she needed to tell her about Michael, and Janice coming. She would write, nevertheless, and merely mention Noel in passing. What would she think if she wrote that another man had come into her life at her age?

Her pace quickened as she remembered the minestrone on the stove and the warm welcome she would receive from Intrepid. She spied in the distance a neighbour walking his Alsatian towards her, but wasn't too sure which house he came from. 'Afternoon,' he said, a tall man in boots and mackintosh; obviously a man of few words. She nodded, her grey eyes combing his face as she walked on by.

Later, he remarked to his wife that he had seen the 'new lady' from River's End walking alone in the rain. 'She had penetrating grey eyes,' he said. It was a peculiar remark for him to make, as his wife had never in their twenty years of marriage heard him mention *her* eyes in any shape or form. She was watching a replay of the women's tennis final at Wimbledon on the television, and wondered if he was going through the male menopause.

On reaching River's End, Marion found the lights were on and music was emanating from its walls. She turned her key in the lock and thanked God for all her blessings.

~XIII~

Thy word is a lamp unto my feet
and a light unto my path.

Psalm 119, v 105

'Marion! Marion? Is that you?' a breathless voice called among the shoppers on Staines High Street. Lost in thought, dissatisfied at the brusque way Patricia Clerk had dismissed her enquiry, Marion had left Clerk and Gamble Estate Agents' offices with Patricia's voice ringing in her ears. 'I really think you should wait a few more months, Mrs Lee. Mr Sloane left specific instructions that he would contact us.' She emphasised the *he* and *us*, drawing them out as if Marion was mentally deficient. 'I did tell you this when you first decided to rent the property.'

Sophie Young diffidently touched her shoulder, aware that the swinging richly coloured hair, Chanel handbag and matching shoes amounted to a smarter version of the Marion she once knew. 'It is you,' said Sophie, 'but I thought you were in Australia. What a surprise!' Familiarly, she linked her arm through Marion's. 'Do say you have time for a coffee. I want to hear all the goss…'

'Well, I, er… why not?' Of all the people she would rather not have run into, it would be Sophie; not because she was unpleasant or disparaging – more in the sense that she invaded your space, gushing like a schoolgirl.

'Charlie's?'

'Lead on.' Marion smiled, rearranging her face, hoping she looked interested at what Sophie had to say, or at least sounded friendly. They sat at a circular bar with cakes and delicacies displayed behind glass; the waitresses in the centre wore purple pinafores wrapped around their bodies emblazoned with a 'C', busying themselves with coffee, hot water machines and stacking crockery.

'You look great – but tell me, what are you doing back here?'

'It's a long story. Shall we order?'

A caramel slice along with an Eccles cake was extracted from behind the glass cabinet. A pot of Earl Grey tea and small jug of milk was dispatched swiftly on the counter in front of them besides a cup and saucer complete with two packets of sugar; also an iced coffee in a tall glass with swirls of cream, sprinkled with chocolate.

Watching Sophie tuck into her caramel slice between mouthfuls of cream scooped off her coffee, Marion was not surprised that her friend's body required nourishment. Her cheeks, once chubby, now sagged. She was wearing a dress that was extremely tight and short, made out of some shiny dark brown material that rode high on her leg, revealing bony knees and stick-like legs. Whatever she had done to her hair Marion could only guess. Once it was fair and smooth but today it seemed to stand up like a broom. Maybe she was being too critical, and Sophie was having a bad hair day. She was heavily made up with various gold chains around her neck and several rings, their gems like rocks on all fingers. She was quite shocked, for at previous encounters at Old Girls' reunions, Sophie, while behaving oddly, always dressed modestly – drably in fact, if she thought about it. 'Well?' Sophie said, between mouthfuls of caramel.

'Leonard died… of an embolism.' She swallowed some tea, omitting to reveal her husband's deception and unfaithfulness, the result being a young man of seventeen now living under her roof. She also omitted to mention her interest in Noel Barker, or that she thought she may be in love with him.

'Poor you, I'm so sorry. It must have been a terrible shock for you, him dying so suddenly. I suppose Anna won't be coming back here to live?'

'No, in fact they have moved to Queensland. Nigel has a teaching position there on the Gold Coast – promotion, actually. Anna writes quite regularly… she's enjoying modelling.' And before Sophie could ask any more difficult questions, she added,

'I have moved back to Laleham. It has river frontage and it's lovely, set back from the towpath.'

'Ooh, nice.' Sophie's eyelids fluttered, aqua cream smeared across, up and over her eyebrows. Thick black mascara had stuck some lashes together. A small mouth painted in glossy brown completed the picture. Marion was nonplussed as to what could have possibly caused this dramatic change. This was nothing like the Sophie she used to know.

Fishing for neutral topics, she remarked. 'I have a dog, a collie. Her name is "Intrepid".' There was little response to this remark, so against her better judgment, she inquired, 'And what about you?'

Sophie, having taken note of the calm sophistication emanating from Marion, decided it had come about because of travel. She herself had not been further than Devon, and that was for a short summer holiday. 'Oh, this and that,' she said airily. 'Actually, I have taken a part-time job at Matthews the florist, in Ashford. And...' she inclined her head close to Marion's, eyes bulging as if to impart earth-shattering information. 'I auditioned for Epone in *Les Misérables* at our local amateur musical society! I'm her understudy,' she said with a flourish.

'Good heavens. I didn't know you could sing?' It was out before she realised it.

'I know, I wasn't in the school choir, but I wasn't interested in all those Welsh songs,' she said, tossing her head and looking affronted.

'Congratulations!' Marion couldn't remember there being any Welsh songs except the National Anthem; which every student learnt, not understanding a word of it, except *Gwlad*, there being no translation given. So that explained the heavy make-up and presumably the anorexic look. Poor Sophie was trying to fit in somewhere but not quite getting it right.

She reflected on the many reunions attended, Sophie retelling wild exploits that no one else ever remembered. Once, when Sophie had imbibed too much Moselle, the chairwoman of the association, Morwena Davies, had leant across the white table-cloth and hissed at her saying, 'Who *is* that?' as if she were responsible.

'St David's Day, you missed a good one there.'

'I did?' It occurred to Marion that she had entirely forgotten about it. Extraordinary, as she was back in England before then.

'You'd better send in your change of address or you won't know future dates.'

'Right… As you can imagine, I've been rather occupied.'

'Christine Samson is divorced.'

'Who?'

'Christine Samson, used to be Christine Jones.'

'Oh, yes, of course.'

'Ran off with the golfing coach.'

'I didn't know she played golf.'

'Oh yes – the team consisted of Janet, Carolyn, and Sandra. They did us proud at the Silver Tassie tournament. Didn't win, but played magnificently with a score of 242. Do you play? Because I know for a fact they have trouble getting a team together.'

'I wouldn't know an iron from a driver.' Neither, she suspected, did Sophie.

'Good for the school. Good for Ashford Manor Golf Club,' she said knowingly. Before Marion had time to digest this piece of information, Sophie added, 'Valerie Trainer's camera shop has gone to the wall and rumour has it that one of the present staff is – you know – with the chaplain!'

'Surely not… you're pulling my leg.'

'I heard it from a very reliable source.'

Marion began wishing she hadn't come to Charlie's, hearing all the supposed infidelities and disasters of 'old girls' she could hardly put a face to. Nevertheless, she ordered more hot water for her teapot and attempted to turn the conversation away from wild speculation. 'It must be nice working in a florist's.'

'Oh, it is, but sometimes we get the strangest men lodging orders. The cards they write! Nor are some averse to flirting. It's unbelievable! I'll tell you what they say!'

Marion looked around the café. A clock said 11.45. 'Look, Sophie, I really have to go. I didn't realise the time. Lots to do still.' She smiled, edging away.

'Oh, but you'll come to the next OGA dinner in August.'

'I don't know if I can… house guests.'

'House guests?' Sophie looked scornful.

'No, really. A young lass from Tasmania, and…' Her voice trailed away.

Sophie shifted beside Marion as she began to move among the chairs and tables, sticking so close that at one stage she almost bumped into her. '*Les Mis*, you'll come to that… I'll send you some tickets.'

'I can't say, that far ahead. You know how it is.' She had reached the doorway of the shop, waiting to see which way Sophie would go.

'What are friends for! I wouldn't dream of you having to buy tickets. Give me your address and I'll send you some.'

Marion fished around in her bag for pen and paper, wondering how she had become involved with the likes of Sophie. She had more important things on her mind. There was Michael, and Janice arriving shortly, then there was the car, and not being able to contact Philip Sloane. 'Ah, here it is.' She retrieved a pen and tore a small piece of paper from her diary. 'Here's my phone number, I think it would be wise to ring me nearer the time.'

Sophie peered at the number, then shoved it down a beaded shoulder bag. 'Well, that's that then. We'll meet soon. I'm off to do some retail therapy. Actually, I'm looking for a place to live, share a house with someone. You should see the woman I share a flat with! She's a fanatic tidier – nothing out of place – drives me mad. You don't know of anywhere, do you?'

'I'm sorry, I don't. Try one of the agents.' And with Sophie's words ringing in her ears, Marion made her getaway. She had intended to browse, buy Michael something he would deem 'cool'. Instead, feeling flustered, she caught the first 218 bus she saw, for home, hoping Sophie wouldn't find out about Michael or her relationship with Noel, it being so soon after Leonard's death. It didn't bear thinking about.

Later that evening she was annoyed with herself for being so intimidated by Sophie. 'Quite ridiculous!' she said as she ran a bath, pouring in rosehip oil she had acquired the previous weekend at the car boot sale with Noel. The woman had become a dangerous menace. Marion slipped into the warm water, feeling its soothing effects and wondering on the vagaries of human behaviour. The last thing she wanted was Sophie calling around, insinuating herself and being a nuisance. What with scandals passed around by Sophie about unsuspecting members of the OGS, she speculated whether it was worth retaining her membership. Then there were the church services using electronic gadgets, and changing well-known prayers with modern translations; the reason given that they were old-fashioned, moreover; and knocking down the beautiful rood screen for a children's corner! She felt the world she had once known had changed irrevocably, like shifting sand beneath her feet causing uncertainties. What was wrong with the old English *Book of Prayer*, that it had been replaced with pamphlets and different prayers? 'Almighty and most merciful Father, we have erred and strayed from your ways like lost sheep...' Beautiful words, prayed humbly within God's house. You couldn't say they were incomprehensible. 'Trespass' was another. Why change the Lord's Prayer? 'Sins' didn't have the same ring to it. Everyone knew the meaning of trespass. Then there were the lessons, once read apart from each other, giving you time to take them in; but now all three were read one after the other, the psalm being squeezed into the middle. What was the point of standing for the Gospel facing east while your mind was filled with the other readings whose contents had no relevance to the Gospel? It defied logic and spirituality as far as she was concerned. People felt alienated and confused. She pulled the plug, dried and dressed, deciding to go in search of Intrepid and make hot chocolate for herself and Michael.

'I could have met you at the station,' Marion said as she handed Michael a hot lemon drink, which he placed beside two Disprin and a glass of water on his bedside table.

It was a new experience, all this fuss and attention he was receiving. He reckoned he'd caught the flu on the day of the downpour, and remembered catching the 6.25 from Waterloo; the carriage windows steamed up with all the wet raincoats and puddles on the floor from umbrellas. On arriving at Staines Station, he had made a conscious decision not to wait another hour for the 224 bus, but to take his chances with Gresham Road and the 218. As it happened, by the time he had arrived at the bus stop on the Staines Road, he was soaked to the skin.

'Now, is there anything else I can get you?' asked Marion.

'I'm fine really. You go off to the Centre.'

'I'll be back around one. If I'd had a car, you wouldn't be lying there sick.'

'As long as I'm right by the weekend...' He sighed, which caused him to cough.

It was like a recurring nightmare for Marion, handing out tablets and expecting everything to be all right. Visions of Leonard lying in bed complaining of a migraine became entangled with the present. She'd felt guilty for days, not calling a doctor sooner.

'I'll get the doctor,' she told Michael, worry and concern etched across her face.

'No need. He won't come anyway. They never do nowadays. If I'm worse by teatime perhaps you'd call him then. Maybe on his way home after surgery he'd drop by.' Michael closed his eyes. Underneath them, dark lines like bruises contrasted with taut skin over flushed cheekbones.

She'd never forgive herself if he became delirious while she was out of the house. She said, 'You'll call me if you feel worse, won't you?'

He nodded, wishing she would go, so that he could go to sleep.

'I'll make us something nice for lunch when I return.' She stood looking down at his flushed face, hair flopping over his forehead. His hands were splayed out on the duvet, showing beautiful, long, tapered fingers. She touched his forehead. It didn't feel too hot.

He opened his eyes. 'Thanks, Marion, I'll be all right,' he whispered.

Quietly, she went down the stairs, checked that Intrepid had her bowl of water and some biscuits, then left for Laleham Heritage Centre. Today she dusted the bone china plates, catalogued the books and itemised pamphlets, maps, and bric-a-brac for sale. Normally she enjoyed these simple tasks, even taking bookings for guided walks of the region; but today she felt distracted by Michael lying sick in bed, not making a decision about which car to purchase, and an underlying apprehensive dread that, come Christmas, she would have to move from River's End.

She was in two minds whether to ring Noel and ask for his advice on both counts, but decided against it. She picked up the phone and got as far as phoning Dr Walters, as he lived in the village, but as she heard a taped message she replaced the receiver swiftly, unable to cope with a disembodied voice. With her chores finished, she went outside to the Wildlife Garden and, bending down by the herb wheel, picked some mint and thyme, behind which scarlet poppies, delphiniums and hollyhocks grew against the surrounding wall. Foxgloves and yellow toadflax grew among a hawthorn hedge, and hop trefoil mixed with clover formed a round lawn dotted with daisies. There was a wooden seat placed near a man-made stream, where marsh marigolds and water crowfeet floated. Along its tiny banks, columbines waved and ground-hugging periwinkle were kept in check by scarlet pimpernel.

Here, Marion sat, enjoying the summer warmth, watching a family of sedge warblers peck at the weed seeds and insects. Somewhere within the garden, a hedgehog burrowed, as did a family of voles, but today she saw neither. Nor did she see the brothers Tom and Terence Mayhew, now in their sixties, who tended the garden on a voluntary basis. The tranquillity of the garden and its inhabitants worked their soothing powers.

The church clock struck twelve, its bell piercing the air. She rose from her reverie to lock up and go home refreshed, trusting that whatever the circumstances she found herself in, she would find the necessary strength and wisdom to persevere. She recalled reading somewhere that it wasn't what happened to you in life that mattered but how you reacted to what had happened. And when she thought about it, she realised how profoundly true this was. Like reading about muggings, murders and world disasters: you could either go into some kind of depression, or you could soldier on, trusting that there was good in the world and that in general man did try to love his brother. She thought of Martin Bryant and all the horrors he had inflicted on persons unknown to him. She offered up a silent prayer for continuing fortitude and some measure of peace for those family members left in the aftermath. She thought of Michael coming into her life, and as a result the blessings she had received, even though they had been born out of adversity. She no longer saw him as a problem or worry but as a person to love and be there for.

A calming spirit like she had received at Mary Knoll came over her, and memories of Sister Ruth reading from a Bible on her lap. 'Come unto me all you that are heavy laden and I will give you rest.' She had explained that if you looked at a problem, or a relationship, or an unpleasant decision you needed to make, differently, if you stepped back only a little way, you would see the persons involved with fresh eyes, with love and understanding rather than anger, hostility, fear or hate. The burden and the stress fall away. The situation may stay the same, but if you don't despair, you don't see it as a problem any more.

Only now did Marion fully understand those words, as she linked others going through her mind from the Gospel according to St John: 'Ye shall know the truth, and the truth shall make you free.'

She arrived home to find Michael making himself a sandwich in the kitchen. 'I felt hungry,' he explained. 'Would you like one?'

'A cup of tea is what I need.' Marion smiled as Intrepid came towards her, tail wagging before licking her hand. 'I think I'll work in the garden this afternoon – and you, my lad, ought to rest in bed.'

'Yes, ma'am,' he said cheekily.

After lunch she went out into the garden armed with trowel, fork and gloves previously purchased from Staines Market Square. A wheelbarrow stored in the summer house served to put the weeds in. An old pillow placed in a black rubbish bag did for kneeling upon, which she found perfectly adequate. It was pleasant foraging among the garden beds. She felt her mind relax, and somehow just kneeling and pulling out stray grasses gave her a sense of belonging. It was therapeutic, being close to the earth with the sunshine on her back, musing about her relationship with Noel. She stretched, leaning back, looking at a few puffy clouds crossing a blue sky, deciding then and there that tomorrow she would buy the blue Ford Focus she had seen in the car yard at Crimbles in Staines. Then a voice called, 'Hello there!'

A man and woman crossed the lawn. He was solidly built with receding sandy hair, wearing a soft green shirt, its collar visible over the lapels of a denim jacket. His jeans showed creases from sitting some length of time in a car, and on his feet he wore suede lace-up shoes.

'Hello,' said the woman. 'You don't know who we are, do you?' She smiled, and her lips, an apricot colour, twitched. She too was wearing denim. Her skirt was knee-length, showed freckled legs, her feet encased in a soft type of golf shoe, off-white in colour, their backs barely covering her heels. She laughed now, turning towards her husband. 'She doesn't know who we are. It's Marion, isn't it?' she said, holding out her hand.

Marion pulled off her gloves, trying to pinpoint the accent, and fascinated by the woman's short reddish hair swept back from her face in small sticky clumps. She presumed that for the style to stay like that, she would have used a tube of gel.

'I'm sorry,' said Marion, looking puzzled, taking the proffered hand as a whiff of lily of the valley passed in the air.

'We're Nigel's parents.' A throaty laugh emanated from her pink open-necked shirt.

Over her right shoulder hung a patchwork leather handbag, which she now transferred to her left as she took hold of Marion's hand. 'Oh, I'm so sorry. I'm very pleased to meet you… I'm Priscilla.'

'Of course – Priscilla.'

'And this here is Neville.' She beamed. Embarrassed to be caught like this, Marion ran her hand through her hair, feeling at a disadvantage.

'I hope we are not interrupting anything…' Neville said, indicating the wheelbarrow.

'Because,' Priscilla interrupted, 'we just had to pop in on our way to Windsor.' She looked around the garden. 'What a lovely spot you live in.'

'Our condolences, Marion. I expect you find it hard without Leonard.' Neville cleared his throat. 'We would have liked to have met him. Wouldn't we, love?'

Priscilla nodded. 'But you still have a charming daughter – doesn't she, Neville. I've always wanted a daughter, but it wasn't to be. Nigel is a lucky man.'

They stood in the garden chatting about the weather, hired cars and airlines before Marion, pulling herself together, suggested they stay for afternoon tea.

'We'll have it in the conservatory, if you like.'

'Would you mind if I used your little room?'

'Of course not. It's through the kitchen in the hall,' called Marion after a hurrying Priscilla.

But Priscilla didn't hear the exact directions, and after fumbling through coats in the hallway she assumed the toilet must be upstairs. She peered in various bedrooms before trying the handle of what she assumed was the bathroom. Someone was in there running water. She stood on the landing, hesitating for a moment, partly concealed by a fern cascading from a hanging basket. Then the door opened and a young man dressed only in a towel came out and entered one of the bedrooms. As soon as he had closed his door she ducked into the bathroom, relieved to see a toilet, assuming that the young man was Anna's brother, although she had never heard of one being mentioned.

Downstairs, pleasantries were passed along with shortbread, chocolate marshmallows and banana cake. Earl Grey tea was poured into fine bone china cups decorated in pink rosebuds.

'Milk, sugar, Neville?'

'Please.' He would have preferred a beer but didn't like to ask the quintessentially English Marion.

'The wedding took place in the church you would have seen on your way here,' Marion said as she poured the tea.

'What's that I heard about a wedding?' Priscilla chortled, re-entering the conservatory, helping herself to sugar and accepting a marshmallow.

'Anna and Nigel, their wedding, and Leonard's Memorial Service was there too… in the village church.' She smiled. 'It's very old, dates back to Norman times.'

'I thought you had the funeral in Tadbury.'

'We did, but I preferred to bring his ashes home. It was a beautiful service. Bells were played and the church was packed.

He used to train youngsters in campanology.' They looked blankly at her. 'Bell-ringing... It was a thanksgiving service, if you like, for his life.'

'I'm not much up in Church protocol. A thanksgiving service, well I never. Have you heard of that, Neville?'

'Can't say I have, my dear. I'll have another slice of that banana cake, though.'

'I couldn't leave him there in Tasmania... it's like the end of the world. He... we belong here,' she found herself saying decisively.

'Right. Well, we haven't been down to Hobart in years, have we, Neville? And I don't suppose we will, now that Nigel is in Queensland.' Priscilla helped herself to some banana cake. 'I'd like to visit Queensland, now it looks as though, if we like it, we might move there. That's right, isn't it, Neville?' She swallowed some tea and then added, 'We thought you might have moved there, to be close to Anna.'

'There were difficulties,' Marion said carefully. 'And to be honest, or should I say, to be fair, I didn't see much of the pair of them when we all lived in Tadbury. Anna and Nigel were both teaching, and I didn't know anyone, friends, you know...' she trailed off.

'I understand... and Anna's brother was still here in England.' Priscilla smiled, nodding her head knowingly.

'Brother?' Marion replied, shocked. 'She doesn't have a brother.'

'Don't be absurd, Priscilla.' Neville frowned at his wife, wondering why she always managed to make outlandish comments. Marion had gone quite pale. He noticed she didn't eat a thing. Priscilla looked abashed.

'I see, you play...' Neville said heartily, nodding in the direction of a violin case.

'Ah, no, that belonged to Leonard's father. It was his only legacy to Leonard. He died during the war.' Marion seemed to have been disturbed by something, and in order to keep the conversation going Priscilla said conspiratorially, 'Marion, do tell us. When are we to be grandparents?'

'I have no idea. I'm in the dark as much as you are. I think we may have to wait some time.'

'Pity.'

'I agree.'

There was a pause in the conversation. Priscilla was quite clear in her own mind that she had seen a young man dressed only in a towel. Neville was thinking it was about time they settled in one place, and Marion was simply wishing they would go.

'I just love your house,' Priscilla said brightly, and standing up, looked around the room.

'It's not yet...' Marion changed her mind. It was none of anyone else's business whether she owned the house or not. Instead, she said, 'You can see the river from the lounge room. I grew up here, so I know all the beautiful spots. I even went to the village school. Leonard and I lived down another lane closer to the village. That too was a lovely house. Anna attended my old school in Ashford and took up a teaching position there. Nigel also found a position close by but we missed them when they left for Australia.'

'I'm sure you did, my dear, but you know what young people are these days. Here today and gone tomorrow.' Neville laughed easily and then stood up. 'I think we ought to be making tracks, my dear. We've a booking in Eton for tonight, and up to Oxford for a few days before returning to London.'

'I mustn't keep you. The traffic will be getting heavy,' Marion said, and they moved towards the side of the house where a silver car was parked. The visitors said their goodbyes, promising to keep in touch and thanking her for providing afternoon tea. It was with a sense of relief that Marion leant forward through the open car window endeavouring to point out the easiest route on the map via Windsor to Eton, and wishing the Creeses safe journeying. She stepped back, only to see Noel roaring up the lane way in his red sports car with the roof down. He pulled over as Neville was reversing out, but not before both of them had a long look at the handsome man at the wheel.

'Did you see that?'

'Yes, dear!' With his eyes still on the rear-view mirror, Neville said, 'He has alighted from the car and appears to be following Marion back into the house, carrying a bunch of flowers.'

'*What!*' Priscilla swivelled around, but by then they had

reached the end of the lane and turning into Staines Road. 'Well, I never!'

'It's none of our business.'

She was silent for a while and then said, 'I saw a young man upstairs going from the bathroom into a bedroom dressed only in a towel.'

'I really wish you wouldn't make up these stories, Priscilla. It's embarrassing.'

'I *did* see him! Who do you think it was?'

'I have no idea.' After a while he added, 'That was quite excruciating. I need a beer.' He followed Marion's directions into Staines and was appalled at the traffic. 'Christ! Keep your eyes open for signs to Windsor. If I get in the wrong lane we'll probably end up in London.'

'Oh, don't be silly! There was something else peculiar. Why have a violin and music stand erected if you don't play? Somebody played that instrument, I'm sure of it; besides, there were piles of classical music sheets. It's all very odd.'

'Don't you fret yourself about it, love. Put it out of your mind.'

'It's probably just as well she didn't go to the Gold Coast after all,' his wife said sagely, shifting in her seat and peering up at the road signs.

'Yes, I'm thinking that too. Let's stop at a pub. Keep your eyes open, my dear. I'm in need of some strong refreshment.'

'It was a beautiful house, though.'

'I'll get you a beautiful house, dear.'

'I'll believe that when it happens.'

Maybe Priscilla was right. Their house in Devonport was very ordinary. It was about time they settled down, travelled less; this driving was becoming a bit of an ordeal, and they weren't getting any younger. He said, 'After this trip we'll take it a bit easier, find a spot we like, hopefully near Nigel. Would you like that, dear?'

She patted his knee, wondering if he would ever settle. 'There's a pub right on the water, the Bells of Ouseley… You'll have to find a turn-off and get across the traffic somehow. There, up there.' She pointed through the windscreen.

'Right, got you.' Neville manoeuvred the car, thinking he'd

had enough for one day. All these imaginings of Priscilla's! What if senile dementia had set in? She'd already complained someone had taken all her underwear while staying at the Spread Eagle in Midhurst, only to find later she, herself, had divided up the clean underwear from those needing a wash in separate pockets of her suitcase. 'We're going to need petrol soon.'

'Yes, dear,' he said. 'Everything in good time,' and deftly parked on the forecourt.

On the evening that Marion's Ford Focus first sat in the driveway, Michael was mooching around in his bedroom. A holdall containing his toiletries, change of jeans, T-shirt and underwear lay on the bed. He leafed through his wallet for the third time and came to the conclusion he would have to ask Marion for money. Earlier in the day, a letter arrived from his mother, which now lay open on the bed. She had explained in answer to his previous note that she hadn't any money to spare, as Craig, the lover she had left with, had now returned to his wife. She hadn't known he was married. She now was stuck down in Wiltshire, having to pay for the one-bedroom flat herself. A postscript stated she would try to send some money for his birthday.

He went downstairs to make a drink, noticing how quiet the house was then remembered Marion had taken Intrepid for a walk. He needed a job locally to tide him over the remaining part of the year, as his scholarship money had all but been spent. A concert booking in October in Cardiff and the imminent Edinburgh Festival would bring in a little, but not enough; besides which, what if Marion asked for board? Wandering through the house, Michael felt completely at ease; there was something about the shape and furnishings that brought about a sense of belonging, of 'home', an instinct not experienced at Number Six, Ferry Lane – quite ridiculous, really, as he didn't belong here either. Marion was kind and more like a real mother, or so he imagined. She was a bit weird at times, but that was to be expected at her age. At least she didn't keep on at him about drugs and sex. He could hear Lucy yelling at him, 'And where have you been? I hope you're not getting some girl pregnant!' Her face would be all shiny and pinched looking, her hair fluffed up, and she'd be smelling of some sickly scent. At least Marion didn't harp on, questioning him as to his whereabouts as if he were a halfwit.

He wandered through the conservatory into the back garden carrying a glass of cider and sat down on the steps, thinking about a girl in the orchestra, a flautist he rather fancied; but as far as he knew she lived Wimbledon way.

'And what do you want to do with your life?' his professor had asked, quite recently. 'Do you want to become a famous violinist?' His long white hair bobbed around on his collar as he closely observed Michael's face, his eyes screwed up, peering over rimless spectacles.

'I don't know, sir,' he had replied.

'Well, you'd better make your mind up, you know, before someone else makes it up for you,' the professor said crossly.

It was all very well telling him to get a manager, but he hadn't the money, not like some of the others in the orchestra, who came from well-to-do families. There was Bruce Banfield and three others who had teamed up with an agency off Fleet Street, playing light classical at dance halls and soirées and the like. He couldn't see himself playing at holiday camps and old-time dances. He couldn't see himself studying overseas in Vienna or anywhere else in 1998, with or without a scholarship. He would rather stay in England. Furthermore, he'd teach if he really had to in order to make ends meet. Prof. Llewellyn imagined he would become a second Yehudi Menuhin. That was quite absurd, and it was another cause for concern. For it was while he was playing some Debussy, with the prof accompanying him on the grand piano, that a suavely dressed man in his thirties with coal-black hair and eyes entered. He was sure the former was dyed as he shook hands. The man introduced himself as David something or other, 'agent extrordinaire', and said, 'What couldn't *I* do for you, young man!' The emphasis on the 'I'. 'You have the talent, so Prof here tells me,' he added with a wink in his direction, 'and *I* have the contacts!'

Michael had heard stories, of course, but to meet David in person made his skin crawl. There was no way he could liaise with and put his career into the hands of a raving queer. Visions of night-time activities he had no interest in swam into view –

strange hotels and peculiar arrangements adding to his consternation. He'd supposed he'd been quite rude. No wonder Prof. Llewellyn was losing patience. He aspired to becoming lead violinist in one of the national orchestras, like the Berlin or London Philharmonic, or even the BBC; however, that was unlikely, as competition was fierce. They would consider him too young.

It was at times like this Michael wished Leonard was around. Maybe he could talk to Noel; he seemed a down-to-earth sort of bloke, he wouldn't talk bullshit… but being a farmer, he really wouldn't be of much help. He took a long swig of his cider before saying aloud, 'If I'm to continue with this lark, I need a mentor. What I need is a mentor!' He raised his voice and waved his arms about in frustration. He stood up, returning to the kitchen in search of food. A sugar fix might help his quandary.

'Michael, is that you?' The back door banged. Marion and Intrepid came into the kitchen, she looking flushed from the warmth of the evening, Intrepid making for her water bowl.

'I thought I heard voices.'

'No, just me.' He looked guilty, with a hand covering his mouth as he savoured his second chocolate marshmallow. Marion laughed, removing her sunglasses, revealing grey eyes sparkling like crystal, or so it seemed to him. 'Eat as many as you like,' she said, crossing to fill the electric jug with water for a cup of tea.

'Let me…' He took Intrepid's lead and looped it over an apron on the back of the door and the thought came to him: what if the owner, Mr Sloane, refused to sell Marion the house. What then? Where would he be? Up the proverbial creek without a paddle! Marion would be all right; she'd go and live with Noel. You'd have to be blind not to notice something was going on between them, at least on Noel's part, but where would that land him? They wouldn't want him. It was amazing she took him in at all, under the circumstances. In the silence that followed Intrepid could be heard slurping water as they watched the jug boil.

'All organised for Edinburgh then?'

'Sort of.' He thought of Graham Sheedy, a trombone player to whom he owed £50.

'The fireflies and midgets are out,' said Marion. 'Intrepid

chased a moorhen. She's hopeless.' Hearing her name, the dog lifted her head, looking at Michael for sympathy.

Bending down to stroke her silky ears, Michael wished his life was as simple as hers. 'She'll get into trouble one of these days.'

Marion nodded, placing two mugs of tea on the table; he didn't really want any tea after the cider, but didn't like to say. 'I see you had a letter from your mother,' she said brightly, helping herself to milk. As he didn't reply, she pulled out a chair from the table and sat down, indicating for him to do the same. 'Is anything the matter?' her voice gently probed.

'Calling you "Marion" – it doesn't sound right.' Whatever made him say that he had no idea; it wasn't what he had in mind. He sat down awkwardly, shifting his mug around in circles.

'Oh.' Her lips twitched. 'Why's that?' He shrugged, and she went on, 'It's not your fault you find yourself in an embarrassing situation. I have another name – Claire. You could use that, if you like. My friends at school called me Clarrie.'

'Clarrie.' He rolled the name around his tongue stretching it out, '*Clarrie*. I like that.' Stumbling, he said, 'When I was little I called... him... Uncle Len, but when I turned eleven he suggested I drop the "Uncle". That's when he gave me the violin.'

'Did he?'

'He was very good to me, gave me lots of toys.'

'Was he?'

'Yes, he gave me a cricket bat and roller skates, but the best was the violin.'

Painful though it was, she asked, 'Did you see him often?'

Michael recalled his eleventh birthday when he opened up the case and saw his very own violin. Up until then he had used one from Halliford, his primary school. There came an occasion when the small school orchestra had an opportunity to go to France and join with a French school for a week. They would present a recital on the last night of works requiring large numbers of musicians. Michael had been very excited, hoping Leonard would pay for his ticket. French students would then come to his school. He could see himself now, ferreting about in the desk where his mother kept perfumed writing paper, gas and electricity bills, and old photos all jumbled up together, looking for his birth certificate, because Mrs Savage at the school said, 'And anyone who hasn't got a passport will need to contact the passport office in London with his or her birth certificate before it will be issued.' Furthermore, she had told them to get on to it quickly. It could take a fortnight or so, and as they were leaving in a month it was necessary, if they didn't want to be left behind.

Michael hadn't understood her properly, but realised he would need money. Luckily, Leonard had given him £20 to put in his post office account for his eleventh birthday. He had found the certificate one afternoon when his mother was out. There it was: mother, Lucy Driver; father: deceased. All through the tour he had felt sick remembering that he had asked Mrs Cherry at the post office how he should fill in the form that she supplied. He'd signed the postal order and she'd done the rest, saying, 'You poor mite.' He had felt like an idiot.

They'd played Brahms and practised Tchaikovsky's '1812' Overture. He'd never told his mother any of it, and a year later he could see the likeness in himself to Leonard, his hair, his eyes, even in the way he moved. He didn't ask who his father was. He could sense it wasn't the thing to do. Leonard never said, nor did his mother. It was the sort of thing like if your dad was in prison – not talked about.

Now, sitting opposite Marion, he said, 'I don't remember much except for birthdays. He usually came over. After I turned eleven he would ring sometimes, and of course I saw him at the church with the other boys bell-ringing. I don't think he saw much of my mother… if he did, I didn't know.'

They were silent, each with their own thoughts. 'Drink up,' she said, because she couldn't think of anything appropriate to say. He looked miserable, so she asked, 'Is there something else bothering you?'

He pulled out a letter from his jeans and laid it on the table. 'It's from the building society… I'm overdrawn.'

'Oh dear.' She saw the statement and read, 'please rectify'.

'I don't know what to do. I need to hire a tux for Edinburgh, and I owe a friend—'

'Shh,' she put hand over his. 'It's all right, Michael, I'll make us another cup.'

'I don't know how this has happened!'

Marion busied herself with the jug, refilling it from the cold tap, thinking to herself she knew exactly why all this has happened. He'd been abandoned by a flighty mother and a father who was too embarrassed to tell his wife of a son born because of an affair begun at an office Christmas party. She saw his stricken face and her heart went out to him. 'Tell me... you have a scholarship to the academy?'

He nodded, then added, 'But that only covers my tuition and travelling to and from home.'

'What about Edinburgh? Who pays your accommodation and expenses?'

'We stay at a school, as it is holiday time, or find our own place... it depends. Sometimes several of us share a flat, but this time—'

'Tell me the itinerary,' Marion cut in. 'I don't know about these things.'

'What do you mean?'

'For a start, what do you do for food?'

'We buy our own. We're playing at various concert halls – that is, the main orchestra is – and several of us have got together to form a quartet. We're playing on the "Fringe", performing works composed by one of the guys, Ray Sterling. I like his stuff, he's very good. There's me; John Campbell, he plays the violin too; then there's Hamish Wilson, who plays the cello; and Ray, who plays the oboe. It sounds brilliant. There's a lot going on at once, so if you are free, you can usually get into what's on at the Fringe: new comedians, fresh acts, modern dance. Tickets are fairly cheap, whereas the main events have sold out before the Festival opens.'

'Do other students get into difficulties? I mean, with money?'

'Well, everyone I know has a part-time job, and there is a lot of borrowing.'

'Leave it with me; I'll think of something. For the present you need a tux, some cash for the festival, and some money in your building society account.'

Michael nodded, thinking that if he had alerted his mother to half of what he had revealed to Marion, she would be screaming at him by now. She came round the table to him, gently ruffling his hair. 'Go and do some practice, you'll feel better. I've got things to do before tomorrow. Ah… there was one thing.' She paused before going upstairs. 'I don't know how to put this. Did Len help out in general… financially?'

'I'm sorry, Clarrie. If it hadn't been for him…'

A numbness spread through her, as if the last seventeen years of their marriage had been a lie. She'd lived in the same house as Leonard, provided his meals, entertained as best she could his business acquaintances, cleaned his house and knelt next to him during the morning service at All Saints', saying, 'And lead us not into temptation' – and she never knew. She had no idea that just around the corner lived his mistress and their son. No wonder Len was happy to go to Australia, to run as far as he could from the situation! And she, being naive, believed the reason for their departure was to be close to Anna. She walked into Michael's room feeling the weight of responsibility she had so innocently accepted. Leonard had paid Lucy Driver on a regular basis, before moving to Australia. She recalled his peculiar behaviour over their telephone number, giving her an unsatisfactory reason for having it changed.

Now, sitting on Michael's bed, she began checking all was as it should be: clean socks, underwear, extra jeans, sweater and T-shirts neatly placed within his holdall. Before she picked up Lucy's letter, tears trickled down her cheeks. She wept. 'If only you knew what I feel like, Len! I sold the house from under your son's feet.' Wiping her tears, she reread the letter, admitting that Noel was right. She hadn't known what she was letting herself in for, playing mother because she so wanted a son. Well, she wasn't going to abandon him now, whatever the cost. She would have a word with Noel. He would have a more realistic idea about what a young man's needs would be financially. Then, in the morning, before dropping Michael at the station, she would visit her bank to transfer a suitable amount on a monthly basis across to his account at the building society in the Thames Road.

The following morning while driving her new Ford, she mentioned Burton's Tailoring. 'It would be cheaper in the long run to buy a tuxedo, Michael. You might be lucky and get one off the peg… and you must buy some shoes!'

'I haven't the money, Clarrie.'

'I know you haven't. I'm coming to that. How much time have we?'

'About an hour.'

'Well, we'll try to get you a tux first, before going to the bank, OK?' Then she said, 'You haven't said anything about my car.'

'It beats catching the bus,' he replied, grinning.

They would have an understanding, she had said. She would take care of his overdraft and deposit £100 into his building society account every month. If he got into difficulties, he'd have to sort it out. She'd draw a line at bailing him out in the future. He'd have to share some of the responsibility. When he returned he would need to find a part-time job until he had decided what it was he was going to do.

'I'm not a free gravy train. Is that clear?' she said quietly, while easing the car over Staines Bridge and into a multi-storey car park. He had kissed her on the cheek and said he wouldn't let her down.

Although they hadn't found a tuxedo to his satisfaction, he had enough money to rent one in Edinburgh and pay for all his needs while away. She felt a sense of relief as she waved him off at the station, in an agreeable frame of mind. This, combined with the driving of her new car, nourished her well-being. The awkwardness between them had dissipated, honest feelings acknowledged. It was as if a barrier had been lifted. Their relationship had stepped up a notch.

Well, that's how it is, she mused, letting herself in at the Historic Centre over an hour late. A new confidence banished past sensitivities of anxiety and guilt as she set to dusting the shelves. The only cloud on the horizon she foresaw was that she hadn't as yet written to Anna explaining any of her new circumstances.

Marion wandered from lounge to kitchen and back again, going over and over in her mind what she would tell Anna. She could hardly ring her up and say, 'Oh, by the way I have a seventeen-year-old living with me, the product of an indiscretion on your father's part.' She sighed, realising there was no easy way of imparting such information, that she, Anna, had a half-brother.

Then, collecting pen and paper, Marion decided to write the whole story down.

'Dear Anna, you remember that house in Ferry Lane neither you nor I were aware your father owned…' She stopped, not knowing how to proceed, and seeing the *Express* she riffled through the paper in order to attempt the crossword, but not before lurid captions caught her eye: 'Boy dies as pet traps him in a tumble dryer'… 'The case of *Blair* versus *Blair*, M'lud' and 'Four held by City squad in £28 billion scam' caused her to pause and reflect on what made news. There were the usual articles about the royal family. Australia's Patrick Rafter had beaten Canada's Greg Rusedski at the US Open, and there was a piece about the heat keeping shoppers off the streets; it was the second hottest August since records began in 1659.

None of this was any help with her letter to Anna, except to say that the weather was lovely. She elaborated.

> His name is Michael, the violin player behind the rood screen at your father's Memorial Service. I didn't know this at the time. I sold the house in Ferry Lane and she – his mother – took off with a lover down to Wiltshire. Michael attends The Royal Academy of Music on a scholarship, but has no other visible means of support. I guess he takes after his grandfather, and in some ways is like your father. He is presently playing at the Edinburgh Festival. Your dad would have been so proud of him. You can imagine the shock when I discovered the situation. I hope you see it the way I do, taking him in, as it seemed the right thing to do.

Marion read through her explanation, adding, 'Michael's presence in no way diminishes your standing in the family. Love as always, Mum.'

After mixing herself a gin and bitter lemon, she decided to seal the letter without mentioning she wasn't able as yet to buy River's End, or referring to her close relationship with Noel Barker. It was too wonderful, too powerful, to be set down in a letter that would probably end up with the rubbish.

The warmth of the evening drew her outside towards the front garden. Intrepid nuzzled her leg as she sat in the porch, vaguely watching the river traffic and individuals out for a stroll. Lost in her own reverie, she wouldn't have been able to say who or what she saw, if asked. Her mind dwelt on images of Noel. She couldn't say exactly when he first crept into her thoughts. She didn't mind the invasion; he was just there, like the river gently flowing along. She sipped her drink, recalling the tone of his voice, the knowledge reflected through his eyes, and the strength emanating from him as he stretched out his frame on a comfy chair. It was a mystery to her how someone so giving could live alone. She knew now that she loved him. It wasn't just a passing attraction. The ease with which they conversed, the understanding which flowed from one to the other without words, allowing for individual space and ideas. She didn't feel obligated, as with Len, recalling anxieties, persuasions, and entertaining people she disliked. How stupid to think at the time that there was some defect in herself, something lacking! It simply wasn't so. Noel seemed quite content with just her company. And she found him restful, as if at last she herself was accepted, enjoyed and (dare she allow) cherished. She felt rather than saw the evening coolness, the silence, except for the odd call of a moorhen, the shadows across the lawn and the peacefulness surround her. Stroking Intrepid, she whispered, 'Time to say goodnight to Noel, my friend.'

~XIV~

Noel stretched, leaning back in his swivel chair, pleased with his handiwork. This was the second time he had been asked to illustrate flora and fauna in the Thames Valley. Already he had reached the letter 'G' in the alphabet, and hoped he would be finished for an October run, the edition glossy, and out in time for Christmas shoppers. Looking now at the page before him, he was satisfied with the vibrant watercolours of the goldfinch, situated centre, its nest of thistledown, moss and lichens below, and the weedy waste areas where it foraged for seeds and insects, around the edges. At the bottom of the page, he had used a delicate script, stating that the goldfinch's preference was for nesting in orchards, and its song reminiscent of Japanese wind chimes. Next, he would move on to the heron, where he would position it atop a bollard on the river, surrounded by frogs, eels, insects and water voles.

He dialled Marion's number. So far he hadn't shared his love of painting with her, nor had he, in so many words, mentioned his love. It nettled him to think that at his age he wasn't sure how to put his feelings into words. Everything was going along swimmingly until the advent of Michael. There was no need for her to buy 'River's End' – she could marry him in due course, and live comfortably at the farm.

---

[*] London Folio Society, 1955, Chapter 14, p.256.

'Well, what's this, then?' said Noel, as he crossed the driveway to meet her. He was dressed in an open-necked blue shirt, the sleeves rolled up halfway, exposing tanned wrists. A wide leather watchstrap circled his right arm, and a gold chain rested lightly on his collarbone. Light coffee-coloured pressed trousers sported a darker belt with a silver buckle. Well-polished brown boots gave him the air of Lord of the Manor, or so Marion thought as she alighted from her blue Ford. She too had made an effort, the invitation having previously been relayed over the telephone, 'Would Madame accompany his humble self to dine at the Farmhouse on the night of August 30th?'

She wore a figure-hugging cream silk dress with high neckline and matching Louis-heeled shoes, teamed with a mulberry-coloured handbag, similar to the hue of her hair, which gently framed her face, in a pageboy style. A watch set within a cream-coloured bracelet completed the ensemble.

'Do you like it?'

'I like it very much,' he said, noting delicate rose-coloured earrings as she turned to face him.

'Silly!' she laughed. Radiant eyes masked by flickering lids turned away from his and back to the car.

'Oh... the *car*!' he said in mock humility, as a waft of gardenias reached his senses. 'Very nice, very nice,' he murmured, appraising it from front to back. 'And here was me thinking you preferred to walk...' His eyes twinkled as he endeavoured to keep his face straight.

They ambled back towards the house, as she explained that if she'd had a car, she could have picked Michael up at Staines Station on the day it poured with rain; he wouldn't have been soaked nor have caught the flu. She didn't add that it gave her a sense of independence, nor did she allude to meeting Janice at Heathrow Airport. They entered the lounge. Memories of her first encounter, filled with noisy guests invited back to the farmhouse after Leonard's Memorial Service, floated on the air.

'This room looks lighter, brighter somehow,' she remarked.

'I've had it painted.'

She could hear the faint sounds of Vivaldi's 'Four Seasons' as she wandered around looking at the pictures. 'I don't remember this one.'

'It's a David Cox.' Coming closer, he handed her a gin and tonic. They stood together, both aware of the charged atmosphere in a pretence of social etiquette. Gentle laughter, she sipping, watching the ice cubes clink, and he, feigning undue interest in the amber liquid within his brandy balloon, quelling a desire to make love there and then, knowing it would ruin everything he had spent time and patience on, so that this evening would go as planned.

'In fact,' she said tentatively, 'I don't remember much about this room except the roaring fire and the leather couches. There was that ghastly woman you rescued me from… Rita Mollock.'

'They weren't your kind of people.'

'It seems so long ago now. The vicar and I sat over there. Poor man, I think he was intimidated as much as I was by Rita. Oh…!'

'What?'

'I didn't realise we were in front of French windows… and there's a patio behind.' She gasped. 'Oh, Noel, it's a conservatory!'

'Do you like it?' He seemed to be saying that quite often, and was amused watching her, something akin to pleasure reflected in his eyes as she remarked upon the table set for two, the vine and its luxurious grapes dangling from tendrils across the glass roof and side panes. He liked the sound of her shoes tap-tapping on the terracotta tiles, and her appreciation of nemesia peeping out from under the fan palms at the far end of the conservatory. She paused, drinking in the perfumes, then turned to look back at him. It was an unfathomable look, which seemed to combine mystery with sensuality, profoundly affecting him.

They steered clear of intimacies, chatting about peripheral events over a light supper of honeydew melon sliced in boat-shaped pieces laced with lemon and ginger, followed by leek quiche and a garden salad, accompanied by a liberal amount of rosé. They talked of the imminent arrival of Janice, and now that Marion had a car how it would make it easier to visit places of interest. Reference to Michael was minimal, only to say that at present he was up at the Edinburgh Festival, after which she wasn't sure of his movements.

'What about next year? Surely he won't be staying with you?'

Choosing her words carefully, Marion explained that from what she could gather he was not very keen to go overseas to gain expert tuition, but would rather stay in England. 'But,' she added, 'he admitted he was too young to be accepted in one of the major orchestras, and had little idea about in what or where he would gain employment.'

'Well, that's not really your concern, is it?'

'I think he finds it all rather daunting,' she replied, helping herself to salad and a sip of wine, putting from her mind worries about Michael and enjoying the warmth in the conservatory as the sun went down.

'Of course he does, but that really isn't your problem,' Noel said.

She made no reply, but privately accepted what he said to be true, only it wasn't as simple as he made out. Changing the subject she asked, 'Do you always eat in here?' *Alone*, she might have added but restrained herself.

He smiled, amused at her not too subtle question. 'You mean, did I prepare the quiche and lay the table just for us? Yes. I'm quite a dab hand after many years of living alone. But no, I usually eat alone in the den.'

'Den?'

'You haven't seen the house properly. Feel free to look around. The den is behind the bookcase near the fireplace. There's a knob on the right side; you push it and the door opens. Another door inside leads to the kitchen.'

Before leaving the den by the way she came in, her eyes focused on the cubbyholes at the back of the desk containing what she assumed were invoices, bills and the suchlike, then down to the drawers. The contents of these were none of her business – or were they? Thoughtfully, she let herself out, Dorcas in tow, to explore the upstairs of the farm.

Meanwhile Noel, having finished the clearing up, brewed some coffee and waited patiently for Marion to return downstairs. *Don't crowd her, let her see for herself.* He changed the CD to Roberta Flack, Matt Monroe, Helen Reddy and Glen Campbell favourites. He remembered being in church on the last Sunday before

Marion left for Australia, seeing her white face, knowing she dreaded leaving her roots. He remembered the joy he'd felt when she returned, alone. His whole life changed from that moment; for years he had been drifting, with no particular goal in sight, and then everything changed. He had so much to achieve, so much love to give, and she positively glowed under his ministrations. Surely she would see where her future lay; tonight was the right time to bring things to a head. He had waited quite long enough. Intuitively, he knew she would open last of all the door to the bedroom designed and furnished for her alone.

Ten more minutes passed, and as she hadn't come down the stairs, he slowly went up. She was sitting on a chair by the small table looking out of the window. He coughed, seeing her just as he imagined she would be, as he leant against the door jamb.

She turned her head. 'Was this your wife's room?'

'Good God, no!'

After a long pause she tentatively mumbled, 'Mrs Davies?'

It wasn't worth a reply, but as she didn't move, he attempted nonchalance. 'Is it to your liking?'

How could I not like it? rang through her brain, but she only nodded, and looked around the room making sure her eyes didn't meet his, quite overcome.

What with several glasses of rosé, entry to his den and all that was within, the bedroom especially for her, and the beautiful conservatory which she hadn't seen before, she didn't know what to say. The words he wanted to hear eluded her. It was as though she had dried in centre stage, not sure which scene she was in. Did she love him? She thought she did, but he seemed to swamp her. He was so thoughtful and kind and good and seemed to really care about her. The silence was an agony for Noel. Why didn't she respond? Disappointed, he turned to go down the stairs.

'Coffee's brewed. Come down when you're ready. Come Dorcas.' The lines rang through his brain: 'Why should we faint, and fear to live alone/ Since all alone, so Heaven has will'd, we die?'

Marion listened to his footsteps retreating down the landing and the occasional creak of the stairs before looking at herself in the bathroom mirror. A face with few lines, grey eyes, attractive hair, though she said so herself; but I am turning fifty-seven next month and for the first time in my life I can make my own decisions, live where I want to, see whom I wish; I enjoy being my own mistress, I enjoy the freedom. Do I want to marry again? What about Michael? Noel made that quite clear some time ago, he wasn't prepared to include him… And River's End – I love it so. Is it selfish to accept Noel's attentions and not give myself in return? I'd hate to lose him. What would my life be like without him? She sighed, the euphoria of the early part of the evening having worn off.

On entering the reception room she moved across to the seat by the bay window, very much aware of the song, 'Tonight I celebrate my love for you' – her dilemma increasing, as each word seemed to be mocking her indecision.

Noel studied her face as she paid undue attention to Dorcas. He had wanted her to sit next to him and had grave misgivings about his choice of music. He crossed to change the CD, but not before Dean Martin's dulcet tones crooned the first lines of, 'Let me go, lover'. He fumbled around to find Chopin's Nocturnes which, to him, seemed to embody a safer, less poignant sentiment, and to fill the void, perceiving she was caught in conflicting emotions. He had had enough of her prevarication. He wanted to know where he stood and plunged in.

'How are things on the home front?'

'Well, Alice is coming with me to meet Janice at Heathrow, and Michael—'

'No,' he interrupted. 'I mean the house. What's the latest?'

She stirred her coffee – unnecessarily, as she didn't take sugar – and avoided the question by commenting on what she saw in his den, the birds and flowers, his garden designs, the delicate paintings, all of which were new to her. She said, 'I like the way the plates are set up. They are exquisite, with the bird in the middle. Is it going to be published?'

He ignored the question and was upset that she seemed to be playing games. He just restrained himself from shouting; instead, he swallowed. 'You do?' he said softly. 'Then why won't you answer my question?' Their eyes met, his demanding, hers bordering on tears.

She parried with, 'Will you kiss me?'

Thrown off balance, he said acidly, 'Is that all you want, an affair? We're a bit old for that, aren't we?'

Then he exploded out of his seat and crossed the short distance between them, gathering her up from the chair in one swift movement, so that, surprised, she let go of her cup, which tipped over, spilling its contents onto the table and down the leg, as he held her and crushed her mouth with his.

She broke away, never having experienced such intensity. Almost losing control, he grabbed her hand, frustration spilling over, 'Is that what you want, an affair? Is it?'

'No – yes – I don't know!'

'I love you, Marion, and I want to marry you.' He slumped back onto the couch. She began ineffectually mopping up the table leg. How could she explain, talk about her feelings towards Michael, River's End, and her awakening to emotions she had never before experienced. She so wanted to be in control of her life, not to be coerced because of circumstances. How could she explain?

'I've made a mess of your table.'

'Mrs Davies will fix it when she comes.'

'You have an answer for everything.' She smiled tremulously. He looked up and gave a rueful grin. 'Not everything... you in particular.'

The intensity of the past few minutes ebbed away, so that she felt a wave of love towards him without any interference from other thoughts. 'I don't know yet if Mr Sloane will sell River's End, and I have no way of contacting him. I can't throw Michael out, in all conscience, and God knows what Anna will make of everything. Oh, and yes, I love you too,' she said, sitting down beside him.

She turned and kissed him tentatively. He responded, and they both felt all impediments fade away. 'Oh, Marion,' he said, the words muffled in her hair, 'I won't stop you buying River's End, if that's what you are afraid of.'

'You won't?'

'No, why should I? But I'd like you to live here with me, if you can bear the thought.'

'Not so fast! It all depends if Mr Sloane will sell the house at all, and at a price I think favourable; but it does seem a bit of unnecessary extravagance.'

'If that is what you want, my love...' Noel gently stroked her hair and traced her face with his finger. All of a sudden emotion swallowed them both, everything else forgotten. Marion was carried along on a wave as he laid her down on the couch, touching, stroking every part of her until she cried out for release. After removing her dress and underwear, he stripped off quickly to the sounds of Chopin, which later, when he reflected, he couldn't even remember.

When the colours finally ebbed away, an exquisite calm engulfed them both. He said, 'Tea, my love?' and turning, wearing only his jocks, he made his way towards the kitchen, uttering as an aside, 'I guess I'll get used to Michael being around... I'll try, anyway...'

On Sunday, 31 August, Priscilla and Neville Crees planned to take morning coffee with their son and daughter-in-law at the Broadwater watching some of the most expensive marine craft in the Southern Hemisphere. All along the boardwalk of Marina Mirage were restaurants catering for every kind of taste, their shade sails flying high above tables of varying size, some with rolled up transparent plastic blinds which could be dropped down in unpleasant weather. They were amazed at the grandeur of their accommodation at the Sheraton Mirage. Fountains splashed into enormous paddling and swimming pools, deckchairs were strategically placed, a floating bar sold exotic drinks. Bright and early on the previous two mornings, they had walked along the beach, gaining access from a private gate. The weather was sublime, the sea deep blue, palms and flowers surrounded the pools. Their suite overlooked the beach from the living room, and a wading pool from the bedroom. That morning at breakfast, Priscilla had indulged herself with tropical fruits, cereals and toasted muffins, wishing she had room for all the exotic delights arrayed in front of her. Neville had commented, 'It's good to be back in civilisation.'

'This is quite something,' Anna agreed; neither she nor Nigel had yet dared to wander through the front door.

'Grand, isn't it?' Neville remarked, pleased to impress his glamorous daughter-in-law.

They crossed the road towards Marina Mirage shopping complex by a pedestrian bridge built in white stone, financed by disgraced entrepreneur Christopher Skase.

'Ooh!' gushed Priscilla, eyeing a lingerie shop. 'Oh! And look at these exquisite shoes!'

Together, she and Anna felt their feet sink into soft white carpet as they feasted their eyes upon strappy elegant footwear imported from Italy, Germany and Switzerland. Anna fell in love with a $400 handbag glittering with rhinestones. Priscilla wished she had slim feet and painted toenails. As it was, she doubted whether there would be any occasion in Devonport to wear such creations, as Tasmania rarely experienced Queensland's wonderful sunny weather. The men strode past Boss suits and Yves St Laurent ties, only interested in the magnificent yachts moored alongside the jetties. 'Beautiful one day, perfect the next,' remarked Nigel.

'Sure is that. Not a bad place to live, son. What's that?' Neville pointed across the canal strip towards a magnificent marble courtyard made up of coloured chips laid in circles, around which statues of nymphs and scantily clad Greek goddesses caught his eye.

'That is Versace. Everything, even down to the dinner sets, has the Versace emblem embossed. Similar to the Sheraton, but it has a beach within the complex.'

'Did you see the birds, Neville, and those cute little turtles inside the wire enclosure?' Priscilla grasped his arm, adding, 'Where to now?'

'Time for coffee, I think.'

All four agreed, so they found a table facing the yachts, saw a tourist helicopter taking off and admired a gondola moored close by. It was during the recounting of their overseas trip that Priscilla commented that they had visited Anna's mother at River's End.

'It's a beautiful house, Anna. Your mother was busy gardening when we arrived.'

'She loves gardening. I'm thinking of going home for Christmas or before, but then Nigel won't be able to come. Mum will be alone.'

'Oh, I don't think you need to worry, dear. She seems to have quite a few visitors, doesn't she, Neville?'

'Visitors?'

'Well, I had reason to go to the bathroom…'

'Priscilla, not that ridiculous phantom story again!' her husband said wearily. 'I tell you, Nigel, your mother has started seeing things. It's time we went home.'

Anna, sensing something was amiss, asked her mother-in-law, 'What are you talking about?'

'I did see him, Neville.'

'See *who*?'

'Priscilla said she saw a young man upstairs at your mother's house.'

'It was when I couldn't find the downstairs loo, so I went upstairs to the bathroom, and just as I was about to enter, a young man in just a towel came out. He didn't see me as he went into one of the bedrooms. I thought it must have been your brother, but your mother said you didn't have one.'

'No, I don't! I can't think who it could possibly be. She hasn't mentioned any young man staying, only a young female student from my home room at St Mary's who lost her mother in a car crash and seems not to have any relatives – but I don't think she is there yet.'

'Don't worry, lass. I didn't see him, and Marion gave no explanation so it seems obvious Priscilla was seeing things. Too many wines the night before,' said Neville jovially. 'She lost her underwear at one hotel, and there was quite a rumpus. Turned out she'd forgotten she'd put it in the side pocket of her suitcase!'

'Anyone could do that, Dad. I'm surprised she hasn't lost you on occasions.'

Neville turned to Anna. 'So, who is the dashing Romeo in the sports car?'

Nigel's eyes looked wary. Anna frowned, not sure of how her father-in-law could have seen her with a photographer from yesterday's photo shoot.

'At your mother's. He drove into her driveway as we were leaving.'

'*My mother*! She wouldn't know a sports car if she fell over it, let alone a dashing driver.'

'Well, she knew this person. She came out to meet him. Tall, good-looking, late forties, I would say,' said Priscilla knowingly.

'That's absurd.'

'And so was the near-naked young man I saw, according to Neville.' She stood up to leave, irritated by Neville's manner. 'I don't care what any of you think. I tell you I saw a young man coming out of the bathroom.'

'Yes, dear, as you said.'

There was an embarrassing pause before Anna said gently, 'I have absolutely no idea who it was, Priscilla.' Anna looked genuinely puzzled, taking Priscilla's arm as Neville paid the bill. A slight tension emanated from the women as they wandered further along the boardwalk, admiring the boats. Nigel and his father strolled behind, murmuring portents about Priscilla's age, and the vagaries of women.

'Oh, look, Neville! An olde worlde pub.'

'Time for a snifter, yes. Nigel?'

'Bit early, Dad. How about I take you both into Surfers for a look around and then on to King's. You have to see it before going home.'

Priscilla dampened his enthusiasm. 'I'd rather go back to the Sheraton. I'm feeling a bit peaky, if you don't mind, dear. It's quiet there.'

'OK with me.' Visions of the various bars at the Sheraton swam before Neville's eyes.

Hiding his disappointment, Nigel swallowed, 'Well, in that case we'll push off, then, and meet you both later tonight, say sixish?'

Arrangements were made. Anna was quiet as they drove back to the flat. 'Do you think your mother imagined she saw a young man?'

Nigel shrugged. 'There's probably some simple explanation.'

'Either your mother is hallucinating or mine is taking in lost boys.'

'Doesn't sound likely.'

'Well, I wish I knew; my mother with a Romeo! That's not

likely, either. She was never one to get about, and as far as I remember, she only went out at night with Dad. It just doesn't fit.'

'Well, it's no use speculating. Ring her up tonight and ask her.' He parked the car in the designated spot for their flat and, hurt by his parents' lack of interest in his affairs, complained, 'You'd think they could show some interest in where I work. But no, not interested. I'd liked to have shown Dad over King's College.'

'I thought they wanted to look at real estate.' Anna clambered out of the car, following him up to their flat.

'Maybe they will tomorrow. But I can't show them over the school tomorrow, it's Monday.' Moodily, he opened the front door for her.

'My dad would have been really interested. I know I didn't see much of him but I miss him. Wished things had turned out differently.'

'So do I, Anna, so do I...'

The following morning Anna collected their mail from a nearby post box. There was quite a bundle. Two bills, a bank statement, the usual wine club specials, a flyer and a letter from England. She recognised her mother's handwriting and opened it first. It appeared quite long; seldom did she write more than half a page. Stunned by its contents, Anna read it through several times, then sat for a while staring at nothing in particular. Finally, she rang Nigel during his lunch hour.

'Your mother was right!' she shrieked down the telephone. Then she gabbled some of the letter's contents.

'Slow down, darling, I—'

'There's no mention of whether I mind or agree,' Anna said tearfully. 'I don't believe it, Nigel!'

Not fully understanding what Anna had said, Nigel promised to be there as soon as he could, then hung up. He looked around for a likely relief teacher who would understand his predicament. Luckily, some teachers were away on camp with grade nine, the remaining ones trying to look busy.

'First period after lunch is free... it's just the other two. Would you mind covering for me, Vanessa?'

He was home in half an hour. He found Anna distraught at the thought of a 'stepbrother', and himself amazed at his late father-in-law's conduct. Neither gave a second thought to the good-looking man in the sports car visiting her mother.

For Anna, the shock of discovering her father's infidelity outweighed any love she had for him. Throughout the remains of the day she repeated, 'To think he had a mistress and son growing up in our village – and now, on top of that,' she hissed, 'Mother calmly offers a roof over the head of a seventeen-year-old boy she knows nothing about. Typical!'

'We don't know that, Anna…' Gently, Nigel tried to pacify his wife as he handed her a gin and tonic.

'Of course she didn't know!' she retorted. 'She hardly left the house. I'm not surprised Dad looked elsewhere. She was dull and boring!'

It was on the tip of his tongue to say, 'Well, she isn't dull and boring any more, is she?' But he thought better of it. Privately, Nigel wished his own mother was less bizarre and more like Marion – quiet and caring. 'There's more to your mother than meets the eye. It's probably only temporary.'

Anna glared. Attempting to sound conciliatory, to defuse the situation, he sprawled in the chair opposite her. 'I wouldn't worry; she's trying to help the lad, probably feels responsible for selling the house…'

'That house was hers – *ours*, if you like. God knows when we shall see any of the proceeds… If I have anything to do with it, this Michael will be temporary. I'll play her at her own game, see if she likes shocks.' Angrily, she hunted around for the Yellow Pages telephone book. 'She didn't consult me or give a moment's thought to our future. Who knows what provisions she'll make for this "Michael" while we're over here and she's being her altruistic self!' Sarcasm rang through her words. 'Well, two can play at that game! I'll surprise her and turn up on her doorstep.'

With that she rang a travel agent and booked a flight to England during the last week of September.

That same evening, relayed on all television channels was the story of the death of Diana, Princess of Wales, apparently from a high-speed car crash the previous night within a Paris road tunnel. They had missed the previous bulletins earlier in the day.

'Good heavens, that's awful!' remarked Nigel.

'Doesn't surprise me. Maybe the CIA knocked her off. Don't look like that! She was becoming a loose cannon… everyone knew that,' Anna said loftily, lost in her own turmoil of family duplicity. She couldn't begin to contemplate the ramifications of a beautiful rich princess riding in the back of a Mercedes and dying in the arms of her Muslim lover. Unlike Anna's distress, Diana's tragedy was brought about by her own behaviour; nevertheless, it created a vast outpouring of sympathy that was felt worldwide. Anna's distress was secret; she had been abandoned. Screaming headlines kept the world informed, and graphic descriptions in the tabloids kept the British public suitably titillated. Private grief became a public display. Not twenty-four hours before her death, Diana was sailing the Mediterranean and sunbathing in St Tropez on the yacht *Jonika* belonging to Dodi Fayed's father. They had been seen off Sardinia's Emerald Coast and so in an attempt to ward off the paparazzi, they made a dash to Paris. The rest became confused, and blame was scattered like confetti.

It was about this time that enjoyable pursuits became entangled in litigation, as an insidious insurance liability came into being without the general population understanding where this would lead to. Premiums went sky-high, notwithstanding only the insurers made money, along with the lawyers. No one was to blame. Right and wrong, though fully understood, were 'shanghaied' by fuzzy concepts, explained away by unfortunate circumstances and semantics, so that the victim was often ignored while the sinner received counselling – to the detriment of the law in many cases. 'Guilt' and 'sin' were words rarely used except from the fundamentalist pulpits. 'No fault clauses' were the catchphrases of the day. Retribution and accountability were laughed at, as sinners blamed their victims, other people, alcohol, drugs or whatever seemed plausible at the time. It was in this climate the crowds invaded London in a desperate need to be part of the drama, relating to it, as in some soap opera.

She was their sister, mother, girlfriend, the Goddess Diana. Thousands placed flowers outside Kensington Palace, to what purpose seemed unclear. Someone else was to blame for her death. Her image was to remain untarnished, in spite of the brutal facts. In some eyes she had ascended into sainthood like Mother

Theresa, and Eva Peron. She became the Queen of Hearts. A few weeks before, her behaviour was decried throughout the land; and within this short period of time she had become the people's idol.

It was in this atmosphere that a young woman flew into Heathrow Airport feeling very excited about her first trip abroad. She was tall, slim and had shoulder-length straight blonde hair. Her face, though pale, revealed high cheekbones, and on removing her sunglasses as she entered the terminal her eyes shone like sapphires. She was close to tears, so she kept her eyes focussed on the back of the person in front of her in the passport queue.

The controller studied her photograph and then her person and smiled. 'Coming for a holiday, young lady?' She looked up and nodded. He was bowled over by the bluest eyes he had ever seen. 'This photo doesn't do you justice,' he declared and handed back the passport document, aware that she seemed to glide past, her mind on other things.

'There she is!' cried Marion. 'That's Janice – poor love, she looks all in!'

Alice scrutinised the tall blonde girl who looked neither to the left nor right. 'Probably tired. It's a long flight.'

After greetings and introductions there was luggage to collect off the carousel. 'What are we looking for?'

Janice choked. 'One black, the other brown,' she said, and burst into tears.

'Oh dear...' Marion put her arms around her. 'What's the matter, love?' She wiped Janice's tears as Alice stood uncomfortably beside the pair. 'It's the car crash. I've tried not to think about it... and everyone was talking about Diana on the plane. The woman next to me was devastated,' she hiccupped, 'and I kept remembering there was only me for Mum! I can't get the sound out of my head... the crash... since hearing people talk about Diana and Dodi. I'm sorry to make such a fuss!'

'Don't be! It's perfectly natural, if you ask me.' Alice smiled and then added, 'Come on, let's get out of this crush and back to Laleham. You'll feel better there.'

Marion gave Alice a grateful look, thanking heaven she had agreed to accompany her to the airport. Handling the driving and

Janice's tears would have been beyond her. She felt quite emotional herself, and was glad she had recounted to Alice Janice's background during the drive to Heathrow. For her part, Alice kept up bright conversation throughout the 45-minute return journey, covering topics from everything Janice had been doing, to some of the places Marion would take her to see.

On arrival at River's End, Janice had quite regained her equilibrium; but the best surprise was the welcome Intrepid gave her that night, and for the rest of her stay, Intrepid insisted on sleeping at the end of her bed in the attic room.

To Janice, early morning walks with Intrepid along the Thames towpath towards Penton Hook Lock were the highlights of each day. It wasn't that she didn't appreciate places of interest, but the crowds murmuring in foreign languages, the queuing, and signs of 'Keep off the grass' instinctively rankled. She couldn't see the point of large expanses of lawn (crying out for bare feet to relish) where you were forced to keep to the paths.

The freedom and sparseness of people along the towpath was similar to her walks beside the Derwent River. She picked many a leafy wild flower alongside the sleepy, tranquil River Thames, which she carried back to River's End, slightly breathless, her hair flying, her face flushed pink. The joy she discovered rising up within her like a crystal spring washed into the crevices of her mind, flushing away depression. Confidences shared with Marion, who understood, whose hand was there in her need, brought back a zest for life, in spite of her uncertain future. This, coupled with the ambience of River's End, made her wish she could stay for ever: the unconventional nooks and crannies; her attic bedroom with its dormer window facing the river; the cluttered kitchen and much-used solid wooden table in the centre; the kettle continuously on the boil.

Then there was the garden, with its dahlias, chrysanthemums and floribunda rose bushes, clumps of aubretia and thyme clinging to the rockery, and gypsophila weaving its way between Michaelmas daisies and marigolds. Marion didn't seem to mind when she came inside carrying armfuls of flowers, looking for a vase; she laughed at her tentative arrangements, suggesting the use of a brick sponge. She showed her what to use, and where her arrangements would be seen to the best advantage. She took her to see Noel's conservatory and greenhouses. He lent her books on wild flowers, birds and river animals.

In a way, Marion and Noel became her surrogate parents, and River's End became the substitute home for the one she'd loved in Norwood Avenue. Janice had felt so alone up to now, in spite of Barbara Mason's efforts to fill the breach left by her mother; but having lost all innocence by the time she was sixteen, matters of sex were given a wide berth.

Here in England she felt secure and free at the same time. She hadn't given Gavin Armstrong a thought; nor had she dwelt upon the tragedy Martin Bryant had created. She began to notice the change in Marion without Leonard and, as a teenager, couldn't quite put her finger on the turnabout in Marion's demeanour since she last saw her in Tadbury. She seemed livelier, more interesting and completely in control. Not once had she mentioned Anna, which seemed odd. Now as she sat in the conservatory bathed in sunshine, reading through *Wild Flowers of Britain*, Janice was immersed in what to look out for on her next morning's walk and decided to cross Penton Hook Weir to the island. She recalled the low-lying gentle fog hanging over the river, and willows leaving heavy dew droplets on the surrounding grasses, not lifting until she had breakfasted, this being the beginning of autumn. Intrepid lay snoozing at her feet, and Marion would be home in a couple of hours from the Heritage Centre. She was content.

$$\sim XV \sim$$

Give me my scallop-shell of quiet,
My staff of faith to walk upon,
My scrip of joy, immortal diet,
My bottle of salvation,
My gown of glory, hope's true gage;
And thus I'll take my pilgrimage.

Sir Walter Raleigh[*]

Michael stood in the doorway of the conservatory regarding his dream. She was about his age, with long blonde hair down to her shoulders, an impish nose and cupid-shaped lips touched with mango-coloured lipstick, looking gorgeous, neatly curled up in a wicker armchair reading a book. She was wearing a white T-shirt striped with yellow, white shorts revealing long slim thighs, and a pair of golden flip-flops were placed beside the chair, their straps highlighted by tiny diamantine.

He swallowed. 'Hello?' A desperate attempt at nonchalance sounded like a croak. Janice looked up, surprised to see a young man with deep-set brown eyes, a mass of tousled curly hair and a crooked smile.

'Hello... You must be Michael.' She laughed, and her heart lurched as she assessed his jeans, navy sweatshirt and violin case. 'You're supposed to be in Edinburgh!'

'I came home early.' Speedwell-blue eyes caused Michael's pulse to beat at an uneven rate.

---

[*] Judith Williams (ed.), *A Gallery of Renaissance Poetry*, Vol. I, p.273.

Swinging her legs off the chair, she thrust slender feet into her flip-flops. Not knowing what to say, Michael watched.

'Marion's down at the visitor centre.'

'Ah! You must be Janice.'

'Yes.' She wasn't making things easy.

'From Tasmania.'

'Yes.' She stood there, looking bemused.

What to say next? He'd never experienced such shock waves. The blood was rushing to his head. 'How long have you been here?' *Feeble, pathetic!* He wished he'd worn clean socks.

'Oh, er, just over a week.' She felt the old excitement rising. *Not again… I'm not going down that road.* She waved a slender hand and said, 'Aren't you going to put that thing down?'

'Ah, yes.' He wanted her to leave; he couldn't practise with those incredible eyes looking on – too distracting. He made a business of opening the case, extracting the violin and priming the bow up and down with a block of rosin.

Janice riffled through a pile of music. 'What are you going to play?'

'Scales… studies…'

'Anything else?'

'What? I'd appreciate it if you left that alone.'

'Why? I'm not hurting anything.'

'Because…' He moved over to the music, taking the pile from her. He smelt honeysuckle. Any more of this and he'd have to go to the bathroom. Why, oh why, wasn't Marion here! This girl was gorgeous; he just couldn't concentrate!

'There's no need to get huffy. I'll sit quiet as a mouse and watch you play.'

'I'd rather you didn't… I'm only going to practise.'

'Ooh, excuse me!' She moved to leave.

'I didn't mean it like that. I practise about five hours a day.' Michael looked stricken.

'Are you always this serious?'

Cornered, he gently placed the violin back in its case, trawling through his mind for something to say. *Television* – she must have watched Diana's funeral… everyone did. 'So, what did you make of "Goodbye, England's Rose"?'

'The what?'

' "Candle in the Wind" – the song composed by Elton John? A mate of mine taped it. The music was great. Four of us got together and had a jam session.' He smiled enthusiastically.

'The lyrics – you must have liked it – a bit sad, though. How did it go?' He smiled enthusiastically and hummed a bar or two of the verse, then softly sang a few words. She stayed quiet.

'Did you see all the Royals walking behind the cortège? It seemed the whole of England was crammed into London. Those of us who were elsewhere…' He trailed off.

Why didn't she say something? What was wrong now? He watched her face crumple, her lips quiver and tears slide down her cheeks. Christ, this was awful!

What if Marion were to walk in now? She would blame him for making Janice cry.

'Whatever is the matter?'

With the back of her hand, she wiped ineffectually at her tears. 'Have you got a handkerchief?'

He withdrew a creased, not too clean article edged in blue. 'Sorry, it's rather grubby. I'll get you some tissues.'

'No, this will do.' She attempted a smile, and, taking it by thumb and index finger, looked for a clean spot. Between mopping and looking at his concerned face she stroked Intrepid's head; the dog seemed to sense unhappiness and so leant against her leg. 'I was in a car crash, in the rain with my mother. She died.'

Michael was appalled. Why hadn't Marion said anything? But of course I wasn't meant to be here. Realising he knew nothing about Janice except that she was a pupil at St Mary's College, where Anna used to teach, it occurred to him that she was fatherless too, and that was why she had come to England for a holiday. He said, 'Marion seems to make a habit of taking in us strays.' The remark brought a tiny giggle. At least that was the right thing to say. He breathed a sigh of relief.

Trying to make amends, he said softly, 'I don't expect Marion has taken you to our local, the Three Shoes, has she?'

Janice blinked back her tears and shook her head.

'It's not far… if you'd like to.'

'For a beer, you mean?'

'Or whatever. By the time we get there it will be open for lunch.'

'OK. I'll get my bag. Better leave a note for Marion, hadn't we?'

'Right. I'll write the note and lock up.'

'What shall I do with this?' She held up the handkerchief gingerly.

He laughed. 'Dirty linen box outside the bathroom.'

Silly to get so upset when she could see Michael was just as jittery as she about where life was going. He talked and she listened as they strolled along the towpath towards the village. He didn't seem at all embarrassed by his background; it was amazing to think he hardly knew her. Fancy telling her Mr Lee was his father, and that Marion hadn't known about it! Michael pointed out Burway Rowing Club; she said she loved sailing, and he said he would take her out in a friend's boat if she'd like that. Before either of them were aware, they had passed Marion's previous house in Blacksmiths' Lane, Alice's home by the memorial, the church, garage, post office and the butcher's. Next to the butcher's stood a small antique shop about 200 yards from the Three Shoes. Janice made a face, peering through the dusty window.

'Can't see much.'

'I've never seen anyone go in!' They both laughed and began to enjoy each other's company. Janice remarked on the olde worlde charm of the pub and ordered a gin and tonic. Michael paid for her and ordered a pint of lager for himself. It was a toss-up whether to sit in the 'cosy' or outside in the garden.

'It's really quaint.'

'Do you like it?'

'Vastly different from the few pubs I've seen.'

'In what way?'

'You do ask a lot of questions!' She smiled, leading the way through to the garden. 'Shove-halfpenny and Bagatelle! Darts… I would love to play Bagatelle. All those old pins and silver balls.' Her eyes roamed the tables, resting on a cedar setting with benches attached under a willow tree. 'Let's go over there, we can people-watch.'

They sat on the far side, facing inwards, vaguely watching the other patrons: young men wearing white, open-necked shirts carrying dark jackets flung over their shoulders; young women in tight navy skirts tottering along in high heels, juggling drinks, carrying files and handbags behind the young men, creating smart banter so that everyone could hear; furtive couples planning imminent liaisons, gazing around to see if anyone recognised them.

'What do you have in Tasmania then, just a bar?'

'No, silly. Some have billiard tables. Most have lunch tables, I suppose to pick up passing trade. And definitely "no dogs".' She spied two King Charles spaniels sitting at the feet of their mistress, looking hopeful, but she was engaged in fluttering her eyelashes at the portly man opposite. A bartender came out with a bowl of water and ceremoniously placed it by the dogs.

'Good heavens! And before you ask, this is some crazy place!' She laughed, shaking her long blonde hair, much to Michael's delight. They seemed enamoured with each other's spontaneous remarks; one fair-skinned, blonde head and forget-me-not blue eyes bent close to a head of unruly nut-brown curls surrounding an artistic face, darker in complexion. It was exciting to be themselves, not knowing or caring if they offended. Physically, you would be hard-pressed to find such opposites and yet, a magnet pulled.

'What music do you like?' asked Michael.

She thought for a while, making sipping noises with her straw. 'Country and Western I suppose… oh, and Enya.'

'No, I mean composer.'

'I don't have one. Who do you like?'

'Mahler.'

'I've never heard of him.' They sat in silence, two disparate souls drawn to each other but with no starting point. Suddenly her mouth twitched and she turned to look at him closely.

'And… what is your favourite plant?'

'What?'

'Your favourite tree or plant.'

'Oh, I don't know… I like mauve flowers.'

'You mean plants like wisteria, lilac, and clematis and…'

'Hold on!' he laughed. 'If you say so.'

'I'd like to work with trees and plants. Like Noel.'

'Talking of Noel, do you think he's – you know – with Marion?'

'Mmm, I see what you mean. I think they like each other,' Janice ventured.

'You know what I think? He wants her to live at the farm.'

'She couldn't do that. She loves River's End.'

'Ah, yes, but it isn't hers, you see. The owner can't make up his mind about selling.'

'Oh… I didn't know.'

'So, I've been thinking I ought to find work and move out. Leave the way clear, so to speak.'

'Has she asked you to?'

'No.'

With their two heads close together, whispering conspiratorially, anyone watching would think they were a couple embarking upon a passionate affair. Nothing was further from the truth as Michael unburdened his worries and future concerns. It was cathartic having a complete stranger to talk with, someone who understood his aloneness, his anxiety of an uncertain career, and a lack of the wherewithal.

'We seem to be in a similar situation, except you still have a mother.'

'She's better off without me,' said Michael. A rueful smile played on his lips, and as their eyes met, she digested this sad information. Words were unnecessary, as their awareness of each other's vulnerability went to the core of their being.

'I think we ought to make tracks.' His face hardened as the noise level around them grew. Expensive cars filled the gravel space behind the hedge as Michael took her hand. She felt his overwhelming protectiveness by this one small gesture. Love gently found a footing, surprising both of them, bouncing from one to the other.

'I make a good spaghetti Bolognaise… Are you hungry?' Janice asked.

'Only if you change that to lasagne. I hate spaghetti,' he said, whispering in her ear.

Letting go of her hand, and before she could retort, he ducked out of the Three Shoes, grinning at a surprised patron walking in. 'Excellent food here,' he said. 'Try the fish.'

Janice followed, trying to suppress her laughter.

Marion found the note, and immediately began to imagine the possible outcomes of harbouring two teenagers under the one roof. Her anxiety multiplied on reading a letter from Patricia Clerk of Clerk and Gamble, saying that Philip Sloane's wife had decided to return to England, but would be staying with friends in Shepperton. There was no need yet for Marion to find alternative accommodation as she, Norma, couldn't decide whether to buy a new property or face the memories of River's End. Apparently her marriage had broken down. Patricia would be in touch when she knew something definite.

Marion stood stock-still, the news shattering all her hopes. This situation couldn't go on, although she was forced to admit that it had been a possibility all along. She would call the tune, make a formal offer and final date, on her terms. She said out loud, 'No more negotiation, Norma Sloane,' and then went upstairs in an agitated state to clean the bathroom.

Autumn mists and crisp air did not deter Janice from her early morning walk with Intrepid. She relished the crunch of paper-thin leaves as she walked. Some were curled, pale yellow, dancing with each puff of wind; others, now brown, congregated in dips waiting for the rain to return them from whence they came. Trying to enthuse Michael to join her met with little success; he preferred a lie-in, as did Marion, who was thankful for the respite. She wasn't sleeping too well and woke with a number of dilemmas on her mind.

On this particular morning she turned fifty-seven, which wasn't something she wanted to broadcast. Caution had prevented her from showing Patricia Clerk's letter to Noel, although she dearly needed to confide in someone. He would only smile in his most beguiling way, repeating, 'Live with me. Marry me.' In all conscience, this wouldn't do as a way out of her dilemma; nor, when she thought about it, was it very seemly with Leonard's ashes lying less than six months in All Saints' churchyard. There was no comparison in her feelings between the two men, that wasn't the problem. Harmony and love flowed between her and Noel, but a sense of loyalty and 'the right thing to do' weighed heavily on her heart, never mind the gossip they would attract by either course of action. Noel didn't seem to realise that gossip would ensue for himself as a churchwarden, by flouting propriety. Wryly, Marion imagined herself singled out as a pathetic case across the village, whereas she was perfectly happy the way things were. She wasn't ready to marry again. It was respectable in the view of others, maybe; however, enjoying her freedom without having to compromise was a gift. This she wasn't about to give up lightly.

Anna would be horrified; that was a scene she didn't look much forward to, considering no disclosure in her letters relating to Noel had been relayed. In fact she had been deliberately circumspect in her correspondence.

Feeling a slight nip in the air, she put on her dressing gown, a dark red velour, hugging it to her body and appreciating its warmth and softness. Then, slipping her feet into lambswool slippers, she went downstairs to make a cup of tea. She filled the kettle, looking out at the back garden beginning to decay, experiencing an uneasy feeling about the obvious attraction between Janice and Michael. Heaven forbid if that got out of control, but how was she to approach the subject? It was none of her business to disclose Janice's past pregnancy – or was it? She placed an English Breakfast teabag in a mug painted with nasturtiums, poured in the water and a small amount of milk, then sat down at the kitchen table warming her hands around the mug. She comforted herself with the knowledge that Janice was to leave in two days' time; maybe she had already told Michael, but on second thought, she doubted that.

If only Michael hadn't returned early from Edinburgh, they would never have met and she wouldn't feel so responsible. It was amazing how they seemed to be quite at ease in each other's company, quite extraordinary when they had so little in common. She would take Janice with her to see Patricia Clerk as it had been over a week without a word from that quarter, favourable or otherwise. She would miss Janice's enthusiasm and love of nature, but the responsibility of looking after her welfare under the present circumstances was quite wearing her down. Rinsing her cup out, she heard Janice returning with Intrepid and refilled the kettle, lit the gas and found a towel with which to rub down the dog.

'I think it's time to put the central heating on,' she said, smiling at the flushed face before her, wondering how Janice could look so beautiful first thing in the morning.

Unbeknown to Marion, the young couple had spent an idyllic Thursday afternoon on Scott Weirs' houseboat when she was at the hairdresser's. What happened was inevitable, given the ambience of the mooring, their age and physical attraction for each other. She needn't have worried, though, for Michael took due care. Janice made it quite clear she wasn't going to take any risks. It surprised her how much he cared for her welfare, restoring her trust in the opposite sex. One day, if it seemed necessary, she would tell Michael about the baby she lost, but not now; this was their moment in time, unhindered and private. She knew he would write and she would reply. They may even meet up again, but when and how was not important. They were like ships passing in the night, each on its own course, acknowledging the encounter while berthed at a safe harbour.

Patricia Clerk saw Marion and Janice entering her office and thought how propitious. 'I was just going to ring you, Mrs Lee. Come in, come in.' This being the first time Janice had been in an estate agent's office, she was peering at various properties displayed on the walls, imagining herself showing clients through expensive houses and drinking wine with wealthy vendors, while sitting on plush couches wearing glamorous clothes.

Surprised by Patricia's cordiality, Marion assumed this to be a good omen. Over the past months she had done her best to avoid her. 'So…' She looked at Patricia's smiling face, 'My offer has been accepted?'

'Well no, not exactly. I haven't heard as yet, but I…'

'I thought…' Marion sat down slowly on one of the two chairs in front of Patricia's desk. Janice took the other, scrutinising Patricia's smooth red hair, flawless complexion and glittering chain necklace.

A smile played on Patricia's lips. 'I did say I would contact you as soon as I heard something definite. In the meantime I thought you may be interested in another property in case the Sloanes reach an unfavourable decision as far as you are concerned.'

At this unexpected turn of events, Marion was speechless. Janice studied Patricia's blouse and jacket, the former of white silk, the jacket pale aqua made of soft suede, with three little matching buttons at each cuff. Patricia continued, 'It's within your price range – in fact quite a bit less than your last offer for River's End.' Marion's face was impassive. Words meaning little. 'Properties of this kind only come on the market occasionally, you know.' An encouraging smile was wasted. Patricia ploughed on.

'The owners are retiring to the country; the damp Thames air doesn't suit them, something about rheumatism. Anyway, as I was saying, their children are off their hands. One is at an art college in London and the other recently married. He, Mr…' – she glanced at the paper in front of her – 'Mr Craddock, is no longer practising as a solicitor because of health reasons, as I stated before…'

'Did you say Craddock. Hugh Craddock?'

'Yes, that's right. The house is very pretty, covered with Virginia creeper, long and low, and almost has river frontage called…'

'…Little Withies. I know, they were our next-door neighbours in Blacksmiths' Lane.'

'Oh… then you know the property?'

'I haven't been inside, if that's what you mean.'

Watching Marion's icy stare, Patricia could see the sale slipping through her fingers. Janice thought, How crass. Marion quietly absorbed this salient piece of information and leant across the desk to a startled Patricia Clerk, delivering a strategy she wished to be carried out on her behalf to Norma Sloane. And yes, she was interested to know that Little Withies was for sale at quite a bit less than River's End, and thanked Patricia for her help in the matter. Satisfied that she could do no more in securing River's End, she bade Patricia 'Good morning', while Janice, astounded at

Marion's composure and command of the situation, watched Patricia's reluctant nod and tight-lipped smile, before following Marion out into the street.

'Wow, that was something in there!' She gave Marion's shoulder a squeeze, as if to an older sister. Touched by her approval, Marion felt a warm glow of affection towards her young charge. Such demonstrative behaviour in a public place was like a breath of fresh air. Anna wouldn't have voiced any such encouragement, but then Anna hadn't understood why she had returned to Laleham in the first place. Janice would never know how much Marion appreciated this one gesture.

They returned home to find Mr Symmonds raking leaves from the grass into a smoky bonfire, and wheeling his barrow with the last of the Peace rose cuttings towards the compost. Michael was practising a difficult study in the conservatory and Intrepid, not appreciating the discords, was lying in her basket in the lounge.

On hearing the women chatting in the kitchen, Michael came through, envious of the ease with which Janice expressed herself as she helped to unpack various items from several large bags with 'Tesco' written on the outside.

'You had a phone call, Clarrie,' he said, staring awkwardly at the shopping. 'I wrote down the message and number.'

'*Clarrie*. You called Marion "Clarrie".' Janice looked puzzled. 'Silly…' she gave him a playful push.

'No, no, it's quite OK. I used to be called that.' Marion smiled across at both of them. 'Makes me feel young again!'

The air seemed electrified, pulsating like a stream negotiating stones too large for the flow to ride over smoothly and forced to skim past. 'You finish putting things away. I'd better see who called.' Marion inclined her head, grey eyes speaking volumes, their message clear. *Sort out your rivalry before I return.*

Saturday passed all too quickly for Janice. Marion felt strongly the emotion running between the two, but not having anything concrete to go on, suggested to Janice she accompany her to Sunday morning service. Janice declined, excusing herself on the grounds she needed to finish packing. Throughout the service, Marion found her mind straying away from worship, interrupted first by Noel's beaming smile as he handed to her a prayer book and hymnal sheet on entering the church. Secondly, she worried about what the two youngsters would be doing in her absence at River's End. Once more, she could hardly remember anything that was said, like the last service she and Leonard attended before leaving for Australia; only this time she grappled with the prayers and psalms, which stayed elusive and out of reach of her soul. Her mind was a jumble of emotions, feeling Noel's eyes on the back of her head and imagining Janice and Michael copulating in the attic bedroom.

Nothing as wild as her imagination had taken place. The young couple had gone for a short walk along the riverbank, without Intrepid. Both yearned for intimacy, but both had a horror of things going wrong. After the service Marion stood on Alice's doorstop for less than five minutes, reminding her that she was expected to dinner that night, whereas previously she would have relayed the gist of the sermon over a glass of sherry. By 12.45 she arrived home to find Michael practising in the conservatory and Janice putting the finishing touches to a chocolate cake.

The evening went well. Alice arrived with a silver bracelet studded with tiny blue glass as a farewell gift for Janice. Noel roared up the driveway in his sports car, watched by Janice through the kitchen window. Elegant, not at all farm-like, she mused, as he entered through the kitchen door carrying a parcel, which he presented to her.

'For you, I saw you admire it while browsing in the study. Would someone take these?'

Greetings all round livened up the atmosphere as Michael took two bottles of wine through to the dining table, while Janice opened the parcel. It contained a 1947 hardback edition of *Wild Flowers of Britain*, complete with colourful dust jacket.

Conversation flowed simply as Janice showed around her treasure. Intrepid sensed the excitement, wandering around the dining table. Noel carved the roast lamb, conversing easily with Michael who poured the wine, a French Chablis and a Spanish red. Two candles within glass balloons glowed in the centre of the table, lighting up bronze maple leaves adorning the spaces between each person's setting. Vegetable tureens passed from hand to hand as Alice regaled everyone with a hilarious account of a dental chair out of control. 'It was as though it had a mind of its own. Poor Mrs Smith…!'

Glasses were replenished as Noel proposed a toast. 'To Janice, her future and a safe journey home.' Murmurs of agreement brought tears to her eyes, and then a tasty gooseberry fool, made by Marion that afternoon and decorated with clotted cream in parfait glasses, was much appreciated. The meal completed, Marion said, 'Come, shall we take our coffee in the lounge? We'll leave all this… Maybe you'll play for us, Michael?'

All eyes locked on his sardonic smile. 'How much?'

'Go on with you!' Marion laughed. As he left the room to fetch his violin, she pondered his future and the seriousness of his career path. Words were exchanged between the four along the same lines, each coming to the conclusion that they were privileged to be sitting here at this particular time of his life.

'Front seats, how much?' joked Noel as he fished around for his wallet. Janice giggled; Alice closed her eyes, waiting to be entertained, and Marion mused, knowing that Noel had never actually heard Michael play.

Michael returned, then dimmed the central light before crossing to open the curtains covering the bay window. The twilight created just the right atmosphere as he sat down to play several Highland laments, followed by 'Auld Lang Syne'.

'This one's for you, Janice,' he said, and launched into the emotive Glen Campbell tune, 'Gentle on my Mind'.

Next, he winked at Marion. 'For you…' The strains of 'Maggie' brought a lump to her throat, and caused Noel's arm, which was resting on the back of the couch behind Marion, to slide across her shoulder.

As Michael played on, coffee was sipped. Intrepid pushed her nose onto Marion's lap as her mistress gazed around at each person in turn, experiencing a joy she knew existed, but never imagined herself to receive. Silently, she thanked God, as Michael brought the evening to a close with 'The Long and Winding Road'. Not long after the party broke up, Janice stood by the back door, waving to Alice and Noel in a flurry of tearful farewells. She watched their cars receding along Beech Tree Lane, then slowly re-entered the kitchen to help with the clearing up.

'Not tonight, my love. You take yourself off to bed. I'll manage here,' said Marion, smiling. She looked around for Michael, but he seemed to have made himself scarce!

On Monday morning, Janice and Marion left early for Heathrow Airport. There was no sign of Michael, who had taken himself off to Penton Hook Lock around five, in order to avoid saying goodbye. The previous evening Janice had looked so beautiful he didn't want to see her leave, preferring to keep his first memory of her sitting in the sunshine, curled up in a chair in the conservatory, reading a book.

Amid the checking of her passport, buying something to read and seat allocation, words of comfort and encouragement floated up and around her. 'I don't know what to say.' Janice's eyes brimmed with tears. 'I've had the best time ever!' She kissed Marion, then just before hand luggage control, she turned and waved goodbye.

Marion felt quite shaken seeing her disappear and went in search of a coffee, grappling with that surreal situation, where one minute you are conversing intimately and the next there is an empty space. She decided to eat something, a sweet bun would do, imagining Janice walking along the various concourses before reaching her gate lounge surrounded by strangers and noise. 'Poor lamb,' she whispered. Airports were terrifying, impersonal, lonely places.

It had begun to rain as she turned into her driveway and was met on the doorstep by a distraught-looking Michael. Several thoughts crossed her mind as she approached the back door; Michael was in love, and it was painful. Thank heavens Janice had left for Tasmania. The implications of living in such close proximity, although partly of her making, were nevertheless completely circumstantial. Secondly, as she bustled in out of the rain she wondered if he had once more overspent. Attempting to lighten his mood, she went straight into the kitchen and put the kettle on. 'Don't look so forlorn! The sky hasn't fallen in, it's only raining!'

Abashed, Michael pulled out a kitchen chair and slumped across the table. She pretended not to notice, collecting two mugs, placing a spoonful of sugar in the one painted with heartsease, his favourite, then a measure of coffee, waiting for the kettle to boil before adding a dash of milk and stirring vigorously. It was times like this she wished Noel was there, being reluctant herself to advise on matters of the heart. Michael said nothing as she sat down opposite him. She could do without this and, feeling unsure how to proceed, she slipped out of her houndstooth jacket, a birthday present to herself, hung it inside out over the back of her chair, then pushed his mug against his hands and waited.

He looked up. 'I can't concentrate. I can't practise. She's everywhere! I didn't give her anything, Clarrie. Noel did, so did your friend Alice. I didn't,' he said dully.

'Does it matter?' She tried not to smile or look relieved.

'Of course it does!' he burst out. 'And, she left me a birthday cake,' he muttered.

'Pardon?'

'A chocolate cake. It's in the pantry.'

She was completely lost for words. It was one of those critical celebrations some families ignored, as in her case, but in other families people made a fuss. Why hadn't she known? Why hadn't she asked? Leonard never missed it, or so Michael had led her to believe. Was it today? Tomorrow? When was it? What could she do to make amends?

'Close to mine!' she said brightly.

'Is it?' He stirred his coffee, watching the liquid going around in circles. 'I didn't say goodbye… I couldn't.'

'It's all right, Michael. She would understand.' She drank, deeply cross with herself for making such a paltry remark.

'It's not all right! But thanks anyway.' Relaxing somewhat, he tried to explain his feelings between mouthfuls of coffee. She was amazed at his perception in one so young. 'Clarrie, she was so beautiful. Why didn't we have anything in common? She made me feel special, even when we disagreed. Do you know what I mean?' Not waiting for answer, he continued. 'I mean, I'm a musician, and a good one…' He trailed off in thought. 'Janice said what she thought, and somehow it made no difference when she made stupid comments – you know – as she knew next to nothing about music, really, and it's everything to me!' He stood up, moving over to the kitchen sink, looking moodily out of the window watching the rain. 'And my mother called. She wants me to move back with her now that she has a flat in Richmond.' He turned to face Marion, a picture of despondency.

'Ah… I see.'

'You don't, Clarrie. I want to stay here with you, or at any rate start making arrangements, maybe move out on my own… or with a mate, you know, another musician.'

'But you are only seventeen!'

'Eighteen today. Please don't say "Happy birthday", cos it isn't. And don't say, "You've got your career to think about." I don't want to study overseas. I want to stay here!'

Marion remembered at eighteen how everyone ignored her wishes, but she was a compliant soul. Looking at the set of Michael's jaw, she knew he was a different kettle of fish, besides which he had a special talent. Picking her words carefully, aware of his artistic nature, she refrained from making a glib remark. 'There hasn't been much time to explain my situation about River's End. As you know, I still don't own it, and Mrs Sloane…'

'…hasn't made up her mind whether to sell. Yes, I know that. Janice told me. Life sucks.'

'I may still have to move. But just because we don't get what we want, it doesn't mean everything is awful.' In a confidential tone she continued, 'I thought like you once, but life goes on, and since that time I've been blessed ten times over. Do you think I ever imagined a year ago I would be here in lovely River's End, talking with you, seeing Janice again, meeting Noel? Life is a journey. Every so often we take a side road, sometimes get lost, but someone comes along and helps us back on the right track. It depends on how we look at setbacks. Our desires get confused with needs, whereas if we looked at the particular situation as a challenge rather than being thwarted, we would save ourselves a lot of unhappiness.

'I have this friend – well, she's not really a friend, just some-one I went to school with… I see her at the Old Girls' reunions. And to be honest, I hardly remember ever having much to say to her. She was just there. But she remembers things differently and latches on to me at the dinners. She is still back there in a time warp, so to speak, going over the same ground, imagining conversations and situations, as if they were important. Most of it's untrue… She's unable to grow up, unable to move on with confidence, to be herself. There was a time those reunions meant a lot to me, but now they don't. I've moved on. I've other exciting things to think about.' Softly, she said, 'At the moment everything looks rather bleak from your perspective, right?'

He nodded, turning to look back at the rain.

'You know, Janice won't find life easy, either. She has no one except a friend of her mother's to advise, comfort and provide for her. Because of circumstances she has had to repeat her final year of school. She has had to grow up experiencing loss, disappointments and some frightening facts. No doubt coming here helped. I expect she told you how we met?' He didn't reply, so she rushed on. 'I'm sure she'll write, Michael. Cheer up! The house seems lonely without her, even Intrepid looks sad, but that's a good thing, isn't it?' He shrugged. 'Of course it is! It would be awful if we couldn't wait for her to go. Come on, this won't do!' She stood up. 'Have you had any breakfast?'

'I wasn't hungry.'

'How did you leave things with your mother?' she asked. She moved across to the sink, making a fuss of running the hot water and swirling the dishwashing liquid.

'I said I'd think about it. She's lonely. She made me feel it was all my fault, everything had gone wrong for her. She's got a flat and a job in an antique shop.' He paused. 'What do I tell her, Clarrie? I don't want to live in a tiny flat. There won't be anywhere to practise!'

It seemed perfectly natural for Marion to put her arm around his young shoulders. 'Oh, Michael.'

How could she explain that Lucy thought by having him with her she wouldn't be lonely? And was it fair to expect him to fill that gap? 'You know, I was often lonely.'

'What, when you lived with my father?'

'Often. Just because you live with someone doesn't necessarily mean you won't be lonely.' Painful memories resurfaced like slivers of glass.

'But now you're not. Not lonely, I mean.'

'No, now I'm not.'

'Because of Noel?'

'Yes, and other things.'

'Are you going to live with him?'

Marion ignored his question; instead she said, 'I want you to know that whatever you decide to do is fine by me. Having you live here seemed so… right. Living here at River's End has been good for both of us. I love this place too, but it isn't mine. It's ironic that what is happening to me is similar to what I did to you and your mother. I thought I would need the money to buy my own place. I couldn't in all conscience stay any longer with Alice, and I wanted to get settled.' She laughed disparagingly. 'Strange how things work out!'

'Now that I'm eighteen, I can do what I like, can't I?'

'Yes, in a way. You can get a driver's licence. You can vote.'

'And live where I like. Think I'll go to Tasmania and see Janice.'

'There's a little question of finance, and, depending how long you intend to stay, you might need a working visa.' She saw his countenance fall. 'And you'd need to find somewhere to stay. Sometimes what seems like love while on holiday doesn't always pan out in reality.'

'But I could, in theory?'

'You're like a dog with a bone! Yes, you could.'

He grinned. 'If I move back with Mum and it doesn't work out, can I come and stay with you?'

'It depends if I'm here; but of course you can. In fact I'd be disappointed if you didn't come to visit now and again.'

Michael cheered up perceptibly after this remark and, retrieving the chocolate cake from the pantry, placed it on the table with a flourish. *'Da-dah!'* he exclaimed. Then, using his index finger, he swept up some of the butter icing into his mouth. Marion collected two plates and, handing him a knife, murmured, 'Can I say it now?'

He shrugged. 'I'm starving!' Deftly he sliced two segments and, much to her surprise, started singing. 'Happy birthday to us, happy birthday to us!'

Joyfully, Marion joined in. 'We'll celebrate together.' She collected two wine glasses from the draining board, left there from the previous night's festivities, and poured some

Chardonnay from a cask in the fridge. 'To us and the future!'

'To us!' His eyes met hers, and he wondered why Anna hadn't bothered to send her mother a birthday card.

It rained consistently throughout the rest of the day, but Marion didn't mind. She liked the steely grey of the river and its banks covered in mist, the freshness of the air when opening the back door, insisting Intrepid needed to go out. With the departure of Janice, Intrepid slunk back into her mistress's bedroom for the night, lying between the foot of the bed and the Queen Anne dressing table. Marion thought, as she prepared for bed, carefully hanging the houndstooth jacket and skirt in the wardrobe, that she preferred built-in cupboards and less ostentatious furniture, like the room awaiting her at Noel's farm; but otherwise she loved the sloping ceiling, the pink flock wallpaper and views from the windows. Before closing the window overlooking the river she listened, hoping to hear it rushing past, but somehow the denseness of the fog swallowed up all sounds.

Tiredness and the emotions of the day did not stop her brain from sorting the secondary issues from the facts of her situation. She stayed by the window, breathing in the cool air and began to pray. 'Our Father, which art in heaven, hallowed be Thy name,' she paused. 'Father, am I right to buy River's End, or am I to look on my stay here as an interlude, a kind of stepping stone, bringing to an end past grievances?' It was like a concerto, she thought. Exposition, development and coming together of all the strands of the theme. She concluded, 'Thank you, Father, for giving me confidence and understanding more about myself and how to love others. More and more I hear an inner voice helping me to have patience and courage when things seem difficult.'

She stopped, staring out into the mist, which now seemed tinged with silver, hearing distant vague sounds and close by the drip of rain. She hesitated before continuing. 'Can you make it clear for me if it is love I feel for Noel, or something more akin to basking in his flattery? Do I fear to be alone?' But deep down she knew it wasn't a fear of loneliness; it was a fear of compromise, losing her independence.

'I love this independence. I love this sense of freedom, to choose whom I like to see, eat what I like and when, stay up to all hours or not, and have my own bedroom. Loneliness doesn't come into the equation; I know that now, as I tried to explain to Michael. Independence and solitude do. Is that wrong? Father, I thank you for bringing Noel into my life, but would marrying him work to the benefit of us both or would I have to... compromise? Most women do. I'm worried about the gossip in the village so soon after the Memorial Service for Leonard. And I'm nervous about people working out who Michael is. What if it got around Laleham that for sixteen years Leonard kept a mistress on the other side of the village, and I didn't even know – never mind having a son! I don't know if I could handle the gossip! But then, maybe no one would connect the article in the paper, "Virtuoso in our midst", with Michael. The only other person who knows is Alice. Father, I'm sorry about all these questions. Please help me to think with my head as well as my heart.'

Thinking fondly of Noel, she prayed, 'Thank you for Noel's change of heart where Michael is concerned. It is strange, now that he expects to play surrogate father, how the situation has changed, as Michael is going to move back in with his mother until he has acquired the finances to do otherwise. But then, I know you know all this... and things are looking up for Michael, and I thank you for the contracts which give him hope for the future.'

She mused over the call from his agent, who was a director of *The Stage* newspaper, and part-owner of a record company. Michael had swept into his office, pleading with him to be his agent, which had led to a lucrative booking for the Academy orchestra, Carols by Candlelight in Hyde Park; moreover, a contract was awaiting his signature as guest artist for the BBC concert series in February, plus several smaller engagements for the quartet during the festive season at various London hotels. Carl Collins was in his fifties and happily married. He was reputed to own a Ferrari, along with several vintage cars. Michael had been elated; she had been relieved. 'Thank you Father for all these blessings; forgive my lack of trust in your goodness, and please take care of Janice as she flies home to Australia. Amen.'

Sliding into bed, she reached for *New Passages* by Gail Sheehy. It had caught her eye while browsing in Smith's bookshop on her way back from one of her many forays to the office of Clerk and Gamble. On the spine were the words, 'Mapping Your Life Across Time'.

She read for a while, then reminded herself to make a note of the date in the back of her diary so that next year she would remember Michael's birthday. Her memory was jolted. Tomorrow at 10.30 she had a dentist's appointment: not something she relished. Still, Alice would be there, which was a comfort.

By ten o'clock the following morning the rain had stopped, and in its place a north-easterly wind was blustering around the house. Clouds scurried across a weak sun. Everything looked saturated. The grass was spongy, the lane full of potholes and the river dangerously high. Any late flowers, almost drowned with the rain, now were battered by the wind. There was a knock at the front door. Irritated at being disturbed, Michael continued to practise his part in a violin duet composed by Yanni called 'Within Attraction', hoping whoever it was would go away, but Intrepid started barking at the persistence of the knocking.

'Quiet!' Michael exclaimed. He pushed the affronted Intrepid into the kitchen, before approaching the front door; then, seeing through the glazed side panel a woman checking something in a small notebook, he opened the door, stunned to see two large suitcases and two vanity cases in matching blue on the step. Before he had a chance to say, 'I think you've come to the wrong house,' the young woman impatiently said, 'I suppose this is where Mrs Lee lives?' and pushed her luggage onto the porch. Michael looked blank.

'Mrs Marion Lee?' The woman spoke as though he was mentally defective. 'This is the address I have. It had better be right; the taxi cost me a fortune.'

'Ah, you mean Clarrie, yes… but she's out at present.'

'No, *Marion*. Out or not, I don't intend standing on the doorstep in this wind. I'm Anna, her daughter. Anna Crees. And you are?' She raised her eyebrows, perfectly aware to whom she was speaking, as the likeness to her father was unmistakable.

She pushed past Michael into the hallway before he had time to reply. 'You can bring my bags in. Where's the kitchen? I need a cup of tea.'

One of the beautiful people ran through his mind. Dressed in a type of woollen cape clipped high at the neck with bat-like sleeves, its colours ranging from dark green to lime, Anna wafted past, leaving in her wake a whiff of some expensive perfume. She wore high-heeled black patent shoes, and her blonde hair fixed in a smooth pleat, creating a glamorous image to one so susceptible as Michael.

However, in spite of an extremely large gold bracelet and exquisite gold drop earrings, Michael found her intolerable, and took an instant dislike to his sibling.

'Don't just stand there, you're letting all the warmth out!'

He shut the door, animosity rising like bile in his throat. 'Don't go in there – we have a dog,' he told her.

'We have a dog, do we?' she teased, ignoring his advice. Intrepid came bouncing out, thrilled at seeing a new face and began circling, landing on Anna's feet and almost tripping her up.

'Oh, God… move this dog, will you, she'll ruin my shoes! I knew Mother had a dog, but I'd imagined a lapdog!'

Ushering Intrepid through to the conservatory, Michael called, 'The kettle is over there. You can find your way around. Clarrie won't be long, she's at the dentist's.'

'Wait a minute!' snapped Anna. 'I've come all this way, so the least you can do is make me a cup of tea. You can make a cup of tea, I suppose?' She flashed blue eyes in his direction with a suitable pout, as if to say, 'Poor little me!'

Michael stood his ground. 'I'm busy,' he explained, and made towards the conservatory.

'You're Michael, aren't you – my father's bastard!' she called.

'And you're a right bitch!' he rejoined, slamming the door of the conservatory behind him.

'Touché,' she sneered, but it was a waste of breath as he didn't hear her. The house wasn't too bad, she told herself, as she fingered the table and chairs, looking around at the china and knick-knacks on the kitchen dresser. A bit old-fashioned, but it had style, she would concede that. There seemed to be something wrong with the electric jug – probably the element, she surmised. Feeling annoyed, she located a kettle that had seen better days, filled it with water and placed it on the gas hob. Understanding how to light it was another matter. She was about to go in search of Michael when the kitchen door opened. 'Bugger it!'

'Hello?' a voice behind her chuckled.

She turned around to see a good-looking middle-aged man laughing at her. 'Excuse the French… You don't know how to light this thing, do you?'

Putting a large cardboard box filled with vegetables on the kitchen table, he strode across to where she was standing. 'I'm Noel, Noel Barker,' he said, and held out a slim, tanned hand above which was a neatly rolled blue and white striped shirtsleeve, the shirt's collar open at the neck.

Anna looked blank, ignoring his hand, and turned back to the stove. 'I've never heard of you. I'm Marion's daughter. I'd hoped she'd meet me at Heathrow, but typically, for some reason she was out when I rang. I wanted to surprise her.' An impatient frown crossed her brow.

Taken aback more by the way she spoke than by what she said, Noel could quite well imagine the surprised look on Marion's face. 'Here, let me try… a bit temperamental, this gas burner. I think Marion uses the left one. You're Anna, right?' She nodded. 'Live in sunny Queensland, correct? Got it.'

The gas flared. 'Mmm.' It was embarrassing talking to a complete stranger in her mother's kitchen.

'You've met Michael, I suppose?'

'Ah, yes, I've met my father's indiscretion; though why he should be here is beyond me.' Her blue eyes locked with his. 'You're not from Oxfam or something similar, are you?' She waved her hand in the direction of the vegetables.

Noel laughed, a deep throaty sound, beginning to enjoy himself at Anna's expense. 'Where's Marion, then?' he asked.

'According to him' – her head inclined towards the sounds of a violin playing – 'she's at the dentist's!' She began ferreting through various canisters. 'Do you know where she keeps the tea?'

'I think in the pantry.' Half amused by her behaviour, and at the same time amazed by the contrast in character with her mother, Noel could well understand why Marion did not wish to live near her daughter. 'Where's your luggage?'

'Still outside the front door, as that cretin refused to bring it in.'

He was not at all surprised to see enough matching luggage in the porch for two people for a month. She was like a disdainful swan, and impossibly selfish. Carting the cases into the hallway, it struck him that maybe she had returned for good. Maybe her marriage had collapsed! Now he'd be stuck with another obstacle to overcome. But then, to be rational, he was sure Marion wouldn't countenance living under the same roof as Anna. He doubted anyone would live in the same house with her for long. Poor Nigel! His thoughts rambled on.

Perhaps it would be to his advantage to get Anna onside rather than stir the pot, so to speak. Completely mystified as to why she was there, he made his way into the conservatory.

Michael seemed relieved, even welcoming his presence, rather different from his usual demeanour. Information was exchanged about his recent career developments and the expectation of his mother. Noel attempted not to look pleased at this last revelation.

'Want a tea or coffee? Anna has put the kettle on,' Noel ventured.

'Don't ask her to do anything! She'll just as soon poison you.'

'She can't be that bad. I expect she's tired. It's a long trip, you know.'

A withering look from Michael caused a change of tack from Noel. 'Marion know she was coming?'

'Not to my knowledge. If she had, she would have made up the attic bed,' he mumbled darkly. Then, picking up his violin, continued to practise the last movement from Vivaldi's 'Four Seasons'. Noel stayed to listen for a short while, impressed by his maturity and visible prowess.

A short time later he joined Anna in the lounge, he with a coffee and she with a Royal Doulton cup of tea, accompanied by a large slice of chocolate cake. His eyes focussed on her as she devoured the cake, knowing Janice had made it specially for Michael.

'I'd forgotten how bleak it is here.' She shuddered between mouthfuls. 'Actually,' said Noel, 'this weather has come on suddenly, shortly after Janice's visit.'

'How was she?'

'What do you mean?'

'Was she quiet?'

'Not to my knowledge. She loved it here. Took Intrepid for walks, adored your mother and fell for Michael.' Laughingly, he added. 'You'll be popular. She made that cake for his birthday.'

Noticing his teasing smile, she shrugged and began to relax. 'You seem to know a lot about what goes on here.'

'Do I? Yes, I suppose I do.'

He smiled in a beguiling way, leaning back into the armchair, quite unnerving Anna. The phone rang. 'Shouldn't one of us answer that?' she asked.

'Uh-huh, I don't think so. It can't be for you or me. Leave it to Michael.'

'Oh, right.' Intrepid barked. A door was opened, then some shuffling and the phone ceased. 'It's strange, being here in her house, I mean.' She looked around. 'This furniture, I've never seen it before.'

'She's leasing… most of what you see belongs with the house.'

'Oh, I thought she had bought it.'

'Not exactly. The owner can't make up her mind whether to sell.'

'That's not what I understood. The way she described it in her letters…' It dawned on Anna that her mother's finances were looking decidedly healthier than she had been led to believe. Confused, she asked 'Where do you fit in?'

'Not here. I own a farm on the other side of Laleham. I've known your mother for years… through the church.'

'Oh, I see. You're religious.' She made a face.

'Depends what you mean by "religious". I would like to make an honest woman of her.' Chancing her reaction to be favourable to this idea, he moved across to the window. 'I want to marry your mother,' he said firmly, then turned to face her. 'There's no need for you to worry. I'm quite successful.' He smiled. 'I employ three staff and a housekeeper, and own—'

'A sports car!' She grinned.

A rueful smile played on his lips, 'I own three vehicles, actually. How did you know about my Aston Martin?'

'Ah, wouldn't you like to know.' She laughed. He wasn't bad-looking in an English sort of way; he didn't have a paunch and his hair hadn't receded. He obviously had money, so he wasn't after her mother's money – or, to be correct, *her* inheritance. But what on earth did he see in her? 'Marry her?' she queried.

'Well, not immediately.'

'What about Michael?'

'What about him?'

'He lives here with Mum! For goodness sake!'

'Only temporarily. Look, I think you had better keep your questions for Marion. It's not my place…' Intrepid barked. 'There she is now.'

The door into the kitchen opened and Anna could see her mother's silhouette through the French windows.

'I saw your car in the driveway, Noel,' she remarked, coming into the lounge and stopping dead still in the doorway. The smile on her face evaporated, replaced by alarm. 'Anna! What are you doing here?'

'That's a nice thing to say, I must say.' Anna attempted to sound jovial but was shocked by her mother's tone. It wasn't the homecoming atmosphere she had expected, nor was her mother's appearance. She looked ten years younger, with her pageboy hairstyle. Her clothes looked chic and she seemed to have a vitality Anna had never seen before. Inanities filled the embarrassing next few minutes.

'I've been at the dentist's.'

'I know.'

'I haven't had time to change the sheets. Is something wrong… is it Nigel?'

'*Hello, Anna, what a lovely surprise! I'm so glad to see you.* No, there is nothing "wrong", Mother, as you so discreetly put it – not with me and Nigel anyway!'

'I'm sorry, but you gave me quite a shock.'

'*I* gave *you* a shock? What about the one you gave me in your last letter?'

There was more of the same, so Noel took his leave. To Marion's surprise, Anna seemed to like Noel and teased her about their relationship, but refused point-blank to be drawn on any discussion involving Michael. In fact, her revulsion concerning him soon abated, as within a few days of her arrival, Marion deposited him and his belongings somewhere in Richmond. On the Sunday Anna attended the morning service at All Saints' with Marion, after which she accepted a glass of sherry at Alice's. Anna was nonplussed as to how such different women could be friends, but then since she had returned to England everything seemed to have changed.

She dined that evening with Marion at Noel's farm, and was greatly impressed by the decor and the meal. It was far grander than she had imagined, so surely her mother could give up her silly idea of owning River's End and release her inheritance now. Anna imagined owning a house on one of the canals in Miami or Sorrento, complete with swimming pool. They could buy another car, she could entertain in style.

During the following week, Anna borrowed Marion's car to go clothes shopping only to return with underwear, as the shops were full of winter wear which she would have no need of in Queensland. She managed to be civil to her mother, but couldn't erase the memory of Michael and what he represented to her. Marion attempted some explanation. 'You see, he was so talented...' But Anna refused to be drawn. 'I don't want to discuss the subject.'

As a special surprise, on Anna's last night, Noel bought three box tickets at the Yvonne Arnaud Theatre in Guildford, to see *Bedroom Farce* by Alan Ayckbourn. They dined in the theatre restaurant before the show and sipped pre-ordered cocktails during the interval. The next day, seeing her daughter off at Heathrow Airport, Marion couldn't help comparing the different feelings both girls had on her equilibrium. Finally, anxious to appear pleased with Anna's surprise visit, she found herself saying she would seriously consider marrying Noel, and when Anna and Nigel found a house to their liking, she would supply the relevant deposit.

She watched Anna looking so self-assured, turning heads, and waved as her daughter disappeared from view. She loathed airports, the crowds and farewells, but most of all for the awkwardness they managed to create, stifling heartfelt emotions. On returning to River's End she was struck by the quietness, but it was a safe haven after negotiating the M25. In fact, that was precisely what River's End had been for Michael, Janice and herself. She stood in the conservatory, missing Michael, his playing and wishing she could tell Leonard all about it.

Like a revelation it came to her then the meaning of the painting on the west wall of the church. God was reaching down, offering unconditional love and all man had to do was receive. In the same way, he used his servants to reach out to others, as she had to Michael and in a lesser sense to Janice. How rich and rewarding her life had been with that one small gesture! And in His mercy, He had planted Noel in her path, something she had never imagined. She remembered the words, 'Take my yoke upon you, it is light,' the confusion while living in Tadbury, her fear, and the hand of Sister Ruth reaching out to her. Now, she had other decisions to make. It was strange she hadn't heard from either Norma Sloane or Patricia Clerk; she would have thought one or the other would be on the doorstep, so to speak. Moving into the hallway, she changed her jacket for a warm car coat and gloves. It occurred to her that she had once again fallen in with Anna's wishes. Was she that weak-willed?

'Walkies!' she called out. Intrepid ran around in circles while she changed her high-heeled shoes for sensible walking ones; and collected a walking stick and the lead.

Now that winter had arrived, she took Intrepid for one long walk instead of two, turning left on the towpath toward Chertsey. Regardless of what the outcome was relating to River's End, she'd made a decision about where her relationship with Noel was going. She watched the river gliding past, a dull grey, even with the weak sun and patches of blue sky; not a bird in sight or any river traffic to ruffle the water. It was as if the whole world had gone to sleep.

She passed the end of Blacksmiths' Lane, where long ago she had been puzzled to see Leonard returning from ringing the bells at Evensong, his explanation not standing up, as he wasn't in the habit of helping little old ladies, as far as she knew. The close proximity of Vicarage Lane alerted her to the next row of houses between it and Ferry Lane, where lawns flowed down to the towpath. She decided to put Intrepid on her lead, as the lawns were an open invitation to those of Intrepid's persuasion to leave a calling card. Before turning the corner into Ferry Lane, she could see the swans, coots, moorhens all gaggled together on the riverbank, and further along the occasional stoic fisherman casting his line.

She walked past the field now, empty of livestock, and at the T-junction turned right towards the Priory and the park. The sycamores and horse chestnut trees now lay bare, their branches dark brown, asleep for the winter. There was a new gate installed at Number Six, causing her to stop and notice *The Hollies* in gold lettering attached to the top bar. The path was now free of weeds, shrubs replaced, and the front door stained a shiny brown. A large brass knocker could be seen under the number '6', and fresh shutters attached to the windows upstairs. Her eyes roamed downwards to where several geraniums were flowering on the windowsill of the kitchen. Altogether, the house looked well cared for. If she hadn't decided to sell the house, she would never have learnt Leonard's secret – well, not immediately anyway; and through it all she had learnt forgiveness, understanding, and experienced self-worth. So much had happened to her since she had returned from Australia; not the least was gaining the courage to abandon fear of the unknown, and to hope instead for what the future might bring.

Turning away from the house, Marion checked on the where-abouts of Intrepid, who, unbeknown to her owner, was foraging in the exact spot where Leonard had stood those many months ago, filled with indecision while listening to Michael playing Mendelssohn's Violin Concerto in E. Strange to think how one action had changed her whole life! She walked on, filled with a sense of purpose.

Recent events had shown her life was not as insignificant as she had thought. Action on her part had strengthened her faith, offering an insight, small though it was, into things unseen. Noel's agenda required her to be his wife. Anna's lobbying made it clear that she claimed her rights financially, and she herself wished to be left to make her own decisions. Only this, she felt empowered to do. Now, as she walked along the avenue flanked by fir trees, she watched Intrepid nosing around the base of a larch, her tail wagging, excited by the smell of small animals; the cause of her frustration was a squirrel sitting upon a branch above, chattering and swishing its fluffy grey tail.

Marion clipped Intrepid once more onto her lead as the avenue ended in a T-junction abutting the road to Shepperton, and took the footpath that led back to the village. Here, she passed the butcher's and the antique shop where Janice, along with everyone else, had found the window covered in grime and no signs of life. She wondered if the owner had died, as she ventured into the GPO corner shop. Intrepid waited patiently outside, tied to a lamp post, recognising this routine would result in a treat. 'Don't tell Noel,' Marion whispered in her ear. 'He wouldn't be pleased!'

Intrepid swallowed a chocolate strip with one crunch, looking for the second. They heard the church clock strike one as they turned the corner, crossed Vicarage Lane, passed The Wee Hoose, its original owner now forgotten in time, and on down Blacksmiths' Lane towards the river and home. There was a West Highland terrier peering out from the railings of her previous home, who set up a furious barking, taking offence at Intrepid as they passed.

She saw the familiar maroon and cream 'FOR SALE' sign of Clerk and Gamble perched against the front of Little Withies, now devoid of its striking red foliage, its suckers of Virginia creeper surrounding the small windowpanes reminding her of a children's book she read long ago about a little grey rabbit. As she passed by heading for River's End, she prayed that her feigned interest in Little Withies had spurred Mrs Sloane into action favourable for herself.

She hadn't been home long before the phone rang. 'Clarrie, is that you?'

'Michael. How are you?'

'Oh, you know, it's not like…'

'I've just been for a walk with Intrepid and saw the Clerk and Gamble signs outside Little Withies.' There was a long silence, 'I couldn't live there…'

'That's what I'm ringing about. With everything going on and Anna arriving, I forgot to tell you. I'm sorry.'

'Forgot to tell me what?'

'You had a phone call from Mrs Sloane. I told her you were out and wrote her number down.'

'Did she say anything you know about River's End?'

'No, just that she wanted you to call her. I'm sorry, I forgot.'

'Is it under "N S"? I think it's still here on the pad.'

'Yes.'

'Funny way you have of writing the number eight. It's like a small fat man on top of a large one.'

'Clarrie… what are you doing for Christmas?'

'Well, it all depends…'

'I was wondering if I can spend it with you and Noel.'

'Of course you can, but what about your mother?'

'She wouldn't mind. When I was small we'd go to a girl-friend's of hers in Twickenham… but that petered out, and she didn't make much of Christmas. We didn't have a tree or turkey, so I'd go to a mate's now and again.'

After this disquieting conversation, Marion put the phone down, whispering, 'God willing, Michael, God willing, you will have Christmas here at River's End.'

A letter with 'Clerk and Gamble' stamped on the envelope had come by the second post. She stared at the envelope for a while before tentatively opening it. An anxious feeling, akin to the fear of bad news, was lodged in the pit of her stomach.

Perhaps if she rang Norma Sloane – if only she knew what she wanted! Either way wouldn't make any difference now. Unfolding the document, she read the note attached to the front:

I have been trying to contact you but with no success.

I am pleased to tell you that Norma Sloane is happy for you to purchase River's End asap, as she is anxious to buy a property further along the river at Maidenhead.

Sincerely yours,

Patricia Clerk

Marion unfolded the contract requiring her signature. River's End would finally be hers. On the final page there was a clause stipulating that the vendor wished to remove certain pieces of furniture on the day of completion, and that she hoped this was satisfactory for Mrs Lee, as she had tried to contact her to discuss the said pieces, but to no avail. Perhaps she would call her at her convenience to discuss the matter. Patricia Clerk also had a list of the required furniture.

It was with a sense of relief that Marion laughed, imagining exactly how she would furnish each room. Norma could take the lot, as far as she was concerned. Let the future take care of itself! Had she imagined the voice in the yew trees outside the church all those mornings ago, as Alice seemed to imply? Or was she privileged to hear that still small voice of calm? One thing she was certain of: Michael would always find a place at her table. This she explained gently to Noel the following Sunday night, while the two of them savoured some mulled wine after they had attended Evensong. She relayed what Anna had previously vowed before boarding her flight. 'When we buy the house we'll start a family.'

'She won't, though – she's not interested in babies! I wish she was. Nothing is exactly how you want it to be, is it?'

Noel regarded with love those knowing grey eyes and, kissing her, thought, But it's not impossible… given time. At least, that's how he saw it.

www.ingramcontent.com/pod-product-compliance
Lightning Source LLC
Chambersburg PA
CBHW060755190726
48285CB00002B/439